LARK AND THE
WILD HUNT

Also by Jennifer Adam

The Last Windwitch

LARK
AND THE
WILD HUNT

JENNIFER ADAM

HARPER
An Imprint of HarperCollinsPublishers

Library of Congress Cataloging-in-Publication Data

Names: Adam, Jennifer (Jennifer Frances), author.
Title: Lark and the Wild Hunt / Jennifer Adam.
Description: First edition. | New York, NY : Harper, [2022] | Audience:
    Ages 8–12. | Audience: Grades 4-6. | Summary: When her brother
    disappears into the Fae realm, twelve-year-old Lark must try to save
    him by solving riddles, fixing an ancient clock, and trusting her new
    Fae friend, Rook.
Identifiers: LCCN 2021051286 | ISBN 9780062981332 (hardcover)
Subjects: CYAC: Magic—Fiction. | Fantasy. | LCGFT: Fantasy fiction.
Classification: LCC PZ7.1.A2285 Lar 2022 | DDC [Fic]—dc23
LC record available at https://lccn.loc.gov/2021051286

Typography by Jessie Gang
22 23 24 25 26   PC/LSCH   10 9 8 7 6 5 4 3 2 1
❖
First Edition

— *This book is dedicated to* —

all the dreamers, doers, makers, menders,
helpers, healers, thinkers, teachers, writers, and
wishers of any age who have ever been afraid of
failure: there's time to take your chance

— *and to* —

my family
for everything, forever

PART ONE

Borderlands

ONE

Broken

LARK MAIREN BALLED her fists and pushed her body faster, stumbling over pebbles in the path and ridges left by tree roots. She plunged through ferns and tangles of bittersweet vine, racing toward the waymarker at the edge of her family's property—the last place she'd seen her brother, Galin.

Melting frost glittered on the grass and soaked the toes of her leather boots as she panted clouds of mist in the chilly morning air, but the ache in her lungs and legs was nothing compared to the pain in her heart. *He'll be there. He has to be there.*

Distant voices called back and forth while thundering hoofbeats drummed echoes from the ground. Search parties followed her in a wide sweep, since she was the only one who had watched the Wild Hunt ride past this stretch of the border. They hoped to find a hint, a clue that could explain why Galin hadn't returned with the other Hunters at dawn.

Had he been thrown from his shadowbred horse? Was he lying injured somewhere?

By the time Lark reached the granite-and-moonstone waymarker indicating the boundary of the Fae realm, her parents were already riding to meet her. "Any sign of him?" she called, but Da shook his head.

She bent forward, bracing her hands on her thighs to catch her breath as disappointment and exertion left her gasping. Last night the wind had smelled of smoke and apples, cinnamon and salted caramel, and the deep green musk of Fae magic. This morning it carried the sour scent of worry and the salt-tang of sorrow.

As she wheezed, her parents argued quietly about how to proceed, their horses catching their nerves and fidgeting anxiously this close to the border.

"Lark, tell us again exactly what you saw," Ma said. Ma— River Mairen, Horsemaven of the Borderlands and five-time Hunter—nudged Legacy, her gleaming black shadowbred mare, closer while Da hunched awkwardly in the saddle of a neighbor's massive bay plow horse. He'd ridden the Wild Hunt once as a young man, Lark knew, but he was a tailor and a dressmaker now. The magic shadowbred horses—part mortal, part Fae—that his wife's family had been breeding and training for generations made him nervous.

They made Lark nervous too, which was why she

preferred to run to the waymarker on her own two feet. Even if that meant she was now too winded to speak.

"Lark?" Da asked.

She had hoped—had let herself *believe*—that no matter what trouble Galin might have found, he would somehow make his way back to this marker to wait for her.

But if he could have made it this far, he would have returned all the way home, wouldn't he?

"Where are you, Galin? What happened?" she murmured.

"Lark, we need to hear every detail you remember," Ma urged. "Perhaps there's a clue we've missed."

Lark had snuck out the night before to watch the stampede of human and Fae Hunters, never expecting to witness her brother's last ride. Guilt and sorrow stuck in her throat like day-old oat bran mush.

"First there was a rush of wind," she said, frowning at a single red toadstool near the base of the waymarker. "Then the pale glow of the White Stag bounding along the border, guiding the Hunters, and the rumble of hooves galloping after him." The image was burned in Lark's mind: a full moon casting silver-rimmed shadows, the surging tide of black shadowbred horses breathing sparkling mist from flared nostrils, racing hounds baying in full song, birds filling the night sky, Fae Hunters in cloaks woven of spiderwebs and starlight. . . .

And the lead rider, wearing a flame-bright crimson

cloak, a golden vest, and a circlet of blazing autumn leaves upon his head. The Harvest King in all his glory, looking right at her.

Lark recalled shrinking back, afraid of getting in trouble. She should have been tucked safely in bed beneath a quilt embroidered with protective sigils and lucky symbols—Wild Hunt nights were full of magic and chaos, even for those who weren't Hunters—but curiosity had tugged her outside.

Her sister, Sage, was riding the Hunt along with Galin that night, and Lark had wanted to see them both. So she slipped from her house and skimmed up the path, past the stable, around the orchard, through the woods, and here to the closest waymarker.

She never expected the Harvest King himself to notice her. Fear curled her toes against the cold ground, but he'd smiled kindly and raised a hand in greeting.

In that moment of distraction, a tangle of brambles and thorns burst from the ground beneath him. Lark now told her parents how vines as thick as her arms erupted like snakes, wriggling and twisting around the legs of the king's magnificent shadowbred. Finger-long thorns ripped into the horse's sleek black coat, raking trails of red-and-silver blood. The shadowbred shrieked and turned to smoke, throwing the Harvest King from his back.

"I screamed," Lark admitted. "And then suddenly Galin was there, riding up on Whimsy. He leaned over, reached out, and gripped the king's hand. Galin pulled the Harvest King up behind his saddle and they raced past the brambles."

"Who else did you see? How did the other Fae react?" Da asked, worry puckering his brow.

"There was a beautiful Fae riding beside Galin, with shining sun-gold hair. She smiled at him when he rescued the king, but I lost sight of them as they rounded the curve of the hills. Sage followed a few minutes later, so I waved to her and ran back to the house. That's all I know. Do you think Galin is still with the king? Maybe he'll be celebrated as a hero and escorted back with honors! We should go see if—"

But it was clear from her parents' expressions that they didn't share her excitement.

"All the other Hunters returned as expected," Da mused. "No major injuries . . . I can't understand why Galin wasn't with them."

"He's always been a courteous boy. Perhaps he stayed a bit longer to offer comfort after the loss of the king's shadow-bred, though I don't see any thorns or brambles now," Ma said, gaze sweeping the ground.

Lark sighed. "No . . . that's the strange thing. As soon as Galin and the king rode out of sight, the vines withered to dust and blew away. Oh!" She suddenly remembered. "I saw something tumble from the king's vest pocket when he fell. I don't know what it was . . . something round and silver." It had smashed in a scatter of tiny pieces while thistles clawed through grass and leaf loam, stretching toward the king. She paced a circle around the waymarker. Perhaps some pieces remained?

"Probably a mirror. The Fae are vain," Ma said dismissively, snapping Lark's attention back to the discussion at hand.

"I bet you're right," Da murmured. "Maybe he simply didn't have time to return to the barn with the other Hunters before the Faevoring ceremony. He's probably in the square at this very moment, and here we are in a panic for no reason." He forced a chuckle and gathered his reins.

Ma nodded but didn't call off the search. "Sage and the rest of the Hunters should be there for the Faevoring now. Go see if Galin is with them." She hesitated before adding, "Just in case he's not, Legacy and I will ride farther along the border. There's a tricky stretch between the waymarker at Hawkridge and the one at Crestview, and if he tried to ride that far with the king behind him . . . Well, I just want to make sure he wasn't thrown and injured. If there was a problem we can't afford to waste any daylight."

Lark glanced reflexively at the sky, even though she knew it was early yet. They still had most of a day to search for Galin if he didn't turn up at the Faevoring ceremony.

However, if they didn't find him by moonrise the border would close. And Galin wouldn't be able to make his way back.

"Galin could still return in the spring when the border

opens for the Mayfair Hunt, couldn't he? If he's somehow been trapped in the Fae realm, surely the May Queen would let him return then?" Lark asked, fretting aloud.

Da bent from the saddle to lay a warm hand on top of her head. "There's always hope—and right now I'm hoping he's waiting for his Faevor with your sister and the other Hunters."

But his lips were pinched in a grim line and Lark's spirits sank like stones in a puddle. Galin *had* to be in the square, otherwise she knew the odds weren't on his side. If he didn't return by moonrise, he'd be stuck in the Fae realm until spring. That would be six moonturns of eating Fae food and drinking Fae water and breathing Fae magic.

By then he might be forever changed. And she had never heard of anyone returning after getting caught on the wrong side of the border.

A worse thought occurred to her, sharp and stinging as a nettle scratch. The brambles hadn't suddenly appeared by accident. What if the Fae king was attacked on purpose? The Twilight Court might be even more dangerous than usual. No place for a mortal.

Still, if anyone had a chance it would be her brother. He'd been brave enough and strong enough to save the Harvest King, so he was brave enough and strong enough to come back too.

He had to be.

"If you find Galin or hear word of him, send a message

through the scouts. I'll check in as soon as I can." Ma sighed and twitched the reins. "In the meantime, Lark, I need you to hurry home straightaway. Take care of the shadowbreds who've returned from the Hunt and wait for us there."

Lark nodded, chewing her lip.

"And watch the road, do you hear me?" Da urged.

"I will," Lark promised. *Watch the road* was code for *Be wary of the Fae.* "You too."

"Luck of the winds!" Ma said, and then she spun Legacy toward the south and cantered away.

"I'm heading to the square, but if you need anything Sarai will be looking in," Da said. "I'll be back as soon as I can." And he rode off too.

After watching him go, Lark pressed a hand against the worry squirming through her belly and turned for home, until a strange croak coming from the fall-faded grass caught her attention.

Surely it wouldn't be a wildkin—not the morning after a Wild Hunt.

Everyone knew the Fae couldn't be trusted, but there were *rules*. Treaties. Traditions . . .

And the most important tradition was the twice-yearly ritual of the Wild Hunt, meant to preserve the balance of power and protect the Borderlands from rogue wildkin magic.

The safest time in the Borderlands was the morning after a Hunt, when any mischievous wildkin had been chased back to the Fae realm where they belonged and the simmering chaos of Fae magic had been temporarily quieted.

Only . . . something had gone wrong on this Hunt and Galin hadn't returned. He was the first Hunter to disappear since the Accords had been signed generations ago, since Mairen Horsemavens had started raising shadowbreds and training riders.

Lark couldn't decide if that was comforting—because then surely Galin would be all right?—or terrifying, because if he wasn't in the square as they hoped, what would it mean? What else could have gone wrong?

The sound came again: a desperate gurgle and a scuffle.

Fear slithered through Lark and she clenched her teeth, tensing her muscles to run. If there was something Fae hiding in that grass she wanted nothing to do with it. But then she saw the tentative flap of a black wing and suddenly realized what she was hearing.

She carefully parted the long stems to find a raven, clearly injured and blinking up at her.

"Ohhh," she breathed, kneeling beside the wounded bird. "You poor thing."

Some of his ink-slick feathers were rumpled, and a small trickle of crimson blood drew a jagged line down his chest. He seemed to gasp for air through his open beak.

"Did you get hurt in the Wild Hunt?" she murmured. Ravens didn't typically fly in the dark, preferring to roost until morning instead. But last night she'd seen a storm of ravens—as well as hawks, owls, bats, vultures, magpies, jays, and gulls—soaring above the galloping shadowbreds and their riders. Perhaps this bird had been wounded in all the commotion.

He blinked one bright eye and clicked his beak. Cautiously, Lark stroked a finger along his wings. One definitely appeared broken.

She hesitated, glancing at the pine and oak trees casting shadows over the waymarker. Although she didn't sense a tingle of magic around this raven, he clearly had *some* connection to the Fae or he wouldn't have been flying on a Wild Hunt night. And that might make him dangerous.

The raven let out a hoarse croak that sounded eerily like *Help!*

Lark couldn't just leave him on the ground. These woods were home to red foxes, prowling cats, brown bears, and even an occasional hunting pack of wolves. A vulnerable raven might be eaten before she even made it home.

Besides, she had a knack for fixing broken things so maybe she could at least offer aid.

"I'm afraid I'll have to jostle you a bit," she told him, "but I'll bring you somewhere safe and I'll try to help you heal." She might not know much about mending wings, but she could ask Netty Greenwillow, the local healer, for advice. At the very least, she could provide food and water away from predators.

Scooting closer, she reached her hands beneath his body to scoop him into a soft pouch made by raising the edge of her blue tunic. As she did, something nicked her finger and she let out a surprised yelp.

Startled, the raven thrashed his good wing and paddled his feet. Worried he would hurt himself worse, she quickly nudged him into her tunic and wrapped the fabric around him. Before she straightened, however, she spotted the sharp rim of a thin circle in the matted grass beneath the bird. A bead of her blood still gleamed on the tarnished surface, oozing slowly into the silver as she studied it.

What was it? It was too large to be a coin. . . .

Was this what she had seen tumble from the king's pocket? It didn't look like a mirror, as Ma had assumed, but in the dirt it was hard to tell.

The raven shifted and clicked his beak. Impulsively, Lark pinched the metal disk—careful not to cut her fingertips on the sliver-thin edge this time—and thrust it into her pocket before hefting the bird in her arms and climbing to her feet.

She hurried home, the back of her neck prickling as though she were being watched the whole way.

She tried to distract herself from worry by imagining what magical Faevors her sister and brother might be awarded for completing the Hunt. Surely Galin's would be something special, since he'd helped the Harvest King?

When he got home, she would help Da fix a special meal to celebrate.

The raven croaked and Lark told him, "Everything will work out. You'll see." But she was trying to convince herself.

TWO

Springs and Screws

WHEN SHE RETURNED home, Lark tucked the injured raven in a small basket she lined with soft moss pulled from a patch by the back door. Then she offered him a handful of dried cherries, seeds, and a stale crust of bread gathered from the kitchen cupboards. As he pecked at the food, she studied the way he held his injured wing. She might have an idea. . . .

But first she needed to check the shadowbred mares. They'd been out all night, racing the wind as they followed the White Stag, and even though they had far more strength and stamina than ordinary horses, the Wild Hunt still challenged their endurance.

"I'll be back shortly," she told the bird. "Don't cause any trouble or I'll put you outside." He settled into the basket nest and blinked at her as though promising he'd behave. She darted out, closing her door with a sharp click.

As she passed Galin's room she had to swallow a knot

of tears and worry. If only the raven could talk—maybe he could tell her what had happened to her brother.

No. Galin will tell us himself. He's likely on his way right now with Da and Sage, in possession of a wondrous Faevor and a daring story, no doubt.

A fresh surge of hope lent wings to her feet. Lark rushed down the stairs and out to the stable yard. When she pulled open the barn doors and stepped inside, she was immediately enveloped in the warm scents of hay, horsehair, oats, apples, and leather—and the dark, wild, rose-tinged musk that was unique to the rare shadowbreds her mother raised.

It should have soothed her, but peering down the row of twelve stalls that held the treasured mares of the Mairen herd, she couldn't help noticing three stood empty. Ma was riding Legacy, of course, and Sage had taken Batwing— too young for this Hunt—out to look for Galin before the Faevoring in order to give her own mare, Reverie, a chance to rest.

But Whimsy, Galin's mare, was still missing.

The remaining shadowbreds greeted Lark with a ruckus, nickering, pawing, or banging their feed tubs in a greedy racket to distract her. "I hear you, I hear you." She laughed, heading to the feed room. They certainly didn't *sound* tired.

Nevertheless, after their hard rides the night before, she mixed extra morning rations for each horse. Inka: half scoop oats, toss of barley; Indigo: full scoop oats; Whisper: half scoop oats, handful of barley; Rumor: scoop of oats, scoop of barley; and so on, with rose petals for all of them. As Lark carried the buckets of feed to the stalls, Sarai Vanbeck—their neighbor and Ma's best friend—appeared in the aisle, her long gray braids wrapped in a knot on top of her head.

"Ah, Lark, sweet little bird. I promised your parents I'd be here to help. I've put some food in your larder—though if you don't like Irma Sweetmeadow's vinegar salad, ignore the blue bowl with the white linen wrapping—and I'll clean stalls so you can rest, hm?"

Sarai's gentle practicality and kind hug brought tears to Lark's eyes and she couldn't respond. Sarai rubbed her back and nudged her toward the barn doors. "Go on, now. I've cared for horses my whole life, and though I've not got your ma's touch with these magic ones, I'm plenty capable of tending them for now."

Lark thanked her but hesitated at the end of the aisle, reluctant to leave the peace of the barn. She wasn't sure she could return to the Galin-sized hollow in her house just yet.

The copper charms tied in the shadowbreds' manes clinked gently as the mares ate, random notes that reminded Lark of plinking music box melodies. The charms prevented the Fae magic in the horses' veins from overwhelming their mortal blood and turning them back into creatures of smoke, shadow, and starlight.

Suddenly a calico cat, fur splotched white, orange, and black, jumped from the rim of a nearby barrel. She greeted

Lark with a rumbling purr, stropping her ankles. Lark bent down to rub the cat's ears. "Good morning, Jinx."

Jinx meowed and wandered off, so Lark finally turned her attention to the idea she'd had for the injured raven. She grabbed a length of baling twine from a hook on the wall and then fetched two fallen twigs from the poplar tree beside the spring in the main pasture. With something to focus on, she hurried back to the house determined to test her design.

Instead of staying in his moss-basket nest as she'd hoped, the raven had perched on the edge of her desk to tap sadly at the window glass. "I'm sorry you're stuck inside," she told him, "but you won't heal if you don't rest that wing! Look, though—I have a plan. I just need you to hold still, understand?"

He bobbed his head and let her approach with her twigs and string. When she reached for his broken wing, however, his temper flared and he snapped his beak in warning.

"I'm not trying to hurt you! But if you keep moving, the bones won't heal properly. This is to hold them in place so they can mend. It's nothing to be afraid of. See?" She held out the twigs so he could investigate, but he tried to snap one in his beak and she had to yank it away. "Quit that! Do you want my help or not? It's not as if I don't have other things to worry about, you know!"

The raven hung his head and meekly held out his injured wing so she could splint it with the poplar twigs, tying them in place with the twine. "There! That wasn't so bad, was it? I'm going to see if I can find Mistress Greenwillow—she's the healer—to ask about possible remedies for you. Her potions always taste terrible but at least they work."

The raven squawked, violently flapping his good wing. "What is the matter with you?" she demanded.

He stared at her and then, without breaking her gaze, covered his head with his uninjured wing.

"Are you tired?" she guessed. "You can sleep there in the nest. I'll close the curtains if you want it dark. . . ."

He clicked his beak and shuffled his feet in irritation.

Wrong guess. "You have a headache?"

This time he rolled his eyes and pecked the desk impatiently before repeating the gesture.

"I'm sorry. I don't know what you're trying to tell me, but Mistress Greenwillow's apothecary shop is just this side of Tradewind Junction—that's what we call our town, in case you didn't know—and it only takes me half an hour to walk there and back. I'll see if I can get you something for pain." *And bad temper,* she added silently.

But again the raven seemed to protest. "You don't want me to find the healer?" Lark asked, and now he bobbed his head triumphantly and settled back in the basket. "But . . . why not?"

He covered his head with his wing and tucked himself as small as he could, nestling into the moss until he was barely visible above the rim of the woven basket. "Ohhh," she breathed. "You want to hide, stay a secret."

With a gleeful croak that sounded a lot like *Right!* he shot up from the nest and bobbed his head so enthusiastically she had to laugh. "Very well. I'll do my best, but you'd better stay quiet or my parents will hear." She frowned at the awkward splint she'd made. "That may not be supportive enough, especially if you insist on fluttering and hopping about. . . . Here. Hold still again."

She took a scrap of old flannel fabric and bound it around the splint, creating a sling to hold the entire wing tucked in safe and close to the raven's body. "There. Maybe that will do the trick."

Instead of returning to the basket, though, he resumed pecking at her window glass. "Quit or it will crack!" she scolded, but he only pecked harder.

Grumbling—this bird was far more trouble than she'd anticipated—Lark flung open the window. The fall air was cool and crisp, but warm sunlight spilled into the room to melt any lingering chill. "There. Don't break yourself worse trying to fly away before you're healed, you hear me?"

He made a cackling sound in the back of his throat and pointed one clawed foot at her window ledge.

"What? The salt and bay leaves are there to keep away any Fae or wildkin."

He pointed again, practically rolling his eyes.

For a bird, he was remarkably good at communicating,

wasn't he? But he didn't smell like a wildkin and she didn't
sense a faint tingle of magic like she sometimes did around
the shadowbreds. Of course, she'd always heard ravens were
clever birds. . . . Frowning suspiciously at him, Lark leaned
out her window to discover a tarnished piece of silver, round
with tiny teeth like a cogged wheel, and a black feather.

She couldn't see anyone, but judging by the raven's
behavior she'd guess another bird had left them for her to
find. Why, though? What did they mean? Was the gear
somehow linked to the disk she'd found by the waymarker?
What was it for?

Lark puttered around the house while she waited for her
family to return. She tightened a loose doorknob, adjusted
a crooked cabinet hinge, swept the floor. . . . Surely the
Faevoring ceremony was over by now? What could take so
long?

Eventually she wandered out to the barn to brush Jinx
and help Sarai clean water buckets, but her worries grew
like weeds with every passing hour. A scout stopped by just
after midday to report that Horsemaven River was riding
past the northern waymarkers, still seeking signs of Galin.
"Wasn't he in the square?" Lark asked, lips trembling. But
the scout pulled up the hood of his green-and-brown cloak,
nodded once to Sarai, and rode away.

"Come, little bird, let's eat some bread and cheese in the

sunshine, shall we?" Sarai suggested kindly, but the pity in her eyes twisted Lark's stomach in knots and she couldn't swallow a bite.

Each moment brought them closer to moonrise. Where was Galin?

Sarai eventually went home—promising she'd be back if needed—and Lark was giving the aisle a last sweep when her sister finally appeared late in the afternoon. Lark's first impulse was to ask about Galin, but one look at the way Sage sagged against the door, exhaustion painted in plum-colored circles beneath her eyes, and Lark already knew the answer.

He wasn't in the square for the Faevoring ceremony. Their fears had been confirmed: he hadn't come back from the Hunt.

"You look done in," Lark said, trying to sound brave. "Go on up to the house. I'll take care of Batwing."

Sage didn't seem to hear. She pulled up her sleeves to study the silver ivy-and-rose-embossed cuffs wrapped around her wrists, marking the completion of her first Wild Hunt. She had earned them last spring, along with a Faevor from the May Queen—a token of Fae magic granted for surviving the Hunt.

Sage's first Faevor had been a leather bridle guaranteeing her horse's safety. Lark wondered what the Harvest King had chosen to give, but she quietly filled Batwing's water bucket and started to mix the mare's evening feed of grain and rose petals. She'd already plucked the petals from one of Ma's Faevors—an ever-blooming rosebush that produced flowers even in the depths of winter, granted by the May Queen when Ma was younger.

"I assumed they would cancel the Faevoring ceremony, with Galin still missing. But they held it anyway," Sage said at last in a daze.

"We hoped Galin would meet you there with the Harvest King," Lark whispered.

"That's what Da said. But the king wasn't even at the ceremony. Lady Mist and two Fae I've never seen before handed out the traditional cuffs and tokens. The emissary didn't look happy about it. I tried to ask her about Galin, but she ignored me. Lark, it was as if he'd never even ridden." Sage crumpled, burying her face in her hands as sobs shook her shoulders.

Tears welled in Lark's eyes too. "What did Da do?"

Sage gulped air and wiped her eyes. "He called a meeting with the Elders."

The three oldest citizens in town—currently Rowana Farstorm, Goward Brassman, and Amalia Heartstone—formed the local governing council. The Elders of Tradewind Junction settled disputes, solved problems, and smoothed the small frictions of daily life in a busy community. Surely their collective wisdom would yield answers.

"They'll figure something out," Lark said, wrapping her sister in a dusty hug. "We'll find him. Somehow."

"There's no time! Moonrise is in less than two hours. I

never should have left him. I have more experience. . . . If we'd been riding together . . ." She cried harder.

"It's not your fault, Sage. When I saw him, he was only a couple paces ahead of you. He rescued the Harvest King. . . ." Lark's voice trailed away. Why hadn't the king been at the Faevoring ceremony either?

Sniffling, Sage drew a brass compass on a slender chain from her tunic pocket and dangled it in front of her, letting it spin. "The emissary gave me this Faevor, though I told her I didn't deserve it after leaving my brother. She said as long as I carry it, I'll never be lost. I wish there was a way to give it to Galin."

"Ma and the scouts are still out searching, aren't they? There's still a chance we'll hear good news. . . ."

But through the barn doors they could both see the sun sinking below the horizon.

While Sage took a quick bath before their parents returned, Lark checked on the raven. She found him proudly displaying a whole collection of black feathers and tiny silver oddments spread across the surface of her desk.

"Where did all these come from? What are they for?" Lark asked, astonished. The raven danced from foot to foot as she gathered up the feathers and slipped them into her desk drawer.

Then there were the silver bits and pieces. Another tiny gear, several springs, miniature screws . . . She kept a box on her desk filled with random parts that might prove useful for future repair projects, so she dragged it closer and prepared to sweep everything in. She could sort through the jumble later, maybe clean the dirt and tarnish off the gears. Right now she was too anxious about Galin to focus on anything else.

But before she could tip the pieces in, the raven flung himself at her hands and croaked so loudly she was afraid Sage would hear. "Hush now or you'll get us both in trouble!" Lark scolded him.

Were all ravens this bothersome or just him? She sniffed the air, but she still didn't smell any sign of magic surrounding him.

He pecked the box and glared.

"Fine, then." She put her hands on her hips and glared back. "What should I do with all these bits? They'll get lost if we leave them scattered about."

The raven tilted his head to one side as if considering her words, and then indicated his moss basket.

"Are you sure? You won't be very comfortable sleeping on them."

He strutted to the basket and, pinching the moss in his beak, lifted it slightly.

"Oh, I see. You want me to hide them under the moss?"

He bobbed his head and fanned his tail, then hopped from foot to foot as if urging her to hurry.

"But why?"

Now! he seemed to croak.

She'd heard somewhere that ravens liked shiny things, but she hadn't guessed they'd be so possessive.

Bemused, Lark carefully tucked the collection of silver pieces beneath the moss in his basket. She had just patted it back in place when he stiffened, flared his tail feathers again, and let out a soft squawk.

"Oh!" She'd forgotten the strange silver disk in her pocket. Withdrawing it, she rubbed her thumb across the scuffed and tarnished surface, avoiding the sharp edge. There appeared to be symbols engraved in a circle, but she couldn't see them clearly beneath the grime. She tilted the disk, trying to get a better look.

Below, the front door creaked open and Ma's voice called, "Girls?"

"Is there news of Galin?" Lark cried, thrusting the silver disk under the moss with the other pieces. She slammed her bedroom door closed and dashed downstairs, Sage a step behind her.

THREE

Cold Toes

THEY FOUND THEIR parents bustling into the kitchen. Da's arms were loaded with baskets of food from concerned neighbors while Ma carried a cloth bag filled with fresh bread and sweet rolls from the bakery, but there was no Galin. And one glimpse of their grim faces told Lark that there wasn't good news about him either. She glanced at the sky through the window and swallowed a sob as the rising moon floated from a curtain of clouds.

It was stained red, as red as the blood of a broken heart.

Her brother was now trapped on the wrong side of the border.

Lark closed her eyes and shook her head, unwilling to believe it.

This was all a mistake. A malicious bit of mischief. A Fae trick.

It couldn't be *true*. It just *couldn't*.

In centuries past, Lark knew from history lessons, mortals were sometimes captured by the Fae and kept as thralls, servants of the Twilight Court. Though this was strictly forbidden once the Accords were signed, they had still faced grievous injury—even death—while riding Wild Hunts with the Fae. But nothing so serious had happened in recent memory, largely because there were now strict rules about who was allowed to participate in the Hunt and stringent requirements for their preparation.

It had seemed like enough, until now.

"What news?" Sage was asking, helping Da unload pie tins and baking dishes wrapped in waxed paper.

Ma sighed and leaned her hip against the edge of the table, folding her arms. Her eyes were pink and swollen, as though she'd been crying. But that couldn't be true either, Lark thought. Horsemaven River Mairen *never* cried.

"No sign of him. One of the trackers found his shadow-bred by the waymarker north of Heron Gap, though. Whimsy had lost most of her copper charms and was too wild to catch, but Legacy and I rode up there and managed to lure her back. I replaced as many charms as I could, but I'll ask Davina Wardspin to come out and add a few once the luckwitches have finished harvesting boundary magic, just in case."

The moon's crimson color faded as it climbed through the stars, sending beams of cold white light slanting into the kitchen. A chill settled in the house and Lark shivered.

While the others unpacked the food, she knelt by the hearth to light a fire.

"Maybe the luckwitches can use that magic to get Galin back," Sage said hopefully.

Lark's hand twitched as she struck the flint fire starter, and she nearly dropped a spark on Da's woven wool rug. Was that even possible?

Twice a year, in the days leading up to the Wild Hunt, the border between the Fae realm and the mortal world grew thin and fragile, letting Fae magic seep through. After the Hunt chased rogue wildkin back across and stabilized the boundary, luckwitches around the Borderlands filled glass bottles with magic-laced earth and collected grass, moss, and leaves that had absorbed traces of Fae power, which they distilled into a shimmering substance used in crafting spellcharms and empowering amulets. The residual magic wasn't concentrated enough for anything spectacular, but it could offer some protection from rogue wildkin and Fae mischief. Was it strong enough to bring Galin home?

Ma's voice was gentle as she answered, "You know it doesn't work that way, girls. The moon has risen. He is caught."

Da coughed—or choked on a sob—and carried a stack of plates to the table.

"But I don't understand what happened," Sage cried. "He wasn't that experienced with the shadowbreds, but he was a *good* rider. And he and Whimsy understood each other. When he kicked her ahead of Reverie and me, I never suspected something might go wrong." Sage dissolved into tears again.

Lark stared at a wisp of blue smoke, watching it curl along a bit of dry tinder. Tears burned her eyes too as a shiver of sorrow chased along her arms. She held her hands out to the spreading warmth of the fire, leaning closer to the hearth.

It was true that Galin had never cared about riding the shadowbreds like Sage, so they were all surprised when he'd announced his intention to enter the Gauntlet, the qualifying race for the more dangerous Hunt.

But Galin raced well and finished in second place. Though no one could catch Sage and Reverie, he and Whimsy came close. Only now Lark wondered if they'd all been too distracted by his unexpected success at the Gauntlet to question *why* he'd suddenly wanted to participate in the first place.

She blurted, "Why did he even want to ride? He wasn't interested before."

"I wondered that too," Sage admitted. "When I asked him, he just said he felt it was time to try."

Da finished setting plates on the table and exchanged a soft, sad, shy sort of smile with Ma. "Perhaps he did it to impress a girl."

"Who? I never saw him with anyone. Never even heard him *mention* anyone," Sage said, pouring cups of cocoa for her and Lark and dark coffee for their parents.

"Why he did it doesn't matter." Ma pinched the bridge of her nose. "I should have made him wait until he'd ridden more."

Da laid a hand on her shoulder. "There's no blame for you to carry. He made his choice knowing the risks."

But Lark wondered if he'd really understood the danger.

There was a moment of silence, punctuated by the crackling flames in the stone fireplace.

Ma finally patted Da's hand and said in a breaking voice, "While we eat, you can tell us what the Elders said. We need to decide what we'll do, these next six months."

Six months. Lark couldn't stand the thought of so much lost time. *Half a year* without her brother. That is, if they could even find him again when the border opened come spring.

They sat around the table, painfully aware of Galin's empty place, and passed dishes of persimmon chutney, roasted potatoes, mashed turnips, and sliced ham generously provided by friends and neighbors. But Lark had no appetite. She picked at her food, concealing tiny bites in her napkin to bring to the raven hiding in her bedroom.

"The Elders weren't helpful, I'm afraid." Da frowned. "Apparently the emissary and the rest of the envoy left immediately after the Faevoring ceremony. I told the Elders what Lark saw at our waymarker, about the Harvest King's fall and the brambles that caused it, but by then Lady Mist and the Fae had already departed and there was no chance to ask about it."

"So what do we do in the meantime, then? Just wait?" Lark asked angrily.

"I'm afraid so," Da told her, dragging his fork across his plate.

Ma added, "Sometimes the best thing we can do is to be patient, as difficult as that is."

Patience seemed a poor solution to Lark. Somehow she had to find a way to help her brother. After all, he would do the same for her.

Later that evening, when Lark was preparing for bed, she tried asking the bird if he'd seen a boy with a dimple like hers and a small scar above his lip—Galin had split it open after trying to skate on a frozen pond before she was even born. "He's about *this* tall," Lark said, reaching her arms above her head a little, "and he always wears a blue felt cap with a gray band. He was riding near the king and a golden Fae. Do you know where they went after the king fell from his horse?"

However, after gorging himself on the supper she'd smuggled in her napkin, the raven hunched in his moss-lined basket nest and promptly fell asleep.

Lark sighed—what else had she expected from a troublesome bird?—and climbed into her own bed, but despite her exhaustion she couldn't find rest. After tossing and turning until well past midnight, she finally gave up and padded down the hall to her sister's room. She eased the door open and tiptoed in, but Sage was still awake too.

"Can't sleep either, hm?" Sage whispered.

Lark climbed into bed beside her, pulling the quilt over both of them. "I'm afraid," she admitted in the dark. "I can't believe he's gone."

Sage's breath hitched and Lark guessed that she had been crying. "Same, little bird," she said. "I wish I hadn't lost sight of him when we were riding. I should have known something wasn't right."

"What do you mean?" Lark asked.

The silence stretched so long she assumed her sister had dozed off, but Sage finally murmured, "We should have been more careful, Galin and I. Something felt . . . wrong, almost from the start. I mean, riding the border is such a rush, Lark. A river of time flows along it, swirling and splashing. You can watch the currents of possibility, the ripples of chance."

"You can see the future?" Lark asked, surprised.

"And the past, and the present, all at once. It's like looking through water and seeing the reflections of endless moments layered across your eyes. You can feel the tug of time from deep inside your bones. . . . It distracts some

33

riders, dazes them and puts them in danger. And then add the tingle of Fae magic singing in your ears . . . It's hard to stay focused. But the White Stag is a beacon in the dark. Behind him there's a moment of calm, a smooth channel between time and magic, a heartbeat when everything is balanced in the midst of motion."

She smoothed a crease in the blanket and said, "It's hard to explain, but last spring, I felt the border steadying as we rode. Closing behind us, as if we were needles pulling thread to stitch a gap in the seam, you know?"

Lark smiled. "Sounds like one of Da's sayings."

Sage didn't laugh. "But this fall . . . everything was different. Restless, somehow."

"Then brambles appeared and the Harvest King fell from his horse," Lark added in the quiet left by her sister's fading voice.

Sage nodded against the pillow. "The Twilight Court holds power in balance, right? The May Queen rules the spring and the Harvest King rules the fall. But if something happens to the king . . ." Sage shook her head. "The border between our worlds is about equilibrium too—between time and magic, Fae and mortal. If something breaks that balance, if the Twilight Court is disrupted, what happens?"

"Our brother goes missing," Lark answered in a cracked voice. "But how do we fix it?"

Sage propped herself up on her elbows and met Lark's

eyes in the dark. "I'm going to get him back during the May-fair Hunt."

"But how? What if *you* end up missing too?"

"Well, everyone in the Twilight Court is encouraged to ride the Wild Hunt, right? So when the May Queen calls everyone to horse, I'll be looking for Galin. As soon as I see him, I'll ride up to him and I won't leave his side until we cross the border and return to the barn together."

"What if he's not with the Hunt?"

Sage hesitated, and then said, "In that case, I'll just have to ride a little farther until I find him. After all, I did get another Faevor, didn't I? A compass that means I'll never get lost. Anyway, I have six moonturns to prepare. I *won't* fail." Sage slithered farther under the covers and added, "Worry won't fix anything tonight. Get some sleep now."

Lark chewed her lip, wishing there was some way *she* could help Galin so that Sage wouldn't have to face the danger of the Wild Hunt again. Something she could do without waiting six whole moonturns. . . .

"Lark?"

"Hm?"

"Get your cold toes off me or I'm shoving you out of my bed."

FOUR

Salt and Spiders

STILL DROWSY THE next morning and feeling Galin's absence like a weight in her chest, Lark could only muddle through her chores.

She trudged to the end of the barn aisle and tugged open the wide doors leading to a large pasture designed specifically for shadowbreds. It was fenced with copper rails showing the green verdigris of age and surrounded by a thick hedge of hawthorns and witch hazel. Charms dangled from the gates, jingling softly in the breeze.

As clear yellow sunlight poured through the doorway, turning the haze of dust to golden glitter, Lark opened stalls and let the shadowbred mares outside to graze. One by one they trotted past her, eager to taste the wind. Watching their exuberance, she could hardly believe they'd raced the Hunt only the night before.

She followed the last mare out and closed the gate, resting her forehead and elbows on the copper rails to watch the herd gallop through the grass.

It was possible to forget what the shadowbreds were when they placidly munched grain or dozed in their stalls. Sure, they ate roses along with their feed, but inside the barn or from a distance they looked like any other ordinary horses. Taller than most, perhaps, and a bit leaner. A more defined arch in their necks, maybe, and longer legs. Fancy and high-strung, true, but . . . nothing Fae or magical or wild.

Out here, though . . .

They raced around the pasture like a thundering river of ink and shadow, their copper charms clinking. A careful observer paying attention to the cadence of their hoofbeats would notice they didn't always strike the ground—sometimes the shadowbreds merely skimmed the surface. A silver gleam swirled in the depths of their dark eyes, and their flared nostrils snorted sparkling mist. The texture of their manes and tails was different too. Rather than the strong, slightly coarse hair of an ordinary horse, theirs was spiderweb thin and silky—and in the wind, the ends melted into wisps of smoke.

But their most significant Fae tendencies couldn't easily be described or quantified: keen intelligence and sensitivity, unusual strength and swiftness, unnaturally long life spans, dauntless courage and stamina.

Characteristics necessary to survive the Wild Hunt.

Journey, the mare Ma had promised to Lark, nickered

and kicked up her heels before plunging into a patch of late clover. Owning a shadowbred was an honor reserved for only a privileged few, and Lark knew she should be more grateful. But while she could easily admit the shadowbreds were beautiful, she wasn't certain they could be trusted.

After all, the magic in their blood meant they weren't far off from wildkin, as far as Lark was concerned. Oh, she knew her lessons well enough and could recite the differences without hesitation—but that didn't mean she was willing to let go of wariness around them.

Wildkin came from the darkness left by Fae enchantments, crawling from the debris of shattered illusions and strung-out spells. The immortal Fae were capricious and sometimes prone to malice—eternity apparently led to boredom, and in their efforts to find entertainment the Fae could be wickedly imaginative. Their tricks left traces in the natural world, creating animals unpredictably influenced by magic.

Some wildkin were harmless. Like hummingbirds that spun rainbows with their wings or sunfish with scales that sparked underwater.

Others, however . . .

Well, it was a fortunate thing that the White Stag had the power and authority to keep them mostly in check.

Shadowbreds differed from wildkin because they weren't ordinary animals corrupted by magic. They were descended from and bred by horses that *were* magic. Like the firedrakes and phoenix birds, basilisks and gryphons,

Fae starshadow horses were pure power and elemental energy. And when bred to carefully selected mortal horses, they produced foals that embodied the best of both ordinary horses and starshadow horses.

But that didn't make shadowbred horses *safe*. Or easy.

Lark chewed a hangnail and kicked a clod of dirt. She was probably the only Mairen girl in history who didn't like riding the shadowbreds. Oh, she loved them just fine when her own two legs were on the ground—she enjoyed feeding, watering, brushing, saddling, and leading them—but climbing on their backs? When she knew they were basically magic and darkness barely contained in thin mortal skin?

No thank you.

She spun on her heel and went back inside the barn. Grabbing a wheelbarrow and pitchfork, she headed to the opposite end of the aisle to start mucking stalls, because even magic horses made smelly messes. Her body fell into the familiar rhythm of shoveling out soiled straw and shavings and spreading fresh pine-scented bedding, but her mind fretted about missing brothers, broken treaties, injured birds, and strange silver pieces hidden under moss.

After chores were done, Sage tried coaxing her to ride, but Lark wasn't in the mood. Besides, she already had a perfect excuse. "Sorry, Sage, but Ma asked me to take a look at the well pump."

"Maybe another day, then," her sister said.

"Maybe." But they both knew that meant *likely never*, and

Sage's resigned sigh plucked a string of sorrow in Lark's chest. How many times had Sage invited her and Galin to ride only for them to refuse? While Lark looked for broken things to fiddle with, her brother had always gone to Da's tailor shop. She still didn't understand why he had suddenly decided to ride this particular Hunt, but now she wondered . . . If he had spent more time practicing in the saddle with Sage, would he have made it home from the Hunt safely?

And then she wondered if Sage had ever felt lonely when they turned her down.

Guilt mixed with grief as Lark grabbed her tools. "I really do have to fix the pump, but . . . thanks for the offer."

Sage smiled back and Lark headed for the well. The pump handle had been sticking for several moonturns and it was getting more difficult to draw water. When she confirmed that the problem was rust, as expected, she scrubbed it away with vinegar, salt, and baking soda. Once everything gleamed, she replaced a washer and tightened some nuts and bolts.

There. Good as new.

She wiped everything down and washed her hands, feeling something like happiness for the first time since the terrible Hunt. It was satisfying to see water once again flowing swift and strong from the well.

She might not be a proper Mairen girl, good at riding shadowbreds, but she *was* good at repairing things. *Just because a tool isn't right for one job doesn't mean it's broken or useless*, she reminded herself.

Speaking of things that needed mending . . .

With Ma and Sage out on a ride and Da working in his tailor shop, Lark had time to check on the injured raven and examine those odd silver parts that had been left on her windowsill. They needed fixing, clearly, but how could you repair something when you didn't even know what it was supposed to be?

The silence of the house tossed disconcerting echoes at her as she climbed the stairs. Galin's room was at the far end of the hall and she couldn't resist peeking in, just in case . . . but he wasn't lying sprawled on his faded quilt. He wasn't sitting at his ink-stained desk or rinsing his hands at his chipped china washbasin. He wasn't rummaging for his favorite shirt in the old wardrobe built by their grandfather and carved with acorns and squirrels.

It was like losing him all over again, though she shouldn't have let her hopes rise. She slouched to her bedroom and closed the door, trying not to cry.

The air smelled unmistakably of *bird* so she raised her window a bit to let in the late-fall sunshine. The raven watched her, perched on the edge of her desk in uncharacteristic silent stillness as she lifted the moss and gathered up all the random little gears and springs and screws. A new project could never fill the emptiness left by a missing brother, but maybe it was just the distraction she needed to clear her head.

She arranged the pieces in a neat line across her desk and then picked up the silver disk. After rummaging for a scrap of wool cloth, Lark began polishing it. When she wiped away the dirt, she discovered there *were* symbols engraved around the edge of the circle. It reminded her of a watch face, only they weren't numbers. Instead, they seemed to be small images.

She tilted the disk near the window to get a clearer view. Yes, now she could see that there were thirteen symbols in total, corresponding to each of the year's full moons: a pine cone, an acorn, an egg. A tree, a hare, a frog. A rose, a dragonfly, a fish. An apple, an ear of corn, a fox, and a bat.

She rubbed the disk with the wool scrap again and noticed another series of images marking a smaller, inner circle: a mountain or boulder, a feather, a flame, and a river or wave. They must represent the four elements: earth, air, fire, and water. Staggered between these were four symbols for the seasons: a snowflake, a raindrop, a blazing sun, a cloud.

But what was this disk for? It didn't look like any clock or watch face she'd ever seen. And how did it fit with the collection of assorted parts?

The raven made a low sound as a flicker of motion drew Lark's eye back to the window.

While she was focused on the strange pieces, a wolf spider big enough to fill a teacup had climbed through the gap in the sash and was now easing itself, one furry leg at a time, onto the sill. It was patterned black and brown, dark and furry.

Lark frowned, a ripple of unease sloshing through her stomach. She wasn't afraid of spiders—she didn't *like* them, but she figured as long as they ignored her she could tolerate a truce.

Only this one wasn't ignoring her. It studied her actions with uncanny interest, waving a leg as though counting the wheels and screws across her desk.

The raven clucked deep in the back of his throat, his feathers fluffed in alarm and eyes wide. He lunged at the window, snapping his beak, but he couldn't reach the spider in the narrow gap beneath the glass.

Was he trying to *eat* the spider?

Ignoring the raven, the wolf spider stretched another leg over the sill—and froze in what Lark could only call dismay. It shook itself, backed away, scuttled sideways, and tried again. And again it froze. It tried a third time, testing the surface of the sill, becoming increasingly agitated.

"What in the worlds . . . ?" Lark murmured, rising to her feet. And then her breath hissed between her teeth. Distracted by worry, she had been slow to notice the green musk scenting the air and the strange tingle shivering across her skin.

Fae magic.

The raven squawked and pecked the glass, scratching at

the sill with his talons. Did he recognize the scent of magic too?

Lark's windowsill was still dusted with a fine sprinkle of salt and three bay leaves—protection against malicious Fae. An ordinary spider might not like the combination of salt and herbs, but it wouldn't be so determined to cross the line—or so frustrated by failure.

This wasn't an ordinary spider. It must be a wildkin.

But the Hunt was supposed to have chased all the wildkin back into the Fae realm. What was a wildkin spider doing here *now*?

Lark shuddered, cold sweat beading on her brow as she bit off a scream. Galin probably would have plucked it up and calmly tossed it in an empty jam jar just like he did to the thousand-legger Da found in his sewing basket last summer, but Lark couldn't make herself move. Logic told her to catch it or smash it so she could show it to the Elders, but creeping terror kept her rooted to the floor.

Just then the wildkin spider tried to jump over the line of salt and ended up in a tortured spasm on the sill, rolling on its back with its legs curled. And then it twitched, righted itself, and sprang out of the window.

Lark and the raven exchanged a startled, shaken look. She slammed her window shut and closed the curtains for good measure, then tucked all the odd silver bits back under the moss in the bird's basket.

She needed more salt.

— FIVE —

Ravens and Rook

AFTER REINFORCING THE salt barrier beneath her own window, Lark ran through her house, sprinkling fresh salt and adding more bay leaves around every window and door. Then she dashed outside to tell Ma about the wildkin spider. The barn was quiet, though—Jinx softly snored on a stack of saddle blankets and a pigeon cooed from the rafters while the shadowbreds grazed in their pasture. Ma and Sage must still be out riding, but Lark had no way of guessing how long they'd be gone.

She could wait for their return, of course, but *a wildkin spider* had just tried to jump through her window. She needed to tell *someone*. Da's shop—Threadneedle's Fabrics—was an easy walk into Tradewind Junction, and maybe she could stop at Mistress Greenwillow's apothecary shop too. She would try to keep the raven a secret as she'd promised, but she was afraid her simple splint and sling might not be enough to mend his wing. Hopefully the healer would have a bird-safe remedy that could help.

The sun ducked behind a dark cloud as a gust of wind shook showers of crimson and gold leaves from the trees. Winter lurked in the sharp bite of the chill breeze and the sensation of watching eyes prickled the skin between her shoulder blades.

Where had that spider gone?

Remembering the way it had studied the scatter of strange silver pieces in her room sent fresh shivers across Lark's skin. She didn't know what all the bits were for or why they had been delivered to her, but she wasn't about to keep them.

What if more spiders or other wildkin came?

The last thing her family needed was additional trouble with the Fae.

Lark never should have picked up that disk. She would take everything back to the Fae border and pretend she hadn't noticed a thing—and then she would ask Da why a wildkin could cross the border after the Wild Hunt.

She hurried back to her room. As she swung a cloak around her shoulders and tucked the collection of silver pieces into a deep pocket, the injured raven grumbled. He clicked his beak, then flung himself awkwardly onto her shoulder. His broken wing, immobilized in the improvised splint and sling, buffeted Lark's cheek as his toes tightened in a painful grip. He flapped his good wing in an effort to regain his balance, the tips of his flight feathers brushing her eyes.

"What are you doing?" she cried, putting up a hand to keep him still.

He croaked in her ear, a sound like *Go!*

"Go? But you can't go with me! I thought you wanted to remain a secret! If I carry you into town *everyone* will be talking about it before sundown!"

He lightly nipped her ear and repeated the sound.

Maybe he just wants to get outside for a few minutes, Lark thought. *Staying cooped up in my room can't be very comfortable for him. . . .* "Fine. But I am *not* taking you to town with me. You can stay in the paddock near the foaling shed—it's not in use this time of year and no one will bother you there."

Walking while a heavy bird perched unevenly on her shoulder was more difficult than she had expected. With only one wing to stabilize his balance, the raven swayed back and forth at every step and his toes dug into her skin hard enough to draw blood.

Lark sighed. How could one bird be so much trouble?

Once she'd managed to navigate the stairs and ease through the front door, she tried to carry him toward the empty paddock so he could safely enjoy some fresh air. But he set up such a protest she could barely move, croaking and fidgeting and nipping her neck until she finally yelled, "Stop that!"

The raven jumped from his perch on her shoulder—half fluttering, half falling to the ground—and flashed her a look of fierce determination. He gestured with one wing and croaked *Follow!*

Lark rubbed the bridge of her nose. "How in the worlds did I get myself into this?" Maybe from now on she should stick to fixing things like wheelbarrows and gates . . . things that couldn't complain.

But she couldn't ignore him. Perhaps he simply wanted to return to wherever he belonged. With a reluctant sigh, she said, "Lead on, silly bird. But this better not take long. I have important things to do."

Croaking indignantly, the raven fanned his tail and hopped forward, moving with surprising speed and agility considering his injury.

Lark followed, feeling slightly ridiculous. "Where are we going?"

The raven didn't respond. He led her through the garden gate, past the pebbled path curving to the barn, around the edge of the main pasture, and through the orchard of apple, peach, and cherry trees her grandparents had planted.

"Wait . . . are you heading back to the waymarker?" It made sense. . . . After all, that's where she'd found him. "This should teach me not to pick up strange things too close to the Fae border," she muttered.

The raven glanced over his shoulder and clicked his beak, urging her to keep going. She sighed and stepped over a lichen-covered log, speeding up past a copse of fir trees and around a fern-covered bend in the trail. He hopped under a tangle of bittersweet vine bright with orange berries and Lark lost sight of him behind a spreading oak tree.

She scrambled through the bracken, branches clutching the edge of her cloak and leaves snagging in her hood. Her boot slipped on a mud-slick rock and she knocked her elbow against the trunk of a slender aspen tree. "Listen, bird, I know you probably just want to go home, but I need to make sure you'll be safe until that wing—"

Lark swallowed a startled gasp as she rounded the oak tree.

A boy-like figure stood before her, cradling the injured raven in both arms. Hair the color of dead oak or beech leaves stood in messy spikes around his head and a smudge of dirt darkened one freckled cheek. He wore doeskin breeches and a loose green shirt, but his feet were bare.

When he saw Lark, his eyes—one moss green, the other a golden brown—crinkled with his warm smile. He pointed to the sling on the raven's wing. "You did this?"

The air smelled of magic—a green tang that made Lark think of clover and honey, pinesap and sugar. Lighter than the dark scent of the wildkin, but disconcerting nonetheless. She blinked and took a step back.

This wasn't a boy. This was one of the Fae.

But how could it be? Once the White Stag and the Hunt had strengthened and sealed the border, the only way for the Fae to cross was through the Oak Gate in the square at the center of Tradewind Junction. They needed official diplomatic permission to do so, and there were all sorts of rules and protocols and—

He was still watching her expectantly, eyes trying to read her face as though it were a page with all her secrets written across it. "Did you do this?" he repeated, pointing again to the sling.

"Um . . ." What exactly did he mean by *this*? Did he understand that she had only tried to help? Was his smile just a trap—would he blame her for hurting the raven? Everyone knew the Fae were tricky and quick to anger, so she had no idea how to answer. She wasn't even supposed to speak with the Fae unless accompanied by her parents.

The Fae looked down at the raven happily nestled in his arms. "Can she speak?" he asked the bird.

"Yes!" Lark snapped. "But you aren't supposed to be here!"

Before she could worry about saying the wrong thing, he grinned at her.

"I know. But I lost Nightbird during the Hunt and it took my bird scouts too long to discover that he'd been injured and then picked up by a mortal girl."

The Hunt! Lark's mouth went dry and she chewed her lip. Here she was, actually *talking* to one of the *Fae*. And he'd been on the Hunt! This was her chance to find out what had happened to Galin. She just had to figure out how to ask the right questions so he couldn't dodge the answers she needed. Buying time to keep him there, she asked, "Bird scouts?" Were they the ones who had left feathers and oddments on her windowsill?

A darker suspicion suddenly scuttled through her mind and she lurched backward. Her salt had repelled the wildkin spider, but was it effective against wildkin birds? The raven had seemed extraordinarily smart, after all, and—

As if hearing her thoughts the Fae chuckled and skipped from one foot to the other. "I don't raise wildkin, if that's what you're worried about. I just have a knack with birds." He glanced down at the raven in his arms. "This sling is neatly done. I'm glad you helped him."

Lark flushed and scuffed a toe in the carpet of fallen leaves and old pine needles. "I suppose I have a knack for fixing things. Only wings are different than wheelbarrows, aren't they?"

The raven clucked and the Fae stroked his head. "He'll heal faster on the Other Side, but I'm grateful you offered him safe shelter in the meanwhile."

"He's quite clever, isn't he?"

"All ravens are, but I found *him* as a fledgling fallen from his nest and raised him myself. I'm afraid my influence has been too strong for him to act entirely . . . well, raven-ish." The Fae smirked as the bird preened his feathers and spread his tail. "He's too proud of himself, for one thing."

Lark couldn't wait any longer. The pressure of her *real* questions squeezed the breath from her lungs. She had to *know*. Voice shaking, she asked, "But how did you cross the border? Or did you just stay here after the Hunt? Why—"

He looked up, brows raised in surprise. "Ravens are pathmakers, wayforgers, trailbreakers. Nightbird can slip through the boundary any time he wishes, and I follow." His eyes darkened and he leaned forward. "But that's a secret I don't often share."

Lark's pulse thundered in her ears. If that was so, then this Fae and his bird could bring Galin back. She had to be careful, here. . . . She couldn't afford to fall into a trap. "Nightbird . . . That's your raven's name?"

"He's not *my* raven. Ravens don't belong to any but themselves, do they? But he is a friend, and I needed something to call him."

Lark blurted, "So what should I call you?" And then she cursed herself for being clumsy. What if she accidentally insulted this Fae? He could be the key to getting Galin back!

He grinned again and tilted his head to the side. The Fae never gave their true names to mortals, but she didn't expect him to ask, "What would you like to call me?"

Trouble, she thought. *Danger.* But aloud she said, "How about . . . Rook?"

"Ah! I like that! Yes, you may call me Rook. And what shall I call you?"

"I'm Lark."

"Lark? Lark Mairen?" His shoulders went rigid, Nightbird squirming in his grasp.

"That's right." Taking a deep breath, she plunged in: "My brother, Galin, rode the Wild Hunt, but he didn't return. Do you or your birds know—"

"Your brother was with the Harvest King."

"Yes! You saw him, then? Where did they—"

Nightbird muttered softly and Rook interrupted, "You're the one who found the moonclock!"

"Moonclock?" she repeated. But her mind started spinning. The silver pieces *did* look like parts of a clock or pocket watch, and the symbols around the disk corresponded to the full moons. . . .

Her heart skipped a beat in sudden panic. If he thought she had stolen it, he would *never* help her get Galin back. Thrusting her hand into her pocket, she pulled out a fistful of gears and springs and held them out. "It was already broken when I discovered the face. I didn't take it on purpose!" she insisted. "I just . . . I have a habit of collecting things to fix, parts that might prove useful. . . . Here! Please. I don't want any of these."

Rook backed away, shaking his head. "I'm sorry, but I sense the moonclock is already sealed to your blood. I'm

53

afraid you're the only one who can fix it now."

"I can't fix it. I don't even know what it *is*. What it *does*. I just want my brother back. Please, tell me where Galin is and you can have all these pieces."

Nightbird let out a harsh cry and Rook jerked his chin up. A moment later Lark heard voices and the steady drumming of hoofbeats.

"We must talk more another time. I do know where your brother is, but if you want to save him you must fix the moonclock. And don't tell *anyone*. I mean it—swear by blood, bloom, and bough that you won't breathe a word of it."

Startled by his urgent intensity, she stammered, "All right. I swear silence. But why—"

"You helped Nightbird so I'll help you. Besides, you aren't the only one trying to save a sibling."

Before she could ask another question Nightbird squawked and Rook slipped through a gap between the trees. The last thing she heard was, "Use the feathers to reach me!"

Lark was left alone in a skirl of colored leaves. She rubbed her eyes, wondering if she'd imagined the whole exchange.

"Lark!" Ma's voice sliced through her daze. "What are you doing out here?" She and Sage trotted up on Inka and Indigo, two of the older shadowbreds, and reined to a stop.

"Ummm . . . well . . . I was looking for you, actually," Lark said, bending the truth. "I saw a wildkin!"

She blurted out the story of the spider and its strange

54

behavior, omitting any mention of moonclock pieces or a wounded raven. "When it realized it couldn't cross the salt line, it leaped from my window and I don't know where it is now!"

Sage leaned forward to rub Indigo's neck. "Ordinary spiders avoid salt too, Lark. It couldn't have been a wildkin—not so soon after a Hunt. Don't worry."

"I know what I saw!" Lark insisted. She also knew the border wasn't as strong as it was supposed to be, but she couldn't tell them that she'd spoken to a Fae. They'd probably say she was imagining things, or Ma would make her stay in the house and she would lose her chance to help her brother.

Lark understood that the Fae couldn't be trusted, but if Rook knew a way to save Galin she had to keep his secrets.

At least for now.

Ma pursed her lips and stared at a spot between Inka's ears. "Well, Da and I are meeting with the Elders tomorrow to discuss Galin's disappearance again. I'll mention your spider to them, all right? Now go on home, where it's safe. Sage and I will meet you there in a little while."

As Lark hurried back to the house, she scanned the trees for signs of Rook or Nightbird. But all she saw were shadows.

SIX

Bloodmoths

WHEN LARK STEPPED inside her house the first thing her gaze fell on was a pair of Galin's favorite fleece-lined slippers in the basket by the door. They were scuffed and worn and she'd teased him mercilessly about their ugliness, and now all she wanted was to hear him shuffling across the floor again. A surge of loneliness stung tears from her eyes as she climbed the creaky wooden stairs to her room.

The Fae she'd called Rook said she could save her brother by repairing the moonclock. She had to focus on that.

After all, fixing broken things was her favorite challenge. And since Grandda Maxim had been a Guildmaster clockmaker before his death, Lark at least had a basic familiarity with the mysteries of clockwork mechanisms. Once Grandda recognized her fascination with tools and tinkering, he had happily demonstrated some of the basic principles of his work.

Unfortunately, that had been a long time ago and she had forgotten too much.

Now she eyed the shelf of clockwork toys he had made for her over the years: tiny horses with jointed legs that pranced and leaped when you wound them up, a bounding fox, even a twirling dancer.

If only she could ask him for help.

Lark pulled her tool pouch from the chest at the foot of her bed and ran her hands over her screwdrivers, pliers, clamps, wrenches, and heavy hammer. Her first pair of pliers had been a gift, but she'd earned the other tools after completing small repair jobs for the neighbors. Everyone in Tradewind Junction knew they could call on her for all the inconveniences a Guildmaster mender didn't want to mess with. Just this week she had fixed Master Amon Miller's flour scales and straightened the hinges on Mistress Falisha Evenrush's garden gate, in addition to mending the water pump outside.

But clocks—even ordinary clocks—were far more complicated. She wasn't even sure where to begin with something called a moonclock. How was it supposed to work? How could it bring her brother back?

She pulled all the pieces out of her pocket and dumped them on her desk.

They certainly *looked* like components of a miniature clock or pocket watch. There were small gears and tiny pins, minuscule springs and screws. . . .

She pushed them around with her fingertip, examining the pattern of cogs and trying to remember everything her grandfather had ever told her about these types of mechanisms.

Blowing hair out of her eyes with a frustrated breath, she frowned at the assorted jumble. Whatever a moonclock was supposed to be, one thing was painfully obvious: she didn't have all the pieces she needed to put it back together.

Did Rook expect her to wait for his birds to deliver more parts? She didn't want to waste any time. . . .

The door banged open downstairs and a clatter of riding boots announced the arrival of her family even before Ma called, "Lark?"

"Coming!"

She'd look for the missing components in the morning, after she'd finished her chores, she decided.

Early the next day Ma and Da went to town as promised to speak to the Elders again. At first they resisted Sage's begging to go with them, but when she pointed out that she had been along on the Hunt and deserved to hear what was discussed, they finally relented. "Lark, you were a witness too. Would you like to come along?" Da offered.

Lark was torn. She *did* want to be included.

But joining them wouldn't bring Galin home, and fixing the moonclock might.

And she couldn't do *that* unless she found the missing components as quickly as possible. The best time to sneak out to the woods and search was while her parents were gone.

"Lark?" Ma prompted.

"I'll stay. Going would just make me feel worse," she said. Which was true, she reasoned. Not a complete lie.

So her parents made her promise to remain in the house until they returned, and they set off with Sage. Lark waited until they'd rounded the bend, then wrapped a sky-colored cloak around her shoulders and tugged up the hood. She hurried outside and slipped into the woods.

She hated breaking a promise, but she couldn't see a way around it if she wanted to fix everything else.

Lark decided to start looking near the waymarker where she'd last seen Galin, where brambles had wrecked a shadowbred, causing the Harvest King to fall and drop the moonclock.

From the base of the waymarker she slowly, methodically worked her way outward, scouring the ground for any glint of silver. She scanned every stone, every hillock of frost-burned grass and brown sedge, but broken twigs and dead bracken blocked her view. The lost pieces would be *tiny*, hidden in the shadows of late-season brush or lost under fallen leaves.

But she couldn't give up. Galin needed her.

She bent forward, squinting at the ground and carefully

brushing leaves and stems aside.

Something rustled in the underbrush, breaking her concentration like a pebble tossed in a pond. "Rook?" she called. "Nightbird?"

Laughter rippled at the edge of hearing and a trickle of fear slid between her shoulder blades. "Rook?"

Lark studied the dappled shade between the trees as she slowly backed away.

She wasn't supposed to linger this close to the Fae border, but she was still on her family's property, and that had always been safe. . . . Of course, if a wildkin spider could creep across the boundary, if Fae could follow ravens through . . . what else might sneak out?

Again that whisper of laughter. *Did she find it does she have it is she hiding it?* The words were a breath in her ear, a sigh on the wind.

Lark hastily pulled a strand of hair loose from her braid and tied it in a luck-knot for protection. Though she was tempted to turn home, she knew the longer Galin spent in the Fae realm the harder it would be to get him out and she was afraid he might be in danger. She *had* to find the rest of the moonclock pieces as quickly as possible, but she wasn't sure when she would get another chance to search.

She knelt on the ground, crawling through the grass for a closer look. Here is where the king had fallen. . . . She remembered seeing the moonclock tumble from his pocket and smash in a scatter of pieces, but then the tide of horses had swept by. It was hard to guess how far the fragments might have been kicked or trampled.

Frustration fizzed in her blood and she took a deep breath. *Patience is often the most important tool when dealing with a problem,* she reminded herself. It was a favorite saying of Grandda Maxim, along with *Sometimes the faster you push, the slower you progress.* She just needed to keep looking. . . .

But another sound behind her dragged her attention back to the woods.

A cloud of moths burst from a clump of ferns and persimmon trees, rising like pale smoke in the air. They twisted and spun—so many Lark could practically feel the flutter of their wings vibrating around her.

She almost laughed at herself. There was no reason to panic. They were just moths.

But then, they didn't look like any moths she'd ever seen before. And it was bright daylight, not dusk. Besides, it was cold. Too cold for moths, surely?

She straightened, brushing crushed grass stems from her knees. Then she frowned and crinkled her nose. Wait. . . . Was that . . . ? Yes. She took a deep breath, smelling the green musk of magic.

Oh no. These were no ordinary moths. They were *wildkin.* Just like the spider.

Lark didn't know if it was common sense or surrender, but she decided it was time to go. She chewed her lip and left the waymarker, watching the hovering cloud from the corners of her eyes as she reached the path home and picked up her pace.

The moths drifted closer, until they surrounded her in a flickering haze of wings and furry bodies with dark, quivering antennae.

Wildkin or no, she told herself, *they're only moths. Moths aren't dangerous.*

Then one landed on the back of her hand.

Lark tried to shake it off, but it clung to her skin with surprising tenacity. Its wings were such a pale white they appeared almost translucent, overlaid with a black pattern as delicate as lace. They opened and closed in a strangely mesmerizing rhythm—an eerie pulse that echoed the exact rhythm of her own heartbeat.

A sharp prick suddenly stung her hand and the moth's wings started turning a deep crimson red, the color slowly seeping toward the outer edges of the black filigree markings.

It looked like the ooze of blood.

Like the ooze of . . . *her blood.*

With a horrified cry, she slapped the moth away and ran.

The cloud of moths pursued her until she passed the fork in the path and cleared the edge of the woods, then they evaporated back into the shadows.

Lark's hand throbbed and every now and then blood

drops spattered the ground, but she didn't stop running until she reached her garden gate. Flinging herself against the fence post, she dropped her head and tried to catch her breath as the ache crept up her arm.

Were wildkin moths venomous?

"Lark?" Ma called. "I told you to stay in the house until we— What's wrong?" She jogged from the stable yard, concern crinkling her brow.

"I was out by the orchard and there were these moths. . . ." Lark lifted her hand, displaying a spreading purple mark. "One of them landed on me, and somehow it *bit* me and sucked my blood into its wings and—" She retched, watching the world slosh dizzily from side to side.

"Moths?" Ma grabbed her hand in a cool, strong grip. Gently twisting Lark's fingers for a closer look, she hissed. "Oh, sweetling. That looks nasty. Come on in and I'll see what I can do."

"Are wildkin moths—" Lark mumbled, her tongue too slow and thick to shape the words banging in her mind.

Was she poisoned?

Ma slung Lark's arm around her shoulders and lifted her, carrying her into their house.

Sage was already inside, preparing noonmeal. "What happened?" she asked, rushing to help Ma ease Lark into a chair.

"Moth . . ." Lark answered, voice slurring. Tiny black and gold sparks burst in her vision and she closed her eyes.

"Run and fetch Mistress Greenwillow. Hurry!" Ma said. Lark heard her sister clattering out the door, and then drifts of wool filled her head and she floated in a soft, blank haze.

She would have been content to continue dozing in that emptiness, but a pungent scent suddenly filled her nostrils. Someone poured a hot, noxious tea down her throat. The acrid, herbal tang swirled in her mouth, burning her tongue.

She spluttered and opened her eyes.

Mistress Netty Greenwillow leaned back and smiled. "There, now. Drink the rest. Quickly, child!" She thrust the mug forward, tipping it so fast Lark gurgled and choked on another mouthful.

Lark grabbed the mug from her and managed to swallow the rest of the bitter tea.

"Good. Show me your hand."

Lark held it out. Heat pulsed beneath her swollen skin, pumping angry ribbons of pain through her veins.

"Ach." Mistress Greenwillow clicked her tongue. "Your ma says it were a moth that did this, eh? A wildkin bloodmoth?"

"Bloodmoths? Is that what they're called?" Lark mumbled.

Ma and the healer exchanged dark looks. "Bit early in the season for moths, eh?" Mistress Greenwillow said, and Ma pursed her lips in unspoken agreement.

Netty Greenwillow bustled around the scarred kitchen table, tossing bits of leaves and flowers into a bowl. Sage busied herself crushing something spicy with a mortar and pestle and when she finished Lark was surprised to see her add it to the bowl as well.

"Hot water, dearie," Netty said, and Sage fetched the kettle from the cast-iron cookstove. She poured boiling water into the bowl and sweet-smelling steam filled the room.

As she stirred the mixture with a wooden spoon, Netty Greenwillow chanted a healing charm, repeating it nine times. Then she soaked strips of clean linen in the bowl and began laying them across the bite on the back of Lark's hand.

The first one hurt like fury, but as the warm poultice soaked into her skin the pain began to fade.

Lark sighed in relief. Her shoulders sagged as her body relaxed. She could almost *see* the venom—or whatever it was—being drawn out of her skin.

"Oh, thank you," she gasped. "That feels so much better."

"I should think so." The healer chuckled. "You were in rough shape, eh?" She plucked off a few linen strips and returned them to the bowl, replacing them with fresh ones. "Where did you say you were when you ran into this bloodmoth?"

"Near the waymarker," Lark confessed.

Netty swirled the bowl. "What were you doing there, child?"

"You were told to stay away from the border!" Ma

65

scolded, worry sharpening her voice.

"I was looking for . . . for Galin," she managed to stutter.

Ma's eyes softened. "Brave, foolish girl."

Netty went back to the kitchen table and rummaged through the canvas sack she always carried. Lark watched her pull out a jar of dark honey, more packets of dried herbs, and a couple of small cobalt-blue glass bottles.

As the healer began mashing honey and herbs together in another bowl, she asked, "Have you seen anything else unusual in those woods, Lark?"

"No," Lark told her. And then she hesitated. She didn't want to reveal any of Rook's secrets, but if the Hunt hadn't chased away the wildkin, people needed to be warned. "But I did see a wolf spider on my windowsill acting oddly. . . . I think it was a wildkin too."

Sage startled and dropped a spoon in the sink. "And we didn't believe you. Oh, Lark . . . I'm sorry."

"I'll notify the Elders," Netty said quietly to Ma. "Although they already lit the message lantern by the Oak Gate to request information about Galin, and Lady Mist hasn't responded yet. She's usually quick to communicate— they can't understand the delay."

Lark fumbled with the edges of her bandage. Maybe the Elders weren't getting answers, but she didn't have to wait for an official response from the emissary. She had her own Fae contact, didn't she? What had Rook said . . . something about using feathers to reach him?

At that moment the door swung open and her father breezed in.

"Who's ready to choose fabrics for their Solstice cloaks?" Lukis Threadneedle called, carrying bolts of rich velvet and warm wool. "I need to start soon since I won't have Galin's help this year." His voice broke and he cleared his throat with an unconvincing cough.

And then he spotted Lark sprawled in the chair, her hand wrapped in a poultice. "What happened, little bird?" He dropped the pile of fabrics on the table and crouched beside her, ruffling her hair.

She ducked her head and swatted his hand away. "Moth bit me."

"A moth? In the middle of the day? And it *bit* you?" Brow furrowed, he turned toward Netty and River. "Mistress Greenwillow, what is this?"

"Evidently a wildkin bloodmoth—"

"Not just one. There were *hundreds*," Lark interrupted.

"Hundreds?" Ma frowned. "We'd better tell the luck-witches too, then. Perhaps people should be warned to take extra precautions."

Netty nodded. "Of course, you folks live closer to the border than most because of your shadowbreds, so maybe this is just an anomaly." She glanced from Lark to Sage and said brightly, "Probably nothing to fret about."

They didn't believe her.

"How are you feeling now?" Da asked, squeezing Lark's shoulder.

"Nearly back to normal, I'd say." Netty patted Lark's knee and removed the linen strips. Gripping Lark's hand in her own, she carefully pressed the skin around the bite. Except for a tiny purple mark shaped like a star, there was no sign of the encounter.

"Pass me that jar," the healer said to Sage, who hurried to obey. Netty held it up for Lark to see. It was filled with a gloppy mixture of honey, beeswax, and dried petals. "Listen carefully, child. Dab a bit of this—oh, about an apple seed's worth?—on that mark three times a day and rub it in. Rub widdershins—counterclockwise, eh?—until both the ointment and the bite are gone. I'll be back to check on you later this evening."

"Won't you stay and eat with us?" Ma asked.

"I'd love to, but I'd best let the Elders and luckwitches know what happened as quick as I can."

"Then let us pack some food for you to take," Da said, motioning to Sage. She obediently grabbed a basket beside the cookstove and carefully wrapped warm slices of bread, soft cheese, a small jar of blackberry preserves, and crisp strips of bacon.

"Thank you for coming so quickly," Ma said.

"Yes, thank you, Mistress Greenwillow," Lark added, staring at the mark on the back of her hand.

"Happy I could help. Don't forget the ointment, eh?" She took the basket from Da with a smile and a word of thanks, and bustled out.

As soon as the door closed Lark's parents rounded on her with identical expressions of fear, frustration, and angry disappointment.

Da raked his fingers through his hair. "Didn't we tell you to stay in the house? What were you thinking?"

"I was looking for a way to help Galin," she said, bursting into tears. Her failure hurt worse than the bloodmoth bite.

Ma leaned a hip against the table and folded her arms. "You getting hurt doesn't help anything! Rust and ruin, Lark, how many times have we told you not to linger by the waymarker? If we can't trust you on your own, maybe I'll have to ask Sarai to mind you like she did when you were an infant!"

Lark's cheeks flushed with prickly heat. "I'm not a baby!"

"Then remember your responsibilities!" Ma snapped.

"River . . . ," Da said soothingly, then turned to Lark. "We understand that you're worried about your brother. We are too. But he doesn't need you impulsively rushing into danger. Let's stop and think a moment, little bird. The Elders have confirmed he's still alive, and that's the most important thing, right?"

She nodded, wiping her eyes on her sleeve.

"He must have had a reason for suddenly wanting to

ride the Hunt. And . . . who knows? Maybe that reason has something to do with why he's still on the Other Side."

"You think he left us *on purpose?*" she cried.

Sage carried dishes to the table. "I did see him talking with one of the Fae just before we set off. It caught my attention because they seemed to know each other impossibly well . . ." She paused, lost in thought.

Lark had a sudden flash of memory, an image of a golden-haired Fae smiling at her brother as he reached for the Harvest King's hand. She shook it away. "No. This is *Galin* we're talking about. He'd rather stitch fabric or skip rocks or catch fish than chase a girl," she said. "And besides, relationships with the Fae are forbidden."

Although . . . she'd struck up something like a friendship with one, hadn't she?

Da exchanged a look with Ma that Lark couldn't read. "In any case, it's not for you to worry about. Let your mother and I handle it with the Elders and the luckwitches, eh? Now let's eat. . . . Everything looks brighter with a full belly."

— SEVEN —

Copper Rings and Acorns

LARK AWOKE THE next morning with a throbbing pain in her hand and the startled sensation that she could actually *hear* the ache knocking through her bones. It took her a bleary second to realize that the sound echoing up the stairs was someone pounding on the door.

She sat up and wiped her eyes. She must have been crying in her sleep because her lashes were stiff with salt and every swallow scraped her sobbed-raw throat. Cradling her sore hand in her lap, she listened as Da opened the door downstairs.

"Good morning, Elders," she heard him say. She flung herself out of bed, ignoring the bloodmoth bite to throw a wool sweater over her head and pull on soft woven leggings.

The Elders! Here, at her house! They must have news of Galin.

Heart thudding, she ran downstairs without bothering

to braid her sleep-mussed hair and skidded to a halt in the doorway of the kitchen.

Sure enough, all three Elders sat at her family's table in their official black scarves. Rowana Farstorm and Goward Brassman clutched mugs of dark coffee in their age-gnarled hands while Amalia Heartstone sipped from a cup of herbal tea.

Elder Brassman twisted his mug, scowling at the rising steam. "We've gotten some mighty odd reports from the trackers, Lukis, but nothing to indicate where your boy actually crossed the border."

Disappointment punctured the bubble of hope that had risen in Lark's chest. They hadn't found her brother, then.

"Odd reports?" Da asked.

"Nothing as serious as Lark's encounter, but a couple mentions of wildkin sightings, ravens and other birds behaving strangely. . . ." He hesitated and then asked, "Why do you think Galin decided to ride the Hunt this season when he never cared about the Mairen shadowbreds or earning a Faevor before? He took your name, right? He was a Threadneedle, your apprentice?"

Da swallowed a sip of coffee before answering. "Yes, he was training to be a tailor, but you remember how young men can be. Sometimes they get an itch to do something daring."

Goward barked a laugh and slapped the table. "We both

did, eh, Lukis? To impress our girls." And then his expression turned serious. "But that's the thing, you see . . ." He rubbed his chin and coughed as though the next words were stuck in his throat.

Elder Farstorm took over. "He's asking because a couple of the other Hunters reported seeing Galin speaking to a golden-haired Fae he appeared to know. Is it possible he *planned* to stay on the Other Side? Did he ever mention anything about—"

Lark's back stiffened. She refused to believe her brother would follow a Fae over the border and desert his family without any word. Unless he was trying to protect the Harvest King, maybe? Galin had already saved him once, and she knew the strength of her brother's loyalty. If he thought the king was still in some sort of danger, Galin would never abandon him.

Perhaps that was why he remained in the Fae realm?

As the questions tumbled through her mind, worry caterpillar-crawled through her stomach. Just how much trouble was Galin in?

"It's the best we can do at the moment, I'm afraid, at least until the luckwitches finish sweeping the boundary for magic residue," Elder Farstorm was saying grimly. "Though Davina Wardspin is worried more magic keeps seeping through. . . ."

Elder Heartstone glanced up then and noticed Lark

hovering in the doorway. "Good morning! You look a bit frayed, child. Sit and have some breakfast. Your father's made apple fritters and fried sausage."

Lark chewed her lip, glancing at Da to see if she was still in trouble. But he wasn't looking at her—he was staring out the window.

Amalia Heartstone patted the empty chair beside her. "Let's take a look at this bloodmoth bite Netty Greenwillow told us about."

Lark sat down and held out her hand, displaying the purple mark.

"Looks painful," Rowana Farstorm clucked.

"It hurts," Lark admitted, "but the ointment Mistress Greenwillow gave me helps."

"Well, this might help too." She plucked a small linen pouch from the center of the table and dumped the contents into her hand. Out tumbled four copper bands inscribed with sigils Lark hadn't seen before. Elder Farstorm gave her the smallest ring, saying, "Put this on and leave it. Do not remove it for any reason, do you hear me?"

"What is it?" Lark asked, slipping the ring on her little finger.

"The luckwitches and the metalsmiths worked together to forge these rings for protection."

Elder Amalia Heartstone hastily added, "Just as a precaution." She passed Lark a plate of apple fritters as Da set a mug of cocoa before her. "By the way," she said, "I need to thank you again for putting my spinning wheel back together after Daisy tried to climb it."

Lark grinned around a mouthful of fritter. Elder Heartstone's prize goat had gotten into her house a week back and left a trail of destruction through almost every room. Ma liked to say goats were creatures of pure chaos, but maybe that was why Lark liked them so much. "I was happy to do it," she said.

Elder Brassman slurped his coffee and set the mug down with a definitive clunk. He pushed his chair back and said, "Well, Lukis, we appreciate the hot breakfast but we'd better head off now. Have to get the rest of the rings delivered as quick as we can."

Da nodded and folded his arms across his chest. "Thanks for stopping in. Take some fritters for the road and stay warm. Looks like an early snow coming."

After the Elders left, Lark stacked the dirty dishes in the sink and pumped water to fill it. Questions burst in her mind like milkweed pods, sending scattered thoughts flying off her tongue. "Da, do you really think Galin chose to stay on the Other Side deliberately? And what are the Elders actually afraid of? I could see it in their faces. What is happening?"

He pinched the bridge of his nose. "The Elders are concerned that the lack of communication with the Fae emissary, the increased presence of wildkin so soon after a Hunt, your brother's disappearance . . . Well, if there's a connection, it might reflect a challenge to our treaty with the Fae."

Lark wiped a plate and set it in the dish rack to finish drying. "What do you mean, *challenge to our treaty*? What's wrong with the Accords?"

He twisted a towel in his hands and looked as if he regretted his answer. "Oh, sometimes negotiations must be updated, that's all."

She could recognize a dodge when she heard one. "But Da—"

Dropping a hand on her shoulder, he said, "Some fears are too big for little backs to carry. Until we know more, let the Elders and luckwitches handle it. Teacher Bardic is coming by this week, isn't he? You have some math problems to worry about at the moment, eh?"

"But maybe I can help. If wildkin are creeping across the border, there might be gaps that Galin could get through too. I could go look—Granny and I used to spend so much time hunting mushrooms and foraging for nuts that I know the woods almost as well as the trackers and—"

"No! The thought of Galin caught in the Fae realm is hard enough. Your mother and I don't want you and Sage wandering into the middle of some Fae trouble too, do you hear me? Avoid the woods, keep close to the house, and wear your ring."

Lark twisted the copper band on her finger and folded her fist around it. "I'll be careful, I promise." She wasn't particularly keen to go back to the forest and risk another run-in with wildkin, but she had to find the rest of the missing moonclock pieces. No matter what reason Galin had for riding with the Wild Hunt, no matter why he hadn't returned, Rook had said the moonclock would help him and the Fae couldn't lie.

"You must promise me you'll leave this alone, Lark. Even in the best of times, the Fae are tricky and unreliable. And now . . ." He sighed and scrubbed a hand through his hair. It was beginning to silver at the temples, and the lines in his face suddenly appeared deeper, drawn in sorrow.

"Just stay close to the house. I'm heading into town for a few hours to work on Solstice cloaks, but Sage and your mother are in the barn." He put the largest copper ring on one of his fingers and bounced the remaining two in his palm. "I'll take these out to them on my way. Get your lessons done and keep out of trouble."

Lark wrinkled her nose and thought about arguing, but she knew it wouldn't do any good. Instead she returned to her room, rubbed ointment on her bloodmoth bite, and obediently dragged her math work out of the pile of books and papers balanced precariously on the desk by her bed. But frustration burned away her focus, leaving her restless and fidgety.

She wished she could have told him about the moonclock, about the Fae who said it would help Galin.

Only, Da probably wouldn't believe her. He'd say that

she had fallen for a Fae trick. He'd tell the Elders, and they would find Rook and punish him. They would accuse him of malice against a mortal, most likely, even though Lark didn't think he had done anything wrong. And then her chance to save Galin might be lost forever.

Maybe that was why Rook had made her promise not to tell anyone about the moonclock. Keeping it secret was probably safest.

She pushed her lesson pages away and pulled out the pieces of the moonclock, tapping her fingers against her desk. After a moment, she opened the drawer and took out the feathers she'd found on her windowsill. Rook had said something about using them if she needed to get in touch, but there hadn't been time for him to explain.

Well, she was desperate. She wanted to ask what he knew about Galin's reasons for riding, and she had to get the rest of those clock pieces.

Making a wild guess, she opened her window, slipped a black raven feather under the sash, then closed it again to pin it in place. Hopefully he would notice and realize she needed to speak to him.

Three days later, as she dumped manure on a compost pile behind the barn, a raven swooped from snow-laden clouds to land on her shoulder.

"Nightbird?" she whispered. His injured wing was already completely healed.

He bobbed his head, shook his tail feathers, and opened his beak to drop a small, grimy wheel in her mittened hand. Then he croaked *Wait!* and flew off.

Lark glanced back at the barn, her breath misting. Sage and Ma were with the saddler, checking tack and making sure any necessary leather repairs were done. Hopefully they wouldn't notice a raven bringing her strange silver clock components, or she'd be faced with questions she couldn't answer.

She studied the wheel a moment before tucking it safely in her cloak pocket. Wind tugged her hood and snow flurries danced in the brittle cold air. Winter Solstice was still weeks away, but the frost had come early. Lark shuffled her feet and clenched her hands, an aching chill seeping through the knitted wool of her favorite mittens. If Nightbird wanted her to wait, he'd best hurry before she froze.

Just as she was about to give up and retreat to the warmth of her house, the raven returned—along with half a dozen of his friends and a small flock of chickadees. She cupped her hands and tried not to flinch as they circled her, dropping small bits of clockwork in her palms. "This is brilliant! Have you found them all, then?" she asked, not expecting an answer.

But a voice replied, "Nearly."

Rook stepped around the corner of the barn, spinning a dead leaf in his fingers. "Look at this beauty."

Lark wrinkled her nose. It was brown and cracked,

barely recognizable as a hickory leaf. "I prefer the colored ones," she said.

He gestured at the trees crowding close to the stable yard and bowing over the pasture fences. Red and gold leaves still clung to a few limbs, but most of the branches were bare. "There's beauty hiding beneath all that death."

Lark took a nervous step back. "Umm . . . the trees aren't dead. They're just sleeping until spring."

"Exactly!" He smashed the dried leaf in his fist and tossed the fragments into the air, dancing a little caper. "The leaves die and fall and turn to dirt, and then buds bloom and new leaves uncurl and the seasons change and it's *glorious*."

He suddenly turned sober again. "That, I sometimes think, is the most powerful magic of all."

"Ummm . . ." Lark's teeth had started to chatter and she wasn't entirely sure it was just from the cold, but she had questions that needed answers. "Did you see the feather I left out? I wanted to talk to you because people are saying my brother disappeared on purpose and you told me I could help him by fixing the moonclock, but you never explained how or why or what it's supposed to do or—" She waved her arms as though she could pull answers from air.

But he hissed and ducked back. "What do I sense on your hand?"

"What?"

"I just want to see." He pointed.

Reluctantly, Lark tugged off her mitten and spread her fingers. "Why?"

"The luckwitches have been creative. That's good. . . . Keep the ring on."

"If it's meant to repel the Fae it can't be very strong," she remarked, and then bit her lip when she heard how insulting that sounded aloud.

He didn't seem offended, though. He chuckled and agreed, "Just so. Still, it will discourage minor mischief. It's better than nothing. Wait . . . what's that mark?"

Lark twisted her wrist. "A bloodmoth bit me, but it's getting better."

He frowned and muttered, "Stars and sorrows. A bloodmoth. Would you allow me to help?"

"Help? The healer already gave me ointment."

"Fae injuries need Fae remedies," he said. "Nightbird, fetch me three petals of bloodbalm, a leaf of purplewort, and a couple drops of moonmilk sap on a patch of moss. Hurry!"

"Oh, but there's really no need for you to make a fuss!" she protested. Although her hand was throbbing again and she had to admit that Mistress Greenwillow's salve maybe wasn't working as well as it should have, she didn't want to owe a favor to a Fae. What would he ask in return?

But the raven sped away and Rook put his fists on his hips. "Nightbird will bring the things you need."

She crammed her hand into the mitten and blurted,

"What I need is for you to tell me about Galin and the moonclock. Why—"

But she was interrupted by Nightbird streaking back, trailing glimmers of magic from the tips of his wings. He landed on Rook's shoulder, a leaf and petals pinched in his beak and a sticky bit of moss clutched in his talons.

Lark gaped at him. Had he already flown over the border and back?

"Ravens are swift flyers," Rook said with a smile. He took Nightbird's collection and mashed it up, forming a dark gloppy mess. "Let me have your hand."

Lark grimaced. The stuff smelled like rotten plums and old bark. "I appreciate your concern," she said politely, "but I really don't think—"

"There's no price to pay," he said. "You were attacked by wildkin on your side of the border so I am honor bound to make it right. Trust me, Lark. I only want to help."

With a sigh, she plucked off her mitten yet again. *Never trust the Fae* was the first rule. She hoped this wasn't a trick.

The instant Rook smeared the paste on the bite, the pain evaporated. A faint tingle, warm and fizzy, ran through her skin and buzzed along her fingers before it too faded.

After a moment Rook wiped away the paste and replaced her mitten. "There. Good and gone."

She flexed her hand and felt immediate relief. "Oh, thank—"

He lunged forward. "No! Don't say it!"

But Lark had realized her own mistake just in time and pressed her lips closed. She'd almost forgotten another rule: *Never thank a Fae.* Thanking a Fae implied that you were in their debt, and they might call in that debt when and how you least expected.

However, Rook didn't seem interested in taking advantage of opportunities to trap her. In fact, he'd tried hard to protect her.

As she studied him, trying to interpret the look in his mismatched eyes, voices seeped through the barn door— her mother's firm but musical, Merrit Saddler's rough and full of humor.

Rook beckoned her behind the barn, ducking beside the massive ever-blooming rosebush that sprawled along the southern wall and fed the shadowbreds all year.

"What do you know about speaking with Fae?" Rook asked.

Not enough, Lark thought. *And it's mostly forbidden.* Aloud she said, "I know that you can't lie." *But you don't always tell the truth we think we hear either.*

"Right. And we can't speak ill of our own."

Lark nodded, though she wasn't sure where he was going.

"So there are details you need to know about the moon-clock and your brother . . . but even when I'm being honest, there are questions I simply can't answer. Do you understand?"

"Yes. So tell me what you can. Where is Galin?"

"You already know. He is in the Fae realm."

Lark frowned at the confirmation. "But where? Near the border? In a house? In a dungeon or a cage? In the castle?"

"I can't say."

"You said you were trying to save a sibling too. What happened?"

His eyes darkened and his lips twisted as he struggled to find words. Beads of sweat glistened on his forehead despite the cold air. After a moment he grunted, "One of my sisters and Galin are . . . friends."

So Galin *did* know one of the Fae. Were the rumors true, then? "Does your sister have golden hair, by chance?" she asked, thinking again of the sunny Fae she'd glimpsed riding beside her brother.

Rook nodded and Lark felt something slip and twist inside her stomach. The Elders had been right. Da had been right. Galin *had* raced the Gauntlet and ridden the Wild Hunt to impress someone—but he hadn't done it for a Tradewind Junction girl. He'd done it for a Fae.

But where had he met her? They weren't supposed to *speak* to Fae! Lark knew her anger was unreasonable—here she was talking to Rook!—but she was too hurt to care. Had Galin deliberately run away to the Fae realm to be with her? Had he left his family behind without even a word?

A burst of bewildered betrayal knocked her to her knees. She didn't realize she was crying until Rook wiped away her tears with his thumb. He snapped a rose from the bush and stripped the thorns with deft fingers, then tucked it behind her ear. She flinched before realizing the concern on his face was genuine. "Beauty to bear your sorrow?" he murmured.

"Mortals usually pass each other a handkerchief when one of us is crying." She sniffled.

He grimaced. "But flowers are so much lovelier!"

Lark tried to smile at him, but her fury blazed even brighter the more she thought about it. They'd been *so worried* about Galin, so anxious to find a way to get him back. And what was he doing all the while? Romancing a Fae and living in a realm of magic. He'd probably already forgotten where he'd come from.

Lark surged to her feet, thrusting a hand in her pocket for the moonclock pieces the birds had brought her. "Tell your sister she can keep him, then!" she snapped. "And *you* can keep your useless moonclock!"

Before she could fling the fragments at him, he clasped her arm and said, "You do not understand, Lark Mairen. It is not so simple."

"Then explain!" she demanded.

"Believe me, I wish I could. But *I can't say*."

His words suddenly sank in, penetrating the haze of hurt and confusion. He hadn't said, *I don't know*. So that meant answering would implicate the Fae in something bad. But if he couldn't speak ill of his own kind, how could she get the answers she needed?

She noticed Nightbird hopping some distance away, muttering to himself as he plucked pebbles and twigs from the ground. An idea took root.

"You might not be able to, but *he* can." She tipped her chin at the raven.

Rook sighed. "He *is* a clever bird, but even though he knows a few mortal words, he doesn't speak your language, Lark, and you don't speak his."

Nightbird gave a *crawk* of indignation and clawed the dirt.

"Doesn't mean he can't answer." Lark picked up a fallen twig and cleared a space on the ground, then drew two circles.

"Nightbird, would you like to play a game?" She labeled one circle *yes* and the other *no*.

"What game is this?" Rook asked eagerly, curiosity bright in his eyes.

Lark couldn't help smiling. She'd heard the Fae loved games, but she'd always thought that was an exaggeration. "You'll see," she told him. She slipped through a paddock fence to rummage in the fallen leaves at the base of an oak tree just on the other side, quickly gathering a handful of acorns.

Nightbird clicked his beak curiously, fluttering from one circle to the other.

"Here's how it goes. I'll ask a question and give one of

these acorns to Nightbird. If the answer is yes, he'll drop the acorn in this circle." She pointed with the twig. "If the answer is no, he'll drop it in that one."

Rook's eyebrows climbed into his hair and he gave a whistle. "Brilliant! Let's give it a try."

"Did my brother deliberately choose to remain in the Fae realm after the Wild Hunt?"

Nightbird looked to Rook for a moment. Then he grabbed an acorn from her hand and dropped it in the yes circle.

Lark's heart plummeted and she threw the rest of the acorns on the ground.

"Wait, Lark! Ask another question!"

"What else do I need to know? Galin doesn't need our help." Her lip trembled and she resisted the urge to wipe her nose on her sleeve. "He decided to stay there."

"Think! Not all reasons for choosing to stay are selfish ones. And even in the Fae realm a situation might change!" The cords in his neck stood out as though simply saying that much had been a strain.

Lark forced herself to bend down and retrieve the acorns. She swallowed her hurt feelings, took a deep breath, and tried to clear her head. "Fine. Did he stay because of Rook's sister?"

Again Nightbird answered yes, but Rook groaned and muttered, "Stars and sorrows, Lark. Be more specific!"

"He wanted to be with her, right? I'm twelve, not *six*. I

know how things go when boys get gooseheaded over a girl."

But instead of answering yes, Nightbird danced back and forth between the circles, flapping his wings and fluffing his tail.

Shame slipped like melting ice down Lark's spine. Was she the one being petty and selfish, thinking only of her own sorrow and loneliness? Clearly there was more going on than she had assumed.

She recalled the brambles bursting from the ground, the Harvest King's fall, the moonclock. . . .

"Someone attacked the king on purpose, didn't they? Only Galin saved him. And maybe he stayed because he was worried the king was still in danger." It was what she'd first thought, after all, knowing her brother's loyalty. If he also remained because he wanted to protect the golden Fae, well, maybe that didn't have to mean he'd rejected his family.

Nightbird dropped his acorn in the yes circle, picked it up and tossed it down again, and then again. *Yes. Yes. Yes.*

Rook nodded, eyes alight and expectant.

Lark sighed. She just wished Galin had told her about the Fae girl. She would have loved to meet her.

Of course, she was keeping Rook secret from Sage, wasn't she? Why were things so complicated?

She picked at a frayed thread on her mitten, thoughts tumbling like dried leaves in the wind. "But you said fixing the moonclock would help my brother. How?" What was the connection? "Wait . . . does the king need the moon-clock?" Was that why he had carried it in his vest pocket? Maybe his safety somehow depended on it. "If he gets it back, can my brother come home? Will things go back to normal?"

Nightbird dropped one acorn in the yes circle and then took another from her hand, spitting it in the no circle.

"Yes *and* no? What does that mean? Is there something else that must happen? Some other problem to solve?"

Nightbird threw three acorns in the yes circle, as though to emphasize his answer.

"Hm. All right. So . . . what's going on?"

Nightbird and Rook both flicked impatient glances at her. That question couldn't be answered by the game. "Can't the May Queen save the king?"

This time the answer was a forceful no.

"Is the May Queen in danger too?"

Yes.

"If the Twilight Court is at risk, are the Fae Accords threatened too?" She was mostly thinking aloud, remembering comments she'd overheard, but Nightbird answered yes again.

"And this is connected somehow to the wildkin still loose on our side of the border. . . . Sage said there was something different about this Hunt. . . ." Lark mused.

Nightbird responded yes, then scratched the dirt with his talons as though upset by the answer.

Rook said, "Speaking of wildkin, I can tell you that my birds tracked down the spider spying on you the other day and I'll pass word along about the bloodmoths, but you must be very careful. It's bad enough that they suspect you've found pieces of the moonclock—if they know you're going to repair it, they'll do anything to get it. Don't speak of the moonclock to anyone. In the wrong hands . . . well, it would be a disaster. Remember your oath!"

"But if the Harvest King needs his moonclock back and the wildkin were sent to find it, why—"

"They don't answer to the Twilight Court. The king has no authority over them."

"Oh. *Oh*. So . . . what could the Harvest King's enemies do with the moonclock?"

Rook grimaced and shook his head. Nightbird shrieked and began flinging acorns into the no circle. "Quiet down or you'll draw attention!" Rook warned him.

"Why don't you just give all the pieces back to the king, then? I'll trade him the moonclock for my brother."

"I already told you it wasn't that simple. The Harvest King . . ." Rook's jaw clenched and Lark could hear his teeth grinding. "He's too weak. He can't fix the clock and"—a tremble ran through his frame as he tried to force the words out—"and he would just lose it again." He let out a gasp and rubbed his throat.

Nightbird muttered and kicked at the acorns scattered through the circles.

"Besides, it's bound to your mortal blood now," Rook said. "Believe me, I wish you hadn't been dragged into this, but it's too late for regrets. You're the only one who can fix the moonclock."

Lark patted the fragments in her pocket. How could something so small—something the size of a pocket watch—feel so heavy all of a sudden?

"What if I can't fix it?" she whispered, but Rook and Nightbird had both cocked their heads to listen to the growing din of hungry horses echoing from the barn.

The afternoon was quickly turning toward evening.

Merrit Saddler was surely almost done and Ma and Sage would be out to gather roses soon. Lark's brilliant idea was working about as well as a square wheel or a stone kite. She still didn't have all the information she needed.

Besides, she was shivering, and as the sun sank lower so did the temperature. Lark sighed and bounced the remaining acorns lightly in her palm, sifting through the questions clamoring in her head to find the most urgent before she ran out of time.

"Is the moonclock some kind of weapon, then?"

No.

"Then how is it supposed to help—"

"*Think*, Lark. It's a moon*clock*," Rook said.

"A clock . . . so it has something to do with time."

Nightbird let out a triumphant croak and tossed an acorn in the yes circle, then preened his feathers.

"But how can time help the Harvest King? He's Fae! He's immortal!"

Nightbird snatched an acorn from her hand and flung it into the no circle, then spread his wings and tipped his head to meet her gaze.

"No? What do you mean, *no*?"

Rusted hinges suddenly squealed—she really should grease them—as a heavy door creaked open at the front of the barn. Merrit Saddler's hearty voice boomed, "I'll get the new saddle to you in a moonturn, Horsemaven. Take care, now!"

"Many thanks, Merrit! Watch the road!" Ma called.

"Hurry, they'll—" Lark felt the brush of feathers on her hair and a whisper of wind across her cheeks, and when she glanced back to Rook she discovered that he and his bird had gone.

Scrambling to erase the circles she had drawn and kick all the acorns away, Lark tried to wrap her head around a mystery suddenly much bigger than a missing brother. How had a mortal become the *Harvest King*? What in the worlds had Galin gotten himself caught up in?

EIGHT

Clockworks

LARK ONLY HALF listened to Ma and Sage talk about saddles and the next starshadow stallion breedings as they all walked back to the house together. While they cleaned up for supper, she ran to her room so she could put her newest collection of moonclock pieces away. Tucking them beneath the moss in Nightbird's old basket didn't seem nearly secure enough, given what she'd just learned.

After a moment's thought, she decided to keep them in a wooden box Galin had made for her one summer. It was crooked and the lid squeaked when she closed it, but he'd carved a rough G in the corner and a tiny bird—a meadowlark, he said, just for her—on the top. Inside he had painted two words: *one chance*. It was something he always said when she hesitated—before jumping in the river, before climbing a tree, before throwing a ball—and it meant *don't waste the moment*. Every time she dragged the box from its hiding place beneath her bed she would remember him.

She was determined to help her brother. Somehow.

But now that she knew how much might be riding on her repairs, she worried that she didn't remember enough of Grandda Maxim's lessons to assemble even a simple pocket watch, let alone something called a moonclock that could save the life of the Harvest King.

Luckily, she knew where to go for help—Brassman's Clockworks.

That evening, as Da passed bowls of beans and bacon around the table, she begged him to take her to town the next morning. "I'll stay out of trouble," she promised. "I just want to ask Elder Brassman some questions."

"Working on a project, eh?" he asked, smiling at her.

"Yes. I'm hoping he'll teach me a bit about clocks."

"If he's busy I don't want you bothering him. . . ."

"If he doesn't have time I'll spend the day helping you in your shop."

He lowered his eyes, sadness tugging the corners of his mouth. Lark knew it was hard for him to step into Thread-needle's Fabrics every day without Galin, knew it must hurt him to work alone. She reached for his hand and gave it a little squeeze.

Da finished his mug of coffee before finally answering, "Very well. As long as you're caught up with lessons and Ma doesn't need you in the barn."

→ ‡ ←

When Lark entered Elder Brassman's shop the next day she was greeted by an oil painting of her grandfather hanging over the gleaming wood-and-glass front counter and by the rumbling purr of a fuzzy gray cat with white paws.

She leaned down to rub the gray cat's whiskered chin as Elder Brassman spun his cushioned stool around to face her. Like Grandda, he'd been a Guildmaster clockmaker before his retirement and still wore the gold pin on his vest to prove it. Though his son, Simon, had officially taken over the business when he was named Elder, old Goward was as much a part of the shop as a gear in a clockwork mechanism, and no one expected him to leave.

"Socks is delighted to have some attention," he said with a kind smile, the cat's rumbling purr filling the spaces between the ticking of clocks. "And I am pleased to see you as well, Lark. What brings you here this morning?"

"I have a favor to ask, actually. Would you be willing to teach me everything you can about clocks? Specifically, how to assemble a small one, like . . . say . . . a pocket watch?" She was so nervous her tongue tripped over the words and she had to swallow twice.

"Ah! You've discovered an interest in your grandfather's work, eh?"

"Er . . . yes. Something like that."

"Well, Lark, although I'd be more than happy to teach you what I can, I'm afraid Simon and I have no need for an apprentice. Perhaps in a few years . . ."

"Oh! No, I'm not asking for an apprenticeship, Elder Brassman, although I thank you for thinking of it. I simply want to learn how the mechanisms work, how they fit together and function. Grandda explained the systems to me years ago, but I was too young to remember."

For a moment he peered at her over his spectacles, arms folded across his chest. Socks leaped to the top of the counter and began washing his ears.

Finally, just when Lark was starting to think there was no hope, he nodded and said, "Cold winter days can be tedious, eh? Perfect time to learn something new. As long as it won't interfere with your lessons . . . ?"

"I am ahead of my class already, Elder Brassman. I can keep up with the work just fine. Teacher Bardic will tell you the same."

"Very well. I would be happy to share what I know. We'll start with the basics. Follow me to the worktable."

As he tugged over a stool for her he noticed her hands. "Ah! Your bloodmoth bite has healed nicely, eh? Netty Greenwillow's salve must have done the trick."

"Erm . . . yes, I certainly appreciated it."

For the next couple of hours Lark memorized the names of tiny clockwork pieces. As she walked home for noonmeal with Da, she recited them like a charm beneath her breath. "Crown wheel, center wheel, balance wheel, main wheel, ratchet wheel, escape wheel. Balance spring, click spring, pins, pivots, bezels." She liked the way the words felt in her mouth.

"Things must have gone well with Elder Brassman," Ma remarked at the table, passing her a plate of roast chicken and sweet potatoes.

Lark nodded, unwilling to say too much.

"Well, as long as we know where you are and as long as Goward doesn't mind . . ."

"He said he likes teaching me."

"Don't you think you should be helping Ma and me search for clues about Galin?" Sage said, stabbing a bite of chicken with her fork.

Lark squirmed uneasily. Over the past few days Sage had decided that the golden-haired Fae she'd glimpsed with Galin must have tricked him into crossing the border, and Sage was determined to unravel the trap. She'd been questioning everyone who'd watched the Gauntlet, everyone who'd seen the Wild Hunt ride off, anyone who might have noticed *something*. Now she'd talked Ma into riding near the border with her in the hope that they could discover exactly where he had crossed.

Sage's efforts so far had been unsuccessful, and her growing frustration had started to spill over onto Lark. Unfortunately, after Rook's revelations by the rosebush, Lark was afraid Galin's rescue was going to be even more difficult than either of them had expected.

"This is really important," she said, wishing she could explain.

"More important than your brother?" Sage snapped.

"Girls!" Da reached out, resting his hands on their shoulders. "We are all under a heavy burden of stress and sorrow, and we each have our own ways of dealing with it. We *all* miss Galin and want to see him returned, but bickering won't bring him home."

"Neither will clocks," Sage whispered when he wasn't paying attention.

Lark wanted to kick her sister under the table, but what good would that do?

She was skilled at fixing things, not riding shadowbreds. It was the only way she knew how to help their brother. Repairing the moonclock might be the most difficult challenge she'd yet faced, but hopefully once she was finished, her sister would understand.

Only . . . when Lark thought about the weak border, the encroaching wildkin, the threatened king, the fragile treaties, she had to wonder what the moonclock could actually do. Would fixing it be enough to fix everything else? Or was it already too late?

PART TWO

Mayfair

— NINE —

Waking from Winter

WINTER'S END BROUGHT maple sugaring time, when Lark's family joined villagers across the Borderlands in tapping trees, then boiling the sap until great cast-iron kettles were full of rich, dark maple syrup. Ordinarily everyone would laugh and sing and taste maple-sugar taffy, a sweet promise of the spring to come. A celebration of hope and new beginnings.

But this season was different.

Lark stood with Sage over the boiling syrup pot and remembered how Galin had loved this time of year. He'd sing funny songs to make them laugh so hard they cried, then tease them into chasing him through the trees. He'd hang from branches to startle their parents and feed the squirrels from his hands.

But now she and Sage weren't allowed anywhere near the wood. "It's safer for you to stay back here, away from the border," Da said before setting off with the other adults to tap the maple trees closest to the waymarkers. Hauling buckets of sap to the fires this far away was more difficult, but the Elders and luckwitches insisted it was necessary.

Lark had endured weeks of being told it was safer for her to stay inside, to wear her copper ring at all times, to focus on her studies and not the spreading rumors of rogue magic and wildkin running loose in Tradewind Junction.

Everyone in the Borderlands was frightened, Lark mused as she glumly stirred the syrup kettle. She could practically feel fear like a fog in the air. Wildkin sightings had spawned stories of strange thefts—people were missing pocket watches, kitchen timers, and alarm clocks—and though the White Stag had been spotted once or twice, his appearances had inspired worry rather than reassurance. He was supposed to be a symbol of balance and blessing along the border, but folks said he was growing weak, losing his power.

Even the Elders were at a loss. Whispers rose and spread, about invoking the controversial Last Protection clause in the Fae Accords, which would allow the use of salt and iron against the Fae. It required incontrovertible proof that the Fae had wielded magic as a weapon against mortals, of course, but the line between harmless mischief and deliberate malice seemed to be growing ever thinner. However, the Elders urged caution rather than confrontation and insisted that the safest thing to do was simply to wait. "We will demand answers from Lady Mist and her entourage when they cross the border for Mayfair," Elder Rowana Farstorm had announced.

As smoke and steam curled around her, Lark kept thinking about what Rook and Nightbird had communicated through their acorn game last fall. It seemed that Galin was somehow involved in defending the Twilight Court from an unknown foe, but Rook and his raven also revealed that the Harvest King had once been mortal. Had that left him vulnerable? Despite the danger, was the May Queen powerful enough to restore peace?

Rook had urged Lark to repair the moonclock, insisting it was the key to saving her brother—and perhaps the Harvest King himself—but she was still missing a couple pieces. How could she find them when she wasn't allowed away from her house? Nightbird and other ravens had managed to deliver a few more springs and screws over the winter, but with trackers patrolling the Borderlands and luckwitches hanging protective charms through the forest, Lark had been afraid to contact Rook. It felt too risky—she couldn't bear the thought of the consequences if he got caught.

"Need a break, Lark?" Sarai Vanbeck's eldest son suddenly asked, dropping another log on the fire beneath her kettle with a dirt-smudged smile.

Her arms *were* tired—stirring the sap as it thickened to syrup was hot, hard work—but it felt good to do something useful. "I'm still all right," she told him, lifting the long-handled wooden spoon to watch the sticky liquid drip off. "Getting closer."

He touched the brim of his cap and left to gather more wood.

Sage glanced up from her kettle a pace away and gave a little wave. Her cheeks were rosy from the warmth of the fire, and the steam had coaxed curls from her dark hair.

Lark waved back, trying not to envy her sister. Sage was almost seventeen summers old, brave and beautiful, with skin the color of smooth hickory and gold-flecked brown eyes. She was everything sweet and sunny, strong and swift.

Lark, on the other hand, was small for her age, with mouse-colored hair as dull as dead wood and eyes an indeterminate grayish-green, the color of pond muck and muddy water. She was pale and plain and entirely unremarkable.

No one would guess the secrets she carried.

What if she couldn't get the moonclock to work? She didn't even know what it was supposed to do.

"Is yours ready to taste yet?" Sage called, skimming foam off the surface of the sap in her kettle.

"Nearly!" Lark called back.

Lark knew Sage was also anxious to help their brother, her resolve growing with the approach of spring. Sage was convinced that she could find Galin and bring him home on the night of the Mayfair Hunt, before the border closed. "My Faevor from the Harvest Hunt was a compass that will keep me from getting lost, remember?" she had argued with Ma just the other day. "Whatever happened to Galin last fall, he'll be doing everything he can to get back to us. If he's riding with the Hunt, I'll find him and guide him home. If he's not, I'll go looking for him."

Ma had pursed her lips sadly. "It won't be as easy as all that. After six months in the Fae realm, his mortal nature might be fading, especially if he has chosen to stay."

Both Lark and Sage refused to believe that. Stubbornly optimistic, Sage had set her chin, squared her shoulders, and insisted, "Reverie and I will find him. I'll ask the May Queen to help."

Now the innkeeper's youngest daughter skipped over to Sage's kettle for a turn with the spoon and Sage came to stand beside Lark. "It's looking good," she said, though her voice was dull, lacking the delight of previous maple sugarings.

"The maple trees are happy this year," Lark commented.

"At least *something* is."

They were both silent for a moment, watching flames lick the bottom of the heavy kettle. Then Sage leaned her head on Lark's shoulder. "It's almost spring," she said, "and soon I'll bring Galin home."

"How?" Lark whispered. "What if he can't join the Hunt? What if he doesn't want to? What if something happens to *you*?"

Sage kicked a branch into the fire burning beneath the kettle and growled, "I'll find him. No matter what it takes."

She looked prepared to drag him home by his ears if she had to. "One chance, remember?" she said, repeating Galin's favorite saying.

Lark twisted the copper ring on her littlest finger and wished she could tell her sister about Rook and the moonclock. But as she studied her sister's determined expression, she suspected it wouldn't change Sage's mind.

A log crackled on the fire, scattering bright sparks. Lark waved smoke away from her face. *Somehow I must fix the moonclock before she rides the Gauntlet; otherwise I might lose my sister too*, she fretted.

Three weeks later the first daffodils bloomed and preparations for the impending spring Wild Hunt began in earnest. Lark was desperate to solve the puzzle of the moonclock and as soon as she'd finished morning chores she spent her time fiddling with the mysterious pocket watch or studying clockwork mechanisms with Elder Brassman.

As the days gradually grew brighter and the Hunt approached, she started heading to the barn earlier and earlier, trying to buy as much time as possible.

"Oh, Lark! Good morning, little bird," Ma said with a smile the day the tulips opened. "Da said you skipped breakfast again and he didn't want you to miss out. Here you are, sweetling." She handed Lark a steaming stoneware mug of tea and a pastry wrapped in waxed paper.

The scent of orange marmalade, cinnamon, and clove

made Lark's mouth water. "Thank you, Ma."

"You must really enjoy working with Elder Brassman."

Lark choked on a bite, wondering what Ma would say if she knew her daughter was trying to cobble together a Fae moonclock that could be the only key to helping Galin. She swallowed the secret and said, "Mmhm."

"Take your time," Ma said. "Sage and I will start cleaning stalls before the lordlings come."

Lark plunked down on a hay bale. She took another bite of pastry and let out a sigh of satisfaction. Warm, sticky orange jam dribbled down her chin.

The nearest horse stuck her head over the stall door to snuffle Lark's face. Lark laughed and shoved her velvet nose away.

"How many lordlings?" she asked, licking her finger. "Isn't it early in the season to start rider evaluations?"

"Not for this Hunt. I want the riders to be as prepared as possible before they even attempt the Gauntlet," Ma said, coming around the corner with a bucket in each hand. "Especially with the shadowbreds acting up."

"Do you know what's bothering them?" Though Lark had been spending more time at Brassman's Clockworks than in the barn, she still helped clean stalls and fill buckets. She'd noticed a shift in the mares' behavior—the shadowbreds kicked their stalls, yanked charms from their manes, and raced like ink and smoke through the pasture. Of course, high spirits were expected with the arrival of spring, especially since this winter had been particularly rough. They were *all* glad to see the sun.

But the shadowbreds hadn't settled. Even Legacy, Ma's wise and generally steady mare, had become hard to handle. At first they assumed it was because she was now in foal to a starshadow stallion, but she'd had three foals before and never acted quite like this.

"They're just agitated. Reacting to our stress, I imagine." Ma waved a hand as though it didn't matter, but Lark could see the pinch of worry between her eyes. "I'm afraid they might be difficult to control on the racecourse, though."

"What if they're responding to the weakness in the border? Do you think they feel the call of Fae magic?"

"Perhaps." Ma frowned and rubbed a hand across the back of her neck. "We may have to adjust their charms before the Gauntlet. But I'm making sure all the riders are ready for whatever comes."

"I know one rider who might be in trouble." Lark smirked, catching her sister's eye.

Sage snorted as she grabbed Whimsy's pail and poured in a scoop of oats and roses. "I still can't believe Brendan Forth had the nerve to challenge me. Wagering a silver coin! As if *he* could beat me at the Gauntlet. Who does he think he is?"

Ma chuckled and stroked Inka's neck. "His father rode the Wild Hunt twice and Brendan is careful in the saddle. He's earned the right to at least try Cinder, girls."

"He'd be better suited to mucking stalls for a year and a day!" Sage spluttered.

"He can't seriously think you might lose. Everyone knows you're the best rider in the Borderlands and Reverie is the fastest shadowbred. I mean, unless he cheats." Lark was suddenly aghast. "Do you think he's going to?"

Sage straightened and swept a strand of shining chestnut hair behind her ear, silver ivy-and-rose cuffs glinting. "Cheat?" she repeated. "He could try, I suppose, but he'll find out you can't cheat the Gauntlet. Not that it would matter. Reverie is faster than Cinder, but she also knows the course better."

"Then why does he upset you? He'll only make himself look a fool."

Sage hefted two buckets and headed for the stalls. "You wouldn't understand."

"Winning the Gauntlet is certainly a worthy accomplishment and an honor to be celebrated, but don't let pride cloud your purpose. The Gauntlet is simply a proving ground," Ma chided. "Preparing for the Hunt is what matters. Friendly competition can be useful motivation and good fun, but this rivalry with the Forth boy shouldn't become a distraction, Sage."

Sage's eyes glittered. "Oh, don't worry. The *Forth boy* won't shift my focus."

Lark knew her sister was thinking about Galin's disappearance and her plan to find him. The last bite of orange pastry turned to sand and sawdust in her mouth and she had to choke it down, gulping hot tea from the mug so fast it scalded her throat. Her stomach churned. Despite Sage's determination, Lark was afraid her sister's participation in this season's Wild Hunt might put her in danger as well.

Lark was running out of time to fix the moonclock. She had to finish it before Mayfair or Sage's brash courage and dauntless confidence might get her hurt.

"We also have Orin Hatchcross and Artur Bowman coming in to ride Secret and Stardust." Ma spoke up, consulting a sheaf of papers she'd taken from the tack room. "I thought last spring's race was enough for Artur, but apparently he's decided to try again. Fool boy's brain is full of Faevor dreams, just like his father's was."

Sage dropped the brush she'd picked up. "But he nearly died!"

Lark cringed. Artur Bowman, despite lessons with the Horsemaven, had lost control of his shadowbred around the first turn of the Gauntlet and ended up tossed in a ditch, both legs broken. He'd recovered with barely a limp, but surely silver cuffs and a bit of Fae magic weren't worth the risk?

"Sage," Lark said, her voice smaller and sadder than she'd intended, "are you sure you want to race again?"

Jinx, the calico barn cat, jumped in Lark's lap to sniff pastry crumbs. Now she gave a *Mrow!* of concern and delicately cleaned her whiskers as Lark stroked her back.

"What happened to agreeing that Reverie and I can't be

beat? That we're the best team?" Sage scowled. "Besides, you know I'm not doing this for glory, Lark. I'm doing it for Galin. *One chance.*"

"But if we lost him, we could lose you too," Lark whispered, tears clogging her throat.

Ma set her papers on a stack of hay bales near one end of the aisle and knelt beside Lark, wrapping her in a hug. "Sweetling, I know you're worried. I am too. But this is what Mairens *do.* It's what we're good at, what we're known for. *Someone* has to ride the boundaries every spring and fall, after all; otherwise we would be living in magical chaos. And Sage is one of the best. She'll be fine. Reverie will make certain of it, right?"

She glanced over her shoulder at the stall behind her, where Sage's mare was blowing bubbles in the water bucket. Reverie looked up, knowing they were talking about her, and whinnied.

Ma chuckled. "See? She knows her job. In any case, I've been speaking to the Elders and the luckwitches about extra protections for this season's riders. It will turn out, you'll see."

Lark's fingers tightened against Jinx's fur and the calico cat jumped down from her lap, giving an indignant tail twitch before stalking off. "But Ma . . ."

Hooves crunched up the gravel road to the barn, voices and laughter breezing through the open doors. "Ah," Ma said brightly, leaning forward to look. "Brendan Forth is here. Sage, would you saddle Cinder with him while I have a word with his father?"

Lark waited for her sister to make some sharp, sarcastic remark, but Sage simply nodded and dusted her hands on her hips. If she didn't know her sister better, Lark might have found the sudden pink blush blooming in Sage's cheeks suspicious.

Must have been a flush from the exertion of feeding and watering the horses.

Lark knew she should get to work too, but she took a slower sip of tea, hoping the warmth would thaw the chill in her chest. Despite Sage's brave words and Ma's calm confidence, she was afraid.

"Luck of the morning to you!" Brendan called as he swung out of his own saddle and tied his ordinary chestnut horse to a hitching rail in the stable yard. He patted the thick-necked gelding on the shoulder and strode into the barn, grinning at Lark as he passed her.

She tried to ignore him, but he was swinging his arms so enthusiastically he knocked into a bucket of rose petals Ma had picked for the horses. The bucket tipped off the ledge by the door and spilled across the aisle. Twelve eager horses nickered and smacked their lips, expecting an extra helping of breakfast.

Lark groaned and knelt to gather up the delicate petals. "Sorry!" Brendan said, joining her.

But then Sage stepped around the corner carrying two saddles and he leaped to his feet, jostling Lark and the bucket again. "Sage!" he exclaimed.

"Clumsy oaf," Lark muttered under her breath, sweeping up the scatter *again*.

"Cinder's down here in the third stall," Sage said, pointing.

Lark watched him from the corners of her eyes as she finished collecting the rose petals. It took him three tries to buckle the halter on Cinder, and when the mare tossed her head he nearly lost his grip on her lead rope. He got her saddled without too much trouble, though Sage had to show him how to slowly ease the cinch tight to keep Cinder from getting annoyed enough to kick.

This was the boy who bragged that he could beat the famed Sage Mairen?

Lark was unimpressed, but Sage's bubbling laughter and bright smile seemed to fill the barn with sunlight. Shaking her head, Lark scratched the tip of her nose and finished helping with the chores.

He was *such* a blunderknuckles. But it was nice to see her sister smile again.

— TEN —

Feathers and Faevors

LATER THAT MORNING, while Ma and Sage evaluated riders in preparation for the Gauntlet and the Wild Hunt, Lark went to town with Da. When he stepped into Threadneedle's Fabrics, she ran down the cobbled street to Brassman's Clockworks.

After an entire winter of memorizing diagrams and assembling simple clockworks, there was still so much to learn. She was anxious to absorb as much information as possible, hoping it could help her with the moonclock.

As Elder Brassman sorted through sales receipts for Simon, Lark practiced calibrating gears and working on winding mechanisms. Socks purred at her feet, the soft rumble a pleasant hum beneath the regular ticking of clocks.

Suddenly, a single chime rang through the shop.

Lark sucked in a startled breath and Elder Brassman's hand jerked, accidentally sweeping some of the papers to the floor. Socks hissed, fur bristling in alarm.

Goward Brassman's Faevor was a clock that kept perfect time. Which meant that every clock in his shop was set precisely the same, so if one clock chimed the hour they *all* did.

But now each clock displayed a different time. The ornate wooden cuckoo clock on the north wall of the shop claimed it was six in the evening, as evidenced by the mechanical moon rising in the polished enamel sky. The grandfather clock standing in the corner showed one in the morning. Meanwhile, the hour and second hands on some of the clocks just bounced back and forth between noon and half past.

"What is happening?" Lark whispered, too shocked to speak out loud.

"I'm not sure," Elder Brassman muttered. "I've never heard of a Faevor failing. I suppose it could just be an anomaly of time, a bubble along the border, but . . . I simply don't know." He shook his head. "Forgive me, Lark, but I need to speak to the Elders. They might have to investigate further." Then he scrawled a note for Simon and flung his black scarf around his neck. Gathering up his staff, he said, "I'll see you tomorrow. If you'd like, you can take those gears home and continue working, hm?"

"Thank you, Elder Brassman." She followed him out the door, hurrying to Da's shop.

Lark tugged open the door of Threadneedle's Fabrics and stepped into a rainbow of satins, silks, velvets, brocades, and spools of ribbons and laces. Da stood at the long work-table, cutting a length of shimmering peach-blush cloth from a bolt of silk.

"Good afternoon, little bird," he said with a smile. "Why aren't you at Brassman's?"

"Da, something strange happened while I was there. . . ." She frowned, watching him pin the peach silk into the shape of a gown's bodice.

"Yes?" he prompted.

"Elder Brassman's Faevor failed. His charmed clock lost time. . . . It just chimed for no reason, and then all the clocks in the shop started spinning at random. It was complete chaos."

Da dropped his pincushion and regarded her with wide, startled gray eyes. "Is that so?"

"Yes. He's calling a meeting of the other Elders right now to discuss it, but . . . what do you think it means?"

Da sighed and smoothed a hand across the fabric. "Perhaps it was merely a quirk."

"Have you ever heard of a Faevor failing?"

"No, but we don't understand precisely how the Faevors work." An edge beneath his mild voice told Lark he was trying to hide his concern—which only upset her more. Why didn't adults understand that honesty was far less frightening than false reassurances, which just left room for even worse imaginings?

He flipped the bodice over and set an iron to heat.

"Don't borrow trouble, Lark. It's nothing for you to worry about. The Elders will see to it, all right?"

Lark scowled and paced a circle around his worktable, fidgeting with her copper ring. "Da, I'm not a baby. You don't have to protect me from the truth. I know that something is happening in the Twilight Court. Galin went missing for a reason, after all, and—"

"Rust and ruin," he suddenly cursed, holding up a short length of frayed thread. It was white or gray—she couldn't tell which. But Da's Faevor was a spool of thread that never ran out, never twisted or tangled or broke, and it matched the color of any fabric. . . .

What was he doing with this piece of common string?

His hands trembled as he examined the needle and thread, face pale with shock. He picked up the spool in his other hand, bouncing it lightly in his palm. "It's never failed before. Not once in the twenty-three years since I earned it."

A sharp icicle of fear pricked Lark's neck and melted in a cold rush down her spine as she realized what he was saying. Da's Faevored thread had snapped. The charm had broken.

Just like Elder Brassman's.

"Well, I was already an accepted member of the tailor's guild before I rode the Hunt," Da said with a shrug after a moment. His face was a mask of forced calm but Lark saw the dismay in his eyes. "I can sew without charmed thread. The general store here carries the basic colors, and I can send a courier to Blomm's and Burghley's in Mer Harbor for anything else. We'll manage someway." He flashed her a brittle smile but she wasn't fooled. He was afraid.

"Da, who granted you the Faevor? The May Queen or the Harvest King?" A creeping dread had struck Lark.

"The Harvest King. Why do you ask?" And then his eyes narrowed as he followed the direction of her thoughts. "Ah. I understand. If something worse than a simple tumble from a shadowbred happened to the Harvest King . . ." He drummed his fingers against the table. "Elder Brassman's Faevor was from the Harvest King too. He is meeting with the Elders now, you say?"

Lark nodded.

He smoothed the peach-colored silk on his worktable and scowled at the broken thread. "Then I'd better tell them about mine too. I hate to make you walk home alone, Lark, but I'm not sure how long I'll be at the meetinghouse, and Ma will need help with the evening chores."

"I'll be fine, Da. There's still at least an hour until sundown and I have my copper ring. I'll hurry."

With a reluctant nod and a tight hug, he said, "Watch the road and be quick, do you hear me?"

Lark hugged him back, promising she would, and dashed out the door. She rushed through Tradewind Junction and along the path leading home, but—with a twist of fear and a prick of guilt—she veered into the trees and headed for the waymarker near her family's maple grove instead.

She had to talk to Rook. The answers she needed were worth the risk.

She almost changed her mind when she reached the waymarker, though. The braided yarn-and-glass-bead cord charm the luckwitches had wrapped around each waymarker in an effort to secure the border was badly frayed. Beads had fallen in the grass and loose threads drifted in the wind.

Even worse, instead of glowing softly to indicate a strong boundary between the Fae realm and the mortal world, the moonstone set in the granite block flickered like a dying lantern flame.

Well, they all knew the border was fragile. Lark couldn't turn back now. If the Harvest King's Faevors were failing, fixing the mysterious moonclock was more critical than ever, but she couldn't do it alone. She needed Rook's help.

Taking a deep breath and straightening her shoulders, she pulled a handful of feathers from her pocket. She had taken to carrying them out of superstition, but now she hoped they would catch Rook's attention.

It was a gamble, calling him like this. She hoped he would be careful enough not to draw notice.

After a moment's hesitation, she pressed three raven feathers into the mud at the base of the waymarker like small flags. And then she added a red cardinal's feather she'd found to show that the message was urgent.

The waymarker's light sputtered again. Trying to get a closer look at the frayed charm—she was no luckwitch, but

119

maybe there was some way she could help fix it while she was here?—Lark stepped around the stone. She froze as a sudden searing flame licked her littlest finger. Her copper ring gleamed, the protective sigils engraved upon it flaring vivid gold. And then the ring slipped off, falling to the ground.

Lark bent to retrieve it and noticed what had been hidden in the soft moss and spring grass beneath her feet.

Bright red toadstools, their caps marked with white spots—a Faery ring.

She'd been caught in a trap for the unwary.

It's not possible, she thought. The Accords strictly prohibited such things.

Why would a Fae do something like this? Why *here*? And why hadn't her ring protected her?

This was a waymarker at the edge of *Mairen* land. . . . Maybe it wasn't an accidental trap.

Wildkin had been after clocks and watches all winter, and though their efforts had seemed random, Lark suspected that was only because whoever sent them wasn't sure how to be more specific. After all, a wildkin squirrel or raccoon wasn't likely to understand that the moonclock was currently just a pile of pieces hidden in a box under her bed. But if the spider or the bloodmoth had reported back, then *someone* surely knew that she was the one who had it.

And maybe they had decided that if they couldn't

successfully steal the moonclock they would just snatch *her*.

Lark's skin started to tingle. Luckily she'd only stepped one foot over the circle of toadstools, so maybe she could—

Salt and rust. When she tried to lift her foot, nothing happened. She couldn't move, no matter how hard she strained. It was as if she had been glued to the ground. She couldn't even wriggle her toes.

She tried to scream, but the air started to shimmer like water around her, tossing her voice back in her face like a malicious echo.

No one could hear her. A fist of panic squeezed her chest as faint strains of Fae music chimed in her ears. She remembered old fireside tales of the time before the Fae Accords had been signed, stories of people trapped in these toadstool rings, drawn into the Fae realm like dust caught in a soap bubble. She couldn't help Galin if she ended up trapped on the Other Side with him!

The air began to condense, taking on a weight and texture altogether strange. It was *pulling* her.

Thinking fast, Lark reached down to unlace her boot, wondering if she could simply leave it behind. But the moment her hand crossed the line drawn by the red toadstools, she lost her balance as the drag of magic intensified. She wobbled, pinwheeled her free arm, and started to fall.

A raven shrieked and suddenly Rook's bird was there, diving at the toadstools and ripping them apart with his beak. He scratched the ground with sharp toes, thrashing and flailing until the circle was a mangled mess of broken mushrooms and splattered mud.

Lark collapsed, breath rasping in her throat. "Oh, Nightbird, what would I have done without you? How did you know?"

He spread his wings and dipped his head, looking for all the world as if he was taking a bow. Then he clicked his beak, folded his wings, and began to preen his feathers, well satisfied with his work.

But Lark was still shaken. A Faery circle! *Here!* And it had very nearly swallowed her.

She gulped air and pointed to the feathers. "I need to speak with Rook," she whispered. "Can you bring these to him?"

"There's no need. I'm here," a grim voice murmured behind her.

She let out a startled shriek, and before she could spin around to face him, a cherry-scented hand slammed against her mouth, nearly sending her sprawling. "Ssssh!" his voice hissed. "No one can know I'm here."

Rook stepped in front of her, his face pale and worried. His different-colored eyes—moss green and golden brown—were wide and dilated, like a disturbed cat's.

Lark glared at him until he released his hand and helped her sit up. "If you ever silence me like that again I will smack you," she whispered furiously. "My lips are bruised."

"I'm sorry," he whispered back, and he really did look contrite. "I panicked."

Lark sighed and brushed at a dirt smudge on her sleeve. "I forgive you, but only because Nightbird saved me. Rook, there was a circle of toadstools here. I was wearing my copper ring but—"

Oh no. Her ring!

She leaned forward, scrabbling in the crushed grass for her fallen ring.

The raven let out a soft chuckle and hopped toward her, the glint of copper shining from his beak. "Oh, you marvelous bird," she said softly, holding out her hand so he could drop the ring into her palm.

She hastily slipped it back on her finger—though she no longer trusted it could do much good—and whispered to the raven, "I owe you a special treat, don't I? Come by my window tomorrow morning and I'll leave you a gift."

Rook mumbled, "I have something for you too." He held out a strawberry-sized burr acorn. "Remove the cap and you'll see."

She pried the fuzzy top off and discovered that the acorn was hollow. Tucked inside were two minuscule jeweled bezels and three filigreed watch hands of slightly different sizes.

"The last pieces, other than the case. I have bird scouts searching for that still. Have you told anyone what you're working on?"

"No! I keep my promises!"

His mouth twisted and he raked his hands through his hair, tiny sparks dancing off his fingertips. "They're getting bolder. By now they might realize the moonclock is bound to your blood. . . . If that's so, they won't give up." He dropped his hands, slapping his thighs in frustration. "Oh, feathers, this is a sour pickle, isn't it? How close are you to fixing the moonclock?"

"If it's meant to be assembled like an ordinary pocket watch, it shouldn't take me long once I have the case." She frowned and rubbed her chin. There were days this past winter when she'd *almost* assembled it, when she could practically see how all the pieces were meant to fit. But then she would notice an extra wheel or spring and confusion would drown her in questions again. At times she felt as if she held her brother's life in that wooden box beneath her bed and the burden of her failure was a constant ache in her heart.

"Will it work in a different case?" she asked. "I've already tried combining moonclock pieces with some of Elder Brassman's spare parts but it never goes well. Everything starts to rattle and vibrate until my fingers ache and my teeth buzz."

Rook acted as if he hadn't heard her, pacing around the waymarker and kicking at the remnants of the toadstool circle as he muttered to himself. "Too much danger for one mortal girl, but it's marked with her blood now and . . ."

He lifted his chin and stared at her. "You need protection."

"These copper rings clearly don't work as well as the Elders and the luckwitches hoped they would," she quietly agreed. "But I'll fill my pockets with salt and sage, and maybe Dame Wardspin will weave me a stronger defensive charm."

"No. . . . You are the moonclock carrier. There's a target on your back and you need to be able to defend yourself. Nightbird says there is a small shed and an unused paddock near your barn. Meet me there tomorrow at dawn's first light."

Lark rubbed a smear of mud off her fingers and twisted her ring. "It's not safe for you on this side of the border, Rook."

"It's not safe for me on the Other Side either," he said in a hollow voice. Before she could question him, he asked, "What did you want to speak to me about?"

She hesitated, shaken by the bleak expression in his eyes. "Faevors have started to fail."

"I was afraid of that. We're running out of time."

"What do you mean? You guessed this was going to happen?" Her voice rose and he shook a finger at her, urging her to stay quiet.

"I can't explain now."

"You have to! Is Galin all right? What about your sister?

What has happened to the Harvest King? Why are his Faevors failing?" She tried to whisper but she was so upset her words came out in a worried squeak.

"Tomorrow morning, Lark Mairen."

He whistled an oddly discordant note. Lark stumbled backward as the air took on a brittle shimmer, almost as though it had turned to glass or water. The waymarker's feeble glow flared to life and she realized she was looking at the magic boundary itself.

A heartbeat later Nightbird launched himself into flight, his powerful wings ripping through the flimsy border. The raven disappeared between one blink and the next, Rook plunging after him.

The air cleared, the waymarker's light dulled, and Lark found herself alone in the woods.

Rook had said ravens were pathmakers, wayforgers, trailbreakers. And the old stories mentioned that they could fly wherever they willed, navigate between worlds, rip through barriers on a whim, skim across the strongest borders.

But Lark had never expected to witness it.

Of course, she had never expected to be friends with a Fae either or thought she would one day have to repair a clock to rescue her brother.

What strange times.

— ELEVEN —

Baubles, Bribes, and Tricks

AFTER WATCHING ROOK and Nightbird disappear, Lark ran home, thoughts racing as fast as her feet.

She could think of only one explanation for the Harvest King's Faevors failing . . . and it was a dark and terrifying idea.

Rook and Nightbird had hinted that the king might once have been a mortal, though Lark knew even the Fae could be killed.

Could he have died?

No . . . there *must* be another reason the Faevors had broken. The Harvest King had shared rule of the Twilight Court since the first mortals had settled in the Borderlands generations ago. It was impossible to imagine a world without him. It was like picturing Mer Harbor without the sea or Dodger Creek without the creek.

But it didn't make sense. All winter magic had seeped

across the boundary, so wouldn't Faevors grow stronger rather than weaker?

Unless the Faevors were linked to the king who had granted them . . . which sent her fears spiraling back in a circle.

If the Harvest King had died, what would happen to the Twilight Court?

What would happen to the May Queen? Rook and Nightbird had warned that the queen was in danger too, but they hadn't given any details or explanations.

A worse thought struck her.

What would happen—had happened?—to her brother, the mortal who'd saved a Fae king? Lark's heart and stomach twisted like twin snakes trying to devour her from the inside out and pain squeezed the air from her chest.

Was she already too late? Had it taken her too long to fix the moonclock?

Was Galin still alive?

Rook would have told her if something had happened to her brother, right? If it was hopeless?

"Tomorrow morning," Rook had said in answer to her frantic questions. But how could she wait?

There was one thing she could confirm. Lark's lungs burned for air and her legs throbbed by the time she shoved through her garden gate. She sprinted for Ma's rosebush behind the barn and tripped to a stop when she saw that it was still blooming. Red and pink roses as big as plums still covered the shrub, weighting the branches and scenting the air.

Her relief was fleeting—before she turned away, she glimpsed a cluster of blackened spots on one of the stems and a creeping rim of brown on some of the petals. The May Queen's Faevor was still alive—but for how long?

She and Rook needed to find the moonclock's case as quickly as possible so she could repair it before they lost their chance to fix everything else.

Too much depended on it.

Lark ran into her house, fear dragging at her heels.

As she washed her face in cool water, Lark tried to tell herself that as long as the May Queen was alive she could still set everything back to rights even if the king was gone. But the Twilight Court of the Fae depended on balance, and if the diseased roses meant the queen was also in danger . . .

Lark hated having to wait until supper to hear what the Elders had told Da about their failing Faevors. But then he sent a runner from the messenger guild saying he was delayed in town and would eat with the Elders, only increasing her impatience. And Sarai was helping Ma with the fractious shadowbreds, so they just grabbed a couple of meat pies, apples, and chocolate biscuits to share before rushing back to the barn. "Stay inside," Ma told Sage and Lark. "I'll be in later."

Lark tried to bring up her fears with her sister, but the Gauntlet was only days away and Sage was too worried about the spring Wild Hunt to be in a talkative mood.

Well, Lark would just have to hear what Rook had to say in the morning. The Fae might play with honesty the way cats played with string, but at least they couldn't actually lie. She planned to pick apart whatever he said until she found the hidden truth.

But she was so tired of *waiting*. She could practically feel time slipping through her hands, and for the sake of both her siblings she couldn't afford to waste it.

Something tapped on Lark's bedroom window at too-early-o'clock the next morning, startling her awake. She pulled her pillow over her ears and tried to ignore it.

It tapped louder.

"Rust and ruin," she whispered, sitting up in bed. What if it was another wildkin? She'd stayed up too late the night before, desperately and unsuccessfully trying to cram the pieces of the moonclock into one of the battered tin cases Elder Brassman had let her borrow. After the toadstool trap from yesterday, had she drawn dangerous attention again?

The tapping grew more insistent and she worried her window might break. Then she heard a soft croak and suddenly realized who was standing on the other side of the glass. She flung off her blankets and leaped to the window, yanking back the curtains and lifting the sash just as Nightbird bobbed forward to peck again.

"What are you doing?" Lark hissed at him. Morning

light barely faded the eastern sky, and a waxing crescent moon still hung above the horizon in tattered clouds.

The raven tipped his head to one side and shuffled his feet, bright eyes peering at her and ink-slick feathers ruffling. He shifted to maintain his balance in a gust of cold wind.

"No!" she told him, guessing that he'd been sent as a summons. "Tell Rook it's too early and I'm tired."

Nightbird clicked his beak and squinted one eye. It was early for him too, she knew.

"Listen, I know that we agreed to meet this morning but the sun isn't even awake yet! Come back in an hour and I'll give you some bacon."

The raven spread his wings with great dignity. Slowly and deliberately, he pecked the wooden windowsill three times and raised his head to stare at her.

His signal was clear. *Come now.*

Lark rubbed her eyes. "Fine. Give me a minute to dress and I'll meet you out there."

He waited until she'd started rummaging through her drawers for clean socks before flying out of sight.

Lark grumbled. She needed to talk to Rook, that was certain, and she knew lying in bed wouldn't help Galin or keep Sage from riding the Wild Hunt.

But still. Another hour of sleep would have been nice.

Jaw cracking in a yawn, she tugged a soft brown tunic over her leggings and wrapped a leather belt around her waist. She braided her hair with deft fingers, wondering how far she could—or should—trust Rook. He had told her he was trying to save a sibling too, and he'd promised to help her learn to defend herself. Besides, Nightbird trusted him. She considered him a friend. . . .

But he was Fae, and that meant he was a creature of secrets and tricks. She had to keep her wits sharp.

With a wistful glance at her warm, rumpled bed, Lark eased her door open and stepped out. Resisting the urge to peek inside Galin's room—no matter how many times she checked, he still hadn't come home when she wasn't looking—she tiptoed past Sage's room across the way. She smirked at the snores Sage would never admit to and hurried past their parents' room, running lightly down the stairs and jumping over the creaky fifth step.

She took her cloak from the hook by the back door and swung it around her shoulders, then held her breath and opened the door. It let out a squeak and a creak and a groan. She froze, but when the silence of the house continued unbroken she darted through, closing it with a soft click behind her.

Her stomach clenched as she crept through the cold dawn. Sneaking out was not allowed. Speaking to Fae was *definitely* prohibited. Though Lark had bent the rules before, she really hated breaking them. But she would do anything for Galin and Sage.

Dew soaked the toes of her boots and dampened the

hem of her cloak as she kicked her way through the spring grass toward a breeding paddock and small shed on the far side of the pasture. She was heartsick at the thought of Galin trapped on the Other Side, of Sage flinging herself into danger after him. And she was so discouraged. . . . She'd worked *so* hard all winter to put the moonclock together, without all the parts or information she needed. How could she hope to succeed facing a wall of Fae secrets?

She was tired and sad and worried and angry and it all felt like a storm stuck in her chest.

Nightbird met her halfway, swooping overhead and then circling away. Frogs peeped from puddles and songbirds trilled, suddenly falling silent when Rook stepped out of the shadows.

"Am I too late?" Lark demanded, eyes blurring with tears she angrily blinked away. "I spent all night attempting to assemble your moonclock, but no matter how hard I tried to force the pieces into one of Elder Brassman's spare watch cases, they *refused* to fit. That's the only way I can describe it. Rook, I *tried*. I've tried *all winter*. Am I too late? Is my brother . . . is he . . ."

She couldn't force the words out. They stuck to her tongue like clumps of cobweb.

"*Galin Threadneedle* is still alive," he said, but something in his voice, in the formality of his tone and the emphasis on Galin's name, pinched her sense of alarm and confirmed her suspicion.

"But the Harvest King is not, is he? Something happened to him. Something worse than falling from his horse. Those brambles that attacked him on the Hunt—they got him, didn't they?" Lark's lips trembled and she pressed her fingers to her mouth.

Rook grimaced and glanced away, but not before she saw a quicksilver tear slide down his cheek.

"What about your sister?" she whispered.

"Both of them—" He pursed his lips and a sound squeaked out, while the cords in his neck quivered and his face flushed red. He strained, sweat slicking his forehead as he choked and pressed a hand to his throat, gritting his teeth. Finally he croaked, "Danger," before coughing and spitting out a jagged green leaf, like one from a bramble.

"Rook!" Lark cried, but he waved off her concern. Then he hugged his elbows and sucked air through his teeth.

Nightbird dove with a shriek, ripping the leaf to shreds with his talons, and Rook slowly straightened.

"You have *two* sisters in danger?" Lark asked.

Rook stomped the ground, raked his fingers through his hair, scowled like a thundercloud. Birds burst from the trees in a swirl of leaves and feathers and soared toward him, spinning around his head until he was nearly enveloped in a shifting curtain of wings and beaks and bead-bright eyes.

Lark took a step back and wondered if she should run to her house.

"We need the mysterymoonclock. It's the only way. . . ." His voice was muffled by the surrounding commotion.

"I need the case."

"*I know*," he snarled, and the flock of birds around him suddenly scattered.

"You'd better not wake my parents," Lark warned him. "So, how do we find the case? Where should we look? When Da came home last night he said the Elders have forbidden anyone from getting within thirty paces of the waymarkers. They decided it's too dangerous, between failing Faevors and increasing instability along the boundary, but maybe we could sneak—"

"It has already been found," he grunted, slamming a hand against his thigh.

Lark blinked. Surely that was a good thing? Why did he sound so angry? Unless . . . Oh no. "One of the Harvest King's enemies has it?"

Nightbird let out a warning croak and Rook frowned. "I might be able to bargain for it. But things are . . . getting complicated, and you need to know how to defend yourself. Pay attention because I don't know when I'll get another chance like this."

He glanced around and whistled a high, clear note that tingled in Lark's teeth and vibrated in her ears. The sound shivered the air, sending spreading ripples around them. He let the note fade, then clicked his tongue, and the air went crystal-still, like a bubble of glass.

"There. Now we can't be observed unless someone

stumbles too close." Rook cracked his knuckles and said, "I'm going to teach you a few small tricks for protection. They won't save you from a fully worked Fae spell, but they could buy you time to get away."

Lark swallowed a lump of unease and pulled her cloak closer. "Tricks?"

"Simple charms that might turn Fae magic aside long enough for you to escape." He grimaced and shuffled his feet. "I'm afraid there are"—he fought to get the words out—"powerful Fae who will do anything to get their hands on you and the moonclock, and since you've managed to elude or escape them so far, they'll only try that much harder."

Lark's knees wobbled like a newborn colt's but she nodded, thinking again how fortunate she was that Nightbird had managed to break the toadstool ring in time to free her. She might not be so lucky next time they tried to trap her.

"But I don't understand what my blood has to do with it. What is the moonclock's purpose? Why do they want it so badly?" she asked, proud that her voice quavered only once.

Rook held up a hand. "Fluff and feathers, Lark. We're not here to talk about the moonclock right now! We're here to talk about how to keep you safe. Anyway, my tongue is tied—I've told you all I can. Now, what do you know about breaking a Fae illusion?"

Lark frowned. She wanted *answers*, not rhymes and

riddles. But she needed Rook's help, and she would take whatever he offered.

With a sigh, she repeated lessons all children in the Borderlands memorized. "The surest way to break an illusion—assuming you know it *is* an illusion—is by peering through a hagstone. Lacking one, a mirror charged in midsummer sunlight, tilted just so, might work too. I've heard that the luckwitches used to make a clearsight salve, but if that's true, I've never seen it. But Rook, I don't understand. I thought you couldn't speak ill of your own kind?"

"I can't. But I *can* speak ill of myself, and since I'm a master of tricks, there are plenty of things I can tell you." He flashed a wry smile. "Do you have a hagstone?"

"Ma does, though she rarely carries it. I think I saw one in our upstairs closet. I'll dig it out. Don't the Fae Accords prohibit the use of all illusions other than glamours against mortals?"

"Promises made of ink and paper are flimsy things. When we're finished here, find that hagstone and keep it with you, understand?"

She nodded, biting her bottom lip.

"How do you stop a Fae from muddling your way?" he continued.

"If you're crossing the Darkmist Moors, you carry a beeswax candle blessed by a luckwitch and wear your shoes on the wrong feet. But no one from Tradewind Junction has attempted the Moors in . . . oh, I don't know how long. Anywhere else, you tie your bootlaces in triple knots and carry a pebble from your own yard in your right pocket."

"Good. So you know the basics."

"But . . . these are folktales. The Fae Accords—"

"Are *fragile*. Don't you understand? What you call *folktales* are important, Lark. It's time your people remembered. Now, how do you turn aside a Fae's attention?"

"Wear your clothing inside out. Carry bread crumbs in your pockets. A red vest with rough-edged seams can be a shield too, according to Da."

"Yes! And if you're being followed by a Fae, walk like this: three strides with a heavier weight on the right foot, then a step to the side with the left foot, then three strides with a heavier weight on the left foot, then a step to the side with the right. Like this, see?" He demonstrated the odd rhythm and made Lark imitate his movements. "It won't work against a determined hunter, but you'd be surprised how effective it is against most Fae. We're easily distracted in the mortal world."

"And in your realm?"

"If you're being followed in the Fae realm, you'd best have some other tricks up your sleeve. Glass marbles make good bargaining tokens. So do other baubles: beads, bracelets, hairpins. Mortal fruits, honey and milk, tea and cake are all good bribes."

Lark adjusted the hood of her cloak and regarded him

with skepticism. "And salt and sage can send a Fae away. Rue and purplewort repel them. These are things all children know."

"In a pinch, they are solid measures of protection. But you should know some charms too."

"Charms? But Rook, I'm not a luckwitch. I can't use magic."

"Not all charms require magic—especially in the Fae realm. The most important thing is just your will—something most mortals underestimate. So, for example, let's say the way is blocked before you. Imagine you are on a path and a log has fallen over the trail. If your need to get past it is strong enough, if your will is hard as iron, if your focus is unflinching, you can clear the path with nothing but your own hands and breath."

"You're teasing."

He shook his head. "I tell the truth. Someday you may have cause to prove it. But this morning, just remember this: press your hands together as firmly as you can, until you feel the heat of your skin flowing between your palms. Go on, do it."

Lark raised her eyebrows but did as she was told, pressing her hands together like a closed book before her chest.

"Right. And if you were to picture your hands as a representation of whatever barrier might block your way, to break it you would visualize the path clearing as you breathe into your palms while slowly opening them. Like so." He unfolded his hands like a swinging gate, blowing through them.

Nothing happened, but he tipped his chin at Lark and said, "Now you."

Feeling self-conscious, Lark copied his gesture.

"You forgot to breathe as your hands open. The breath is an embodiment of your will—it is what clears the obstacles. Do you see?"

No. "Um, sure." She tried again, and this time he was satisfied.

"Yes. Remember it, in case there's ever a time when you truly need to use it. Only then will it work." He paused as if waiting for her to express astonishment or wonder or something, but Lark wasn't sure she believed him.

After a heartbeat Rook shrugged and said, "If you are ever caught in a snare, take a piece of red thread or yarn or ribbon and weave it around your fingers like this. . . ." He pinched his fingers and a red string suddenly appeared. Then, twisting his hands first one way and then another, he looped the string around his fingers in a simple pattern. "Say: *Caught and bound, by string surround until the cage comes unwound.* Chant it three times, and mean every word. On the third repetition, flick your fingers like so—" He did something sharp and sudden with his hands, and the string fell loose. "And say *the power of three shall set me free* three times. If your intention remains strong and steady and sure, you'll find yourself able to walk from the trap. Are you listening? This is critical!"

"Yes! It's just . . . these are nursery rhymes and ribbon games. How do you know these charms will work for me? I mean, it's easy for you to *say* they do, but you have magic!"

"I wish I could promise that they will. All I'm saying is that if you want them to bad enough, they might."

"That's not very reassuring," Lark told him, frowning. Was he just playing with her?

"It's the best I can offer. Now concentrate . . ." He continued reciting simple chants and small charms until a raven's call echoed inside the shimmering circle Rook had cast around them. He snapped his fingers, letting it dissolve in a sparkling swirl. "Fluff and feathers, Nightbird says your parents are awake. We'll continue tomorrow. Don't tell *any-one*."

"Rook, as much as I appreciate all of this, I still need answers about the moonclock."

"I know. But I also need to keep you safe. I'll see you here tomorrow at dawn."

TWELVE

Salt and Iron

LARK WENT TO bed early that evening so she'd be prepared for more lessons with Rook at sunrise, but sometime in the middle of the night a commotion outside awakened her family. Lark and Sage wrapped fleece-lined flannel robes around their nightgowns and padded downstairs together, clasping hands when they saw their parents standing before the open door.

Da had lit the oil lamps in the front room and in the pale glow Lark recognized the luckwitch from Signal Ridge as well as Dame Davina Wardspin—Tradewind Junction's own luckwitch—along with several neighbors. A man in front wore the linked circle badge of the messenger guild. The shadows clinging to their faces made it hard to read their expressions.

Fear caterpillar-crawled up Lark's spine and nested at the base of her neck, tickling her hair. Were they bringing bad news?

One of Sarai Vanbeck's sons spoke in a low, urgent tone, gesturing with the lantern he held so flickering light splashed the night.

Lark's stomach felt like a bog puddle of eels and duckweed, all tangled and writhing in slippery knots, and her skin went cold. What had happened? She stepped forward, but Sage drew her back with a hiss of dismay, fingers squeezing around Lark's wrist.

Lark tried to pull away, but Sage's cheeks had flamed pink and she dragged Lark in front of her. "What are you doing?" Lark asked.

Sage jerked her chin at the cluster of people by the door, and then Lark noticed Blunderknuckles Forth. "I'm in *my* robe," she whispered, teeth grinding on the words.

"So? It's only Blunderknuckles. Now let me go. I want to hear—"

"Girls?" Da glanced over his shoulder, worry pinching his brows and something like fear drawn in white around his eyes. "Get back to your rooms, make sure your windows are closed and latched, then climb under your patchwork protection quilts. Quickly now. Go on!"

Lark stared at the luckwitches, at their pale green cloaks embroidered with gold symbols, at the loops of beads and bells around their necks and the dried flowers woven through their long braids. Her mouth had gone dry as dust. "Wildkin?" she whispered.

"No, Lark, it's—" Brendan started to say, voice soft.

She frowned at him. What was he even doing here?

The man with the messenger badge answered Lark's unspoken question with a pleased smile, gesturing at the insignia she hadn't noticed pinned to the vest Blunder-knuckles wore beneath his cloak. "Brendan's the newest member of our guild."

The luckwitch from Signal Ridge clucked. "No time for tongue-wagging. We must draw the wards and move to the next place."

"What *happened*?" Lark demanded. She wasn't about to hide in her room until she knew what was going on.

"We caught some fool with salt and smuggled iron at the Crestview waymarker while patrolling the border. We notified the Elders, but given the state of the boundary and the lack of communication we've had with the Fae emissary for the last few moonturns . . . well, out of an abundance of caution we've sent luckwitches throughout the area to weave a shield around every home. Just in case," Dame Wardspin said.

"Just in case *what*?" Lark asked.

"Girls, don't argue. Go to your rooms and get back to sleep. Let the luckwitches move on with their work. We'll talk in the morning," Ma told them.

But the messenger answered, "Just in case the Fae decide he broke the Accords."

Lark and her sister exchanged wide-eyed glances. There had been so much talk about the Fae breaking the treaty—Lark had never considered that a *mortal* might ignore the Accords.

"If the Fae find out a mortal brought iron to the border . . ." Sage murmured, horrified.

"He said he was invoking the Last Protection clause. It would mean war," Brendan agreed grimly.

Lark squeaked and the luckwitches looked at her. It wouldn't just mean war—it could mean the destruction of the entire border. But Dame Wardspin said, "Oh, child. Don't worry. This isn't going to go further—we're here to make certain of it."

"Please, Lark. Follow your sister and climb under your quilt. Let the luckwitches work in peace," Da said.

As her parents stepped out onto the porch with the others, Lark noisily clattered up the stairs after Sage and whirled into her sister's room. The dull chime of copper bells filled the night outside and a shiver of magic rippled across her skin.

Sage unfolded her quilt and waved Lark closer. Lark shut the door and leaped for her sister's bed, jumping on the soft mattress. Sage wrapped the quilt around them both and Lark felt her tremble.

Cut-out tin stars covered the lantern on Sage's desk, casting star shadows across the walls. Lark leaned back on her elbows to count them as Sage smoothed a hand over the patchwork quilt. Each square was embroidered with different sigils and symbols of protection, designed to keep young children safe on Wild Hunt nights. They were a tradition, the pattern handed down within families. "Granny Juniper and Da made these for us before we were even born," Sage murmured. "And Galin patched mine two springs ago."

But Lark barely heard her. "What's the punishment for someone smuggling iron into the Borderlands?" she asked.

"Didn't Teacher Bardic mention it in your history lessons? Permanent exile."

Lark couldn't imagine leaving her family, her friends, her *home* forever. "That's terrible."

"So is risking the peace between our realms."

Lark couldn't argue. "Why do you think he did it?" she whispered.

Sage was quiet for a moment, and then she said, "Fear makes people desperate."

Lark agreed. After all, she was so desperate to save her brother—so afraid of what he might be going through at this very moment—that she'd been working on a secret moonclock despite wildkin attacks and toadstool traps. But Rook had been taking chances too, hadn't he? Every time he snuck through the border with Nightbird. And he'd taught her defenses against his own people. He must be desperate to save his sisters as well. Just how bad were things within the Twilight Court?

She pulled the quilt up to her chin. "Sage, I think the Harvest King is dead. I think that's why the Faevors he granted have failed."

Sage went still, and then she said, "He's too powerful to be killed."

"What if I told you I . . . came across . . . information hinting he might have been a mortal once?"

"Impossible. The Fae would never accept a mortal as their king."

"But what if he *was*?" Lark insisted.

Sage sighed. "Even if he was once a mortal, he's not any longer. He's been in the Twilight Court for centuries. *Centuries*, Lark."

"He could still be killed."

"Yes . . . yes, that's true. If he had an enemy powerful enough."

"*Someone* sent those brambles to trip his horse. Think about it, Sage. It would explain . . . well, everything."

Sage chewed her thumbnail thoughtfully. "I suppose you could be right, but surely the May Queen would have sent an emissary to tell the Elders? I mean, if your theory is correct, *she's* obviously still alive because her Faevors are still working. Ma's rosebush is still blooming."

"But the roses don't look . . . healthy. Haven't you noticed the spots? She could be in danger. Or she could be wrapped too deep in grief. She and the Harvest King were together for all those centuries you mentioned. Surely she would mourn his loss? And besides, the Court depends on balance."

"Well, I guess we'll know for certain soon, eh? It's nearly Mayfair." Sage eyed the silver ivy-and-rose cuffs on the corner of her desk. "As long as that fool with salt and an iron nail doesn't convince any friends to salt the boundary with him, to hammer nails between all the waymarkers . . ." She shuddered and clutched the quilt in both fists.

The full significance of what could have happened crashed on Lark like a rockfall. If salt and iron broke the border a permanent rift would form between the Fae realm and the mortal world—a gap no one could cross.

She would never see Rook again.

And Galin . . . Galin would be lost forever.

Lark choked on a sob at the thought of everything she could lose and Sage wrapped her in a hug. "Don't worry, though, little bird. It's almost time for the Wild Hunt. I'm going to win the Gauntlet, and then I'll ride the Hunt and get Galin back. The May Queen and the White Stag will strengthen the boundary and everything will settle down once more. You'll see."

Lark didn't need Nightbird to wake her the next morning. Though exhaustion weighted her eyelids, she hadn't been able to fall back asleep after the arrival of the messengers and luckwitches. Afraid her restlessness would bother Sage, she'd drifted back to her own room. As soon as the first blush of dawn lit the horizon she pulled her clothes on and ran outside.

She was in such a rush she almost didn't notice the strange symbols drawn on the door in white chalk or the garlands of knotted yarn, bits of wood, and shells draped across her house. But the tingle of magic was unmistakable and she lurched to a stop to stare at what the luckwitches had worked in the night.

This was a strong shielding charm—perhaps the most powerful she had ever felt. And as she turned, gaze sweeping the garden gate and the yard, she saw more wards placed in the corners and hung over the posts. Additional symbols were painted across the barn doors and bundles of dried herbs had been nailed to the eaves.

It was meant to keep away all Fae—and that meant Rook couldn't enter the property.

Lark twisted her fingers in the hem of her cloak and considered her options. Should she risk looking for him at the waymarker?

No. She glanced at the wards protecting her family's house and barn and decided too many people had worked too hard to keep her safe.

Besides . . . how would she explain the wards? If she mentioned salt and iron, he would know a mortal had considered invoking the Last Protection clause, and then what would he do?

Even though he had helped her, she and Rook were on opposite sides of the border . . . maybe in more ways than one.

As she stood on her porch studying the symbols swirled across the weathered wooden boards of her home, Sage stepped through the door. "Oh! I'm glad you're here. I told Ma to rest a while longer. We can manage the shadowbreds together, eh?"

Then she noticed the wards and whistled. "I've never seen such intricate shields before."

"They feel strong," Lark remarked, reaching out to touch a white star and then changing her mind.

"The only advantage to the weak border, I reckon." Sage nodded. "More Fae power to use against them."

The offhand comment bothered Lark, burrowing in her heart like a barbed thorn. She knew the Fae were danger-ous, tricky, mysterious . . . but she didn't want to see magic used against Rook. She had come to think of him as her friend, as strange as it felt to admit that.

Before she could frame a response, though, Sage was already hurrying toward the barn, and Lark had no choice but to follow.

Inside the barn, the shadowbreds were restless and irri-table. Smoke drifted from the ends of their tails and sparks crackled from their nostrils as they blew frustrated snorts.

They kicked their stall doors, leaving silvered scars in the wood, and whinnied to each other across the aisle.

Tension tightened Lark's shoulders. She barely trusted the shadowbreds on a good day—this morning she found them frightening.

Sage handed her a bucket and gave her a gentle shove. "They're reacting to the magic in the wards, I imagine. But they won't hurt you."

Are you sure about that? Lark wanted to ask, but instead she hauled the bucket out to the rosebush and began picking petals. She had a feeling it was going to take more than usual to satisfy the shadowbreds.

She tried to ignore the slowly spreading black spots leaching up the stems and the curl of brown along the edge of some of the roses.

Once Rook makes his bargain for the moonclock case, I'll assemble it. And then we can fix everything—as long as there's still a border to fix.

Lark left a black feather outside her window that afternoon hoping Nightbird could somehow still get a message through, but several days passed and she didn't see either Rook or his raven.

She desperately hoped they were recovering the moonclock case, because the situation in Tradewind Junction continued to fracture. The Elders even called an emergency town hall meeting. The last time Lark remembered such a thing was the summer she'd turned six, when a lightning strike sparked a wildfire and everyone in town had to form a bucket brigade to save the sawmill. Galin had thought it a grand adventure but she'd tasted smoke on the air for days.

A restless, angry crowd already filled the meetinghouse when Lark and her family arrived. Ma and Da took their seats along one wall while Lark followed Sage up narrow wooden steps to the wide loft overlooking the main floor of the stone building.

Blunderknuckles Forth and his friends leaned against the railing on one side. Lark scowled and started to stalk past them to a cluster of girls she used to fish with on the opposite end. To her surprise, though, Sage breezed directly toward Blunderknuckles with a bright smile.

"Sage! What are you doing?" Lark hissed, plucking her sister's sleeve. But there was no time to talk—they squeezed past a knot of younger children playing a dice game and reached the front railing just as the three Elders took their place on a small wooden platform at the front of the hall. One of them rapped her staff on the floor and reluctant silence swept through the building, broken by a cough and the scrape of boot heels on wooden planks.

Elder Rowana, with her fierce hawk nose and sternly braided hair, cleared her throat and announced, "We've called this meeting to discuss the upcoming Mayfair Hunt. We—"

"They've broken the Accords!" a man in a blacksmith's

leather apron and high boots cried.

A woman near the back of the room raised her arm and called, "I can't let my little ones out to play for fear some wildkin will wander from the forest and hurt them. Where's the White Stag?"

"Why should we join their wicked Wild Hunt when the Faevors they promised have failed?" someone else yelled.

Elder Rowana tried to calm the rising tide of anger, but people shouted about Fae tricks and timeslips and thorns growing through garden walls.

Elder Goward Brassman fidgeted with the watch chain looped to his vest pocket in a nervous gesture Lark had come to recognize. He thumped his staff on the floor. "Silence! There will be time for questions and comments later, but first you must listen to—"

A man in a green-and-brown tracker's cloak shouted, "It's time to invoke the Last Protection clause! They broke the Accords first and now we've lost control of magic and time along the border. We need salt and iron!"

The woman beside him stamped her feet and began a chant: "Salt and iron! Salt and iron!" It was picked up by the people around her, rising like a storm in the hall.

"How many times must we remind you? The *instant* the Fae sense you sprinkling salt along the boundary, the moment you press the first iron nail into the ground, they will send all their magic against us in retaliation," Elder Goward cried, hands cupped around his mouth so his voice carried through the entire hall.

Lark and Sage exchanged a dismayed glance. "I thought the Elders and luckwitches had resolved this. I assumed the man they caught was exiled," Sage murmured.

Brendan leaned closer and gestured to the agitated crowd. "Evidently he isn't the only one who feels this way."

A man shouted, "It's the only way to stabilize the border! Bring your salt and I'll grab a hammer and nails. Problem solved! Let's go, boys!" And he waved an arm as though prepared to lead an army out.

"No!" Lark gasped. "Galin—"

Blunderknuckles glanced at Lark and nodded as though hearing her thoughts. She frowned. He might be a messenger, but that didn't mean he knew anything.

Her scowl deepened when she saw him lay a hand on Sage's elbow and squeeze. Then he put two fingers in his mouth and let out a shrill, piercing whistle that sliced like a knife through the chaos.

"Have you forgotten? There's another way to fix the breach in the border," he cried. "Five of us must ride the Wild Hunt four nights from now. As we have done for generations."

"Why should we risk the ride if their Faevors can't be trusted?" someone shouted back.

"Because it's never been about the Faevors," Ma said, stepping closer to the Elders. "Brendan is right. The Wild

Hunt has *always* been about bringing balance back to the Borderlands, building peace between our people."

Lark narrowed her eyes at Brendan. She didn't trust his sudden heroic stance. More likely Blunderknuckles just wanted his chance to race Sage.

Someone in a gauzy gray-and-black skirt with strands of shells and beads looped around her neck entered the hall and threaded her way to the Elders. Lark leaned forward and recognized Dame Davina Wardspin, Tradewind Junction's luckwitch.

"These are troubled times," the luckwitch agreed. Her voice was soft and measured, and yet somehow it carried to every corner. "And it would seem the answer is to simply close our lands, eh? Break the border with salt and iron, and by doing so break a trust and a treaty that has held since your families first laid their roots here. But there would be a cost, my friends. Their magic sustains *us* too, whether you wish to admit it or not."

Cries of protest rattled the room but she held up a slender hand and they subsided. "The healer's best potions and poultices are laced with scavenged magic. Tomsin Bridger, when your heart gave out last summer, it was magic that brought the breath back to your lungs. Eddis Rowman, when the grappling hook down at the dockyards shredded the skin off your arm, it was magic that cleared the blood-sickness from your body. Lia Crofter, when your child had the scarlet fever, what saved her life?"

"Magic in the syrups you and Netty Greenwillow mixed for her," Lia admitted in a subdued voice.

"Yes, the Faevors are failing," the luckwitch went on. "But we need answers, not anger. Discussion, not destruction."

"We'll speak with the Fae envoy at Mayfair," Elder Rowana Farstorm announced. "Perhaps they are unaware of the situation on this side of the border."

Lark doubted that, but the adults on the main floor shifted their weight, scratched their beards, smoothed their aprons, and allowed themselves to be persuaded.

"Besides, even if the Faevors have failed, we can still purchase charms at the Midnight Market tomorrow," someone pointed out, answered by ripples of agreement.

A flicker of excitement quickened Lark's pulse. The Midnight Market was a chance for mortals and Fae to talk, trade, barter, and bargain. Although carefully regulated, magic and marvels would be offered for sale, and she was *finally* old enough to see it all for herself.

"Yes, with caution," Elder Heartstone warned. "Something has clearly changed in the Twilight Court, and until we understand what it is, we must all take care."

"But it's the nature of *mortal* things to change. Not the Fae," Blunderknuckles murmured to Sage. She didn't answer, her gaze fixed on the crowd of adults below.

It wasn't in the Fae nature to die either, Lark thought to

herself. And yet it was possible.

Should she tell them what she knew, what she suspected? Would they believe her? Would the knowledge fix anything, or make it worse?

And if she *did* reveal even part of her secret, how could she explain where the information had come from without endangering Rook?

While she hesitated, wrestling with her doubts, the moment passed and the Elders thumped their staffs to signal the end of the meeting.

"So. We are agreed, then. Mayfair will begin as planned tomorrow, but I urge you all to be wary. Be observant. Remember the rules for dealing with Fae, wear your copper rings, and *watch the road.*"

"Where does that expression come from, I wonder?" Blunderknuckles asked. "Why not just say *be careful* or something?"

Oh, so the know-it-all didn't know *everything*? Lark smirked and waited for Sage to say something sarcastic, but her sister just smiled.

"It comes from the days before the Accords were signed, when the Fae liked to play really nasty tricks on people. You've heard the stories, how they liked to lure people through the mists with flickering lights, only to lead them over the edge of the cliffs. Or how they would twist the paths to confuse people, leaving them wandering lost in lands they should have known. So *watch the road* means keep your eyes open, keep your wits about you, and stay safe," Sage explained.

"Ah, of course," Blunderknuckles said earnestly. "You're so smart."

Lark rolled her eyes.

Ma raised her hand. "One announcement before we all go," she said. "I will enter nine shadowbred mares in this spring's Gauntlet. I've been evaluating riders for the past few weeks and will make my final determination in a few days. If any of you wish to try the Gauntlet on one of these horses, come to the barn tomorrow unless I've already seen you ride. But everyone must be aware that the issues with the border have made the shadowbreds skittish, so this spring's race will require exceptional strength and steadiness from the riders."

A fresh tide of fear sent a surge of blood rushing in Lark's ears as her heart pounded her rib cage. The Gauntlet was in three days, the Wild Hunt one night later. Even if she *did* manage to fix the moonclock before Sage rode, how was she supposed to use it to help Galin?

— THIRTEEN —

The Midnight Market

THE MAYFAIR CELEBRATION surrounding the Gauntlet race and the Wild Hunt traditionally began at sundown with the opening of the Midnight Market, and Lark was eager to experience it for the first time.

She'd been too young before, required to stay in the children's tent at the edge of the town square. Though she had enjoyed playing games and gorging herself on frosted flower cakes, it wasn't the same as exploring an entire market of magical things.

Lark hurriedly changed her clothes and filled her pockets with protective charms in preparation for the evening ahead, feeling the reassuring weight of her hagstone and the enticing jingle of coins and glass marbles for bargaining. Her entire life she'd heard stories of wonders and whimsies beyond imagining for sale, and now she looked forward to the distraction of one night of delight.

She needed the reprieve, because her worries just kept growing.

Although the Elders had mostly calmed talk of salt and iron, the threat of war with the Fae still hung in the air like a bad smell. Questions swirled—would the Fae emissary even arrive? Would wildkin interrupt the celebrations?

And Rook *still* hadn't responded to Lark's feather. If he couldn't get the moonclock case, Sage would be left trying to save their brother on her own. Lark couldn't let her do that—especially not when she knew how unsettled the Twilight Court had become.

But she had to admit she worried about Rook because she cared for his friendship. Since he had told her his sisters were in trouble, she was concerned for his safety too. She hoped his absence had simply been a precaution, a reaction to the luckwitches' wards, rather than a sign of something more sinister.

The truth was, she missed Rook and Nightbird more than she had expected. In the midst of all the danger and despair, Nightbird's drama and Rook's wry humor had brightened her spirits. Their games had made her smile and she longed for their company again.

"Excited?" Sage asked, glancing at Lark as they followed their parents out of the house.

"Yes, but nervous too." The Fae Accords strictly limited the sorts of magic that could be brought across the border, setting precise guidelines for the sale and trade of Fae trinkets. Small whimsies, like solidified raindrops strung on spidersilk or sunbeams caught in clear glass, were permitted in the Midnight Market. But greater magic, like true spells or strong enchantments, were expressly prohibited.

Only, if those treaties were broken . . . could they trust the magic on offer tonight? Even simple Fae trinkets could have unintended effects. . . .

"It's fun to look, but be careful before you buy anything," Sage said, as though reading Lark's mind. "Remember the whispering lily I found at my first Market?"

Lark snorted a laugh. "How could I forget? That thing was a menace."

"The Fae who sold it to me said it would share secrets—I just didn't realize it would whisper *mine*. Thank goodness Da knew how to get rid of it. When it told Ma I actually hated her pork-and-apple skillet and Da that I didn't like the purple skirt he made me, I thought I was going to die of shame."

Lark laughed again as they walked down the lantern-lined street through the center of Tradewind Junction, but the blush on her sister's cheeks sparked her curiosity. What secrets would the lily whisper now? "I'll be careful," she said. "I know Fae magic can be tricky. Like Galin's dog whistle."

Sage grinned. "He had every dog in Tradewind Junction following him wherever he went, and some from the villages too. Took the luckwitch three tries to break the charm." The smile slipped from her face and Lark wished she hadn't mentioned their brother.

She'd never realized how painful a funny memory could be when you missed someone.

"There it is!" Ma called from ahead of them, pointing to a small park and breaking the sad silence.

Heritage Park had originally been the town square, until Tradewind Junction's expansion made a larger area necessary. For most of the year the park was a quiet, forgotten space bordered by low stone walls and shaded by two spreading sycamore trees, grazed by a couple of wandering goats. But this evening the placid space had been transformed.

Impossible lanterns made of colored paper and candles floated above the Market while burning sweetsap torches chased shadows from the darkest corners. Strings of golden light like garlands of stars draped over the many booths, casting their wares in an otherworldly glow. Fluttering ribbons and clinking wind chimes hung from the bone-pale sycamores.

Across the park grounds, a narrow path snaked through tents, tables, and stalls. Fae traders and mortal merchants pushed wheeled barrows of trinkets past knots of people.

Lark stood on her tiptoes, staring at the marvels before her. Despite all the reasons to dread the Fae, there was beauty in their magic too.

Wooden stalls swathed in shimmering fabrics woven of sunlight and summer winds offered moonbeam ribbons and dewdrop pendants. Long tables displayed vases blown from waterfall glass and baskets braided from rare grasses the colors of sunset. Through gaps in mist-colored tents Lark glimpsed bowls of glowing gems and carved chests hiding treasures nestled in velvet. . . .

But instead of plunging into the magic of the Market, Ma and Da paused at the entrance. Ma tugged her braid. "Something feels different."

The air was permeated with the smell of magic, but it wasn't the clover-and-cherry scent Lark associated with Rook. It wasn't the dark, tangy musk of the wildkin either—but something spicy and green, like winter pine and cinnamon.

Da took Ma's elbow, beckoned Sage and Lark to step closer. A crowd surged around them, Fae with bright, cunning eyes and mortals wearing dazed, dreamy expressions. Someone with starbursts painted across her cheeks jostled Lark and she stumbled against her sister. A boy spun and kicked up his heels, splashing the girls with honey mead from a battered tin flagon.

"Perhaps we should skip the Market this evening and try again tomorrow," Da suggested.

"But tomorrow's the Welcome Feast and you and Ma will be busy with the Fae envoy," Lark protested. "And then there's the race and the Hunt and the Market will close!" What if Rook and Nightbird were among the Fae crowding the Market? What if she could find a useful bit of magic?

She was so close—she couldn't resist the curiosity

tugging her forward. "Please!" she begged, not wanting to miss her chance.

Ma hesitated. Lark knew she mistrusted magic, despite—or perhaps because of—her experiences as Horsemaven and her connections with the Fae. Ma might be proud of the Faevors she'd earned over the years, but she wasn't keen on what she called bartered baubles and traded tricks.

"The Elders and the luckwitches are monitoring things, see?" Lark persisted, pointing to Elder Farstorm, thumping her staff as she shuffled past a booth of night-blooming flowers in fragile china cups. Ma and Da exchanged a look. They couldn't argue with that, Lark knew.

"I suppose you're right. But—"

Ma was interrupted by the arrival of a mahogany-skinned woman in a flowing green headscarf and pale blue robes edged in yellow. "Horsemaven River Mairen!" the woman called, her smile flashing bright in the flickering glow of the Market. "I'm glad to catch you before the Gauntlet! Last spring I spoke with Lady Mist about arranging a breeding between one of your shadowbred mares and one of my wild sand stallions, but I haven't seen her yet to discuss the terms. I don't want to interrupt your evening with family, but perhaps later we could have a chat?"

Ma pressed her palms together and inclined her head. "You must be Motheress Alina am Banor. It is my pleasure to greet you. Please, walk with me and we can talk. Lukis, stay with the girls. Meet me at the entrance to the square by moonset if I don't join you earlier, all right?"

She turned to Sage and Lark and, in a soft voice, said, "Watch the road and stay close to your father."

And then she and Alina am Banor hooked elbows and skirted the edge of the Market, already deep in conversation about horses and foals and the marvels of the wide southern sands.

Da pinched his lip and said, "Well, girls, where would you like to begin? I think it best if we stick to the fringe . . . the deeper you get in the Market, the darker the magic."

Lark danced toward the entrance, tugging Sage along like a kite on a string, and together they stepped inside the Midnight Market, struggling to move against the swelling tide of people.

A stout man in a captain's canvas vest strode past them with a rolling gait, saying to his companion, "Told my brother not to trust that bloody Faevor of his and I was right, weren't I? Having a compass that always points to land is a rare, fine thing, sure as sunlight, but if it fails when you're halfway through the Sea of Secrets and leagues away from the closest coast it doesn't do a lick of good. At least the skies were clear that night and my steersman knows the stars."

"What are we at the Market for, then?" the other man said. He was thin and bowlegged, with the weathered skin and blue-ink tattoos of a sailor or dockhand. "Thought you said no magic aboard your ship ever again?"

"Aye, well . . ." The captain coughed and stroked a hand

over his long, salt-bleached beard. "I may not trust it, but our next voyage is across Bluestorm Bay and a wind-knot charm to keep the skies calm and the breezes fresh might mean the difference between our fortune and our foundering. Oh, pardon me," he said, easing past Lark with a smile and a nod. He and the sailor were soon swallowed by the shifting crowd.

"He has a point, Da," Lark said. "Look, there's a table of fabric and thread. Maybe you can find something to replace your Faevor."

Sage nodded thoughtfully. "And I'll look for something to help Reverie and me in the Hunt. Dame Wardspin's luck-charms are all well and good, but if I'm going to find Galin in the chaos of the Hunt I might need something stronger."

A swell of happiness and hope lifted Lark's heart. She was finally here in the Midnight Market, rich with Fae magic and potential all around her. But before she reached the first booth, a knot of giggling girls with glowing pink hair—no, not girls; they must be Fae—knocked Lark away from Sage and Da, blowing bubbles in her face.

Lark frowned and tried to disentangle herself, but she was caught in their midst as they sang nonsense rhymes and skipped circles around her. Between their dancing bodies and swirling skirts she glimpsed a display of pocket watches and mantel clocks, hourglasses and sundials. She strained to see who was at the stall. Could it be Elder Brassman and Goodman Simon? Would they go to the trouble of packing up their wares to sell here at the Market when they had a perfectly lovely shop in town?

Just then the Fae with candy-pink hair darted away and Lark found herself standing alone in front of the booth. But it wasn't minded by one of the Brassmans—or any other mortal, for that matter.

A Fae with long green hair like creeping bindweed stood behind the table of clocks and watches, black tongue flickering as she licked her lips and smiled. She wore a birch-bark vest over a linen tunic, and a string of hollow hickory nut shells dangled from her neck.

Lark glanced over her shoulder, looking for Sage and Da, but they'd been swept away by the crowd.

"Are you wanting something special, girl?" the Fae asked in a voice like scraping branches.

Lark turned back. "I—" she started, and then her eye caught a glint of silver. Amid the pocket watches scattered on the table, one case in particular drew her attention.

Almost without conscious thought, she drifted closer to get a better look.

"Ah . . . you like my pocket watches, eh?" the Fae said. "I have all sizes. Silver, gold, copper, brass, tin . . ."

They were each lovely, it was true. Every case was different, engraved with intricate designs or graceful scrollwork. Some held watch faces of polished shell or mother-of-pearl; others boasted jeweled hands or fancy chains. But there was something strange about them. Lark blinked. "None of them work!" she blurted. Each delicate face was frozen, motionless. A couple were even empty, feathers and beads filling the space that should have held wheels and springs.

None kept time.

The Fae's eyes flashed and she slammed her hands on the table, startling Lark back a step. "The beauty of time isn't its passing!" she snarled. "Only mortals wind and watch their clocks day after day. *We* don't feel the need to measure every moment as it slips away." Her sneer was cruel.

Lark gaped at her, and then realized that for an immortal Fae time meant something different, of course. They never felt its limits. Still . . . No, she must have imagined the note of envy in the Fae's voice.

"My apologies," she stammered. "I intended no offense. All of these are beautiful."

"What a kind girl you are," the Fae said, instantly mollified. "If you see something you like, I'll make you a good deal."

Lark hesitated. Sage had warned her to be careful before she bought anything. She should wait for Da and her sister. . . . But that silver case drew her attention again. . . .

Rook had said another Fae had the moonclock case. Was it possible that *this* might be exactly what she needed?

Her fingers hovered over the table, and the Fae, guessing which one she was interested in, plucked it up and thrust it into her hand. "A fine choice, a fine choice!" she crowed. "Ready to fill with your own time!"

It was heavier than it looked, with a hint of intricate engravings hidden beneath a layer of tarnish. There was an inscription inside the cover that Lark couldn't read. A tingle of magic shivered across her skin as she rubbed her thumb over it.

Could this be the missing moonclock case?

Or was that simply wishful thinking? What if this was just a Fae trick? Still . . . it appeared to be the right size, and the condition of the silver seemed to match the pieces she'd been cleaning and polishing. It almost hummed with magic, though she couldn't tell if that was just from the Market itself. . . .

Lark balanced it in her palm. The Wild Hunt was just days away and if this might save Galin she had to try, didn't she?

"What would you like to trade for it?" she asked, and then immediately regretted the question. Sage had also warned her not to give the Fae the lead when negotiating. "Make the first offer so you're in control of the bargaining," Sage had instructed.

Too late now.

The Fae grinned—a sharp, hungry smile. "Well now," she hummed. "That depends. What are your plans for it? Have something in mind, do you?"

Lark was a terrible liar, but she clicked the case open and closed as though evaluating its possibilities and said in an airy tone, "I like to collect things, and I think this would make a lovely container." Which was true . . . in a manner of speaking.

The Fae tapped her lips with a long white nail. "I know who you are, Lark Mairen. You're the bird who likes to fix things."

Lark sucked in a breath and her fingers twitched, nearly dropping the case. But she smoothed her expression and said, "Yes. So an empty watch case doesn't trouble me at all, the way it would most customers. I'll trade you three coppers and a silver star mark for it, just because I think it's pretty."

Those were all the coins she had, unless Da was willing to lend her more. She looked around again, hoping to spot him and Sage. Surely they couldn't have gotten too far away. . . .

The Fae's laugh was a creaky, splintery thing that made Lark's stomach shudder. "Coin? What need have I for coin?"

"Glass marbles, then? I have different colors," Lark suggested, trying to hide her desperation. The longer she held this case, the more certain she was that she needed it.

"Pah." The Fae flicked her fingers as though brushing away a fly. "Marbles. I'm not some silly sprite selling giggle water and sugar kisses." She slammed her hand on the table again, rattling the clocks and watches. "You can have it for five hairs." Her smile was slow and seeping, reminding Lark of a rotten log splitting open.

"Five . . . hairs?"

"Yes. Yours." And she held out her hand, those long white nails curling.

Lark chewed her lip. Luckwitches made charms of hair and feathers, blood and bone, shells and stone. That meant the Fae likely did too. What might they do with *her* hair?

She frowned at the case in her hand, tilting it in the glow of the lanterns around the booth. Squinting, she could just make out the symbol of the triple moon: waxing, full, and waning. She rubbed the marks, again feeling the buzz of magic.

The situation felt like a trap. But Galin had been missing for almost six moonturns, and if this might bring him home, she had to take the risk.

"Three," she said, proud that her voice stayed steady and clear.

"Done."

Lark plucked out three hairs and handed them over, clutching the case in her other hand. "Pleasure doing business with you," the Fae said, tucking the hairs into a small smoke-colored glass jar.

"Likewise," Lark responded, and then dashed away from the table before the Fae changed her mind. She concentrated on the triumph of finding the case, and tried not to think about the consequences of giving away three of her hairs. The moonclock was worth it. It had to be.

She dropped her purchase in her pocket and spun in a slow circle. Where *were* Sage and Da?

"Pretty ladyling," a rasping voice called. "Come see my treasures! Only a penny for your thoughts!"

The words sounded like tumbling stones and Lark turned her head. The Fae caught her gaze and grinned, showing a mouth of pointed rock-teeth splitting his craggy cheeks. His eyes were as black and glittering as polished obsidian from the islands to the east.

Lark stepped past his table but he held up a small jar of swirling green mist. "What thoughts would you like, pretty little ladyling? Thoughts of adventure?" He grabbed another jar, this one filled with rose-colored clouds. "Thoughts of love? Only a penny! Takes but a moment to pour them in your ear!"

She smiled to be polite but shook her head. She'd stick with her own thoughts, thank you very much.

Craning her neck and standing on tiptoes, she scanned the busy Market for sight of her family, but the strings of paper lanterns stretching from one side of the park to the other cast swaying shadows over everyone, and it was hard to pick faces from the crowd. "Sage? Da?" she called.

She turned back but suddenly couldn't recognize the way out of the Market maze. She'd gone only a few paces, but where was the booth of clocks? This one offered piles of glittering fruits she'd never seen before, and beside it was a table displaying tiny bottles of amber, cobalt, and emerald glass with cork stoppers and neatly printed labels.

A Fae with gray eyebrows that drooped all the way

down her cheeks and pointed ears sang out, "Maiden's tears! Forgotten wishes! Secret kisses!" She held a cobalt-blue bottle out to Lark, twisting it so the label was clearly visible. *Broken Dreams* read the spidery writing. The Fae leaned forward and whispered, "Delicious when sprinkled on apples."

Lark shuddered and spun in a circle, but the Market seemed to lurch and shift around her. Now she stood before a stall with silver pendants in strange shapes, and beside it was a booth of flutes carved from hollow bones.

The air was clouded with strange scents—spices and nose-tingling perfumes she'd never smelled before. Haggling voices filled the air and muddled Lark's mind until dizziness sloshed in her ears.

"Sage? Da?" she cried again, louder. A raven called overhead and she craned her neck. "Nightbird?" But she strained to see the bird against the dark sky and was soon jostled again and forced to return her focus to the path in front of her.

She tried to follow it through the Market but the way twisted and turned, looping back around until she couldn't guess which direction led to the entrance. Fear flickered in her chest, burning the back of her tongue. Ahead she glimpsed a figure with tousled hair and a green tunic. With a rush of hopeful relief she called, "Rook?" But before she could run to him he disappeared behind a cluster of boys throwing balls of blue flame back and forth.

Perhaps she hadn't recognized him after all. She'd never felt so alone.

Faces leered at her; laughter echoed in her ears. She patted the watch case in her pocket and tried to quash any sense of regret or reluctance. She *finally* had the last piece of the puzzle. She was going to save her brother, no matter the cost.

But first she had to get out of the Midnight Market—

Wait. What was the charm Rook had taught her, about brushing obstacles aside? It had seemed too simple to work, but now . . .

She heard Galin's voice in her memory, repeating, *One chance!*

Clenching her teeth, Lark pressed her hands together as hard as she could. The tendons in her wrists protested and the veins in the backs of her hands bulged. She poured all her frustration into the skin of her palms and squeezed. . . . And then, visualizing a clear way out of the Midnight Market, she blew her intention into her hands and slowly opened them.

The crowd split, raucous people and rowdy Fae somehow dancing away like tumbleweeds in a summer wind. At her feet a path opened, heading straight through a row of tables and out of the Market.

Lark ran as fast as she could, half-afraid the way would close again before she could leave the snares of the Market.

"Look, there she is! Lark!" a voice called. Lark spied Sage, waving frantically, Da right behind her.

She lengthened her stride, racing past a table of seafoam

lace and one stacked with old books bound in brass and leather. When she finally tumbled out of the Market, she flung herself into Da's arms just as Ma ran around the corner.

"I've looked everywhere and—Oh! Lark! We were so worried!" Ma cried, wrapping Lark into another hug.

"Where did you go?" Da asked, relief softening the edge of anger beneath his words. "I told you to stay close! One second you were right there, and then you were gone and we couldn't find you anywhere. You knew you weren't supposed to wander off!"

"I didn't intend to! Truly! But those girls with pink hair surrounded me and when they finally skipped away you and Sage were missing."

Ma rested a hand on her shoulder, rubbing a small circle on her back. "The Midnight Market often has mysterious ways, though tonight it certainly felt more capricious than usual. At least we've found each other again. Come, let's head home. I'd rather not waste the last of the moonlight."

Lark's eyes flew to the sky in surprise. Sure enough, the moon hovered low above the horizon. "But I couldn't have been in the Market for more than an hour!" How could she have lost most of a night?

"Time does odd things around Fae magic," Ma said, urging them out of the park and down the road. "And this season is stranger than usual."

— FOURTEEN —

The Moonclock

THE NEXT MORNING, after she'd snatched a few hours of restless sleep and helped Ma and Sage tend the agitated shadowbreds, Lark returned to her room and added more raven feathers to the bedraggled one still pinned beneath the window sash. Though she thought she'd recognized Rook and Nightbird at the Midnight Market, either she'd been mistaken or they hadn't been able to talk to her.

Worry sat like a snapping turtle in her chest, heavy and pinching. Where were they now? Even if Rook couldn't make it through the luckwitches' warding to visit Lark's house, Nightbird should have been able to. After all, ravens couldn't be contained with borders and charms.

She stood at her window chewing her lip, then forced herself to focus on the task at hand. At least she finally had a case for the moonclock. She had a chance to help Galin so Sage wouldn't have to race into danger. Bright hope battled the worry-turtle inside her as she took a wool polishing cloth to the silver pocket watch case.

She hoped it was worth three hairs. What if she had made a mistake and it was nothing more than a tarnished, empty bit of cheap silver-plated tin?

But as she wiped away the grime of dirt and age, a complex design of vines and trees slowly emerged. She saw the triple moon again, and a swirl of stars across the upper curve of the case. When she pressed a minuscule catch shaped like an ivy leaf, the case snapped open to reveal a hollow for the clockwork gears and that odd inscription in symbols she couldn't decipher.

She pulled out the wooden box her brother had made and ran her hands over the crooked joints and tiny scratches. "I'm going to get you back, Galin," she whispered. "One chance, brother."

Taking out all the watch pieces, Lark arranged them in a neat row around the case, beginning with the strange clock face marked with the thirteen full moons she had first found. She recited the name of each part aloud as she identified and sorted them, like a chant for luck. Crown wheel, center wheel, balance pivot, balance wheel. Click spring, main wheel.

It was time to test her skills.

Using a pair of tiny tweezers and a magnifying glass, Lark began layering the wheels and pivot points, springs and screws.

This moonclock was far more complicated than

anything she'd attempted to repair before, and despite her lessons with Goward Brassman she still wasn't sure she knew enough to get it right. Her previous attempts hadn't exactly built her confidence.

Squinting in concentration, she blew hair out of her face and set another wheel in place. She'd gotten this far before, but without the case she couldn't keep everything aligned just so and always had to quit. Now, however, she could assemble the layered mechanism and see how it worked. . . . Her hands trembled with excitement and she took a deep, steadying breath.

But as she reached for the next piece she dropped a screw, muttering a curse. It took her too long to locate it, and by the time she connected the next wheel and pivot she had a headache. For days she had told herself that all she needed was the case, but she'd forgotten just how complicated the clockwork mechanisms seemed to be. . . .

Then she pricked her finger on the sharp edge of a wheel, a single drop of blood welling up before dripping into the watch case.

"Rust and ruin!" she snapped, scrabbling for a cloth to wipe it away. But when she turned back to the clock, the bead of blood had vanished. She wiped the tip of her finger instead and frowned.

That was the second time this clock had swallowed a drop of her blood.

Focus on what matters.

Chewing the inside of her cheek in concentration, she added a tiny spring. At least this time the pieces didn't buzz and burn her fingers the way they did when she'd tried to assemble them in one of Elder Brassman's spare cases. This *had* to be the right one.

She muttered to herself as she worked: "Escapement wheel, then balance wheel, then crown wheel . . . no! Wait. Center wheel *then* crown wheel, and here's the winding wheel. . . . Three case screws, the bridge . . . the faceplate and hands . . ."

Lark fastened the faceplate and the silver band that protected its edge, then snapped the case closed with a gentle click. She pressed the tiny ivy leaf and the case popped open again.

She had done it. She had put the broken moonclock back together!

For a moment she simply held it in her hand, admiring its delicate details and intricate design. *I really fixed it!*

"Now let's see how you run. . . ." But when she tried to turn the winding knob, nothing happened. It was frozen.

Her heart plunged.

What could she have missed? She was convinced this was the correct case, and Rook swore she had all the other necessary pieces. As far as she could tell they only fit together one way. Sighing, she raised her magnifying glass and tiny screwdriver again. She had to keep trying.

The engraved inscription caught her eye again. The

swirling symbols must be Fae and that meant Rook could translate when she saw him again.

Only she didn't know when that would be and she couldn't afford to wait.

Lark tapped her chin and considered her next step.

Elder Brassman could explain why a pocket watch might not wind. Despite the commotion and chaos of Mayfair, he'd likely still be in his shop.

Grabbing paper, a jar of black ink, and her favorite fine-nib pen, she hastily sketched the clockwork mechanisms, including detailed studies of each individual component as well as the strange inscription inside the case. She traced each symbol as precisely as possible, admiring the flourished lines and swirls even though she couldn't guess what they meant. She had promised to keep the moonclock a secret, but she needed help. Sharing a couple drawings surely couldn't hurt anything.

But once she'd finished the diagrams, Lark impulsively dropped the moonclock in her pocket as she hurried out of the house.

Tradewind Junction was bustling. The Fae emissary, Lady Mist, and her envoy would be officially welcomed at a community feast that evening and despite concerns she might not arrive, villagers had made extensive preparations. Because it was spring, the May Queen's colors—rose pink and robin's-egg blue—hung all over town. Pink ribbons and light blue banners spanned doorways and rooftops while bouquets of early spring flowers—jonquils and lilies, hyacinths and tulips, dewdrops and pansies—filled barrels at every corner.

Women with kerchiefs tucked over their hair and aprons tied around their waists swept winter bracken and dead leaves out of the road. Men in leather vests and stout boots climbed ladders to repair thatch and clean windows.

The sound of hammering filtered through the festive din as others decorated the pavilion that would welcome Lady Mist and her attendants.

Lark tried to hurry through the market district but found herself snagged in knots of people speaking different dialects. She slowed down and concentrated on weaving through without banging too many elbows or knocking too many hips.

Tradewind Junction sat at the crossroads of two major trade routes: the Salt Road, running east and west, which linked all the Free Cities and helped distribute everything from salt and spices to fruit, grain, vegetables, and livestock; and the Silver Road, running north and south, along which silver, copper, glass, gemstones, and certain perfume oils were transported.

Rumors claimed illegal iron ore was also occasionally smuggled along the Silver Road—the only reason the Junction employed two guards at a checkpoint leading into town. This close to the Fae realm, breaking laws against the sale, transport, and use of iron was dangerous, especially with everyone already on edge after the earlier incident near the border.

Everything seemed to hang in a precarious balance and Lark hoped she had time to figure out the moonclock before the worst happened.

The wind shifted, bringing the damp green smells of fish and river water to her nose. A few leagues from Tradewind Junction was the Snakesong River, with its long, lazy, looping curves. The great port of Mer Harbor was a two-day easy float downriver, but another wide road—called Fish Run by locals—allowed the quick transport of shellfish, seafood, and other trade goods from port to market.

Galin loved to spend summer evenings standing on the banks with his old fishing pole and a pail of bait.

Lark sighed and sped up. She was used to crowds and the daily haggle of merchants, traders, and customers. But today's busy commotion was even worse than usual. With the opening of Mayfair and the Midnight Market, as well as the impending arrival and welcome of the Fae emissary, a crowd of curious visitors had flooded the Junction. She could pick them out by the slightly dazed expressions on their faces, the aimlessness of their wandering—and the fact that they seemed to be in everyone else's way.

Ducking past a woman in a gown so wide she could hardly squeeze her skirts between the rows of wooden produce carts and merchant tents, Lark finally reached Brassman's Clockworks.

As she stepped beneath the Faevored silver medallion above the lintel—advertising the fact that Elder Goward had earned a Faevor in a Wild Hunt—an iridescent green beetle scuttled into a crack behind the embossed ivy-and-oak-leaf border around the insignia of the Twilight Court. She caught a whiff of the green, musky scent of wildkin, but when she looked again the beetle was gone. Good riddance.

She shuddered and tugged open the door.

"Lark! How are you this afternoon?" Elder Goward perched behind the counter as Simon polished a beveled glass.

"I'm doing well, thank you. But I have a couple questions for you, if you have time?"

He chuckled and waved a hand at the walls of clocks. "I have nothing but time, my dear. What do you want to know?"

"Well, first of all . . ." She hesitated, and then took out the drawings she had made of the moonclock and its components. She spread them on the counter and asked, "Have you ever seen anything like these before? Would a clock like this actually work?"

He pressed the top page flat and leaned forward, tracing the lines she had drawn. "Ahhhhh," he breathed, opening a drawer behind the counter to take out a magnifying glass and adjusting the papers so they lay in a bright patch of light from the windows. "What an elegant concept. Is this a design of your grandda's?"

Lark shrugged. She honestly knew nothing about the moonclock's origins.

"A clock or watch like this would be quite complicated, wouldn't it? See, there are essentially two separate gear trains. One to drive this mechanism here—probably for a large increment of time—and then another to drive this one here. I don't know what it might indicate. Could be anything. A cycle of seasons or . . ."

His chin snapped up and his eyes widened. "Seasons! But of course! I've seen this before."

"You have?"

He bustled around the shop, opening drawers and flicking through record books, his joints creaking and popping as he bent to peer in the back of dusty cabinets. After rummaging for several moments he finally withdrew an old leather folio tied with string. When he opened it, she saw a stack of flimsy vellum sheets and fine linen papers, covered with neatly inked diagrams. He gently shuffled through them.

One of the pages immediately caught her attention. It was stained with age, the ink faded brown, but there could be no mistaking that watch face with its thirteen symbols and graceful designs depicting the four elements and four seasons.

What she couldn't understand was why *he* had a drawing of Rook's moonclock.

"Wait! Where did that come from?" she asked.

Goward Brassman set the fragile paper on top of the others and gently smoothed the corners. "This particular drawing has been in my family for more than two hundred years, believe it or not. Maybe longer," he said. "My great-great-grandda used to say that if a Brassman wasn't making clocks, the moon would forget to rise."

Lark gaped at him. *Moon.* "What did you say?"

He chuckled. "I always wondered if Maxim and I could create something like this, but we never seemed to have time. And then he passed on, and . . . well, I figure I'm too old to attempt something so sophisticated and complex by myself, and I doubt Simon would help. He wouldn't believe it could even run."

"Why not?"

"Well, to my best judgment, this clock was designed to mark every full moon and each season. But this inner ring here, with these elemental symbols? What would it measure? And these mechanisms look as if they require *two* winding methods. One is a simple wind stem that just needs twisting, but this . . . well, I suspect it would take a key. And where's the keyhole hidden?"

Lark's knees sagged and she leaned against the counter, her pulse jumping like crickets. *Two* winding mechanisms.

And a *hidden* keyhole. She still needed a key!

But the wind stem hadn't turned either. "Have you ever assembled a pocket watch and not been able to wind it? I mean, if all the pieces fit together perfectly, what would make the winding mechanism freeze?"

He removed his spectacles to wipe them on the hem of his shirt and settled them back on his nose, lips pursed thoughtfully. "Well now, I'd have to see the watch in question to say for sure. . . ."

Lark stuck a hand in her pocket, feeling the cool heft of the moonclock. It would be so easy to give it to him, to let him figure out why it wasn't running and what needed to be done next.

But she'd sworn an oath to Rook, so she told Elder Brassman, "The watch in question isn't mine. I just wondered what ideas you might have?"

"Well, assuming the mainspring isn't overly stretched—which is generally the most common cause of winding issues, in my experience—I'd suggest examining all the balance pivots and making sure everything is in perfect alignment. Look for dust, tarnish or corrosion, broken jewels."

Lark nodded. "I had a feeling that's what you would say." She would check the alignment again, though without the lost key it might not even matter.

"If you'd like me to take a closer look, feel free to run it by whenever you can." But she could tell he was distracted, glancing from her sketches to his old papers. He scratched

186

his chin. "I wonder why Maxim had copies of these diagrams, although he *was* always fascinated by the most whimsical conceptions. . . . Sometimes I had to remind him of the physical practicalities. But oh, how he loved a creative challenge! If his Faevor had been the ability to put any gear into motion instead of tweezers that never put a piece wrong, there would have been no limit to his imagination."

"You said that drawing had been in your family for centuries?"

He chuckled and waved a hand. "That's how the story goes anyway. Family lore says a distant ancestor fell in love with a Fae and disappeared, taking the secret of this clock with him. His brother took over the business and we Brassmans have been making watches and clocks ever since."

"He fell in love with a Fae? But what was this clock for?"

"It's only a fanciful drawing, Lark. Who knows what was in his imagination when he designed it?"

Lark pointed to the lines scrawled in one corner of the paper, matching the inscription she'd copied from inside the moonclock case. "What about those symbols?"

Goward squinted. "Can't say I've ever seen anything quite like them."

"What do you think they mean?"

"I couldn't begin to guess, assuming they *have* a meaning. They look decorative to me. Teacher Wil Bardic might know, though, if anyone would."

"Thank you for the information, Elder Brassman." She

glanced to the clocks hanging on the walls around the shop. They all seemed synchronized once more and her shoulders relaxed. "Your Faevor has been restored?"

"Hm?" He followed the direction of her gaze and his brow crinkled. "Oh. No, I'm afraid not. But we Brassmans can keep time without Fae tricks. I just set the clocks myself—they may be off by a minute or so, but at least they're all the same."

"I'm so sor—" The door burst open and a man in a dove-colored suit and a pale green cravat strode in. A visitor from one of the northern dukedoms, Lark assumed.

"Good afternoon. Show me your best grandfather clock," he ordered.

Elder Brassman winked at Lark while she gathered her satchel. She gave him a quick wave and ducked out as he said, "Certainly, my good man. If you'll take a look at this fine piece . . ."

When Teacher Wil Bardic wasn't visiting his students, he could often be found helping in the small library at the corner of the market district. The head librarian, Megrim Inkler, had also ridden in a Wild Hunt as a young man so the silver medallion of a Faevored business hung above his door too. His Faevor, he'd once told Lark, was an ink bottle that never ran out and never spilled, but what use it was to him she couldn't tell. He had atrocious handwriting.

A strand of copper bells jangled as she stepped through the door.

"Hello?" Teacher Bardic called, his tone more demanding than friendly.

"Good afternoon!" Lark answered. "Are you busy?"

"Oh, Lark! I'm sorry—I've been on edge all day. Master Inkler is away from the library so I'm keeping an eye on things for him. What can I help you with? Your lessons?"

Lark swallowed a tiny prick of guilt—she hadn't even opened her books in several days—and shook her head. "No, Teacher. But I came across something curious and I wanted to ask about it."

His eyebrows quirked a question. "Oh?"

She opened her satchel and rummaged among the sketches until she found her copy of the strange inscription inside the mooncity's case. Laying it on the front counter, she flattened the creases so he could clearly see the symbols. "Do you know what these mean?"

"Well now," he breathed, rubbing his chin. "Where did you find this?"

"A book." The lie tasted like sour gooseberries, but she had to conceal the clock's existence.

He prodded the page with a callused, ink-stained finger as if he could shift the curved lines and swirled flourishes around simply by intention. After a moment he said in a quiet, serious voice, "These are First Words. Forbidden to any but the most powerful Fae in the Twilight Court. To speak them to a mortal means the harshest punishment—a death sentence, or so the old records indicate. How did you discover these?"

"First Words . . . what do you mean?"

"This is their sacred language. I don't know where you found this or what text it came from, but this paper should be burned immediately before anyone else knows you've seen it." His voice was stern and frost-coated, and Lark shrank back. "Rust and iron, Lark. This is *dangerous*." He crumpled the paper in his fist.

Lark grabbed his hand and snatched the inscription back. "Wait! If it's so secret, how do *you* recognize it?"

"I've studied the Accords," he admitted, tapping his fingers on the counter. "The original treaty, I mean. It is written in the common trader's tongue on one side . . . and in the language of the Fae on the other."

"But anyone can read the Accords, right?" She tried not to sound too eager, but he cast a sharp glance at her.

"Yes, Lark, anyone can view the original document. But if you reveal a fascination with *that*"—he pointed to the paper in her hand—"you'll find yourself in the worst sort of trouble. Let it be."

She chewed her lip and asked, "May I see the Accords?"

"Lark—"

"The law says they must be kept on display." She tried to look as innocent as possible.

He sighed and shook his head. "Only for a moment, then." He stepped behind the counter to unlock an ornately carved wooden cabinet with glass doors, withdrawing a scroll from the collection of tomes on the shelves inside before locking it again.

"The Accords," he announced, carefully unrolling the parchment.

Lark's eyebrows tried to climb into her hair as she stared at the original treaty, signed with a dozen names that shimmered faintly in the light. This document defined everything she knew about life in the Borderlands and her community.

The bells jingled over the door and he turned away, rolling the parchment back up. "I'm sorry, Lark. We'll have to continue this conversation another time."

"Wait, Teacher . . . could I take a closer look at that?"

"At the Accords?" He lifted the scroll and a crease puckered his brow. "Lark, I told you to leave the First Words alone."

"I just want to see what the treaty says about the Wild Hunt. Please? I'll be careful."

"Is anyone here?" a woman's voice called. "I'm looking for a book—"

"Be with you in a moment!" Wil Bardic answered. He glanced from the scroll to Lark and chewed his lip. Finally, with a sigh, he nodded and handed it to her. "Only while I take care of this patron," he said. "Longer than that would be against regulations, I'm afraid, without an Elder here to supervise."

"That's all I need. Thank you."

As soon as he stepped away, Lark gently smoothed the treaty and grabbed a scrap of paper and a pencil. Working as quickly as possible, she used the Accords to build a translation key that could unlock the code. By comparing what was written in the Fae language with the common trader's tongue on the other side, she could figure out what each symbol meant. It wasn't perfect—some words couldn't be transcribed exactly, and she was working with a fairly small sample—but within a few minutes she had a usable alphabet.

"Bees? Try this book on apiary management," Teacher Bardic was saying, walking to a set of shelves across the room. "It includes a section on harvesting honey contributed by our own Hivemistress Miram Honeywell and I think you'll find it interesting."

The woman murmured gratitude and a few moments later they walked to the other end of the counter. Lark heard the click of his library stamp marking the date beside her name in the borrow ledger.

Lark's pencil scratched across the paper as she scribbled another row of symbols with two possible translations, and then she decoded the moonclock's inscription: *Time is what the immortal lacks.*

But if the Fae were immortal, didn't that mean they had endless time?

The bells over the door jingled as the patron left. Lark hurriedly shoved her paper in her satchel. By the time Teacher Bardic had stepped around her side of the counter again, she was twisting the end of her hair and pretending to read.

"Sorry, Lark, but I need to return that to the bookcase. If you want a replica I can bring you one when we go over lessons."

Since a copy wouldn't include the First Words, Lark smiled and shook her head. "Thank you, but I've read enough." She carefully handed him the scroll and rose to her feet. "I'm glad I got to see the original document, though. It looks like my mother's family signed it."

"Yes. The Mairens were early settlers."

The bell over the door jingled yet again and he scrubbed a hand over his face. Lark tossed a quick smile at the patron—a woman she'd seen in Da's shop once or twice—and said, "Well, I'm sorry I took up so much of your time, Teacher Bardic. Thank you for the information."

"It was my pleasure. Remember your lessons, and tell your sister I wish her the luck of the winds, eh?"

FIFTEEN

The White Stag

LARK HEADED TOWARD Threadneedle's Fabrics, her thoughts clicking and spinning like clockwork cogs.

Comments Rook had made, offhand remarks, now took on new significance. He'd said that he would have given the moonclock to someone else if he could, but he'd never acted as if he wanted it for himself. And after the moonclock absorbed the first drop of her blood, he'd said it was bound to her.

Bound to *her*, with her *mortal* blood.

Elder Brassman had a diagram of the moonclock—and a family legend about a long-forgotten ancestor who designed it before falling in love with a Fae and disappearing.

Rook had hinted that the Harvest King had once been mortal. Had Goward Brassman's ancestor been the Harvest King? It sounded impossible, even in the stardust spaces of her own mind, but there were too many pieces pointing in the same direction. . . .

What if the moonclock could only be *used* by a mortal?

Is that what the inscription meant? *Time is what the immortal lacks.*

Lark was still pondering the mystery of the moonclock when a raven suddenly swooped from the roof of the storefront ahead of her and skimmed to the chimney of the tavern on the corner, cocking its head to meet her eyes.

Nightbird?

She dodged a man in a tall black hat and wove around two women with baskets on their arms to get closer to the raven. "Nightbird?"

He took to wing again, drifting to a lantern post several paces away. Lark followed, wondering if she was chasing an ordinary bird—until he turned to look at her again, clicking his beak. When he knew he had her full attention, he slowly and deliberately ducked his head beneath his wing and hunched as low as he could.

She recognized the gesture from his days in her room. It meant a secret needed keeping.

Lark eased closer, curiosity dragging her forward. And then, in a shadowed courtyard between the meetinghouse and an old inn, she glimpsed Rook's tousled hair and doeskin breeches.

Giddy relief turned to apprehension. If someone saw him, or spotted *her* talking to him, there could be terrible trouble. But they had to discuss the moonclock—the Hunt was just days away.

Heart leaping in her throat like a pond frog, she ran toward him—and froze when she saw his grim expression.

He beckoned her before darting farther into the court-yard.

Nightbird kept watch from the lantern post as Lark flung herself into the mossy shadows of the old inn. They wouldn't have much time to talk so she blurted, "I found the case, no thanks to you. And I assembled the moonclock, but—"

"You *found* the case?" His eyes glittered. "Where?"

"At a booth of clocks and watches in the Midnight Market. It just caught my eye. I couldn't tell for certain it was the right one, but something told me to get it, so . . . I did."

Lark expected Rook to be relieved she'd found it, or surprised or glad or *something*. Instead, his face went stone white and his eyes darkened. "They were supposed to nego-tiate with *me*. What did you pay?"

"Um . . . three hairs."

"Fluff and feathers, Lark! You gave a Fae *your hair*?" His anger practically sparked in the air. "Did no one teach you what they do with it? If they eat your hair they can see through your eyes, sometimes even hear the whisper of your thoughts!"

She stumbled away from him in horror, knocking her elbow against the stone wall. Was a Fae looking through her eyes at this very moment? How would she know?

She stiffened her spine. Galin was worth the price.

"What else was I supposed to do? She wouldn't take coins or marbles or anything else I had, and *you* said I needed to fix the moonclock. You were nowhere to be found. I couldn't very well mend it without the case, could I?"

"No . . . you're right. I'm sorry. It's not your fault. I should have been there." He slammed a fist against his thigh and spun around, pacing the small shadowed alley like a prowling cat. "But you got the moonclock repaired? It will work?"

"It's assembled, anyway." Lark pulled the moonclock from her pocket and tried to hand it to him. "Here. I can't wind it, but at least it's in one piece. Is that good enough? Now bring Galin back. If you can cross the border, then he can too."

Rook skipped back so fast she barely saw his feet move. "No!" He waved the moonclock away. "You must hold on to it. I told you, it's bound to your blood."

"This thing has caused me nothing but trouble. I've been spied on by wildkin, bitten by a bloodmoth, and nearly trapped in a toadstool ring. I've spent *months* learning how to assemble pocket watches and putting this together. I bought the case with *my hair*. My hair! You promised the moonclock would save my brother, so *here*. Take it and go save him!"

"I *can't*. Don't you understand how much I wish I could? It must be you."

"But I don't know how it works or what it's supposed to do, Rook. You haven't told me anything!" She scowled at the clock in her hand. "Besides, it requires a key."

"A key!" He smacked his forehead and groaned. "The king never said it needed a key."

"Well, it does. Any idea where it might be?"

"No." Rook grimaced.

Lark sighed and tried to ignore the sloshing tide of unease in her stomach. The key would be *tiny* and it could be anywhere. How would they ever find it? Had the Fae sold her the case knowing it was useless without a key? Was this just another trap: waiting for her to put it together before they made another attempt to capture her?

It was the cruelest kind of hope, taunting her by staying just out of reach, and the worst kind of lingering threat.

Rook puffed his cheeks like a blowfish and kicked a pebble out of the alley. Nightbird dove for it, muttering and snapping his beak. "I'm not even sure the king was carrying it when he fell."

"Who else knows about the moonclock?"

"More than I'd like, but don't fret. I'll find the key someway. I'll send the birds out searching again."

Lark dropped the clock back in her pocket. "It has to be used by a mortal, doesn't it?"

His eyes flickered, but his face remained still. "I can't answer that."

"Nightbird, bob your head once if the answer is yes."

Nightbird peered at Rook before glancing to Lark and bobbing his head with a satisfied little croak.

"But if the moonclock must be used by a mortal, what happened after the Harvest King stayed in the Fae realm and started to lose his mortality? Did it lose power? Is that . . . wait. Is *that* what the inscription means? You lose time without a mortal to work the clock? But if you're immortal, why do you need time? I don't understand—"

Rook gripped her by the wrist and gave a squeeze, glancing over his shoulder. "Hush! That's enough. We need to find the key. Remember the charms I've taught you, do you hear me? They know you have the clock and now they have your hair. . . . I tried to put them off your trail, but my influence has dwindled."

"But who are *they*?"

"Foes of the Twilight Court. Bullies, breakers . . . *briars*." His teeth ground together until they squeaked and his voice cracked as if thorns had scraped his throat. Nightbird snapped his beak, spreading his wings in alarm.

A clatter suddenly echoed from the other end of the courtyard and the door to the meetinghouse groaned open, spilling voices.

Rook whispered, "You'd better tell your sister not to ride. It isn't safe." With a breath of cherry-scented air, he cast a glamour over himself and disappeared in a swirl of clover and feathers.

Nightbird launched himself into the air, circled three times in the sky overhead, and then sped northward, vanishing in a wisp of cloud.

As she crossed the town square and wove through the crowds, Rook's warning hissed in her ears. Lark wasn't surprised, but hearing the threat confirmed felt like floundering in cold water—like the time she'd slipped on a patch of slickweed at the river's edge and nearly drowned. Galin had dragged her out and thumped the river water from her lungs.

Now it was up to her to save both her siblings. But without the key, what could she do?

She passed a cluster of tables outside the bakery and caught snatches of conversation that sent fresh chills through her blood. "The luckwitch up by Piney Trace said the waymarker out that way was broken. Cleaved in two, if you can believe it," someone said. "She stabilized the timeslip and rewove the wards, but wildkin are practically roaming free."

"Where's the White Stag, then?" a man with a pipe dangling from his lip muttered.

"The Hunt will set it back to rights," someone else said dismissively.

Farther on a woman in a yellow kerchief muttered, "There are rumors coming out of Yewberry Hollow of people aging suddenly or temporarily regaining their youth. And I doubt it's the only border village with a time problem."

Her companion commented, "Tomorrow is the Gauntlet

and then the Wild Hunt. The boundary is always a bit thin this time of year, but once the Hunt rides it will—"

Lark passed them as they paused near the tavern, but ahead of her a group of women in long, swishing skirts and high lace-up boots carried on a similar discussion. "I say we forget races and Hunts and focus instead on salt and iron, no matter what the Elders say," one said, kicking the hem of her flame-red skirt.

Lark brushed past with a polite murmur of apology and slipped inside Da's shop, her ears still ringing.

"Good afternoon, little bird," he said with a crooked smile. "I thought you were staying home to help bathe the shadowbreds?"

"Sarai and her sons came over to help. They've got more patience than me. And anyway, I had to ask Teacher Bardic a question."

"Well, I'm glad for your company. I'm nearly done here and we can walk home together to get dressed up for the feast, eh?" He chuckled, but there was worry beneath the forced cheer.

As he hemmed a pale blue gown of watery silk, Lark said, "People keep talking about the Last Protection clause."

He mumbled a curse. "Is that still the gossip around the square, then?"

She nodded. "Some of it."

He sighed and smoothed a hand across the fabric. "Before the Elders could invoke that clause, they would need proof the Fae have used magic as a weapon against us. Simple mischief—no matter how malicious—doesn't qualify without clear intention. Let's hope it doesn't get that far. Perhaps once the emissary arrives and the Hunt rides, things will settle down."

He gestured at his worktable and Lark handed him his scissors. "Da, I . . . I stumbled across a phrase or a quote I don't quite understand. *Time is what the immortal lacks.* But that doesn't make sense, does it? I mean, they're immortal. They have nothing *but* time, right?"

"Your mother could explain more clearly than I can since she knows the Fae better, but that's actually a misunderstanding. Time causes birth, growth, death. The Fae are virtually immortal because there is no natural time in their realm. But without time, there can be no change either."

"What do you mean?"

"Time *creates* change. It drives the forces of nature, right? Erosion and decay, tides and currents, life and death and life again. The Fae possess the magic of illusions and shadows, starlight and secrets—but, lacking time, they can't actually craft anything new and permanent. They can't change anything, grow anything, *make* anything. For all their magic, without time the Fae are like . . . marble figures in a garden or statues in a museum."

Lark bit her lip. "So what's causing the strange time bubbles or swirls along the border? Some women in town were talking . . ."

"Timeslip? Well, think about pulling the plug from a water basin or puncturing a hole in a bucket. What does the water do? Sometimes it splashes up a bit before pouring out, sometimes it swirls, sometimes it pours out in a rush. Sometimes it just drips or trickles. The mortal world is like a bucket full of time, and the Fae world is empty. If something rips a hole in the border, the flow of our time is disrupted as it rushes into the vacuum."

Lark chewed her thumbnail as she considered this. "So if the Fae need time and we need magic, why not just eliminate the border entirely?"

Da snipped a loose thread and set an iron to heat. "Before the Wild Hunt was established, one of the Fae tried to do just that. He argued that the boundary between the realms only created reason for conflict, and that both Fae and mortals would benefit if their lands melded. Without the border, he believed mortals would gain longer lives and Fae would share the power of change. But he miscalculated the consequences. Instead, Fae living in the mortal world lost their magic. And any mortals living near the edge of the realm, where the lands touched, discovered that time actually sped up—cutting their lives short rather than extending them as expected."

"But I thought mortals living in the Fae realm became immortal too?"

"Oh, they do! Or they *can*, assuming the Fae allow them to live. But only with the border in place, protecting the balance of time and magic."

Lark paced a circle around his worktable. "And that's why the Hunt started? To keep time on one side and magic on the other?"

"Partly, at least. It was also meant to enforce the Accords and send any rogue Fae and wildkin back where they belong. It preserves order, while binding the mortal realm and the Other Side together."

He draped the gown over the edge of the table and began steaming out the creases, humming as he smoothed the fabric.

But Lark's mind kept spinning. She knew from her history lessons that before the Accords were signed, both mortals and Fae had nearly destroyed one another. If the border was broken and war came again, the destruction would be unimaginable.

Perhaps someone in the Fae realm wanted war, though. To take the Twilight Court—or to try to expand Fae territory too?

But how could the moonclock stop it? And how was Galin involved?

"There. Finished!" Da announced, slipping the gown over a dress form. "Lady Southwinds will come to collect it first thing tomorrow morning."

"It's lovely, Da."

He smiled as he tidied up the work space. "Are you ready?"

When they left the tailor shop the sun was slowly melting toward the horizon and the air was cooling quickly. Outside Tradewind Junction town limits they stepped into the shadows of the woods and a whispering breeze raised goose bumps along Lark's arms. Early fireflies blinked above dew-damp grass.

Lark tipped her head back to spot the first star. When she heard a rustle in the ferns and bracken along the side of the road, she snapped her chin down. She stopped, staring into the bruise-dark shadows between the trees as Da kept walking.

A twig cracked and dried leaves crunched beneath the weight of something moving through the woods.

"Da?" she murmured.

He paused to glance back at her. "What is it, little bird?"

"Da . . . ," she breathed.

A gleaming white stag appeared beneath the sweeping limbs of an ancient oak tree. Thorny brambles clung to his majestic antlers and a strand of ivy wreathed his neck. Pale shimmers danced across his coat like moonbeams on water.

The White Stag.

He was the guardian spirit of the Borderlands, the Lord of the Wildkin, and the leader of the Wild Hunt. He preserved the balance of time and magic by drawing the Hunters—both Fae and mortal—along the boundary, tracing a line linking the waymarkers and following a path between the worlds that only he could sense.

Lark had seen him from a distance, his shining starlit form like a silver blur as the Wild Hunt pursued him. But she had never dreamed she might stand this close, near enough to notice the fringe of his eyelashes and the texture of his coat.

He blinked once, twice.

Did he always look so thin in spring? Now Lark observed the curve of his ribs, the angular jut of bones against skin. He was majestic and magical, yes, but there was something sad in his gaze.

Had his efforts to keep the broken border in place weakened him? Was that why he seemed so worn?

Or . . . the memory of thorns erupting from the earth to destroy the Harvest King's horse filled Lark's mind. Those brambles on the Stag's antlers hadn't been there before, she was nearly certain. She squinted in the blue glow of dusk at scratches on his bowed neck, noted the hollows around his eyes. Were the tangled thorns draining his energy?

"Da, we need to help him," she murmured. "We need to get those brambles off."

But as she said it, a sudden scuffle shook the ferns beneath the trees beside the Stag, ruffling the new fronds. A branch cracked.

The White Stag's nostrils flared and he turned his head, slowly, as if the brambles wrapped in his antlers were a weight too heavy to bear.

His eyes widened in alarm.

Two figures lunged from the shadows in the woods, larger than mortals, with tree-bark skin and twiggy fingers. One wore an acorn-shaped cap and the other had a long mossy beard. Mossbeard began swaying and stomping his feet in an odd rhythm, humming low in his throat. The other Fae jumped in with a peculiar counterpoint, slapping his hands on his thighs and chanting nonsense words.

A shiver built along Lark's skin, like the prickle in the air before a summer thunderstorm or the crackle of cold, winter-dry ice. It stirred the hair on the back of her neck, and the copper ring on her little finger started to burn.

This was deep Fae magic.

"Da, what is happening?" she whispered.

The White Stag tensed to run, muscles shifting beneath his moon-glow coat—

And then an arrow sped from behind a tree trunk, from an unseen bow, to pierce his shoulder. Lark screamed as a crimson stain bloomed across his white coat, and she kept screaming as his legs buckled and he collapsed.

Her father pulled on her, shouting something, but she couldn't hear past the roaring in her head.

"Lark!" Da shook her shoulders, finally catching her gaze. "Lark, we need to get out of here. *Hurry*."

With a mighty rattle of dirt and pebbles and the crash of creaking limbs, the forest burst across the road, swallowing the path in a thick, gnarled mass of trees. Briars wove between the trunks, black roses blooming like rot, while brambles covered in poisonous-looking berries and dagger thorns crept over the verge.

"Lark! This way!" Da tugged her by the hand and together they ran along a detour: past the straggling houses on the outskirts of town, across the bridge over a creek still rushing fast and foamy with snowmelt, through a tunnel of elms and oaks, up a hill, and through the garden gate.

Da bent over, palms to his knees as he gulped air.

"Why, Da? Why?" she cried.

"I don't know, little bird. Let's find your mother."

But Lark was afraid she knew. Whoever had hurt—killed—the Harvest King had just killed the White Stag too. Someone *wanted* the border to fail. Someone *wanted* the wildkin to wreak havoc through the Borderlands.

If that was so, then the Wild Hunt would be more treacherous than usual—and perhaps even more critical, since Da had told her that without the border, magic would die and time would speed up.

Was that why Rook insisted she would have to use the moonclock? Maybe it wasn't just to save Galin but to stabilize time and magic somehow. . . . Was it supposed to save *everyone*?

Lark pressed her hand to the weight of the moonclock in her pocket and felt the weight of the world.

Where is the key?

— SIXTEEN —

Arrival

"YOU HAVE EXCELLENT timing," Ma said briskly when they burst into the stable. "Stardust caught her mane in a tree branch and lost half her charms. I'm having trouble keeping her calm enough to braid some back in. Would one of you hold her, please?"

"River," Da said. "The mare can wait a moment."

"But we'll be late for the Welcome Feast. . . ." She glanced up impatiently, hay stems stuck in her hair and a smudge of dust darkening her cheek. Concern sharpened her eyes when she noticed their expressions. "What is it? What happened?"

"Lark and I . . ." Da frowned and scrubbed his hands across his face.

"What?" Her voice held a brittle edge. Several shadow-breds stuck their heads over their stalls to nicker nervously in response to her rising alarm.

"We saw the White Stag," Lark started, "only—"

"The White Stag? But that's wonderful. The Elders were concerned that his absence was causing the wildkin to grow more aggressive. . . . What's wrong?"

"River . . . he was shot," Da explained. "While we watched. With a Fae arrow, silver-tipped and fletched with black feathers."

"Oh no." Her knuckles whitened where her hands gripped her crossed arms. "Is he . . . ?"

"Dead."

A rustling, swishing, snuffling silence filled the stable as they stared at each other amid two rows of restless shadowbreds.

After a moment, Ma took a deep, shaky breath. "We need to tell the Elders."

"There's more." He told her about the two Fae calling the woods across the road with deep magic.

Rubbing the back of her neck, Ma said, "The Fae emissary is going to have a lot of explaining to do tonight at the feast."

"Assuming Lady Mist appears," Da said darkly. "The Elders have lit the message lantern a dozen times and never received a response."

"She understands the significance of this tradition. I hope she comes." Shaking her head, Ma grabbed a handful of copper amulets to keep the shadowbred grounded in her mortal nature.

"I'll help, Ma. It will go faster," Lark said.

Ma dumped several into Lark's palm and tipped her chin toward a spool of red thread on an overturned bucket near Stardust. While Da held the mare steady, Lark and her mother quickly braided charms into her mane. As they worked, Stardust settled down, becoming more solid somehow.

Earthbound.

Ma finished by singing a chant as she wove a single strand of her own hair into the mare's mane along with a piece of green thread and a small white feather. "For luck," she murmured. Stroking Stardust's neck, she led the mare back into her stall and made sure it was latched.

"Thank you both for helping."

Da clasped Ma's hand and they left the stable yard in silence.

"Where is Sage?" Lark asked.

"I sent her out to deliver the formal race invitations and horse assignments. She should be back soon— ah, there she is," she said as Sage waved from the porch. "Good—let's get ready for the feast as quickly as we can, eh? We have much to discuss with the Elders and the Fae envoy."

Up in her room, Lark tucked the moonclock in the box under her bed and rocked back on her heels, pressing her palms to her eyes as though she could wipe out the image of the majestic White Stag collapsing. Horror and grief sat like boulders in her belly and she couldn't imagine eating a bite at the Welcome Feast.

Jinx the cat had followed her in from the barn and now leaped on her lap to snuffle her chin. Lark stroked the soft calico fur and blinked away tears. She wanted to stay home, wrapped in her blankets, with the cat for company.

"Lark! Hurry!" Ma called from the hall.

She sighed. "I am!"

After one last rub for Jinx, Lark splashed water on her face, washed her hands, and wiped her arms and legs down with a wet lemon-and-rose-scented cloth. Sage, already dressed, swept in with her arms full of fabric and trailing a length of ribbon. "I'll help you," she said. "Since we're in a rush."

Grumbling, Lark let her sister drop a cool chiffon dress over her head. She always felt foolish in fancy clothes, but as Sage tied the laces in the back of the gown Lark smoothed her hands over the skirt and felt a grin pulling the corners of her mouth upward.

Sage spun her around to judge the effect, straightening the neckline and tugging the waist so it draped perfectly over Lark's hips. She caught Lark's expression and smiled back. "Da knew this would suit you."

Instead of the stiff, formal gown Lark had dreaded, Da had made her a loose, simple swirl of cream and cocoa chiffon, with tiny seed pearls and soft feathers accenting the neckline and hem. Long ribbons of pale blue floated from the waist, like streamers of sky. "It's perfect! I can't believe he finished it in time."

"Ohhh, aren't you a pretty bird?" Sage smiled. "It's your first chance to join the adults at the Mayfair Welcome. Da wanted you to wear something special."

But Lark stared at her older sister. "Sage . . . you look *beautiful*."

Sage's gown suited her perfectly too. It had a pale buttercream bodice and a layered skirt slowly darkening to rich gold, as if she'd been draped in sunbeams. She wore a gold headband that gleamed in her dark hair, but she wouldn't stand still long enough for Lark to admire the effect. She twitched her skirt aside and showed Lark where she had pinned a protective charm of feathers, thread, and dried rue and vervain. "Make certain you pin one too," she suggested.

"I don't need to pin anything. My dress has pockets." Lark stuck her hand in one and grinned. "Da knows what I like."

As soon as Sage skipped downstairs, Lark dropped her hagstone, lengths of ribbon and thread, marbles, salt and sage and other herbs in her pockets. Then she slipped her feet in dainty leather shoes that tied around her ankles with brown velvet ribbons and sped down the stairs, hoping the night wouldn't be a disaster, hoping the Fae emissary would have answers and a resolution for the terrible tragedy she'd just witnessed. . . .

Sage and her parents waited by the front door, fidgeting impatiently. Ma wore a dress in mauve and seafoam green—Mairen colors—with divided riding skirts, silver embroidery twining along the hem and neckline. Da wore a seafoam vest over a cream-colored shirt and brown trousers, and Lark ran to hug him.

"Da! I love this dress! Thank you so much!"

He laughed and ruffled her hair. "My pleasure, little bird. Both of you girls look lovely."

"You and Ma look wonderful too," Sage said as they left the house, but Ma wasn't smiling and Lark understood her mood all too well.

"Girls . . . I don't know what we're facing tonight," Ma said. "I want you to stay together, and watch the road." Da quickened his step to match hers, bending close to murmur something in her ear.

Lark fell back a pace beside Sage. She told her about the White Stag and the Fae who'd controlled the wood. "I really don't think you should race this season," she said. "I have a bad feeling."

Sage clucked her tongue and tossed her head, shaking off the warning. "Lark, that's exactly why I *must*. It's the only way we can find Galin. And our only chance to stabilize the border. I'm the eldest daughter of the Horsemaven—how can I ask others to take a risk I refuse?"

Lark choked on a protest and Sage hurried to reassure her. "I'm not saying *you* have to! But I willingly and happily accepted the responsibility. I can't just set it aside if I'm nervous."

Again Lark wanted to argue, wanted to tell her sister

that Galin's absence was a lot more complicated than they thought. She wished she could explain that *she* had a chance to save Galin—and maybe the Twilight Court—too. Yet despite all her efforts, without the key there was no way to make the moonclock work.

Discouragement dragged Lark's spirits down. She tucked her chin and kicked a rock across the road as Da led the way toward the detour around the Fae forest magic, feeling as if she'd failed *both* her siblings.

Other travelers joined Lark's family when they neared the outskirts of the Junction, their cheerful conversation and eager anticipation of the upcoming Mayfair magic a strange contrast to the apprehension that had swallowed Lark. These folks didn't know, yet, that the White Stag had been killed, and she wished she could share in their carefree excitement.

Though the May Queen herself wasn't expected to arrive until the next day to watch the racing of the Gauntlet, her representatives—the emissary, Lady Mist, and various Court officials with business to conduct among mortals—were supposed to spend the evening feasting and talking, dancing and trading.

They had a lot to answer for.

Lark chewed her thumbnail. Ma's Faevored roses had dwindled even worse these last few days. . . . Without the White Stag, was the May Queen strong enough to lead the

Wild Hunt? Did she have enough power left to reign over this half of the year and restore balance to the Twilight Court?

Rook had warned that Sage shouldn't ride, but he and his birds hadn't found the moonclock key yet and Lark didn't know what else to do. How could she stop her sister? They were running out of time and Sage was determined.

Would the May Queen let Galin come home safely?

Distant music and delicate bells filled the air with a festive promise as they rounded the last bend into town, and Lark's spirits slowly lifted like the colorful silk kites swooping through the clouds.

There was still a chance that things would be all right.

After all, Grandda Maxim loved to say, *One of the first tools you need when fixing a problem is faith that it has a solution.*

As she passed Brassman's Clockworks behind her parents, Lark glanced in the wide front window and stumbled to a stop. Instead of waiting at the town square to begin the official Welcome ceremony, all three Elders clustered in the doorway of the shop, and Elder Brassman looked upset. Simon and a handful of other people rummaged through the store—

Oh no! The store! It looked as if a stormwind had blown through, tearing clocks from the walls and smashing them to bits. The glass case in front had been shattered, pocket watches and small clocks scattered across the floor. Files had been emptied, papers tossed about like fallen leaves.

But who would have done such a thing?

"Wait!" Lark cried to her parents, darting across the road to Elder Brassman's side. "What happened?"

"Lark, don't you look lovely," Elder Brassman said with a weary smile. Then, glancing over his shoulder, "I'm not really sure. Simon says nothing is missing. It's almost as though whoever did this was looking for something, but what they hoped to find is beyond my guess."

Lark's family had gathered behind her. "Oh, Elder Brassman, what a disaster. I'm so sorry. Any idea who is responsible?" Da asked.

"Dame Wardspin stopped by on her way to the square and said there were traces of a Fae presence, but beyond that we can't say." He frowned and rubbed a hand across his chin. "Odd way to begin a Welcome, eh?"

A flush of guilt left Lark trembling. She had come to the shop asking questions about the moonclock. She'd made Goward Brassman dig out those diagrams, drawn him into talking about things left long hidden.

And she'd given a Fae three of her hairs. Had they been peering through her eyes, or had a wildkin spy followed her?

Either way, she was the one who had brought Fae attention to his store. She was sure of it, and the knowledge made her sick.

"What can I do to help?" She slipped past the Elders and peered around. "I can stay and clean while you prepare for the Welcome."

"That's a kind offer, but we can manage."

"Please, Elder Brassman. It's the least I can do after all the time you've spent teaching me about pocket watches." She turned to plead with her parents. "I'll meet you in the square shortly. Let me stay and help."

They hesitated, but Goodman Simon looked up from where he was cleaning inside the store and smiled. "I truly could use her assistance, if she's willing. I'm too tall to easily reach into those lower cabinets." He pointed toward the back wall, where small cupboards held drawers of tiny screws, springs, gears, wheels, and other spare pieces. "If she could just tidy them a bit, I'll pick up the larger clocks and sweep the glass off the floor and then we'll join you."

Lark's parents exchanged a glance, and then Ma nodded. "Very well. Just don't dawdle."

Simon put his hands on his hips and surveyed the wreckage. "I don't think the damage is quite as dire as it looks. Shouldn't take us long."

"Thank you both," Elder Brassman said, adjusting the ends of his black scarf. "Come on, everyone. Let's clear the shop so they can work."

Lark knelt beside the cabinets and quickly sorted through the tiny pieces, sweeping them into their proper places. But when she tried to slide a drawer of springs back in, it hit an obstacle and refused to budge. She pulled the drawer out and bent forward, peering into the dark space behind. What was blocking it?

Reaching inside, she fished around until her fingers felt a small wooden box. It clinked and rattled when she withdrew it, tickling her curiosity. Thinking it might be more parts that needed sorting, she raised the lid and discovered an entire collection of keys. *So many keys.*

There were brass ones, bronze ones, silver ones, gold ones. Tarnished ones. Long ones, short ones. Simple ones, fancy ones.

"Simon . . . what are all these keys for?" she asked, shaking the box.

"Hm? Oh . . ." He leaned the broom handle against the wall and walked over to see. "Da wondered where that box had gotten to. Must have slipped behind a drawer at some point." He plucked a slender bronze key from the collection and held it up, examining the sharp teeth along the shank. "These are spare pocket watch keys. It used to be a Brassman tradition—whenever someone ordered a key-wound pocket watch, three keys were made. Two for the customer, and one for us to keep just in case they lost both of theirs. According to family lore, the first Brassman got so tired of people misplacing keys and asking him to make new ones, he decided to keep an extra here. Easier to copy a key than make a new one, you see."

He dropped the key back in the box and grinned at her.

"Eventually, a Brassman decided to solve the missing key problem by charging extra for replacements, and people got better at keeping track. It's bad luck to throw out a key, though, so here we are."

Lark stirred the keys with the tip of her finger, a wild thought winging through her mind. No matter who the Harvest King had really been, if the moonclock had been designed by a Brassman then there was a chance that the missing key was in this box.

Simon noticed her interest. "They're pretty bits of history, aren't they? If you see one you like, feel free to take it. It might bring you luck, and I can assure you no one else will come looking for it."

He turned back to his broom, humming under his breath. "Thank you!" Lark called to him, but her voice wobbled.

If nothing was missing from the shop, then the careless wreckage must have been the result of someone—or something—searching in a hurry. . . . Could it have been Rook and his birds looking for the key? Somehow she didn't think so. They wouldn't have left such destruction.

But other Fae knew she had the moonclock, and if they had figured out that it required a key, they might have decided this was a likely place to look.

Could they see through her eyes? If they realized Lark had found this box, they might return. What if they were on their way back at this very moment?

Panic isn't productive, she reminded herself, hearing her grandfather's calm voice in her memories. *Just find the key as quickly as you can.* . . .

Crouching behind the cabinet, where she was less likely to be seen from the street outside the windows, Lark dug through the assortment of keys. The one she needed would be silver, that much was certain. Other than that, she couldn't tell. She hadn't noticed a keyhole in the moonclock case, though she hadn't had a chance to look very closely. Still, she could assume the key would be quite small. . . .

They clinked and rattled as she rummaged around. She suddenly spotted one engraved with a triple moon. The same design was on the moonclock case, hidden in swirls of ivy. But she had to be sure. . . .

Perhaps there was a way to prove whether or not this was the right key.

A rough splinter of wood stuck out from the back of the cabinet and, wincing, Lark purposely pricked her fingertip on it until a spot of bright red oozed from her skin. Then she picked up the tiny tarnished silver key. A bead of her blood smeared the surface . . . before slowly seeping into the metal, just as it had done on the moonclock face and the case.

Third time's the charm, Lark thought. The moonclock truly was bound to her blood.

Triumph lifted her shoulders and raised her chin. She'd

done it! She finally had the last piece to the puzzle. As soon as she got home, she would wind the clock so she and Rook could save Galin.

And then Sage might be convinced not to ride after all. Lark could keep them *both* safe.

"Goodman Simon? May I have this one?" She balanced the silver key on her palm.

He glanced over. "Of course. Whichever one you want."

"Where should I put the rest?"

"Oh, just tuck them in that case there. Beneath the basket of pendulum weights. Da can figure something out later. Hey, are you ready to head to the square? I don't want to be late."

She tucked the key in her pocket, curling her fingers around it protectively. It might be the key to fixing everything.

By the time Lark and Simon made their way to the town square, the streets of Tradewind Junction had become even more clogged with curious onlookers, concerned citizens, and other Mayfair revelers. Despite the air of unease, people were still doing their best to celebrate. Lark dodged a man herding his children away from a temporary tent selling clouds of spun sugar on sticks and Simon put a hand on her elbow to guide her past a throng of people watching a flame juggler.

Copper bells around Tradewind Junction began to ring

and Simon said, "Oh! Hurry or we'll miss it!"

They squeezed through the crowd. Those who recognized Simon nudged their neighbors aside, whispering, "Elder Brassman's son!"

Lark was grateful for his presence; otherwise she never would have made her way through the press of people gathered in the square.

Visitors from villages across the Borderlands had come to greet the Twilight Court delegation, but an undercurrent of anger buzzed through the excitement. Everyone faced the Oak Gate at the far corner of the square, murmuring impatience as they waited for the first glimpse of the Fae envoy in months.

The Oak Gate was a massive live oak with a split trunk, creating a natural gateway directly through the tree. Usually, the cleft oak was a simple landmark. But twice a year, during Mayfair and Harvest, the air inside the hollow of the trunk would shimmer and open into the Fae realm on the Other Side.

Today the Oak Gate was decorated with garlands of spring flowers and pink and white ribbons. Tiny blue robin's eggs made of paper hung from the branches, along with charms to stabilize the flow of time through the trunk. Tightly woven baskets filled with early roses, lilies, hyacinths, and tulips were piled near the roots of the tree and lined a path across the square and up to the pavilion.

But Lark couldn't help noticing that there were far

fewer people carrying bouquets or waving ribbon wands to mark the occasion than in seasons past. The hard winter had chilled feelings toward the Fae, though hope that the May Queen would restore peace and security drew residents expecting good news from the Fae envoy.

"There are your parents. Follow me!" Simon said, weaving a path toward someone Lark couldn't see. She darted after him, suddenly afraid of getting separated.

"Perfect timing!" Da said when he spotted them.

Lark settled in beside her parents and her sister, patting the key in her pocket. The ember of hope inside her burned brighter.

"Won't be long now," Ma said, tucking a strand of dark hair behind her ear, gaze fixed on the Oak Gate, where the three Elders and a circle of luckwitches stood waiting for the Fae. "The welcome bells have already rung."

But they waited, and nothing happened.

For the first time in living memory, the Fae emissary was late.

As the crowd grew restless, Elder Goward Brassman checked his pocket watch and frowned, muttering something to the other Elders.

"Where are they?" Lark whispered to Da.

"I don't know, little bird," he answered softly, "but time works differently in the Fae realm."

She knew that, but . . . "They've always been prompt

before," she mused, mostly to herself.

He just shrugged.

Lark clutched the key in her pocket so tightly she was surprised the teeth didn't pierce her skin. She could guess why the Fae envoy might be late.

They had lost the moonclock. How could they measure time?

Ugly grumbles erupted, defying calls for courtesy and quiet. "What further proof do you need that the Fae are no longer our allies? They have broken the Accords and they disrespect our traditions," someone growled. Lark heard whispers hissing, "Salt and iron! Salt and iron!" But she couldn't identify who was speaking.

Elder Farstorm raised her staff and shouted, "Be still or be gone! The envoy will arrive any moment and you must show respect!"

But the throng of people filling the square grew increasingly impatient, voices rising in a shrill murmur. Children let their welcome kites swoop and dive, shrieking and giggling, ignoring the admonishments of their parents. A musician played a mocking tune on his fiddle and someone else called out rude jests that made his neighbors laugh, the mood in the square darkening like the sky before a storm.

The Elders shuffled their feet and leaned on their staffs, stern gazes fixed on the Oak Gate.

Ma and Sage tipped their heads close and spoke quietly

about the shadowbreds and the upcoming race, but Lark could see the tension in their shoulders and tight eyes.

The wind shifted, carrying bits of paper and flower petals.

This was not the way the Welcome was supposed to go.

A trickle of sweat slid between Lark's shoulder blades and she couldn't tell if it was caused by nerves or guilt or the afternoon heat. She rocked back on her heels, shrugged to loosen her tense neck, and hoped they wouldn't have to wait much longer.

"At last!" she heard one of the Elders say.

Lark looked to the Oak Gate, studying the shimmer of the open border through the hollow in the huge trunk. The buzz of anticipation swelled until the first rider—on a black shadowbred sold by the Mairens years earlier—appeared, and then the eager murmurs receded, leaving respectful if grudging silence.

This was a tall, broad-shouldered figure with weathered skin the tone and texture of hickory bark, wearing leather breeches with high boots and a vest fashioned entirely from leaves and fern fronds. Twigs and vines were so densely woven about his head it was difficult to tell if he had any hair, and his brows looked like curls of dark moss or fuzzy caterpillars perched above his golden eyes.

He rode to the pavilion, stopped, and bowed slightly from the saddle to the waiting Elders, the Horsemaven, and then the watching crowd.

The next Fae to ride through the Gate was nearly as tall, but willow-thin. His skin had the golden-green cast of new stems. Downy fuzz—like the velvet of a tightly closed bud—covered his chin. The strange wooden hat he wore atop his head reminded Lark of an acorn cap, and his vest and trousers looked like they were made of birch bark.

He did not pause to bow, immediately turning to gesture to someone waiting in the oak.

Lark craned her neck to see. Would this be Lady Mist, emissary of the May Queen?

No—the delicate form riding through was unfamiliar to Lark. She wore a gossamer skirt and a bodice that appeared to be made of pansy petals. A cloud of violet-colored hair brushed bare shoulders that gleamed like moonlight on night-blooming jasmine. Her shadowbred tossed his head as she guided him to a spot beside the other Fae and dismounted.

Lady Mist finally appeared, the last to ride through. She perched on a sidesaddle, wearing a gown of rose petals and raw silk, antique lace and velvet ribbon. A cloak woven from spiderwebs floated from her shoulders and a strand of tiny pearls was looped through her shining silver hair.

A quiet murmur of relief swept through the waiting crowd and Lark thought she saw some of the tension drain from the Elders.

The emissary had arrived. Now they could set things to rights.

Lady Mist dismounted at the pavilion, handing the reins of her shadowbred to the Fae with the acorn cap. "Well met, most gracious folk of Tradewind Junction and friends from regions far! I bring greetings from . . . the Twilight Court. We are honored to share this feast and privileged to witness this season's running of the Gauntlet." Her lilting voice carried clearly above the crowd.

The Elders stepped forward, offering the traditional gifts of welcome: a jar of honey, a jug of mead, glass wind chimes, and a leather pouch containing three silver coins. "Lady Mist, treasured guests, we greet you in the spirit of sweet friendship," Elder Rowana Farstorm said, offering the jar of honey and jug of mead.

The small Fae in purple accepted it with a gracious curtsy, but Lark was distracted.

Lady Mist had changed the words of the ritual greeting. Every spring until now she had invoked the name of the May Queen. Why had she said the Twilight Court instead?

Everyone knew the Fae were masters of wordplay. They never said anything without reason, and those who weren't careful all too often ended up thinking they'd heard something that hadn't actually been said.

Lark wondered at the omission, fearing the worst, but the Elders didn't acknowledge the strange wording. Elder Amalia Heartstone continued with the formal proceedings, presenting the wind chimes to Lady Mist. "We greet you with the chimes of clear communication and harmonious words," she said.

Then as Elder Goward Brassman started to hand Lady Mist the symbolic pouch of silver coins, the Fae in the acorn cap swiftly reached from his saddle and plucked it from her grasp, tucking it into his own vest pocket. For a startled moment Elder Brassman just blinked. "We greet you with the gift of silver, token of our long-established trade partnership, diplomatic treaty, and mutual trust," he finally managed to say, stumbling over the words.

Lady Mist completed the ritual, her face serene, but Lark had seen a flash of anger and . . . fear? . . . when the other Fae took the purse of coins.

Perhaps the gesture was meant to be helpful, but Lark was certain Lady Mist had not seen it that way at all.

Something was going on.

The three Elders thumped their staffs on the ground three times, in perfect unison. "We, the Elders of Tradewind Junction, welcome the members of the Twilight Court to our community and officially declare you welcome to Mayfair! Let the celebration begin!"

The crowd dispersed, wandering toward the market tents and tables spread around town. "Let's pay our respects," Ma said.

So Lark and Sage shuffled forward to be scrutinized by the emissary and her entourage. Sage smiled confidently—she was already known by the Fae—but a hot flush bloomed in Lark's cheeks and she fidgeted with her skirt.

"Ah! The brave Sage! We remember you from previous Hunts. You made quite an impression," Lady Mist said, and again Lark thought she saw something worrisome flicker in the Fae's expression. "Young Lark! Will this be your first Gauntlet and Hunt?"

"No, Your Grace," she stammered. "I'm only twelve summers."

But Lady Mist was already embracing River, kissing both her cheeks before turning to clasp Lukis's hands. "So lovely to see you both again." As they talked about the shadowbreds and possible future breedings, Lark was distracted.

The acorn-cap Fae stared right at her, an ugly look on his face and a knowing gleam in his eye. She gripped the key tight in her pocket, glad she had left the moonclock hidden under her bed.

She just hoped the protective charms around the Mairen property would be strong enough to keep it safe until she could get home to use it.

SEVENTEEN

The Welcome Feast

WHILE LARK'S PARENTS discussed the death of the White Stag with Lady Mist and the Elders and prepared for the evening's business, Lark and Sage were free to explore the festivities together—though it was hard to celebrate after everything that had happened.

Still, Lark was glad to dart away from the evil glances of the acorn-cap Fae.

The Welcome Feast began just before dusk in an open meadow outside Tradewind Junction limits. Lanterns hanging from wooden posts marked a winding trail to the clearing. More lanterns swung from tree branches, already lit and flickering like fireflies in the gloaming. Benches and stools and mismatched chairs crowded close to dozens of long wooden tables resting on trestles. Candles glowed in pewter candlesticks or floated in bowls of water with rose petals and violets, scattered between heaping platters of food.

Mingled voices, laughter, and music drifted over the meadow like fog. The crowd spilled into the surrounding trees, sitting on fallen logs or mossy roots as they balanced plates of food on their laps. Somewhere just out of sight a steady drumbeat thumped like a pulse and people danced beyond the tables.

Distant visitors who didn't know what the winter had brought, who weren't aware of the White Stag's death or the wildkin raids or the pervasive worry that had plagued the people of Tradewind Junction, celebrated the arrival of spring with joy.

Lark tried to swallow her own fear and cling to hope. She had the moonclock key at last and could finally fix her family's sorrow. She could bring Galin home and keep Sage safe, and then maybe she and Rook could figure out a way to repair the border for the benefit of both their realms.

That was worth celebrating, she decided.

"Come on, Lark! Your first proper Welcome Feast," Sage said with a bright smile. "You don't have to stay in the children's tent."

Lark grinned and followed her.

However, as she plunged into the crowd, she found herself startled by the noise and wild behavior. Although the Welcome Feast was traditionally a time for revelry and merriment, there were strict standards of etiquette for both Fae and mortal attendants. From a distant vantage point it had always seemed elegant and sophisticated to Lark.

This evening, though . . .

Slender figures with cotton-floss hair in all the shades of the rainbow leaped over tables to cram turkey legs and venison haunches down their too-wide mouths. Giggling underneath the tables were short, stocky creatures with potato-shaped noses and beards down to their bare, frog-webbed feet. Wisps with gold and silver wings spun through the shadows while a pair of pale figures grabbed bones from the roasting spits with fingers like spiders and crunched them out loud.

Lark tugged Sage's elbow. "It's not usually like this, is it?"

Sage frowned and shook her head. "I've never seen this sort of outrageous behavior before."

She gestured at a Fae wearing a dark leather vest and a kilt of feathers who suddenly leaped from his bench to dance a jig, guzzling mead from a heavy tankard in one hand. When he opened his mouth to belch, a cloud of bats burst from his lips and circled overhead.

Another Fae, dressed in a gown so black it almost hurt the eyes, drifted among the revelers. As she passed a mortal man, she plucked a hair from his head and dropped it on her impossibly long tongue with a low grunt of satisfaction.

Something prickled behind Lark's eyes as she recalled the three hairs she'd exchanged for the moonclock case. Was a Fae listening to her thoughts even now? Peering through her lashes?

Did they know she finally had the moonclock key?

"Dance with me, my beauty!" Lark was suddenly jostled and bumped as a thick Fae with the gray skin and gravel voice of a rocktroll tried to grab Sage's arm.

Lark kicked him in the shin before she could think better of it, bruising her toes against his stone skin. "She doesn't want to dance!" Lark cried.

"Didn't your mother teach you it isn't polite to refuse a partner?" he growled, yanking at her hair. "But if your sister won't dance, you'll do." He tried to heave Lark from her feet, pulling her arms and bruising her wrists.

"We are here to help our parents. Not to dance, I'm afraid," Sage said with ice-cold politeness, but her efforts to dissuade him without further provoking his temper failed.

"They can wait. Pretty girl like you needs to dance." He thrust Lark aside and reached for Sage again.

"And a big old troll like you needs to leave a girl alone," Lark said with venomous sweetness to catch him off guard, salt beneath the honey of her voice.

Literal salt. She'd reached inside her pocket and with a whispered chant she breathed a pinch of salt and vervain into his face.

Cursing, the rocktroll stumbled backward. "His Majesty will hear about this!" he shouted, and then clapped a clumsy hand over his mouth and lumbered away.

Lark and Sage stared at each other, stunned.

"*His* Majesty?" Lark repeated, a slow horror sending

roots through her bones. Was this confirmation that the May Queen had been defeated like the Harvest King?

"He's a rocktroll. He probably just got confused and forgot this is the spring Hunt, the queen's Mayfair rather than the king's fall Harvest festival," Sage tried to assure her.

"I don't think so," Lark said quietly. "You've seen Ma's Faevored roses. They've been fading for weeks." And besides, if the Harvest King had died, who would have taken his place?

Sage was only half listening, frowning as she watched three slender Fae in translucent silver gowns corner a couple of mortal boys wearing the stiffly formal suits of the noble houses. Bemused, the boys let the Fae kiss them—not noticing the unnaturally long fingers plucking memories from their minds like fruit from a tree. "This is not right," she said.

Lark had to agree. Dread pounded in her ears, echoing in time with the thudding drumbeat rolling through the party. "Sage . . . this afternoon Lady Mist said she brought greetings from the *Twilight Court*. Not the May Queen. And someone killed the White Stag. Faevors are failing." She took a breath. She'd been trying to keep Rook's secrets safe, but this was too big to hide. "I think something terrible has happened in the Court."

Sage looked as if she wanted to argue, but then she sighed and nodded. "I'm afraid you're right. We need to tell our parents and the Elders about all of this." She yanked Lark aside as a mossgoblin cartwheeled past, chuckling as he knocked people off their feet.

They hurriedly threaded their way through revelers until they reached the pavilion where the Fae emissary and the Elders were just taking their seats at a long table. Their parents sat at one end with other prominent members of Tradewind Junction and a select few honored guests from towns and provinces across the Borderlands. Fae representatives clustered at the other end.

Though the decorations throughout the meadow and the town square were pretty, here they were even more elaborate and lovely. Bouquets of spring flowers filled silver pitchers and spilled across the table. Candles floated in cut-crystal vases. Covered silver dishes and gleaming plates waited at each person's place, with linen napkins folded like swans or lilies.

Here there was none of the raucous clamor Lark and Sage had left behind. Soft music drifted from a nearby harp, played by a woman in a white gown. Conversation—measured, polite—flowed from one end of the table to the other.

If the general Mayfair Welcome was meant to be a festival, this particular corner of the feast hosted a ritual of diplomacy. Every rule precisely observed, every point of protocol carefully followed. Tucked away in the pavilion, guests would never guess the chaos outside.

At least, until Sage and Lark stumbled up the pavilion steps, interrupting the elegant proceedings with panting breaths and flushed cheeks.

Elder Amalia Heartstone surged to her feet, knocking her chair back. "Is there a problem?" she demanded.

Lukis and River jumped up at the same time, rattling the table. Candle flames stretched and wavered while sparkling wine sloshed in crystal goblets. "Girls? What is it? What's wrong?" Da asked.

Ma twitched her skirts aside so she could hurry past the corner of the table toward them. "Has something happened?" she asked.

"Here, now," an unfamiliar voice spoke from the mortal end of the table. Lark didn't recognize him: a florid man with a greasy beard and fat fingers clutching his napkin. He must be one of the merchants from Mer Harbor. "What is the meaning of this intrusion?"

One of the Fae closest to Lady Mist, wearing anger on his pale, pearl-slick face, clicked his tongue. "This is most irregular. Explain yourselves!"

"No," Sage squared her shoulders and lifted her chin. "*You* need to explain. Where is your queen?"

A hiss issued from a Fae at the end of the table.

Elder Brassman frowned. "You know it is not customary for the May Queen to attend tonight's feast. She will arrive tomorrow to observe the Gauntlet and recognize this season's Hunters."

"Will she though, Lady Mist?" Sage demanded.

Lady Mist's lips twitched. A muscle in her neck jerked, and the pastry she had been holding when the girls ran up to the pavilion fell from her hand.

Lark caught her breath. The Fae could not tell a lie, and they could not ignore a direct question. But it was clear Lady Mist was fighting her own words.

"Do you intend to tolerate such rudeness?" the merchant spluttered, slapping the table and accidentally knocking over his goblet of wine.

Before he could right it, a cloud of humming creatures with iridescent indigo wings surrounded the spill. They looked like a cross between dragonflies and giant moths, but when Lark squinted she saw their tiny faces. They weren't insects at all—they were flickerwixes, tiny Fae drawn to sweet red wine and sparkling ciders. Though they looked harmless, they—

"Ouch! It bit me!" the merchant bellowed, shaking his hand.

"Ah, the flickerwixes are drawn to feasts. A minor nuisance," Elder Brassman said. He lured the flickerwixes away by popping the cork on a fresh bottle of wine and pouring it into a bowl on the other side of the pavilion while Elder Farstorm wrapped the merchant's hand in a clean cloth.

"They're not venomous," she reassured him, but he shoved away from the table with a growl.

Elder Heartstone, flustered at the momentary distraction,

gently chided Lark and her sister: "I hope you have a good reason for interrupting this formal dinner; otherwise you must apologize and return to the Mayfair celebrations in the clearing at once!"

Ma had come to stand beside Lark and Sage and now she said, "Hold a moment, Elder Heartstone. Let's hear them out. Something has obviously upset them. What is it, girls? What happened?"

"A rocktroll tried to steal a dance, and—" Sage began, but the merchant interrupted.

"That's no cause for disrupting important discussions! If you can't handle the excitement, perhaps you should return to the children's tent," he snapped.

Da leaned over him. "She wasn't speaking to you. If you can't mind your manners when someone else has something to say, perhaps *you* should return to the children's tent. Go on, Sage."

Lark stifled a giggle at the merchant's shocked expression but Sage managed to hold her composure. "The rocktroll let something slip when Lark and I sent him away. I think the emissary can explain. . . . Lady Mist, once again I ask, will the May Queen arrive tomorrow?" Sage repeated in her most polite and polished voice.

The other Elders turned to regard Lady Mist.

"The ruler of the Twilight Court will certainly attend the Gauntlet, as tradition has dictated for centuries," she finally said.

Sage nodded as if this confirmed her suspicions, and a surprised rustle swept the Elders. "The ruler, Lady Mist?" Elder Brassman frowned at the emissary, catching the ambiguous phrasing. "Not the May Queen?"

The Fae called Mist looked away, mouth tightening. When she glanced back to the table her eyes were dark and fierce. She clapped her hands three times and all the candle flames were extinguished in a single curl of smoke.

"Thank you for your meat and wine, grain from field and fruit from vine," she recited formally. "Breaking bread and sharing food weaves the bonds of friendly mood. And with the ending of this meal—" She coughed and tried again. "And with the ending of this meal—" Her throat spasmed and she couldn't speak.

"There's no need to end the night so soon." The merchant glared at Lark and Sage, heavy brows knitted over deep-set eyes. "They're just younglings making trouble."

But the Elders ignored him. They knew as well as Lark did that if Lady Mist couldn't finish the ritual words of parting, it was because she couldn't speak the lie. Elder Farstorm passed the emissary a cup of wine, as if they could pretend the problem was nothing more than a dry tongue.

Lady Mist ignored the offered cup. She backed away from the table, wringing her hands and trying one last time. "Thank you for your meat and wine, grain from field and fruit from vine. Breaking bread and sharing food weaves the bonds of friendly mood. And with the ending of this meal—"

Your luck and safety we now seal, Lark mouthed silently.

But again Lady Mist couldn't finish speaking. With a look of dismay—almost apology—she flung her arm in a sweeping gesture and a sudden swirl of fog enveloped the pavilion.

Lark grabbed Sage's hand as the chill cloud swallowed them whole, evaporating as quickly as it had come.

When the air cleared, all the Fae at the table were gone.

EIGHTEEN

Music and Mayhem

THERE WAS A moment of silence, a collective gasp, and then the bearded merchant cursed, "Rust and ruin! I had important negotiations to conclude!"

"Do you think all the Fae have gone? Perhaps we should send everyone home, just to be safe. . . ." Ma suggested, ignoring his selfish outrage.

Elder Farstorm frowned at him before turning back to the others. "Let's check the festival meadow and the town square to evaluate the situation before we—"

A rising sound interrupted her.

Thump ba-boom, thump ba-boom. The evening breeze carried a clear drumbeat. Another drum, deeper and more resonant, picked up a low pulse. *Boom-boom, boom-boom.*

A scream shivered through the air, echoed by eerie horn blasts rising like howls over the background drumbeat and fiddle music.

"Sounds like trouble," Davina Wardspin said, racing toward the noise with the other luckwitches.

"What in the stars?" Elder Brassman cried, and they all rushed to follow.

Torchlight leaped and flickered in the evening breeze, casting strange shadows over the festival meadow. It was hard for Lark to see what was happening, but Sage suddenly cried, "Brendan?"

Lark squinted in the direction of her gaze and spotted Blunderknuckles Forth. He ran past them, frantically playing a fiddle with flushed cheeks and a sweat-damp curl stuck to his forehead. As he ran, he jerked his knees in an odd dance.

"Help me!" he shouted, spinning in a lopsided circle before jogging down the road.

"I didn't know Blunderknuckles played the fiddle," Lark said, alarmed at the sight.

"He doesn't." Sage frowned. "It's a Fae trick. It has to be. We need to stop him!"

"I'll fetch a luckwitch," Ma said. "If I can figure out where they went. Follow him and make certain he doesn't hurt himself."

Sage was already hurrying to catch him, and Da ran after her. Lark accompanied Ma. Musicians scattered around the meadow and into the square were all playing at once and a wild, random cacophony of jigs, reels, and ballads filled the air. Blunderknuckles wasn't the only one caught in the enchantment, Lark realized as a luckwitch rushed toward a woman who had just collapsed on the ground, dropping a slender flute as she fell. Beside her a Fae continued playing his fiddle, laughter stretching his moss-colored face.

"The luckwitches are already doing their best," Lark pointed out. "Maybe we need to find the healer instead."

She had noticed a woman wearing a crimson gown and golden slippers dancing in a small clearing amid the crowd. Something in the woman's posture—back rigid, arms stiff, muscles quivering—didn't seem quite right and her flashing feet moved quicker than Lark thought possible.

The dancer started spinning. Fast, and then faster. Her skirts swirled out like the petals of a flower, revealing green leggings underneath. Golden hair laced with silver threads of age spun in a halo around her white, frightened face. A slow scream rose in her throat like the cry of a wounded deer.

Red stains seeped through her velvet slippers as she danced her feet to blisters and blood.

The Fae only laughed.

"They're toying with us," Ma said grimly. "Oh, thank the stars. There's Elder Farstorm with Netty Greenwillow. Come on!"

Ma ran toward the healer and the Elder, Lark struggling to keep up as dancers leaped and kicked, swayed and circled out of control around her. Other mortals carrying protective charms strong enough to help them resist the spell scurried through the chaos, anxiously trying to help or desperately trying to flee.

Lark lost sight of Ma, and as she frantically looked around, her gaze fell on a couple of short Fae with long, twiggy fingers and wicked smiles. They were the ones pounding drums.

Ba boom da-da-dum, Ba boom da-da-dum. When the rhythm of the drums changed, the energy of the crowd shifted subtly. Eerie music stretched and wavered, wandering through notes and harmonies that sounded strangely discordant to Lark's ears.

If she could distract the drummers and stop the music—even just for a few moments—maybe she could give the luckwitches and the healer a chance to restore at least some semblance of order and stillness.

Ducking behind a large man with a brass horn pressed to his lips, Lark slipped through a gap in the unruly crowd and passed a young boy jumping and tumbling in the dark. She edged past four girls skipping in a wild circle around a bonfire and darted into the shadows beyond the reach of the flames.

Holding her breath, Lark crept closer to the Fae drummers. One step at a time.

A rustle in the trees on this side of the green startled her, locking her in a silent crouch. But as she strained to see through the night gloom, a burst of sparks from the bonfire illuminated the darkness and she noticed the quick flicker of a raven's wings.

Nightbird! Did that mean Rook was nearby?

She eased nearer to the drummers, her belly a knot of nerves.

A raven's harsh croak made the drummers miss a beat and the crowd fell back, the music sinking for one brief second. The Fae drummers resumed their enchantment, but the magic was weakened, confirming Lark's suspicion.

If she silenced them . . .

One of them looked up and caught her eye.

So much for creeping. Pretending to be caught in their spell, she danced in a circle that carried her closer . . . closer . . . closer . . .

She was almost within reach of the first drum when the Fae crouched behind it leaped to his feet. "Hey!" he cried, scowling at her.

Rust and ruin. He realizes I'm not enchanted.

Lark stumbled, missed a beat. The other Fae drummer fixed his glare on her.

Suddenly, a raven burst from the trees, swooping low over the drummers with another cry. Talons reaching, he dove past their heads, tearing at their ivy hair.

Howling, they tried to fend off the angry bird.

Lark seized her chance. She leaped toward the drums, kicking them until the thin skins stretched over the frames broke.

Still fighting the raven—Lark couldn't tell if it was Nightbird or another—now pecking and clawing at their faces, the drummers screamed at Lark. "You'll pay for this!"

"So will you!" she screamed back, all her worry igniting into anger.

The Fae drove the raven away with their drumsticks— which looked like slender lengths of old bone—and lurched toward her, fury burning in their eyes. One of them began to hum, a low and sinister melody that buzzed in Lark's ears like a swarm of bugs. Her copper ring burned her finger and she was afraid the protections in her pockets wouldn't be strong enough to resist whatever spell he was trying to work against her.

She tried to run, but a crowd of dazed, exhausted dancers surrounded her, stumbling in her way. For a moment she panicked and forgot to breathe. But Rook had taught her charms for a reason, hadn't he?

Rummaging in her pockets, she hurriedly pulled out a bundle of dried herb stems bound with red thread. "Bay and vervain, sage and rue, cast the magic back on *you*!" She tossed it at the Fae, clapping her hands three times.

But they only laughed. "Oh, look at the twiggy youngling with her dead weeds and red string!" One grinned, showing far too many teeth. "She thinks that tiny charm can pinch the likes of us!"

The other lunged and grabbed her shoulder, his fingers digging bruises into her muscle. "Don't you know who we are?" he growled. "We're the Twilight Court's own drummers, not some wildkin to chase away with thread and words. You'll pay for your disrespect. Let's see what else you've got in your pockets. . . ."

Lark tried to twist away. "Let me go!" she yelled, kicking at his shins and flailing her arms. But his grip was strong, and beneath his fingers Fae magic prickled her skin like the sting of nettles.

"Take your hands off her!" a familiar voice suddenly ordered. Lark looked up to see Rook, Nightbird croaking as he flew angry circles around them.

"Or what, Prince of Birds?" the Fae drummers taunted.

Rook raised his arms and a rush of wings filled the night sky. Shrieks and calls and a low questioning *Who who whooo?* drowned out the discordant music as hundreds of owls swept low over the heads of the drummers. Barn owls, screech owls, great horned owls, small attic owls, and the elusive secret-keeper owls. Snow owls and hedge owls and swift golden owls.

Their talons tore and scratched at the two drummers, drawing lines of blood. The owls pecked at the faces of the Fae, giant wings buffeting cheeks and noses.

"You've overstepped the bounds of your authority!" one of the drummers growled, but they fled, arms still frantically beating away the onslaught of pursuing owls.

Lark choked on an incredulous laugh, rubbing her sore shoulder. "So you can call owls as well as ravens, then, hm?"

It was as close to thanks as she could give a Fae and she hoped he understood what she wasn't saying.

Rook didn't smile. "I may not be able to help again. Remember everything I've told you, Lark Mairen."

Before she could respond, before she could tell him that she had found the key to the moonclock, he dashed into the shadows and disappeared.

For a moment, guilt rooted her feet to the ground. She'd been so focused on saving her own family she had let herself forget that Rook's sisters were in danger too. What trouble would he face, now that he had confronted other Fae to save Lark?

What a tangled mess it all was.

She clutched the key in her pocket and lurched through the crowd of confused, shuffling people. Some had collapsed, moaning, but the wild dancing had stopped. The music had ended, replaced with dazed murmurs.

Ma raced across the green when she spotted Lark, dodging people. "Netty Greenwillow will tend to any serious injuries, and the Elders are sending everyone home. At least all this"—she waved a hand around—"has settled down. I saw you destroying those drums. You took a terribly dangerous risk, but it was brave and I'm proud of you." She hugged Lark and murmured, "Let's find Sage and your father, shall we?"

"Yes!" Lark gasped, following her closely.

"Oh, there they are!" Ma waved. "Lukis! Sage!"

While they made their way home Sage described how

Brendan had been released from the enchantment: "All of a sudden he dropped his fiddle as though it burned his fingers," she said.

Lark was tempted to make a snide remark about Blunderknuckles and his clumsy hands, but in all honesty she was glad he wasn't hurt. And she was too worried about Rook for jesting.

When they were safe at home behind the luckwitches' wards, Ma and Sage changed their clothes and headed to the barn to check the shadowbreds while Da went into the kitchen to heat milk for cocoa. Lark rushed to her room to make sure the moonclock was safe.

As she tugged the wooden box from beneath her bed, though, something flashed across her vision and for a second it felt as though she were looking through a curtain of water. She blinked and shook her head. *My eyes are tired*, she thought. *Or maybe smoke from the bonfires has irritated them.*

She unlatched the box and was relieved to find the moonclock still safely hidden.

And now Lark finally—*finally!*—had the key to fixing everything. Heart racing and hands shaking, she took the silver key from her pocket and weighed it in her palm. Her skin tingled with the faint trace of Fae magic.

Her eyes blurred again and she pressed a fist into them, trying to rub away her exhaustion. She *had* to try the key.

Too much depended on her and this strange little clock.

With an apprehensive shiver, she made sure her curtains were closed so no spies could see what she was about to do. Then she turned up the flame in her oil lantern, flooding her room with a warm golden glow. Finally lifting the moonclock from the box, she searched for a hidden keyhole. It would be small—about the size of a grain of rice, she suspected, or maybe a pearl of barley—so it could easily be concealed amid the engraved leaves and stars and crescent moons decorating the case. . . .

She ran her fingers over the silver surface, looking for indentations or holes. When that failed to reveal anything, she started pressing elements of the design to see if they might spring open and show where the key should fit.

"Lark? Want a cup of cocoa?" Da called.

"No thanks!" She was *so close*. . . . She couldn't stop now. She had to discover the secret of the moonclock. The Gauntlet was tomorrow. She couldn't let Sage try to save Galin on her own.

But after almost an hour of unsuccessfully pressing, prodding, poking, and pushing the moonclock with her fingers, it occurred to her that the key itself might be a magic trigger. So she spent the next hour pressing, prodding, poking, and pushing the moonclock with the key.

Nothing happened.

Tears of frustration stung her bleary eyes and aching

exhaustion throbbed in her temples. She was *so* close. How could she be good at fixing things if she couldn't fix the things that really mattered?

With a soft groan, she crossed her arms on her desk and dropped her forehead with a thump. What else could she try? What if it didn't work? Too much was at stake.

The floorboards in the hall suddenly creaked and Da's voice murmured through the door, "Lark? Are you still awake? It's late and there's a long day ahead of us tomorrow. Blow out your light, little bird, and sleep."

"Good night, Da," she called, but when she tried to look away from the moonclock something yanked her gaze back. It felt like a tug inside her head. . . .

She started trembling as the horrible truth dawned on her. If one of the Fae ate her hair, they could see what she saw. . . . Suddenly her blurred vision made horrible sense.

Something else had been staring through her eyes.

Swallowing a scream, she drew protective sigils over her eyelids with a shaking finger. *Get out of my head!*

The sensation passed with a burning chill, but she felt no relief. Lark jumped into bed, wrapping herself in the special protection quilt for Wild Hunt nights. She squeezed her eyes shut and clutched the moonclock in both hands, the useless key pressing into her skin.

She was afraid to let go.

And the Fae still had two hairs left.

PART THREE

A Wild Ride

NINETEEN

The Gauntlet

RACE DAY DAWNED pink and gold, mist rising from the damp earth in tattered veils. Lark couldn't savor the morning's peace, though. She hadn't slept all night and her heart still pulsed with fear.

And she wasn't the only one fighting anxiety.

Apprehensive riders and nervous watchers crowded the stable yard, an undercurrent of fear shadowing their conversations. By now most knew the Welcome Feast had taken a dark turn and they tossed questions to Ma in a blur of words: "Are you worried that this Gauntlet will be more dangerous than usual? What about the Hunt? What did the emissary mean when—"

Some, on the other hand, seemed to think it was all just part of the Mayfair experience, thrilled by the excitement and magic. "What can we expect from the Gauntlet?" they wanted to know. "How many Fae will be there? What sort of obstacles?"

"You'll know when it starts, won't you?" Lark snapped, struggling to wind her way through the restless crowd while carrying buckets full of grain.

Ma clapped twice. "Everyone out except riders and stable hands!"

She hurried to Lark and said quietly, "We have a problem. Thadeus and Izak have withdrawn from the Gauntlet. Their families say the Fae broke the Accords and they refuse to participate in the race or the Wild Hunt. What's worse, they're petitioning the Elders to cancel the Gauntlet."

Lark mixed wild rose petals—a barely adequate substitute for Ma's dying Faevor—in the breakfast buckets as Sage said, "It's not up to the Elders, though, is it? The Mairens started the Gauntlet with Fae representatives to select the best riders for the Wild Hunt. This is your decision. And there are still enough riders competing in the Gauntlet. You only need the top five."

Ma rubbed the bridge of her nose. "But if word gets out that for the first time ever riders have refused their invitations, others might panic and withdraw as well."

"Well, dozens of people were eager to give a shadowbred a try. Just choose the next best. Lark can run and fetch them while we finish getting ready for the race."

Ma patted Sage's shoulder. "I think I'd better go. They'll want an explanation. . . . While I'm gone, Lark, would you and Sarai oversee grooming? Make sure no one misses anything. A burr in the wrong place or a fly bite beneath tack could kill a rider, and I've already got my hands full."

"Of course!"

"Thanks. Try to keep everyone calm until I return." Ma strode out of the barn, muttering curses to herself.

Once all the shadowbreds had finished eating, Lark and Sarai meticulously brushed each one, making sure the horses gleamed. After picking dirt from the mares' hooves, they combed their tails and counted the charms in their manes. Then Lark and Sarai proceeded from rider to rider, helping them tack up. They examined saddle pads and girth straps, bridle buckles and bits. Everything had to be perfect.

Sarai hummed as she worked, soothing the horses with her low, sweet voice and steady, experienced hands. But Lark spent the whole morning fretting. Why hadn't she found a keyhole for the moonclock? What was she missing?

What would the Fae with her hair do next?

When Ma returned with two replacement riders, Lark scurried off in search of Sage.

She reached her sister and Reverie just as Sage double-checked the length of her stirrups. "Everyone ready?" Sage asked. "How's Brendan?"

"Blunderknuckles? Clumsy and stubborn as ever, I suppose. Listen, Sage, I don't think you should ride the Hunt. And that means you need to skip the Gauntlet. It's too dangerous. Your Faevors won't work. What if instead of finding

Galin you get lost yourself? Or hurt?" Lark clenched her hands and blurted, "Besides, what if I have another idea for saving our brother?"

She'd promised Rook she wouldn't tell anyone about the moonclock, but the Fae already knew she had it. At this point, what harm could mentioning it do? And if sharing the secret would keep Sage safe, Lark couldn't keep it to herself. "If you come to the house with me for a quick minute, I'll show you—"

But Sage interrupted. "Lark, we talked about this already. Someday this stable and all these horses will be my responsibility." She ran a hand down Reverie's neck, tapping the copper charms braided in her mane. "What sort of Horsemaven would I be if I let fear keep me from the saddle? Besides, I can't let *them*"—she gestured toward the other riders, but Lark saw her eyes land on Brendan—"race if I'm too nervous to join them. I won't leave Galin behind again. I promise I'll be careful."

"But there might be another way! Let me just—"

"Lark, now is not the time. Go see if Ma needs more help."

Lark reluctantly drifted back to the barn and picked up the handles of the wheelbarrow, feeling like a failure. Sage was taking a risk to help Galin, and what was she doing? Shoveling muck.

→ ╬ ←

By the time the shadowbreds and their riders stepped out of the barn, most of the morning's crowd had dispersed along the road curving around Tradewind Junction to the stands near the start of the Gauntlet.

It was time for the Parade of Horses to begin.

River Mairen wore a white tunic with elbow-length sleeves to show off the silver cuffs she'd earned on her first Hunt. Over it was a ceremonial leather vest embossed with her personal sigils and runes. And though the magic may have faded, she still wore Faevors from her Hunts: a silver whistle hanging from a cord to call starshadow stallions, silver earrings shaped like honeybees to keep bugs away, and soft leather gloves that were supposed to ensure the safe delivery of every foal.

She gripped the reins in one hand and twisted the other in Legacy's mane. Setting the toe of her left boot in the near stirrup, she glanced down at Lark. "Don't look so worried, little bird. All will be well." She sprang lightly up, swinging her right leg over Legacy's back and slipping her foot in the off-side stirrup. She settled gently in her saddle—another Faevor, meant to guarantee she'd never fall from her horse—spine straight and shoulders relaxed.

"But, Ma . . ."

"I already know your concerns, Lark, and believe me, I share them. But with or without the White Stag, regardless of any Fae mischief, our only chance to secure the border is to follow the laws of tradition. What other choice do we have? It's either this or the Last Protection clause, and that would be worse. I've spoken to *all* the riders, your sister included. They are as prepared as they can possibly be. Whatever unrest plagues the Twilight Court, we must see this through. Try to have faith." Then she smiled, stroked Legacy's neck, and lightly squeezed her calves against the mare's sides.

Legacy pricked her ears and arched her neck, proudly marching off. She was bold and beautiful and when the throng of people in the stable yard saw her they let out a collective sigh of admiration.

But all Lark could see was the regal White Stag in the moment before his death.

If only she'd wound the moonclock and seen what it could do. . . . She wished she could be brave and successful like Ma and Sage. *There's a tool for every job and a job for every tool*, she reminded herself. But she felt like a hammer trying to loosen a screw. She still felt like a failure.

Ma rode through the stable yard, graceful as a queen, and circled the barn three times for luck while the day's riders rang tiny copper bells.

The shadowbreds tossed their heads and pawed the ground, eager to race.

Ma called, "Riders up!" The stable yard filled with the creak and swish, rattle and scuff of riders mounting restless, ready horses.

Lark held her sister's shadowbred, hands trembling as Sage mounted smoothly. She checked one last time to be certain Reverie hadn't shaken any charms loose. "Are you *sure* you want to do this?"

"Lark!"

"Just asking. Luck of the winds be with you," Lark said with a worried frown, swallowing dread.

Sage grinned, eyes fierce. "And joy of the sky be with you," she answered, brushing a speck of dust from her silk tunic. She wore Mairen colors: mauve and seafoam green, and Reverie's saddle blanket matched.

All around them other riders and their chosen grooms exchanged the same formal blessings. Each shadowbred wore a white saddle blanket trimmed in seafoam green to mark Mairen ownership, but the riders had chosen their own colors in different shades of blue, green, gold, orange, and red.

The stable yard was a sea of rainbow silk and satin black horses.

Sage bent down and said in a low voice, "Watch the road, Lark."

Lark didn't have time to respond. A horn sounded one long, ringing note followed by a quick rill and Ma waved her arm, gesturing for all the riders to follow her.

The line of horses wound through the yard and out onto the road. Cheers rose from the waiting crowd as the legendary shadowbred mares and their brave—or reckless—riders passed.

Journey and Whimsy followed the group, wearing wreaths of ivy and roses. Ma had invited Lark to ride Journey with the parade, but there was something in the air today that made her especially glad to feel the solid earth beneath the soles of her boots. And Whimsy was Galin's horse, her bare back a bleak reminder of why the race and the Hunt were necessary.

Lark let her eyes follow the riders as they passed her one by one, guessing who wasn't likely to finish the course. Romin Brookings gripped with his knees so tightly his mare hunched her back and sucked in her belly, taking short, choppy strides. If he didn't relax, she would dump him over the first fence.

Rik and Antonus Greensfeld—replacements for Thadeus and Izak—held their reins in white-knuckled hands, elbows stiff. Their horses mouthed the bits and flattened their ears. They'd be thrown off at the first obstacle too, most likely. They were decent riders, but Lark suspected they had underestimated the coming trial. She had a feeling they now suspected the same thing.

There was a big difference between riding a shadowbred in the arena and trying to race one through the Gauntlet. And yet no matter how many times a rider was injured on the course, there were plenty eager for the challenge, hungry for the risk, desperate for a Faevor from the Hunt.

Well, there would have been in any other season. The Greensfeld brothers were brave enough to ignore the strange circumstances surrounding this spring's Gauntlet and Hunt. Lark had to give them credit for that, even if they did look anxious and overwhelmed now.

Another note sounded and the horses began to trot.

Lark sped up, noticing which riders hunched forward or bounced in the saddle. Artur Bowman's shoulders were tense and his jaw clenched, but he knew what to expect and wore an expression of fierce determination. Stardust arched her neck under him and marched along steadily, and Lark hoped they'd both finish safely. Julienna av'Amberli, a merchant's daughter from one of the Free Cities, rode Whisper as if they heard each other's thoughts and Jinniver Tennet from Mer Harbor smiled atop Inka. But Brendan Blunderknuckles Forth followed on Cinder, his face a distinctly greenish hue like he was fighting not to vomit. Then Kerigan Cormick brought up the rear on Indigo, and as they passed Lark the mare tried to bite his boot.

What would happen if five riders couldn't complete the Gauntlet? The Accords specifically stated that at least five mortals had to ride with the Fae in the Wild Hunt. . . .

Where the road curved, Lark decided to take a shortcut so she could watch the shadowbreds enter the grassy staging ground before the Gauntlet. She plunged into ferns as high as her knees, wading through greenery, stepping over tree roots and bluebells, until she stumbled upon a thorny tangle in the path ahead. . . .

Brambles.

She sucked in a breath as the barbed vines twisted toward her, black buds swelling and bursting as evil-looking berries filled the air with the scent of magic and rotten fruit.

Jumping over a boulder, Lark ran down a grassy slope and darted between hickory and maple trees. Twigs snagged her tunic and branches scratched her, but she couldn't slow down. If the brambles were mere steps away from the Gauntlet, whoever controlled them could interfere with the race. She had to reach her sister, had to warn the other riders.

She tumbled out of the trees and lurched to a stop, whipping her head around to make certain the brambles hadn't followed.

The Gauntlet spread out before her.

Lark knew Da was already waiting in the spectator stands and Ma would be near the finish line, but she hesitated. Across the course was a pavilion for Fae spectators, draped in white and blue to shade the May Queen and her entourage. Only it didn't look right. . . .

She squinted, shading her face with one trembling hand. No. That pavilion was silver and black, and instead of the May Queen's emblem she saw a knot of thorns. Brambles.

"Sage!" she panted, pressing a hand to her burning chest and running toward the starting line.

Three long horn blasts pierced the sunny morning and the horses took off.

She was too late.

Lark scurried up a small knoll so she would have a clear

view of the entire course. Sage was easy to spot, with her long, dark hair and pale green tunic. She and Reverie had an early lead, swiftly skimming the ground.

The first obstacle appeared to be a simple wooden fence with hedgeroses climbing the sides. Reverie tucked her knees neatly, cleared the fence, and . . .

Disappeared in an expanding rush of roses and vines.

There was a collective gasp from the crowd, and then applause. To most, the challenges on the course were simply entertainment, magical obstacles designed by Fae representatives as a surprise each time.

But their lives weren't at stake.

Lark leaned forward, holding her breath. Where were Sage and Reverie? Caught in a maze of briar roses?

A heartbeat later Reverie galloped out, Sage leaning over her neck. Lark sighed in relief. As soon as Sage was through, it went back to looking like a straightforward wooden fence. Three rails, reasonable height.

One shadowbred horse balked at the fence—not trusting her rider to know what he was doing—and he pitched over her neck. Though she couldn't tell for sure from up on her perch, Lark suspected that had been one of the Greensfeld brothers on young Batwing. Another shadowbred jumped the fence but threw in a gleeful buck for good measure and her rider bounced out of the saddle—probably Romin Brookings.

The next shadowbred to clear the fence with her rider

vanished in the burst of roses, but Lark didn't see how long it took them to escape because Sage and Reverie were already approaching the next obstacle.

This was a stone wall with a deep puddle behind it. Rie soared over the wall and didn't hesitate when she hit the water, splashing through it boldly and surging up a small hill.

There was a groan of disappointment from some in the crowd who wanted to see more excitement, but others cheered Sage's name and stomped their heels to urge her mare onward.

Lark had seen a flicker in the water, though, and she suspected the obstacle was more than it appeared. She watched closely as the next horse cleared the wall and entered the puddle. The rider was out of balance, bobbling the reins as the shadowbred stretched her neck. Suddenly, a green wave rose from the water and swallowed them both with a crash of foam and spray.

Lark glanced back at the hedgerose challenge and was dismayed to see two riders on the ground and a chestnut horse—a mortal horse, entered by a daring rider who didn't believe in the dangers of the race—limping off the course.

Meanwhile, Sage and Reverie had widened their lead. As they raced around a turn toward a brush tunnel a cheer went up from the stands. Someone waved a pocket watch in the air and Lark guessed that Sage and Rie must have broken their previous record.

They soared over a small combination fence and through the brush tunnel, galloping smoothly down a grass slope. It ended in an awkward corner fence with a twisted tree reaching out to snag the riders. Lark couldn't bear to watch—if Rie lost her footing and fell, Sage would be crushed—but she couldn't turn away either.

Eyes burning, pulse stuttering in a rhythm that matched a horse's gallop—*ba da da dum, ba da da dum*—breath caught like a bird in her chest, Lark craned her neck to watch Sage and her mare.

Reverie flew over the corner fence and turned neatly, smoothly, stretching out as she raced across the ground. Three fences in a tricky combination and her hooves barely touched the ground.

Here the Gauntlet entered a narrow, twisting trail between a copse of silver birch trees. Even from where she stood, Lark could see a shining mist curling between the slender trees. This was without a doubt another magical challenge, but what sort of difficulty it might pose she couldn't guess.

Heart in her throat, Lark started whispering every chant she could remember for safety and protection. She recited the words so fast they melted together in a sibilant hiss of desperation and fear.

Be safe, Sage. Be safe, Rie.

A shout rose from the stands and Lark's gaze flicked to another rider, clinging to the neck of her horse as she tried to regain her balance after a dirty jump. They wobbled a bit, but the mare straightened and sped up, galloping after the others.

There were just nine riders left on the course now. Two were only a few paces behind Reverie, three at least a league back. A couple of stragglers on mortal horses.

Lark fastened her gaze on the birch copse. Beads of sweat trailed down her back and between her shoulder blades. *Be safe be safe be safe.*

Rie and Sage did not emerge. Another shadowbred plunged after them—Cinder and Brendan? Lark couldn't tell—and then a few minutes later a third. None emerged.

"Sage!" she screamed.

Two more riders fell and their horses charged off the course, but Sage and Rie and the others were still concealed in the birch glen.

Murmurs rose from the anxious spectators, some rising to their feet.

A raven swooped low over the shimmering leaves and let out a long call. Lark chewed her lip. *Where are you, Sage?*

There! Sage and Reverie burst from the trees and leaped over the highest fence yet—which Rie cleared in a perfect, graceful arc.

The finish line was only ten paces away now, and Lark counted every stride. Sage and Rie flowed like one creature, two wills bent to a single purpose.

They streaked through the shining silver ribbon, winning the Gauntlet to a deafening cheer from both the mortal and the Fae stands.

Lark sank to her knees, relief turning her bones to bread pudding. "They did it! Oh, brilliant ride!"

The remaining riders galloped across the finish line long minutes later: Brendan, Julienna, Jinniver, Artur, and Kerigan.

Lark shoved herself to her feet and scrambled toward the finish to congratulate her sister and rub Reverie's neck, but fear still twisted like a thorny vine—like the brambles and briars she'd seen—around her heart.

The Gauntlet was only the first part of the ordeal. The *real* challenge was surviving the Wild Hunt tomorrow night.

TWENTY

The Briar King

LARK ELBOWED HER way through the crowd at the finish line until she reached Sage. Flinging her arms around her sister, she said, "You did it again! You and Rie are amazing!" *But now you have to ride the Hunt.*

Da jogged over, cheeks flushed and hair rumpled. "Well done, Sage! I'm so proud of you and Reverie!"

"Thanks, Da!" She kissed his cheek and slung an arm over Rie's neck. "Look, she's not even winded."

"But what happened in the birch trees?" Lark asked.

"I'm still not sure, to be honest. We were swallowed in mist." She shuddered and smoothed Reverie's mane. "I couldn't tell which direction we were facing, where the track was. I couldn't remember what we were supposed to be doing. And then these whispers started up. . . . They crawled inside my head and swallowed my thoughts and I felt so tired. . . . But a raven croaked and my mind suddenly cleared. I could hear other riders behind me so I called to them to follow me."

Lark's heart soared. Nightbird must have offered guidance!

"And what about the hedgeroses?" Da asked. "Were they terrible?"

Sage choked out a laugh. "Only until Reverie took a big bite." The mare tossed her head with a snort and Sage rubbed her nose.

"Well, *I* think you're a brilliant mare and the fastest shadowbred ever to run the Gauntlet," Lark told Reverie, scratching her withers. When the mare curled her neck around to regard Lark with shining eyes, Lark leaned forward and whispered, "Thank you for keeping my sister safe."

Then the crowd surged around them, chanting and cheering, "*Sage Mairen! Sage Mairen!*" People reached for Reverie's tail, begging for a strand of hair to bring them luck. Rie clenched her lips in irritation and threatened to kick as Ma waved them away.

"Let's get to the pavilion for the awards," Da suggested.

So they pressed through the crowd, pausing in front of the pavilion, which had just been draped in swathes of green-and-mauve bunting to match the Mairen colors in honor of Sage's victory. Brendan Forth and the other finishers were already there, holding their restless shadowbreds as they waited.

Brendan grinned when he saw Sage. "Guess I owe you a silver coin, eh? Best one I ever spent."

Sage—to Lark's disbelief—actually blushed and *giggled*.

Lark tried not to roll her eyes.

"Seriously, though. That was an incredible ride. You and Reverie are a force of nature."

"Thank you. You and Cinder raced well too."

Why was Sage complimenting *Blunderknuckles*? Although . . . a twinge of guilt forced Lark to admit he'd done better than she expected on the Gauntlet. He wasn't a bad rider after all.

His ears turned pink and he shuffled closer to Sage, Cinder snorting at Reverie.

Lark smirked but before she could tease them a horn blast split the air.

Ma murmured to Da, "I haven't seen Lady Mist or the May Queen yet. I wonder where—" She was interrupted by a harsh call.

"Make way for the Thornguard! Make way for the Thornguard!"

Lark retreated with her parents into the surge of people surrounding the pavilion while the Gauntlet finishers lined up with their horses. But . . . the Thornguard? She didn't like the sound of that.

She craned her neck to see five Fae with thorns woven in their hair, eyes glittering red as holly berries and grins like black slashes in pale stone faces, marching toward the pavilion.

Behind them, Lark recognized a Fae with a mossy beard and another with an acorn cap. "Da!" she whispered urgently, clutching his wrist. The pair looked like the Fae they'd seen the night the White Stag was shot.

"I see them," he muttered grimly.

A tall Fae, muscles knotted beneath skin the color of sun-bleached cedar, followed them. Dark hair shaded pine green curled below a silver crown of briars, and the sigil on his vest was a richly embroidered knot of thorns. Like the Fae ahead of him, he carried a spear with black and silver streamers flowing from the pointed tip.

As he moved to the center of the pavilion, one of the Thornguard Fae announced, "His Most Supreme Majesty, the Briar King of the Twilight Court, wishes to congratulate the brave Gauntlet finishers."

Ma gripped Da's arm and Lark pressed against them.

Stunned whispers hissed through the crowd. "Did he say *Briar King*? Who in the starry worlds is *that*?" someone said.

"Where is the May Queen? I promised my daughter she'd get to see the Faery Queen," a woman grumbled.

"Show your respect!" a Thornguard growled, leveling his spear at the knot of gaping onlookers. Thistles and thorny brambles burst from the grass at their feet, heaving out of the ground and filling the air with a sharp green scent. Most people dropped clumsy curtsies or rough bows while the rest just scattered like dried leaves in a stormwind.

The Briar King smiled, a toothy sickle blade splitting his face. His black cloak, silver specks glittering like starlight along the hem, swirled as he spun to regard the people staring at him. He spread his hands and called, "Greetings, friends! Yes, *I* am the Briar King of the Twilight Court."

A murmur of unease swept the square. *"What is happening? Who is this?"*

"I hear your worry, my friends," he said. "As I am sure you have noticed, the border has been unsettled due to troubles in the Twilight Court. But a new era is at hand, a new opportunity for cooperation and mutual benefit here in the Borderlands. I will restore stability."

It wasn't much of an answer, but to Lark's surprise people seemed reassured. The Twilight Court was a mystery anyway—they just wanted someone to tell them it would be all right.

He continued, "But change is built upon the foundations of tradition and history, and so today we recognize the six riders who successfully completed the Gauntlet. Sage Mairen, you have won the Gauntlet and proven your courage. It is my honor to present your prize."

Sage stepped forward as he pulled a perfect red rose from beneath his cloak, each petal limned in gold. Tiny diamonds sparkled like dew on the leaves. She curtsied and accepted the blossom as Reverie tried to nibble the petals. "The honor is mine, Your Majesty."

"And to each of you, for completing the Gauntlet so bravely and boldly, I present these tokens of recognition. Sage Mairen, Brendan Forth, Julienna av'Amberli, Jinniver Tennet, Artur Bowman, and Kerigan Cormick." As he called their names in order of completion, he presented a silver horse-shaped pin to each of them.

"The first five finishers are honor bound to ride the Wild Hunt with us, but . . ." He took a breath and looked around at the crowd. "In the spirit of this new era, I have come to welcome *any* who wish to join the Wild Hunt."

There was a moment of confusion broken by scattered applause. He waited for silence and then said, "Yes! You did not mishear me. I said *any who wish to join the Hunt*. In the past, only the five fastest riders of the Gauntlet were allowed to participate. You were told this was for safety. For protection. But why should the honors of the Hunt be limited to five? Why should Faevors go only to the most fortunate? Why should magic be limited to a rare few? No, I say it is time for new traditions! From this night forward, I welcome *all* riders!"

From the corner of her eye Lark saw Da grab Ma's hand and hold it tightly—in warning or comfort, Lark wasn't sure. An angry flush bloomed in Ma's cheeks and the tips of her ears. Her eyes blazed and a muscle in her jaw twitched. "He will kill them," she whispered, grinding the words between her teeth. "He'll kill every brave fool."

"It won't come to that, River," Da said quietly.

But Ma shook her head. "This is trouble, Lukis. Big trouble. Without a shadowbred, they won't be able to keep up. He's tempting them to their deaths!"

"If you wish to prove your courage and experience the adventure of a lifetime," the king was saying, "my Huntmaster will record your marks."

He indicated a taller Fae behind him, with a bear's pelt flung over his shoulders. The Huntmaster held up a scroll and a slender silver blade.

At first no one moved. Then a disturbance near the edge of the square revealed the Elders making their way to the pavilion, thumping their staffs on the ground. "Your Majesty," Elder Rowana Farstorm cried in her crinkle-paper voice, "this is a matter for discussion first. Let us wait until—"

The king ignored her. "Come! Any who ride with the Hunt from dusk to the break of morning will receive Faevors and silver cuffs! I am a generous king; I place no limits on these honors!"

Kerigan jumped off the pavilion steps, waving a hand. "I'll sign! I want to join the Wild Hunt!"

"Kerigan—" Ma started, but Da laid his arm across her shoulders and gave her a gentle shake.

Kerigan turned to meet Ma's eyes. "I earned it,

Horsemaven. I completed the Gauntlet, even if I finished sixth."

The Briar King spotted her and a slow smile crept across his face. "River Mairen. Horsemaven and keeper of Fae horses. You should be delighted by our new policy! Think of the market for your shadowbreds! Together we will usher in a new age!"

Realizing he meant what he'd announced, others started shoving their way toward the Briar King and his Huntmaster. Kerigan approached first. The Huntmaster grabbed his thumb, pierced the skin with his silver blade, and pressed it to the scroll. A man in a leather vest and green felt cap followed. "I'll join the Hunt!" he yelled. After his thumbprint had been taken, he veered away, clenching his hand and shouting boasts of his bravery.

A group of young boys pushed forward next, clamoring for a turn to mark the scroll in blood. "Edrick Birchman, you'd best get your knobby knees back here this instant!" a mother cried, but the Huntmaster sneered and gripped the boy's hand.

Scattered voices began to protest, but the Briar King's temptation proved too strong and an unruly, boisterous line began to form.

Lark saw some of the lordlings her mother had turned down, a couple of girls too afraid to race the Gauntlet but who'd apparently now decided the promise of a Faevor was worth the fright, and several men who reeked of mead and likely didn't know what they were lining up for.

The horn blew again and the king's voice rose. "Now, let us have music and dancing! We will celebrate Mayfair and the start of our long and prosperous friendship!"

Shivering bells rang across the town square and a wild melody swirled through the air.

Sage wove through the crowd to reach her family, concern on her brow. "We haven't seen Lady Mist since she vanished from the Welcome Feast. Now this Briar King has taken the May Queen's place? Who is he?"

"He's the one who killed the Harvest King, I'm sure of it," Lark murmured. And it appeared he'd killed the May Queen too. Not only that, but now he would lead the Wild Hunt, without the White Stag. A surge of fear for Sage almost made her sick to her stomach.

Sage leaned against Reverie. "But that would mean a coup in the Twilight Court and—"

One of the Thornguards took a step toward them, letting the tip of his spear lower slightly.

"Enough! This isn't the place to speak of it," Ma warned.

Just then Brendan led Cinder closer. "The other riders have started back to your barn," he told Sage. "Care to join me?"

She smiled. "It would be a pleasure."

"Watch the road," Ma said. "Da and I need to check with

the Elders for a moment and then we'll follow. Lark, are you going with your sister or waiting for us?"

"I will—" Lark started, but a raven called overhead and distracted her. *Nightbird*. He was circling a food tent on the far side of the pavilion.

"I'll wait for you, but can I grab something to eat first? I skipped breakfast."

Da frowned, but Lark was anxious to see Rook, so without waiting for his reply she broke into a jog. She had to use her elbows to nudge her way past matrons in aprons and straw hats, around lordlings in velvets and ladies in impractical gowns, through groups of giggling girls from the Free Cities and sailors up from Mer Harbor. Trailing curses, she managed to avoid most of the Fae and finally lurched to a stop in front of the fragrant food tent.

Smoke and steam hovered above the woodfire and the smell of roasting meat coaxed a growl from her empty belly. There were skewers of beef and vegetables, hot pies filled with pork and gravy, bowls of rice and chicken, fried fish and potato wedges, bread pockets stuffed with lamb and lentils. . . .

But Lark had come for a reason and she turned her head, seeking the raven.

"Sage shouldn't have raced," a voice whispered in her ear.

She startled, then breathed a sigh of relief when she

recognized Rook. "But I have the moonclock key! If you tell me how to use it, we can fix everything!"

He shifted his weight, avoided her gaze. "You hungry?" he asked.

"Rook, we don't have time to waste! Tomorrow night is the Hunt and I have to know what I'm supposed to do with—"

A small Fae with flame-colored hair and a cloak of golden dandelion blooms skipped past, pausing to offer Rook a low bow. He inclined his head and the Fae drifted away, but when a couple of Thornguards looked their way Rook tensed. "I haven't tasted mortal food in ages," he said.

Was food the price of information, or just an excuse for distraction? "What do you feel like? A meat pie? Pan bread? A hot bowl?" Lark asked, glad she had pocket money.

"Surprise me. I'll be over there." Rook nodded to a row of pine trees marking the limits of Tradewind Junction and darted away faster than Lark could follow.

After standing in line longer than her patience could tolerate, she bought two grilled vegetable skewers and two meat pies before hurrying to the pines.

Rook waited in the shadows beneath the trees. Nightbird perched on a bough to act as sentinel. "Smells good," he said. "What did you bring?"

Lark handed him a meat pie and a vegetable skewer, settling herself cross-legged on a soft carpet of fallen needles.

"Now hurry up and tell me how the clock works! What am I supposed to do with it?"

Rook pulled a roast pepper off his wooden skewer with his teeth and swallowed it without chewing. "I often marvel at the fact that all you mortals walk around with your own personal clocks ticking away in your chests, counting out the moments of your lives, measuring your own rivers of time in the flow of your blood and the rush of air through your lungs."

Lark grimaced. "That's . . . rather grim."

"I find it beautifully magical." He swallowed another bite while she choked on her frustration.

"Rook! Stop dodging questions!"

"Everything is linked, but I can't explain *how* because I don't understand the mechanisms. As for *what*, that's obvious—it's always about balance. Pay attention to the moon." He licked grease from his fingers.

"What does the moon have to do with everything?"

"The moon draws time just as it does the tides. All currents are connected."

Lark slammed a hand on the ground. "And all clocks measure time. It's *what they are for.* What makes this one special? The fact that it indicates moonturns rather than minutes? Seasons rather than hours? Rook, stop speaking in riddles. *I need to understand!*"

He waved a dragonfly away and tossed a bit of meat up

to his raven. Nightbird caught it with a quick snap of his beak, dancing on the branch in satisfaction. "Think, Lark. Why would the Fae want the moonclock so badly if it can only be used by a mortal?"

"If I knew I wouldn't have to ask!"

"We're running out of time."

"I *know*. That's why I'm—"

"No. You're not understanding me. *We are running out of time.*" He stared in Lark's eyes, willing her to make sense of his words.

Lark bit into her pie and thought about the engraving in the moonclock. *Time is what the immortal lacks.* The Fae had magic, mortals had time. Sometimes they shared.

"You need mortal energy," she breathed.

Rook leaned forward and whispered, "The Briar King didn't know the moonclock existed until the wildkin told him." Even as pain twisted his expression he fought to continue speaking. "He still doesn't believe such strong magic will answer to a mortal, but without the moonclock, the Court will crumble. We will find ourselves suspended in an endless moment of sameness, forced to steal into the mortal world for a taste of change." His jaw clenched and he began to shake. "He wants to rip the border down, but . . ." The ground rippled and the green tang of magic filled the air, a scent like wood smoke and pine needles blended with blackberries and roses. It tingled in Lark's nose and chilled her skin.

Thorny vines wriggled from the pine needles, sharp leaves quivering as they uncurled.

Rook leaped to his feet, shoved the pie in his mouth, and ran away. The brambles sank back into the earth as abruptly as they'd appeared.

Lark stared at Nightbird in dismay. She still didn't know where the keyhole was or how to use the moonclock. "Tell me this, at least," she said to the raven. "Is Galin still alive?"

Nightbird bobbed his head twice and she took that as a yes. There was still hope, then. But for how much longer?

Appetite gone, she tossed him the rest of her food. He gulped bites down and took to wing while she ran back to the town square to find her parents.

"There you are! Ma's been worried frantic," Da said. "Let's get home and settle the horses. Tomorrow will be a long day."

Tomorrow night was the Wild Hunt. They were *all* running out of time.

TWENTY-ONE

The Wild Hunt

LARK STAYED UP too late that night unsuccessfully fidgeting with the moonclock, looking for a keyhole and trying to decipher how it worked. What if it could somehow *make* time rather than simply measure it? That might explain why it required a link with a mortal. . . . She examined the way the wheels fit together, studied the three hands.

Why was this the thing that would help Galin?

Every few moments she blinked and rubbed her eyes, terrified a Fae might steal a peek through them, until eventually falling asleep at her desk. She woke with a headache the next morning.

When she dragged herself out to the barn, she found an argument brewing.

Romin Brookings and Rik and Antonus Greensfeld all demanded the right to ride a shadowbred in the Wild Hunt despite failing to complete the Gauntlet course. Ma refused, standing firm even when they resorted to shouting threats.

"I am saving your lives," she told them, jaw clenched tightly, "whether you believe me or not."

"Fine!" Romin kicked the ground, scuffing his newly polished boots. "I'll ride my uncle's horse. Kestrel's fast and he likes to run."

"Please, Romin, remember the agreement you signed when I invited you to ride," Ma urged. "You promised to abide by my decisions. Wait and try the Gauntlet again next season. This is not your time."

"Romin, mortal horses can't keep up with the Wild Hunt!" Sage cried, leaning over a stall door. "Listen to the Horsemaven. No one questions your courage, but don't be a fluffheaded fool, especially not with this . . . this *Briar King* leading the Hunt!"

He flashed a rude gesture, spun on his heels, and stormed away. The other boys followed, spitting curses as they went.

"How many more reckless featherbrains are thinking the same?" Ma fretted.

While the shadowbreds spent the day resting, Lark went back to her room to experiment with the moonclock again. As Rook had remarked, her heart *did* feel like a clock counting down the minutes until Sage would ride the Wild Hunt. What if she couldn't figure it out in time?

She tried staring at it through her hagstone in case the keyhole was hidden by an illusion, but if it was the concealment was too strong to break that way. Then she tried chanting some of the charms Rook had taught her, before realizing that didn't make much sense since the moonclock had been designed and intended for use by a mortal. Why would a Brassman ancestor go to the trouble of hiding the keyhole with a *Fae* charm?

She chewed her lip and drummed her fingers on her desk. It was bound to her blood, but what if it needed a drop of Fae blood too? After all, there had to be some link between mortal energy and Fae magic. Though if that were the case, wouldn't Rook have said so?

Lark stood up to pace. The problem was, the Harvest King had clearly kept the existence of the moonclock quiet. Rook hadn't even known it required a key. What else was he missing?

When Sage came up to her room to take a brief nap, Lark dashed across the hall and flung her arms around her sister. "I've been trying to figure out a way to keep you and Galin safe," Lark cried, "but nothing works and—"

Sage laughed softly and hugged her back. "Don't fret, little bird. It will all turn out right, you'll see."

"But there's no guarantee that Galin will be joining the Hunt, and you can't ask the May Queen to help! The Briar King and his Thornguards—they're dangerous, Sage. I'm worried about you."

"The luckwitches made me a special finding charm to locate Galin if necessary and Reverie has her own sense about things. We'll be fine . . . if I get some rest before I ride."

By late afternoon Lark was no closer to solving the mystery of the moonclock, and the crushing weight of failure dragged at her feet as she slowly made her way to the barn.

The shadowbred riders gathered in the stable yard, checking tack and getting last instructions from Ma. "We've never had a Wild Hunt led by this Briar King," she warned. "You must keep your wits about you."

Lark chewed her lip, desperately wishing she had fixed the moonclock. Her gaze snagged on Kerigan Cormick's wide-eyed face. Beads of sweat glistened at his temples and above his tightened mouth. He nudged his horse closer to Sage and Ma. "I've changed my mind," he said in a low voice.

"Oh, but you *can't*," Ma told him grimly. "When you spilled your blood, you bound yourself to this Hunt. If you forfeit, you yield your freedom."

"What do you mean?" he asked, voice quivering.

"Should you choose not to ride, the Fae will take you as a thrall. You'll serve the Briar King or anyone he forces you to obey, for as long as it pleases him to do so. And when they get bored with you—and they will—you will be killed."

Kerigan's chin jerked and he gulped. "Very well. We can stick together, right? All we have to do is ride one end of the boundary to the other. Once we return to the standing stone, the obligation is fulfilled and we get our Faevors."

A wry laugh broke from Sage's throat. "It's that easy, eh? You think the Gauntlet and all the days of preparation are what . . . just for show? For fun?" She shook her head. "You're an even bigger fool than I thought." And she nudged Reverie away, joining Blunderknuckles and Cinder.

Ma mounted Legacy and trotted to the edge of the stable yard, shaking her head.

Pity uncurled in Lark's belly and she told him, "Don't take their growling personally. They're just concerned, that's all. Luck of the winds to you, Kerigan."

He nodded once and trotted away, melting into the shifting crowd of riders.

Ma gave a two-note whistle and all the shadowbreds pricked their ears. "May the luck of the winds carry you on, Hunters, and a smooth path bring you home at dawn," she called. "Follow me!"

She and Sage trotted out, leading the other riders to the square in the center of Tradewind Junction for the Blessing of the Hunt. Lark followed on foot with Da, the moonclock in her pocket.

As they walked through the last stretch of woods between the Mairen property and Tradewind Junction, they discovered that someone had collected antlers shed by bucks earlier in the season and tied them in the tree branches with white ribbon. Bundles of dried flowers and ivy hung from their points.

Da explained quietly, "The luckwitches must have sensed the White Stag's death and left a tribute. Or else the Elders have spread the word."

"Will another White Stag come to take his place, to lead this Wild Hunt?" Lark asked, a sudden blur of tears filling her eyes. "The wildkin need a new lord, don't they?"

Unless that had been the whole point of his killing.

"I don't know, little bird," he answered, voice grim. "I just don't know."

"What if—"

"Let's not borrow trouble." But he wore a frown between his brows.

Lark stifled a groan. Trouble was already here.

The town square was more crowded than Lark had ever seen it before and it took her and Da several minutes to spot Sage and Ma. Horses of every size and color jigged, spun, or pawed the ground. They snorted and whinnied while their riders laughed, yelled, and carried on.

"Someone's going to get kicked or stomped," Da fretted, tugging Lark out of the path of a spooking brown horse with four white legs.

"All these people really want to ride with the Hunt?" Lark was appalled at the sheer number.

Da rubbed his chin. "Some are brave enough to think they can help fix the border. Others . . . well, the lure of a magic prize is strong when you aren't used to living with the risks of that magic."

Lark hoped none of them would come to regret it. "Oh, there's Sage!" She pointed and grabbed Da's elbow as they shoved, squeezed, and sidestepped their way closer.

A horn blast sounded, the clear, brassy note hanging in the air until the Briar King and his Fae retinue appeared. The hickory bark Fae with an acorn cap and the moss-beard one were first, closely followed by the Briar King, his Thornguards, and the bearskin Huntmaster.

Lady Mist and her companions were nowhere in sight. What had happened to the envoy after the Welcome Feast? Had the Briar King harmed them?

And where was Rook? It was too late for Lark to fix the moonclock—her last hope had been begging Rook to ride beside Sage, to guard her and maybe guide her to Galin too. . . .

But despite standing on her tiptoes and craning her neck, she didn't glimpse him.

The Fae contingent climbed the steps of the pavilion, joined by Davina Wardspin. Her layered skirts were spring colors: pale green and gold, rose and cream, robin's-egg blue. Tiny copper beads flashed along the hem as she shifted her weight and bells chimed from the ribbon tied around her waist. She wore a brown shawl embroidered with satin blossoms, her braided hair woven with flowers and feathers. Long strands of beads looped her neck and glittering amulets hung between her breasts.

Luckwitches from across the Borderlands flanked her, all wearing long green gowns with ribbon sashes and spring blooms in their hair. After conferring quietly with Dame Wardspin, they formed a curving line.

None of them looked happy.

The milling crowd, however, continued laughing and shouting, lending a festival atmosphere to what should have been a sacred, serious moment. Lark waited for the Briar King to silence them, but he spread his arms and reveled in the chaos.

Dame Davina Wardspin tugged at her ceremonial shawl as the other luckwitches fidgeted nervously.

"Friends! Neighbors! Riders! *Hunters!*" the king finally called. "We gather for the Blessing of the Hunt, asking for luck and fortune to guide us and guard us on our wild ride. When dusk falls, we will gather by the standing stone"—he pointed to the giant granite boulder barely visible on the hill outside Junction limits—"to carry on the tradition of the Wild Hunt long established by the Accords. Together, we will ride the border."

The crowd gave a round of resounding cheers that startled some of the horses and led to further chaos.

The king grinned and went on, "Anyone who made their mark"—here his Huntmaster unrolled a scroll containing dozens of bloody thumbprints, prompting more applause and shouting—"will earn my Faevor should they ride all the way to dawn."

The response was an enthusiastic roar and fists thrust in the air.

"Let us get on with the Blessing of the Hunt!"

The Huntmaster stepped forward at a gesture from the

king and blew a long, high whistle. From beyond the edge of the square, behind the row of pines, came a chorus of baying, barking hounds. A moment later they burst into view, pouring through the crowd and diving beneath the bellies of the restless, prancing horses. They were accompanied by a figure in a black vest and red tunic, riding a shadowbred draped in crimson and carrying a silver whip.

Where was the May Queen's Mistress of Hounds?

As the pack of dogs swirled through the square, the terrifying new Master of Hounds cracked the whip and they all sank to their haunches. Some were white with black ears and splotches, others white with red markings. They were larger than the farm dogs commonly kept in the Borderlands, standing well above Lark's knees.

"The moment the sun slips below the horizon, we ride," the Huntmaster growled in a loud, rasping voice. "Our course will loosely follow the border, riding west to east."

But the Hunt was supposed to follow the course set by the White Stag. Lark glanced at Sage's resolute expression, knowing her sister well enough to recognize the concern in her eyes.

Dame Davina rapped a staff against the wooden planks of the pavilion floor until relative quiet sifted through the restless crowd. Stacked bracelets clinked on her wrists when she raised her hands and bells chimed around her ankles. The other luckwitches spread their arms, palms facing the ground.

Two Fae glided through the crowd and ascended the steps to the pavilion. They bowed slightly to the luck-witches and then stepped to the side. One of the Fae had gossamer wings hanging like a cape down her back and the other had golden antlers rising from a thatch of moss-colored hair. Swirls of gilt ink covered their dark skin and even from where she stood Lark sensed the power emanating from them.

In all the years she'd seen them appear like this, she'd never heard them speak. They seemed to be acolytes of the White Stag, who had protected the woods on both sides of the border for as long as anyone could remember.

Until his shocking death.

Lark held her breath, hoping another stag had risen to take his place. Maybe things weren't as dire as she feared.

As the two Fae joined hands, they began to sing a word-less melody that rose and fell like the wind in the trees or the tides of the sea. Their voices blended in effortless har-mony, magic shimmering in the air around them as their song summoned the White Stag to bless the Hunt.

But a White Stag did not appear.

Da rubbed Lark's back while she choked back tears. How could they all stand here cheering as their friends and fam-ily rode into danger? The Briar King and his Thornguards had threatened the peace of long tradition, the Twilight Court was crumbling, and the one thing that could have fixed things was a heavy, useless weight in her pocket.

She had failed everyone.

The Briar King—who appeared neither surprised nor upset at the absence of the Stag—raised his arms and cried, "I give this Hunt my blessing! And now, refresh yourselves and prepare to ride at dusk!"

As the sun sank, a parade of Hunters left town and started climbing the hill toward the standing stone. Lark had searched everywhere for Rook, assuming he would join the Wild Hunt, but she couldn't find him. A couple of Fae gave her strange looks as she passed and she wondered if they sensed the magic of the moonclock hidden in her pocket. She was grateful Da had insisted on accompanying her because his steady presence was reassuring.

"I know you said you're looking for a friend, little bird, but I don't think we're going to see them. It's getting late— let's find Sage before she has to ride out."

They made their way back to Ma and a moment later Sage trotted up on Reverie. She leaned from the saddle to ruffle Lark's hair and laughed when she grimaced. "Try not to fret. I'll be home by sunrise, and with any luck Galin will be with me. Remember? I have a special charm from the luckwitches."

Sage pulled something from her pocket and dangled it off the ends of her fingers. Lark glimpsed a short length of thin rope—she thought it was cut from the stuff Galin liked to use on his bait traps when fishing—and his favorite silver thimble, but her vision suddenly swam and she had to close her eyes.

She recognized the sensation and shuddered in revulsion. She could not let the Fae with her hair spy on her sister. Sage was in enough danger already—the Fae shouldn't know her plans. Lark pressed her hands to her eyes and imagined herself *pushing* the Fae out of her head. . . .

"Are you all right, little bird?" Sage asked.

Lark took a deep breath as the feeling passed and blinked up at her sister. One hair left.

She gripped Sage's ankle. "This isn't right."

"I know," Sage said. "But I'll be careful. Besides, it's my fault. . . . I should have been with him that night. This is my last chance to make it right."

"It's my fault too," Lark said. "I—" Her lips trembled, but of course she couldn't finish. *I couldn't fix the moonclock in time. I'm not the right person for the job.*

Blunderknuckles trotted up beside them. "Evening, Lark," he said, tipping his chin. "Sage, we'd better head out."

"I'll see you at dawn!" Sage said, then grinned at Blunderknuckles—oh, stars, was she *blushing* again?—and they rode after the others. At least Sage wasn't heading out alone, Lark thought. If Blunderknuckles could give her a reason to smile despite the danger, then . . . maybe he wasn't *too* clumsy.

It was hard to hear the first sounding of the horn over the noise of the crowd, but a shiver rippled across Lark's skin and she went still, straining her ears. Yes—there: a long, rolling blast on a hunting horn.

"Come on—let's find a place to watch," Ma urged, leading them away on her mare. Lark and Da jogged after her, down Trader's Row—mostly abandoned now that everyone was busy with Mayfair festivities—and through a gate in the town wall. They ran down the outer road, along the Snakesong River, until they reached the bridge. Instead of crossing, they left the cobblestone road and plunged through knee-high grass all the way to the crest of a rise overlooking the Junction. Opposite stood the tallest hill, with a massive stone pointing to the slowly darkening sky like a granite finger.

Legacy let out a long whinny and Ma settled her with a soft two-note whistle.

Lark spotted the Briar King in his shimmering black cloak, mounted on a tall black shadowbred. Silver embossed swirls of thorns decorated his horse's tack. He carried a gleaming hunting horn, and when he blew another long, clear note, clouds of luminous fog spilled from the end of it.

The dusk air filled with the scent of pine and blackberry, sage and clover.

Fae magic.

Lark's chest hurt. The absence of the White Stag was a shadow in her heart, and fear for her siblings clogged her throat.

The Huntmaster gave three short blasts on his own

horn, followed by one long note.

A pale glow rose in the trees outside the town, a shining mist seeping between the trunks. It poured along the ground in radiant swirls and eddies, and then a pack of hounds erupted from the woods. The baying hounds streamed down the hill and converged at a spot near the road with the new Master of Hounds.

Lark squinted to see better, but the dim silver light wasn't enough to hold back the coming of night.

A long line of Fae Hunters—riding shadowbred horses raised by generations of Mairens—rode past, two by two. Their cloaks billowed behind them as the horses trotted toward the pack of waiting hounds and the rest of the riders already on the hill.

A storm of wings swirled through the sky and Lark raised her chin to stare at them. Owls, ravens, crows, starhawks, even fuzzy little bats—they clouded the stars in curtains of feathered darkness. And there was Rook, perched unhappily on a shadowbred with Nightbird clinging to his shoulder.

"Look, there's Sage." Ma pointed and Lark's gaze followed her finger to find Sage and Brendan.

Rook, keep them safe! Please!

The Briar King raised his horn and blew another long, wailing note. Then he dug his heels into the belly of his horse. The shadowbred gelding reared up and pawed the air before plunging into a reckless gallop, scattering a group of onlookers who had gotten too close.

The rest of the Fae followed, yipping and screaming, laughing and shouting, cheering and calling, hooting and bellowing, singing and making such unearthly noise Lark's head ached with it.

Sage and the other mortals were swept up in the rush, their horses racing with the tide. Enveloped in that eerie glow, the Wild Hunt tore along the road and charged out of view . . . taking Lark's sister and her friend Rook with them.

Lark and her parents headed home in a preoccupied silence. After helping Ma and Sarai feed those shadowbreds not in the Hunt this year, and leaving fresh piles of hay and clean water to wait for the ones that were, Lark collapsed at the kitchen table and rested her forehead on her arms.

Da fixed a pot of lentils and roasted vegetables and Ma put a kettle on to boil. When the meal was ready, they ate quietly, lost in their own thoughts. Afterward, Lark cleaned the kitchen and Da stirred the fire on the hearth, coaxing it to a bright, cheery flame.

Lark curled up in a chair by the fire, tucking her legs beneath her. Her parents tried to talk her into going to bed, but how could she sleep knowing what was out there? How could she sleep listening for the drumbeat of hooves or the baying of hounds or the cries of some magical creature that had crossed the border and needed to be chased back where it belonged?

How could she sleep knowing her sister was riding,

knowing Galin wasn't safe? And—worst of all—knowing she had failed to get the moonclock working?

So they let her keep vigil by the fire, sipping tea and staring into the flames.

Would this Hunt restore the balance, return things to the way they had been before, even without the White Stag?

Lark didn't think so.

When she shivered, Ma pulled the patchwork protection quilt from her bed and laid it over her. "Sage won't be back until dawn. Are you *sure* you don't want to—"

"No. I can't sleep. I'm fine right here."

"All right. If you insist. Would you like another cup of tea?"

Lark gratefully nodded and held out her empty mug. "I've got a couple of mooncakes left too," Da said, passing her a plate.

She took a cake and nibbled it, though worry turned it to ash and sand in her mouth. "Who do you think this Briar King is?"

Her parents exchanged a look and then her mother shrugged. "We don't know. But the ways of the Fae are not for us to understand. We simply have to uphold the Accords and do our part to maintain the integrity of the boundary. In the end, that is all that matters."

"But if they've broken the Accords—"

"Lark, it's probably best if we don't discuss matters that don't concern us," her father said in a strained voice.

"But they *do* concern us and—"

A sudden rattle at the windowpane startled her so badly her hand shook and she splashed tea over the rim of her cup.

Da said, "Dark things wander the shadows tonight, Lark. We mustn't draw their attention."

She buried her face in the steam from her cup and swallowed her questions.

"I'm going to run out and check the horses in the barn again," Ma said.

Da asked, "Are Sarai and the boys coming back?"

"I told them to stay home and be safe tonight. We're too close to the border and I don't trust—"

Da held up a hand and Ma bit off the last of her remark. Then he turned to Lark. "I'll be right back, little bird. I'm going to help your mother."

"Do you want me to come too?"

"No . . . stay in the house. Finish your tea and rest."

Lark stared at the dregs of tea leaves and wild herb petals floating in her cup as the front door thumped closed. Wild Hunt nights were always intense, but at least with the May Queen or the Harvest King leading in the wake of the White Stag, there was comfort knowing that the Accords would be upheld. That mortals would be as safe as the rules could keep them.

The Briar King, however, seemed to break rules like twigs snapped for kindling.

Lark set her cup on a small side table and took the

moonclock from her pocket. To come so close only to fail at the last moment was a bitter frustration.

She turned the strange pocket watch over and over in her hands, feeling the thrum of magic she couldn't quite unlock. *Pay attention to the moon,* Rook had said. But why?

She dug through her pocket for the tiny silver key and clicked her tongue as she examined the case in the firelight yet again.

Where is the keyhole? What was she missing?

A moonbeam slanted through the window beside her and glinted off the silver case, sending strange shadows shifting across the shining metal surface. What had appeared slightly dull by daylight now gleamed brightly.

The sensation of waiting magic grew stronger.

Pay attention to the moon. . . .

Shifting in the chair, Lark held the mysterious clock in the white light of the moon and caught her breath as new shapes appeared: swirls and circles, stars and knotted triangles. She squinted at them in wonder, annoyed with herself for not understanding sooner.

It was, after all, called a *moon*clock.

She tilted the case, admiring the play of soft light over the silver, when a strange mark caught her eye.

It was dark and uneven, tiny and all but invisible beneath an embossed ivy leaf. But as she studied it, she was reminded of . . . a keyhole.

Heart thudding in her ears and fingers trembling, she

pressed the tiny silver key into the hidden slot and . . .

Something clicked.

A faint chime sounded at the edge of hearing, like the last echo of a harp string, and the moonclock began to hum. Biting the inside of her cheek, she slowly turned the key. One quarter turn, one half turn, three quarters . . .

And there was that odd prickle behind her eyes again, that feeling of split sight as someone else peered through her lashes. Lark gasped and closed her eyes. The Fae couldn't know she had gotten this far.

The door swung open and Lark dropped the moonclock and the key into her pocket. Da stepped in carrying a disgruntled calico cat. "I think it's a good idea to keep her close tonight," he said, setting Jinx down on the floor.

Jinx immediately fastened her green gaze on the window and hissed.

"What do you see?" Da hurried to it, peering out at the night.

But Jinx settled a second later, tail curled neatly over her front paws and ears perked. She met Lark's gaze and calmly licked her nose.

"I'm going to fix some cocoa to take out to the barn. Do you want some?" Da asked.

"No, thanks."

As he bustled around in the kitchen, Lark burrowed under the quilt. She would wait for him to leave and then try again as soon as she was certain the Fae couldn't use her hair to spy again. She'd paid with only three and that should have been the last, but what if the hairs were cut to offer more opportunities? Would they still work?

Sick with worry, she must have slipped into a shallow pool of sleep, dragged by a current of exhaustion despite her intentions to stay awake, because an irritated *mrow!* broke her doze as Jinx jumped in her lap sometime later.

Da had settled in a chair with a basket near his feet and a bright oil lamp close by. He'd selected a lilac gown and was ripping out the hem, humming softly to himself as he worked. "Da, thanks again for my dress. It was beautiful," she mumbled sleepily.

"Glad you liked it, little bird."

"How were the horses? You were gone awhile."

"Ruffled," he answered, scrubbing a weary hand through his hair. "But Dame Wardspin came by to check the protective charms in the barn rafters and Sarai decided to stay after all, so I think they'll make it through just fine. I've got some mending to do but I'll run out and check on them again in a while."

Jinx curled up in the folds of Lark's quilt, kneading her paws in the down-filled fabric and starting to purr. Lark stroked a finger under the cat's chin and smoothed her whiskers, grateful for the company. Could she risk pulling out the moonclock while Da was distracted with his mending, or should she wait a bit longer? Now that she had finally fixed it, she was desperate to find out what it did.

On the other hand, if it involved time it might be too dangerous to experiment while Da was in the room.

Outside the windows a furious baying suddenly erupted and goose bumps pebbled Lark's arms. Jinx stiffened, eyes going wide in the flickering firelight. The fur on her back bristled and her tail flicked side to side.

Da froze, tiny brass scissors suspended as his attention flew to the windows.

Thunder rumbled outside—no, Lark realized, not thunder. *Hoofbeats.*

The Hunt was *here.*

Jinx leaped from Lark's lap and ran under the chair, hissing and spitting. Da shoved the gown from his lap and lunged for the door.

"Da! You can't go out there!" Lark cried, frantic. If an ordinary Hunt was a rush of chaos, how much worse might this one be without the White Stag?

"Your mother—"

"She wouldn't want you to run out either! She's safe in the barn. You said yourself the luckwitch is there. The Hunt will ride past in a minute. . . ."

But the cacophony intensified. Baying hounds, whinnying horses, galloping hooves, blowing horns, shouting voices . . . and then an unearthly shriek rattled the windowpanes and sent sparks swirling across the hearth.

Blue smoke billowed from the fireplace and began to fill the room, and a moment later tiny cindersprites leaped into the air.

Jinx growled and retreated farther under her chair.

Da grabbed a broom and batted at the tiny soot-colored cindersprites, chanting charms before they burned down the house.

Lark pulled a copper bell from the hook by the door and rang it as hard as she could, but the sprites only laughed and darted to the curtains. The fabric singed where they touched it, threads of smoke curling beneath their clawlike fingers and toes. Their wings—wispy things like tattered fog—shook ash everywhere, leaving the acrid tang of burned coals hanging in the air.

"Grab the pail of water!" Da cried.

Lark raced to the sink and filled the tin pail with cold water. She ran back to him, holding out the sloshing bucket. He grabbed it and flung the contents as far as he could reach.

When the water hit a cindersprite, the Fae creature vanished in a puff of steam. After Da had extinguished at least a dozen of the tiny menaces, the rest flew back into the fireplace and swirled up the chimney.

Soot streaked Da's cheeks and the ends of Lark's hair smelled singed. Jinx peeked out from under the chair, but her nose twitched at the scent of smoke and she retreated again.

The sounds of the Hunt continued to rage outside, but

Lark and her father had enough distraction putting out smoldering embers in the curtains, on the chair cushions, even along the quilt Lark had been curled under just minutes earlier.

"How did they get in?" she gasped, smacking yet another spark with a wet cloth. "That's never happened before, has it?" Although the Hunt had certainly come close to their home in the past, the May Queen or Harvest King led the riders away before any damage could occur, chasing mischief from the house.

"Well, we are near the boundary," Da said, wiping a streak of ash across his forehead with a grimy hand. "And the Stag isn't leading them."

But Lark wondered if the moonclock had drawn them.

"I thought we were better prepared." Da threw on a cloak, saying, "I'm going out to the barn. Stay here and calm Jinx down."

"But the Hunt is still too close!"

"And what do you think the shadowbreds left in the barn will do knowing their kin run outside? I need to make sure your mother is safe! Stay put!" he called, and the door slammed.

Lark ran to the front windows, peering through the dim glass to see that Da made it to the barn unharmed. At least she had a chance to try the moonclock again. "Watch out, Jinx. You should probably wait in my bedroom. . . ."

She was just turning away and reaching for the key when

a tide of roiling black swept past the house—dozens of horses, moonlight gleaming on their sweat-slick skin, racing the night wind. The riders were beautiful and terrible—Fae with gilt-tipped antlers or shimmering wings, skin like tree bark or smooth as marble. She could make out the Briar King and his Thornguards in the tumult, mortals trailing in a ragged line as hounds bayed in the distance.

She pressed her nose to the pane, moonclock temporarily forgotten as she looked for Sage and Galin and tried to locate Rook in the plunging rush.

Where were they? For a moment she was tempted to run outside for a better view, but the last time she'd snuck out of the house she had seen the Harvest King fall from his horse. Too much was at stake tonight—the best way to help her siblings was to solve the puzzle of the moonclock, not dash outside into danger.

As if responding to her thoughts, the moonclock suddenly buzzed in her hand, flashing in the moonlight that spilled through the window. Lark gripped the tiny key, slipped it back in the keyhole, and finished winding the clock: another quarter turn, half turn . . .

Click.

For one breathless instant, the world lurched. The moon bobbed in the sky like a buoy on the ocean and Lark blinked as stars burst in her mind. Magic poured through her body, humming in her blood with the promise of endless possibility, infinite potential. . . .

And then, between one heartbeat and the next, the sensation faded. She was just a mortal girl, leaning against a misted window, holding a cold silver pocket watch in her sweating palm.

Jinx let out a soft *mrow* and stropped her ankles. Though relieved that the cat hadn't gotten caught in a timeslip, Lark was too confused to be comforted. She'd felt . . . *something* . . . when she wound the moonclock, but what had changed? Had anything actually happened, or had she just imagined it?

All her hopes crumbled like ash in a dead fire and she nearly hurled the moonclock against the wall in disappointed anger.

She might have done it too if she hadn't heard Da's boots clomping on the porch just then. Wiping bitter tears away with her sleeve, she dropped the moonclock in her pocket and knelt on the floor to bury her face in the cat's soft fur.

Jinx licked her nose with a raspy tongue and a thought suddenly struck Lark with such startling clarity she laughed aloud. Of course the moonclock hadn't changed anything! She was on the mortal side of the border, in a world where time was woven into the very fabric of life.

What would the moonclock do in the Fae realm?

TWENTY-TWO

Missing

SUNLIGHT PRIED LARK'S eyes open the next morning. She blinked and rubbed a knuckle across them as cobweb dreams gradually cleared. A surge of optimism sent her pulse leaping. The night had ended, the Hunt was over— and maybe Sage had succeeded in bringing Galin back with her.

After all, Lark had repaired the moonclock. She'd put it together, found the key, and wound it. What else had Rook expected her to do with it?

"Sage? Galin?" Tossing off the quilt, Lark swung her legs down from the chair and stretched. She wished she'd been able to stay awake to welcome the Hunters back to the barn. Untangling her hair with her fingers, she padded into the kitchen half expecting to see her sister and brother at the table eating griddle cakes drenched in maple syrup or sweet cream.

But the house was empty.

No laughter and conversation. No Sage, no Galin.

Lark swallowed her unease. Sage must still be in the barn caring for Reverie. The Hunt took longer than usual, that's all. Especially if Sage had followed her charm to find Galin. . . .

She threw a change of clothes on, dropped the moon-clock and key back in her pocket, and lurched out the front door to blink like an owl in the bright citrus sunshine. Squinting, she stepped off the porch and jogged toward the stable yard.

As she neared the barn, muffled voices thrummed in the morning air and a wave of relief swept away the residue of her anxiety, lifting her spirits even higher.

"Good morning, Hunters!" she called, swinging through the open barn doors.

But instead of a tired and giddy group of Hunters, Lark saw her parents, the healer Netty Greenwillow, and the three Elders standing in a cluster of concerned friends and family. Brendan's older brother paced the aisle, pounding his fist against his thigh and agitating the horses.

The scuff of hooves pawing straw, the rustle of shad-owbreds circling nervously, the *shushshushshush* of swishing tails filtered through the worried murmurs and tense con-versation of the people clogging the barn. Even Jinx was upset, lashing her tail from her perch on one of the rafters as she kept a wary eye on everyone.

But six empty stalls gaped forlornly.

"They're not back yet?" Lark asked, the words tasting of ash and despair.

No one answered. They were too wrapped up in their discussion to notice her.

"We saw hoofprints all the way out by Hogman's Mill," Elder Brassman was saying. "But it's hard to tell which way they went from there. Ground's too rocky. I sent a runner out to fetch Tracker Joniss. He might see something we missed."

"How do you know the Hunt passed that way?" a stout man in rumpled velvets asked, the hook of an argument sharpening the question. "The mill is at least a league away from the Fae border, isn't it? Don't you think it's more likely that someone simply rode there to drop off grain or pick up flour?"

He wasn't a local, then. Lark leaned forward and noticed the sigil embroidered on his chest: a duck standing on a fish. This must be Lord Tevin Brookings of Mossbrook Place, father of Romin.

Da shook his head. "Hogman's Mill is always closed during Mayfair and doesn't open until the morning after the Hunt, once all the riders have returned. Too much risk of mischief otherwise—the Fae love to make messes of the millworks. No one rode that way for honest business, I assure you."

"Besides," Elder Brassman said, "these hoofprints looked to be coming from dozens of horses galloping at once, and there were pawprints from a pack of hounds."

"What were they doing all the way out there, though? The border swings deeper into the woods, away from the river," Brendan Forth's mother, Mistress Lillen, cried.

Elder Farstorm leaned on her staff, face weary. "They may have been forced to range farther afield to chase down all the rogue Fae and wildkin. We've sent runners out scouting the traditional paths, but keep in mind the Wild Hunt is not a pleasure ride along a marked trail and does not follow a parade route. They go where the White Stag and the hounds lead—well, where the hounds lead, anyway—and the hounds follow their noses, not a map."

"I know *that*," Lillen Forth snapped. "Even so, the sun is fast approaching midmorning and they should have been here hours ago."

"Until we know how far they rode, we have no reason to panic," Elder Heartstone said. "We must wait for the scouts to report back."

"But I heard three bodies have already been recovered near Sycamore Point," someone Lark didn't recognize said.

Lark's heart sank like an anchor stone and she leaned against the wooden wall. This was precisely what they had feared.

"Bold fools on carriage horses. We tried to warn them," Elder Brassman said sadly. "It grieves me deeply."

"My cousin said they heard shrieks and howls out by Goodwin's Gap and her niece claimed she saw the pack of hounds running past Oakhill. If that's the case, it could be well after noon before we see them," someone else said.

"And old man Twyll told me the horses thundering past his place just after midnight nearly rattled the whole cabin down around his ears. Claims a window cracked, though his eyes are getting dim so could be he just never noticed before," a man in a sheepskin vest added.

"But he lives up by Dodger Creek! The Hunt never goes that far into the Borderlands," a red-faced man with a triple-arrow sigil protested, wringing his hands. Gold rings gleamed on his fingers and Lark suspected he was the father of Artur Bowman.

One of the women said, "Without the White Stag, there's no telling how far they may have roamed."

"Or if they'll return at all," another remarked darkly.

Elder Rowana Farstorm thumped her staff on the ground, startling the remaining horses. Jinx hissed and streaked out of sight. "We will know more when we speak to the runners. Panic is not productive."

"Well," Ma said, tightening the leather lace tied around the end of her braid. "I'm not going to stand around waiting while my daughter is still out there somewhere. I've already lost one child to this iron-blasted and blood-damned Hunt. I refuse to lose another. I'm taking one of the horses out to find them. Lukis can stay here and feed them griddle cakes if by some chance they return before I do."

Da folded her in a hug and rested his chin on top of her head. "River, I know you want to go after Sage, but we must stop and think. There was a purpose to all of this, some plan of the Briar King. The best way to save our children is to discover what it is and then respond accordingly. Racing out to the border isn't going to solve anything—think of the weeks you spent looking for Galin. We already *know* where they both are. The challenge now is to find a way to bring them home."

"Of course we know where they are! I'll ride through the Oak Gate before it closes and confront the king myself if I have to," she growled.

"I'll go with you!" Lark blurted. She would take the moonclock and explain everything to Ma on the way. She had been keeping secrets for too long.

"Lark!" Da rubbed his forehead. "We thought you were still sleeping."

Ma tugged her braid. "I appreciate your courage, but this is something I need to do. It's too dangerous for you."

Lark took a breath to argue but Elder Rowana thumped her staff, and worried silence sifted through the barn. "Horsemaven River, hasn't it struck you that the Fae might have targeted your family for some reason? You know the Fae love tricks and traps; perhaps their purpose was to bait you. No one else handles the shadowbreds as well. . . ."

"I'm not leaving my children on the Other Side again!" Ma cried.

Elder Amalia Heartstone laid a soothing hand on her shoulder. "If we can't locate a Fae representative on our side, I agree we should discuss sending *someone* through the Oak Gate to confront the Fae. They owe us answers. But we must not be hasty. If we antagonize this new king, who can predict how he might retaliate?"

"Isn't that what the Accords were *for*?" someone snorted. "To protect us from their whims and follies? At this point they owe us more than answers."

Elder Brassman rubbed his chin thoughtfully "There's a risk that the timeslip might make passage through the Oak Gate impossible for a mortal, but if the luckwitches will help stabilize the flow before the border closes—"

"But I can help!" Lark started to say.

Just then Journey flung her head up and snorted. A moment later Lark heard it too: the clatter of hooves and the huffing breath of a winded horse.

"Sage?" Lark and her father both said at the same time. Sharing a relieved grin, they bolted from the barn.

But it wasn't Reverie they saw approaching. It was Inka, carrying a slumped rider—Jinniver Tennet.

Inka trotted to the barn doors, slightly favoring her right front leg. Her skin was sweat-soaked and mud-splattered, brambles snagged in her tail.

Jinniver had finished the Gauntlet in fourth place, but now she could barely balance in the saddle. Her glassy eyes were dazed and unfocused. Dirt smudged her cheeks and a thin red welt along her neck showed where a whip-thin branch must have slapped her as she rode. Her vest and tunic were sweat-damp and stained.

When Inka staggered to a stop, Jinniver's cramped hands struggled to release the reins. Even from where she stood, Lark could see the blisters on her fingers.

"What happened?" someone cried. "Where are the others? Why did you leave them?"

Jinniver closed her eyes and swallowed, a grimace of pain twisting her features.

"*Where are they?*" the restless crowd demanded.

Mistress Greenwillow shoved her way through the people pressing close to the exhausted mare as Ma gently eased Jinniver's clawed hands open and took the reins. "You rode well," she said, "but we need to know—"

"I'm sorry," Jinniver whispered. "It was all a trick. We were ambushed." Her chin hit her chest and she sagged sideways in the saddle. She would have fallen if two men hadn't lunged to catch her.

"Carry the girl inside," the healer directed. "It's likely strain, stress, and exposure, but I need to examine her."

Ma led Inka into the barn. "Get the liniment, Lark, and the jar of meadowbright paste. And some leg wraps. Luckily Inka will recover quickly. Maybe the others are still on their way." Hope flickered in her voice.

Lark couldn't imagine what Inka and her rider must have been through. Shadowbreds were far stronger, swifter, and sturdier than ordinary horses. For the mare to look this rough, for her to be limping and sore . . . the run with the Hunt must have been brutal.

Working quickly, Lark and her mother pulled off the mare's tack and sponged her with cool water. While Ma applied the meadowbright paste as a poultice to ease the swelling in Inka's sore leg, Lark rubbed her muscles with an herbal liniment to soothe away aches.

Inka dropped her head and sighed. "Poor girl is completely ragged," Ma said.

"How far do you think they rode?" Lark stroked Inka's neck.

"Farther than they should have." Ma finished wrapping the mare's leg and led her to her stall.

Too tired to eat, Inka slurped some water and shuffled to the back corner to sleep.

Lark kept expecting Reverie and Sage to trot in and her gaze flew to the barn doors at every sound, but after a few minutes she followed Ma to the house to see if Jinniver could tell them anything.

She was still unconscious. Mistress Greenwillow said, "I managed to get a little tincture of raspberry leaf, willow bark, and elderberry in her, but she hasn't revived enough to speak. Could be a head injury, though she has no other bruises to make me think she fell from the horse. I did find something strange, however."

The healer lifted Jinniver's arm and turned her hand, pointing out a livid ring of cuts and scrapes around her wrist. "I pulled out a thorn. Didn't recognize it. Feels Fae." She carefully set Jinniver's arm down and covered her with a light cotton sheet.

"Poisonous?"

"Possibly. The luckwitch is on her way to have a look."

Ma clicked her tongue and turned away. Lark could read the worry on her face.

Elder Farstorm said, "I'll send some of them"—she gestured at the people muttering around the kitchen table— "out to walk the trade roads in case the other riders turn up. Perhaps someone has noticed a sign. The rest of us should go to the Oak Gate. Perhaps we'll find the emissary there."

"I don't like this. I still think I should ride across—" Ma began.

"It's a good idea," Da said firmly. "We need to find out what's happened in the Court, from the Fae. Not by wandering into a potential trap and getting caught when the border closes. Lark, wait here in case any other riders return. Netty, Dame Wardspin, you'd better stay too. They may need care."

TWENTY-THREE

Unexpected Allies

WHILE MISTRESS GREENWILLOW pounded herbs for Jinniver with her mortar and pestle and Davina Wardspin whispered charms, Lark drifted back to the barn. She didn't know what to do. Her siblings were still missing and she couldn't shake the thought that it was her fault, her failure.

Jinx slinked around the corner and stropped her ankles, purring. Lark perched on an upturned bucket and let the calico cat jump in her lap. "They have to come back, right?" she said, rubbing the spot beneath Jinx's soft chin.

Closing her eyes, Jinx raised her chin, whiskers quivering with the force of her rumbling purr. Suddenly, her green eyes flashed open and she sprang from Lark's lap, streaking back into the shadows.

Hoofbeats drummed the ground and Lark's spirits soared. Someone else had arrived!

She ran to the barn doors and watched a group of

shadowbreds galloping toward the stable yard in a blur of smoke and pounding legs, riders hunched low in the saddles. As they approached, she checked off their names in her head: Brendan, then Artur and Kerigan, and there was Julienna. . . .

Sage wasn't with them. Neither was Galin.

Lark swallowed a sob. Somehow she'd known even before they made it back to the barn that her siblings wouldn't be returning.

"I'm so sorry, Lark. I tried to—" Blunderknuckles cried, jumping from the saddle when he saw her.

She ignored him, focusing instead on one task at a time: pulling tack, brushing horses, checking hooves, rubbing liniment on tendons, sending riders to the house for the healer to examine . . . until Blunderknuckles gave up trying to talk to her and went inside as well.

As soon as she was alone in the barn, she took the moonclock and the key from her pocket. She was desperate— Rook had said it would save Galin and he couldn't lie. Maybe she should wind it again and see what happened.

Only when she looked at it, she couldn't see the keyhole. She guessed where it was and tried inserting the key, but it didn't work. She needed moonlight.

Lark tucked the moonclock away and headed for the house, a daring plan taking shape.

If she waited until nightfall, it would be too late for Sage and Galin. The border would close.

She couldn't wait another six moonturns to save her siblings.

And besides, she suspected the only way the moonclock would truly work was if she took it to them. It didn't seem to function in the mortal world, but in the Fae realm she might finally see what it was meant to do.

Rook had guessed—known?—as much, hadn't he? Maybe that was part of the reason he had taught her so many defensive charms. Perhaps he had been preparing her for this all along.

Filled with resolve, she entered her house and found the riders sprawled on blankets or the couch near the hearth. Dame Wardspin and two other luckwitches sat at the kitchen table, talking quietly with the healer.

Without a word, Lark went to her room to gather the things she might need.

"What are you doing, Lark? Where are you going?" Blunderknuckles asked, following her to the threshold of her doorway.

She spun on her heel, emotions spilling out of her control. "You left my sister behind! How could you ride off and *leave* her? You're a coward, Blunderknuckles Forth!"

Slamming her bedroom door in his face, Lark grabbed her wool traveling cloak, softest boots, a small purse of coins and glass marbles for bargaining, her pouch of tools, and a flint fire starter from Da. She already carried a hagstone and thread, feathers and herbs and salt.

Pulse galloping in her ears, she flung her door open, shoved Blunderknuckles out of the way, and clattered down the stairs.

He fell back a step but caught up with her in the hall, taking her by the wrist. "We were tricked, Lark, else I never would have let her go," he said quietly. "I swear to you by my blood, bones, and breath. And I swear I'll go with you to find her."

What did he mean, *tricked*? "I don't need your help. Get out of my way."

He dropped her hand. "You might believe I'm a dunder-headed fool, Lark Mairen, but if you think I'm going to sit around your house doing nothing while your sister is trapped on the Other Side then you're a bigger fool than me."

"Children, your tea is ready!"

"This is none of your business," Lark told him. "Stay here and rest. Drink Mistress Greenwillow's tea before she has conniptions."

He scowled at her, miserable and determined. "If you don't let me in on your plan, I'll tell them you're trying to sneak out to find Sage. How far do you think you'll get then?"

"You wouldn't!" she gasped.

"You would do anything for your sister, I know. But guess what? *So would I.* Anything except waiting here like a useless lump. We go together," he insisted. "Besides, I'm the last one who saw her."

"Where? Tell me what happened!"

"Only if you take me along."

Lark sighed. Stars knew she would need help to rescue Sage and Galin, but was it fair to drag someone else into danger? And did that help have to come from *Blunderknuckles*? "We could get in serious trouble," she warned.

"Sage is gone. This so-called Briar King has taken the Twilight Court, and on our side of the border there's talk of salt and iron. Aren't we already in trouble?"

She barked a grim laugh. "True enough. But I don't know what we'll be getting into. I'm not even sure we'll be able to cross the border . . . or if we'll be able to return." She pressed her lips together for a second to keep them from trembling. When she said it out loud it sounded absolutely impossible. "You *really* don't have to do this."

"Yes, I do."

When Lark hesitated he stepped toward the kitchen. "Shall I tell them what you're up to . . . ?"

"All right! You can come with me," she blurted. "We'll hurry out before—"

"Brendan?" one of the luckwitches suddenly called. "Tell us again what you experienced on the Hunt. I'm making a record. . . ."

"Give me just a moment," he begged Lark. "When they're distracted we can slip away."

Lark considered leaving him behind—he was just the diversion she needed—but the look in his eyes wiped the impulse from her mind. She'd already told him he could come along. She wasn't about to let Blunderknuckles make her a liar, and she needed to hear what he had experienced.

"We have to leave as quick as we can," she warned.

"I know."

"Brendan?" the luckwitch called. "Lark?"

"Coming!" he answered, raising a brow in Lark's direction. She sighed and nodded.

Lark rolled up her cloak and tucked it in the cabinet under the stairs with her boots, then followed Brendan into the kitchen. Netty Greenwillow handed her a steaming mug of tea. Lark sniffed her cup—chamomile and mugwort to make her drowsy—and set it on the table untasted.

"Brendan, we need to record your story. Describe the Hunt," Dame Wardspin said, a feather quill poised over a curling sheet of parchment.

"It seemed like a traditional Hunt at first, although without the White Stag. The Briar King led us along the border, faster than I'd ever ridden before. The hounds chased out the sort of rogue Fae and wildkin we expected: a stone-goblin near the old ruins, a pack of toadriders, and then a boggart thinking he could hide in a rotten log. They fled to the Fae realm when they saw us coming, and I figured the chase was just for show. Only . . ."

He swallowed and ran a hand through his hair. "He took us across the Borderlands, weaving between both the Fae and the mortal worlds. The Fae . . . the Thornguards . . .

they weren't just chasing wildkin back over the border. They *killed* them. And then . . ."

He choked and Mistress Greenwillow poured him a steaming cup of tea too. His smelled of feverfew and chicory, willow bark and elderberry. Something for pain and agitation. "Drink that. The rest of your tale can wait," she said. She scowled at Lark, gaze sliding pointedly to the cup Lark had ignored.

Lark bit her lip. The rest *could not* wait. She and Brendan needed to leave.

Brendan gulped his tea, wincing at the steam and—Lark guessed—at the taste. When he had finished all but the dregs he passed it back to Mistress Greenwillow and said, "Then the king led us to a pixie grove in the Fae realm. It was the most beautiful place I've ever seen—silver birches in beds of bluebells and violets, with tree houses built high in their branches. And bells—tiny wooden bells—hanging from every limb so the wind made a sound like . . . like a forest chuckling. Everything glowed. . . .

"I hadn't expected the Hunt to take us so far over the border, and most of the mortal horses balked. A couple of the king's Thornguards peeled away from the main pack then, leading their riders on a different course. I . . . I don't know what happened to all of them." He wiped his eyes with a shaking hand.

Dread cooled on Lark's skin. She'd thought Brendan clumsy and awkward, but she shouldn't have doubted his courage or called him a coward. He was practically vibrating with fear and shock, and yet he was prepared to cross the border again just to help Sage.

He continued, "We rode beneath the largest tree and a pixie with brilliant green wings peered over the edge of the platform. 'The Hunt has no passage here,' she said, and I remember the anger and surprise on her face.

"'I am the Briar King,' he said, 'and I take the Hunt wheresoever I choose!' She fanned her wings and cried, 'Until the White Stag recognizes your authority and blesses your crown, you are no king of ours!' I think those were her words. And that's when he ordered one of his men to shoot her with a silver arrow. She tumbled from her perch, and the air filled with the screams of a dozen voices at the far edge of hearing. Even the trees seemed to shriek."

Brendan rubbed his hands together, scraping the knuckles as if to wash away the filth of his memories. "He killed her in her own home, before her own people," he said, voice like midnight. "And then he slung her body over the back of his horse and said that we had fresh prey for this Hunt. He made us ride through all the pixie groves, and he killed one from each clan. Then he took them and—"

Horror and sympathy knotted Lark's stomach. "Oh, Brendan . . . ," she breathed.

He closed his eyes. "This wasn't really a Hunt at all. It was . . . a massacre. Innocent Fae with the courage to defy their new king cut down like weeds. . . . I told Sage we should ride back home, leave the Hunt to its wicked chase. But she was afraid that if we broke away from the pack the Briar King would come back here and do something . . . do something terrible. She said we needed to keep looking for Galin, needed to see it through."

Lark smiled through tears. That sounded like Sage.

Dame Wardspin's feather quill scratched across the parchment, whisking cages of ink to capture every detail of his experience.

"One of the hounds split off and the Briar King told us the dog scented some harmless wildkin—a rabbit or fox or doe with a glimmer of magic—and he ordered us to chase it back across the border. After what we had just witnessed, it seemed a relief to do something so simple."

"That's what the Wild Hunt is *supposed* to do," one of the other luckwitches said with a frown.

Brendan nodded sadly. "Just so. Anyway, we followed the hound until we realized it was heading away from the border, into the Fae realm. Sage suggested we use the opportunity to look for Galin instead, since we hadn't seen him with the Hunt. The other Gauntlet racers agreed, so we turned aside and tried to follow her charm. It led us into a valley and then it quit spinning, as though the trail had simply . . . ended. While we rested the shadowbreds and discussed what to do next, a whistle sounded and a rider appeared on the ridge. Sage recognized Galin and kicked her mare up a rock outcrop to reach him." He rubbed the back of his neck.

"I followed her, but at the same time another Galin whistled from deeper in the valley, and then a third from a hill on the other edge," he continued. "We scattered, all chasing different illusions. By the time we realized what was happening, we were swallowed in an unnatural fog."

He clenched his fists. "I believed Sage was with me. We couldn't see each other, but I heard her voice. . . . I thought I was right beside her. Until we finally rode out of the mist a few leagues from here and I discovered that she was gone." He turned red-rimmed eyes to Lark. "I would *never* have left her on purpose."

"How did you get back here?" Lark asked.

"We gave the shadowbreds their heads, just as your mother told us to do if we found ourselves in trouble. They carried us home."

One of the other riders started moaning and Netty Greenwillow bustled through the kitchen, boiling a fresh kettle of water and mixing new herbs. The pungent scent of yarrow and ginger filled the room. The luckwitches huddled at the end of the table, speaking softly.

"What happened to Galin, then?" Lark asked quietly. "Was one of the figures really him, or were they all just illusions? Did you see where they went?"

"No, but I might be able to find the last place I saw Sage,

and then . . ." His whisper trailed away, because neither of them could guess what might happen next. They just knew they had to try.

And Lark hoped the moonclock would work its magic.

They watched the adults, waiting for the right moment to sneak away. . . .

Then someone burst into the house shouting about an injured rider found on the narrow bank of the Snakesong River. The healer grabbed her satchel, told the luckwitches to keep an eye on the riders, and dashed out the door.

Lark motioned for Brendan to wait while she took advantage of the disturbance to slip into the pantry behind the kitchen. Ignoring the flutter of fear in her belly, she filled an empty flour sack with a couple of apples, a packet of dried cherries, a hard round of cheese, a loaf of bread, dried meat, and some potatoes that could be roasted over a fire. She wasn't sure how long they'd be in the Fae realm, but eating Fae food was dangerous.

After a few minutes Brendan joined her. "They're preoccupied."

Lark handed him another empty flour sack. "Then we'd better hurry."

"What do we need?" he asked, eyeing the shelves.

She handed him supplies and he carefully packed them inside. She said, "There's a lantern and a medical kit we can take from the barn, and a couple of spare blankets. I'm just not sure how long we'll be, and . . ." The enormity of what she intended to do crashed over her like a tidal wave and she swayed beneath the cold wash of doubt. What did they need? Luck, courage, determination, strength—but you couldn't pack those.

"If I run back to my house for some things, will you wait for me?"

Lark met his worried gaze. "I will wait for you—but be quick! We've already dawdled too long. Time passes differently in the Fae realm, and we still have to get through the timeslip. Remember Miles Ryebrush? Stayed out too late one Hunt night and stumbled through an opening in the border. He managed to make it home before the Gate closed, but he aged twenty years in the process."

"I know. I'll be right back." Brendan touched three fingers to his forehead in a promise before slipping out of the pantry.

Lark twisted the copper ring on her finger and swallowed a surge of wild terror. The only way she could think to fix everything was to break the most important rule of all: *Never look for an entrance into the Fae realm. Never go to the Other Side.*

But that's where her siblings were. That's where Rook was. And she would go anywhere, do anything, to make sure they were safe.

PART FOUR

The Twilight Court

— TWENTY-FOUR —

The Other Side

LARK KNEW SHEER desperation and determination didn't make much of a plan, but she had the moonclock and she had Rook's friendship and now she had Blunderknuckles too. She had to believe that would be enough.

She just hoped Rook was still all right. Blunderknuckles had described a horrible Hunt . . . what had it been like for Rook?

Fighting back her trepidation, she hefted the two flour sacks of food and wondered how she would explain them if anyone asked. But she needn't have worried. By the time she stepped out of the pantry, Jinniver had started raving about briar thorns and mothwings and everyone in the house was busy calming her.

After grabbing her cloak and lacing her boots, Lark ducked out the door and hurried to the barn. Inside, she refilled all the horses' water buckets and gave them extra hay.

She had just retrieved a medical kit from the tack room—containing a pot of salve, a roll of linen for a bandage, and some healing herbs and charms—and lifted a small lantern when she heard hoofbeats.

"Sage?" she cried, hope blooming as she rushed outside.

It was Reverie—but riderless.

Lark's disappointment swelled like a thunderhead until it burst in a storm of fear and fury. "Where is she?" she demanded of the mare. "Why did you just leave her? You were supposed to keep her safe!"

Reverie hung her head and snorted silver mist, then shook her mane until the few remaining copper charms clinked with a dismal chime.

Lark stamped her foot. "You and Whimsy both *failed*. You left my brother and sister on the Other Side. How could you?"

A scream rose in her throat and she had to swallow swallow swallow to keep it from breaking her wide open. She couldn't let anyone in the house hear or they'd come looking for her, see her packs, and guess what she was about to do, but the cost of keeping the secret was the taste of pain.

Reverie flicked her ears, her skin quivering. An air of exhausted dejection hung over her, but Lark was too angry for sympathy.

"You're *part magic*," she growled. "What good did that do my sister? All that means is that you can't be trusted.

You and Whimsy should never be allowed to carry a rider again."

In fact, no shadowbred should carry a rider again, as far as Lark was concerned. For one wild second she was tempted to open the barn doors and set them all free—let them all run back to the Fae realm, where they belonged.

"Lark, it's not her fault. Look at her legs." Brendan's gentle voice startled her. He wore a pack on his back and a brown cloak tossed over one shoulder.

"You shouldn't sneak up on people," she snapped.

"Look at her. She's not to blame. She barely escaped."

Scowling, Lark scanned the shadowbred—and her anger evaporated as she finally noticed the bleeding wounds ringing the mare's legs. "Oh, Reverie! I'm so sorry," she murmured, bending forward to examine the lacerations. "I didn't notice. . . ."

Rie's skin was torn and ragged just below her front knees and around her back fetlocks, and Lark discovered thorns still stuck in the cuts. An image of the Harvest King's shadowbred turning to smoke and shadow last fall flashed before her eyes and she swayed unsteadily. Brendan caught her by the arm. "Easy there," he said.

"I yelled at her. I told her it was her fault. . . ." Lark murmured, running her hand down Reverie's legs so she could pluck out the thorns as carefully as possible.

"I'm sure she understands," he said softly, lifting off the

saddle and removing the mare's bridle.

Reverie snuffled Lark's hair, her whiskers tickling Lark's neck.

Lark led her to her stall and smoothed ointment on her injuries. "I don't have rose petals, I'm afraid, but I'll grab you some clover." She knew she needed to hurry, but she owed Reverie an apology first.

Blinking back tears, she settled the mare in her stall before picking a handful of clover from a patch near the gate. "I'm sorry I shouted at you," she said, offering Reverie the sweet stems. "It's not your fault. I'm just scared and upset, but I shouldn't have taken it out on you. Don't worry, brave girl. I'll find Sage and fix things."

Somehow.

Rie lipped Lark's palm, munching the clover, and then folded her legs to rest. Lark wiped her face on her sleeve and joined Brendan outside the barn. "Are you sure about this?" she asked him.

"Yes. I'm glad you didn't leave without me."

"Told you I wouldn't!"

He shrugged. "Just happy you didn't, that's all."

She handed him the second sack of food. "Ready?"

"Are you?"

No. "Yes," she said. Her insides wobbled like huckleberry jelly but her voice was clear and firm.

She had to do this. Galin and Sage needed her.

It was a terrifying thing, to feel like someone's last hope. But it was even worse to feel like everything was her fault. If she had just fixed the moonclock in time, or prevented Sage from riding . . .

Lark glanced at the sky. The sun was too close to midday. There was just over half a day left before dusk.

Once the moon rose, she'd have a chance to use the moonclock—assuming she could figure out how. But there was a chance she might get caught in the Fae realm like Sage and Galin too.

Of course, time did odd things on the Other Side. What if the moon *didn't* rise?

Well, some worries weighed too much to carry all at once. *Even things that look impossibly broken can be fixed, one bit at a time*, she reminded herself.

She sped up, leading Blunderknuckles through the stable yard and out a small gate between two of the paddocks. They ran across the hayfield, satchels thumping their backs, and skirted the edge of a blackberry thicket. Lark showed him where to duck under a screen of cedar trees and they emerged on the trail that led up to the orchard.

She paused to catch her breath and wipe a sheen of sweat from her forehead. The day was warm and golden, but she took no joy in it. "Are you *certain* this is what you want to do? We might get trapped when the moon rises. . . ."

"I wouldn't be here if I wasn't sure. Lead on."

Lark straightened her shoulders and adjusted her pack. "All right then. I don't think anyone could have seen us from the house, but let's hurry."

"Where do you plan to cross? The Oak Gate?" he asked, jogging to keep up.

"No . . . my parents and the Elders are there, hoping to meet with the Fae emissary or a representative. But if the border isn't sealed, we should be able to cross anywhere. I'm thinking we'll go through by the waymarker."

It was as good a place as any to break into the Fae realm.

She couldn't believe they were about to break into the Fae realm.

The wind suddenly shifted, carrying the sound of voices coming up the path behind them—scouts or trackers. "Follow me!" She ran through the maple grove and across the pine-hemmed clearing, then lurched to a stop by the waymarker.

Brendan breathed, "Rust and ruin. Look at it."

Before them the air shimmered with magic like the ripple of heat on a blazing summer day—the border, wavering precariously.

"I don't feel the timeslip yet. If we're fast enough, we might ease through. But first . . . put this in your right pocket and tie your bootlaces in three knots." She handed him a pebble from her front yard, remembering Rook's lessons from weeks ago.

"What?"

"Just do it. It's a charm to keep the Fae from muddling our way. I don't know if it will work or not, but it's worth a try."

He crouched to knot his laces again. "Should we wait for a luckwitch?"

Lark glared at him. "She would send us home to wait and worry, and . . ." She hesitated. How much could she tell him? She chewed her lip. "And . . . I think we have a better chance of rescuing my sister and brother than anyone else does." Before he could ask for an explanation she wasn't ready to give, she demanded, "Have you lost your courage?"

He scowled at her. "I'm no coward, Lark Mairen." And he plunged through the glimmering curtain of magic marking the Other Side.

"Oh, rust it all!" Lark cried, bolting after Brendan. She ran into his back with a muffled *oof*.

"Took you long enough to get here," he said. "Having second thoughts?"

Lark snorted, assuming he was teasing—and then saw by his face that he was serious. "Wait . . . what do you mean? I ran after you! Couldn't have been more than a few seconds behind."

Brendan shook his head. "Felt like five or ten minutes. I was starting to worry."

They stared at each other. "Fae time," they both said at the same instant.

Or lack of it.

Lark repressed a shudder, glad they hadn't gotten caught in a timeslip tide pool. "I'm sorry," she told him. "I should have thought. From now on we'll stay together, right?"

He nodded, his shoulders still tense. "So . . . the last place I saw Sage, before the fog enveloped us, was on a bluff just above the valley where the Galin illusions appeared." He looked around, narrowing his eyes. "It was two waymarkers past yours, I think, so it's going to be a long walk. . . ."

Lark turned, trying to get a sense of direction, but the waymarker behind them had disappeared. "Umm . . ." she said. "Is distance like time here? Because if so, navigating might be a challenge."

Brendan hesitated.

"Doesn't matter. Forward it is!" she said with a forced grin. But she paused to tie a couple of raven feathers to a tree branch with red thread, hoping Rook or Nightbird would notice them and realize what she had done. She and Brendan could use their help. . . .

He nodded with renewed spirit and forged ahead, striding down a leaf-strewn track through tall oaks and pale-barked sycamore trees.

As she followed him, Lark carefully took the moon-clock from her pocket, keeping it concealed in her hand. She wasn't ready to show it to him quite yet—what would she say? Here's a thing I put together and I know it's magic and it does something with time but how it works is still a complete mystery? But now that she was actually over the border, she half hoped it would reveal more, give her some clue or sign.

Only, it looked the same as it had back in her house. The hands were still, the magic dormant. She gave it a little shake, but nothing happened.

She hoped the moon would rise.

But if she couldn't make it work she had a backup plan. Rook had said the Briar King didn't believe the moonclock would answer to a mortal. If the new king was so fond of tricks, she could play one of her own and offer him the useless clock in exchange for her siblings.

She dropped the moonclock back in her pocket and scurried to catch up to Brendan, until she spotted something and stopped him with a hand on his arm.

She put one finger to her lips, warning him to silence, and pointed to a deep green pool fed by a trickling creek. Willows arched over the water, their branches tangled in a curtain of spring leaves.

Brendan quirked a brow but waited quietly while Lark scanned the pool. As they watched, a webbed mottled-green hand shot into the air and snatched a hovering dragonfly before vanishing silently under the water, without even a ripple.

He scrambled backward, eyes going wide.

"Bog sprite," Lark whispered, thinking back to stories

she had heard. "We'll probably have to pay a toll to purchase our way past." She reached in her pack for a handful of dried cherries.

Hoping her hunch would work, she scattered the cherries across the surface of the water. The frogskin hand shot up once more, grabbing at the dried fruit.

A swirl of bubbles burst near the center of the pool and a figure suddenly rose, with hair like fringes of algae and pale, swollen features. It opened its mouth wide, gurgled with glee, and tossed the cherries in before diving under again.

"Let's go," Lark said.

"Are you sure it's safe?"

No. "Sure. I paid a toll, didn't I? Now hurry before it demands another."

They crept around the edge of the now-placid pool, ducking under the willows and easing through a stand of cattails. Lark kept a wary eye on the water, prepared to throw more cherries if she had to.

But nothing stirred, and in a dozen or so steps they had passed out of the wooded tunnel and found themselves standing on the edge of a wildflower meadow. At their feet, where the dappled shadows of the trees could still reach, a swathe of bluebells and violets extended in a dusk-colored carpet. Past those, swirls of yellow, orange, and red marked clusters of buttercups, poppies, lilies and hollyhocks, irises, and tulips.

She couldn't see a path through, but there seemed to be a bluff ahead.

"It's beautiful," Brendan breathed.

"Which means we probably need to be very, very careful." Lark scanned the shifting ocean of color in front of them, watching honeybees and butterflies drifting above the petals. A quick twinge in the back of her hand reminded her of the bloodmoths she'd encountered, but the scene remained peaceful and pleasant.

Rook had warned her that apparent serenity was a favorite trap of the Fae. They needed to stay alert, needed to keep their wits sharp.

She glanced around again, looking for any sign of a trail or a track they should follow, but the meadow spread unbroken in all directions.

Wondering if Rook's way-clearing charm would work here, she pressed her hands together and then blew in her palms as she opened them. Nothing happened.

Well, the only way through is through, she told herself.

"Keep your eyes open for sudden movement, anything that looks out of place. I think we have to cross it, but there could be hidden dangers."

"The whole thing looks out of place!" Brendan complained good-naturedly.

"Do you see a better route?"

"No," he admitted.

"Well, then—one chance. Let's go."

"One chance?"

Her cheeks flushed. "Just something Galin used to say. It means don't hesitate because you might miss your moment."

Holding her breath, Lark took a tiny step, carefully placing her foot between two swaying bluebells so she wouldn't accidentally crush a flower. The instant she crossed the edge of the meadow a cool, tingling sensation swept her skin like a rainshower. The copper ring on her finger stung for a second and then subsided.

They had left the Borderlands and entered all the way into the realm of the Fae.

"Are you coming or not?" she called over her shoulder.

Brendan grimaced and eased one foot into the wildflowers, cautiously testing the ground with the toe of his boot. Lark saw the sudden widening of his eyes and involuntary shiver as he felt the full magic atmosphere of the Fae realm.

He pointed across the meadow to a narrow trail curving along a ridge of hills. "That looks familiar."

She shifted direction as he asked, "Hey, why were you hanging feathers back there? Is that some sort of charm or what?"

Lark crept forward, another cautious step, and wrestled with guilt. Brendan had boldly flung himself into this quest to save Sage and Galin and she didn't feel right keeping *all* her secrets from him. She finally said, "If I share a secret, do you promise not to tell?"

He snorted and spread his hands. "Who am I going to tell?"

Lark chewed her lip, tiptoeing over a patch of violets.

"Seriously, Lark," he said, "we've already broken every rule I can think of. Your secrets are my secrets now."

She skirted a clump of poppies and finally said, "I have a friend called Rook. He's one of the Fae." She swallowed hard. "I think he has some kind of authority here. I left those feathers as a message for him. When he realizes we've crossed the border, he'll help us."

She heard the quiet huff of Brendan's breathing as he navigated his way through the flowers. "Do you trust him?" he asked.

"As much as anyone can trust one of the Fae. He's helped me before."

"Why didn't you tell your parents? The Elders?"

"I promised I wouldn't. And I didn't want Rook to get in trouble. Also . . . I guess I was afraid they wouldn't believe me." Lark lost her balance and had to pinwheel her arms to keep from stomping a flower.

"What's our plan once he finds us? Lark, I think the Briar King used Galin to trap Sage on purpose. I . . . I am afraid we'll have to go to the castle to find her."

"I agree. And . . . I might have something we can use as a bargaining tool to get her back. I guess we'll have to see what develops. Are you having regrets?"

"Me? Of course not. I would do *anything* for your sister.

I just want you to understand the danger." He sounded so earnest.

Lark figured she probably understood better than he did, but she didn't say that. "Does she know how you feel?" she asked instead.

His ears flushed pink as he crept through a patch of hyacinths and crocuses. "I doubt it."

"You haven't told her?"

"No! I can't tell her. Not until I've proven myself."

"Is that why you wanted to race? Just for her?"

Brendan met her astonished gaze with clear, steady eyes. "I told you. I would do anything for her."

Lark didn't know what to say to that. But she suddenly felt terrible for calling him Blunderknuckles.

After an awkward pause she said, "Well, for what it's worth, I think she must like you too." At least that would explain Sage's frequent blushing.

They picked their way past a stand of sunflowers in silence, and then Brendan swore, "Oh, rust and ruin!"

"What happened?" But Lark didn't need to ask—when the wildflower meadow suddenly began to seethe around them, she knew he must have crushed a flower underfoot. "Watch your step!"

"I'm trying, but there's no path!"

"Try *harder*!" Lark sped up—the sooner they crossed this field the better—but her calves and ankles ached from the effort of taking small, awkward steps. Despite her caution, the ball of her left foot brushed a cluster of buttercups and clover too. A sharp sting immediately burned her ankle.

"Ouch!" Brendan cried, and she guessed he'd stepped on another blossom.

All around them tiny meadowflits rose from the flowers, dragonfly wings buzzing in anger. Their clothes were cunningly crafted from leaves and petals, giving them a bright, colorful beauty. But their yellow eyes flashed with furious threat and their sharp, grasping fingers plucked at skin with venomous nails.

Lark shook one off before it could sink its translucent, toxic nails into her wrist. She wasn't quick enough to dislodge one from her calf, though. A quick, searing pinch like a bee sting made her eyes water.

Brendan swore again, swatting at a cloud of meadowflits darting and ducking around him.

"Don't make them angrier!" Lark cried.

But his hand connected with a flit, sending it tumbling through the air. It landed in an ungainly heap in the cup of a tulip bloom and an ominous hum filled the meadow. "Too late!" he yelped.

Another flit sank its nails into the back of Lark's neck. She clapped a hand to the sting. "We're sorry!" she cried. "If you let us pass, we will leave you in peace! We didn't mean any harm!"

But the meadowflits weren't listening, and when one caught the edge of her ear, Lark shrieked, "*Run!*"

The Prince
of Birds

"I'M SORRY, I'M sorry!" Lark cried, sprinting through the last few paces of the wildflower meadow. Flits dove at her face, clawed the backs of her hands, and clung to her wrists no matter how madly she waved and swatted at them. By the time she plunged through the hollyhocks at the rim and climbed a rocky ledge, dozens of burning red welts covered her skin.

Brendan fared worse. When he finally stumbled out of the flowers and clambered up beside her, his neck and ears were swelling. Blotches marked his arms, his ankles—the meadowflits had even managed to tear his shirt. Fever glossed his eyes and clammy beads of sweat gleamed at his temples.

"Brendan? Are you well?"

He blinked slowly at her, and then his eyes rolled back in his head and he collapsed.

"Rust and ruin!" she cried, kneeling beside him to feel for a pulse. He was still alive—thank the stars—but his breath was fast and shallow and she started to panic.

"Hang on, Blunderknuckles!" she told him, lightly slapping his cheeks. "Stay with me! I've got something to help. . . ." She rummaged in her satchel until she found the little pot of salve. Her own hands were swollen and sore so it took a few tries to unscrew the cap, but she hastily scooped out globs of herbal cream and coated the injuries the meadowflits had inflicted.

The salve was supposed to take away some of the sting, but it didn't seem to help Brendan. If anything, he only got worse. Every breath rattled in his throat and his skin—where it hadn't been scratched by meadowflits—looked pale and waxy.

Lark couldn't help thinking about the bloodmoth that had bitten her. She wished Netty Greenwillow were here to help Blunder—Brendan. Or better yet, Rook and Nightbird, who knew how to use Fae remedies to fight toxic magic bites and stings.

His eyelids fluttered and he mumbled groggily, "What happened?"

"You stomped on a flower and woke up all the meadowflits," she said. "Turns out their venom is pretty hard on you."

"That figures. I'm allergic to bee stings too," he said, the words thick and slurred.

"Why didn't you say so? I would have tried to find another way!"

"There was no other—" His head lolled and he sank back into unconsciousness.

"Brendan!" Lark cried, patting his cheeks and thumping his chest. "Wake up! Please!" She looked around for help, discovering with a chill of fear that the meadow had become an impassable stretch of thistles, brambles, wild hedgeroses, and thorns.

Was the Briar King going to capture her and Brendan too? Was her quest a failure so soon?

"Please!" she wailed. "Wake up!"

She rocked back on her heels, panic beating black wings in her chest. Fixing a person wasn't at all the same as fixing a rusted well pump or a broken gate latch, but she had to try. Her eyes roved over the thistles and briars. Mistress Greenwillow used stinging nettles and thistle sap in some of her remedies, so maybe Lark could craft something that would heal Brendan. She had water and flint to start a fire for boiling. . . .

But as soon as she reached for a thistle stem, the world lurched. She blinked—and found herself surrounded by stone and sand. It was as if something had sensed her intentions and thwarted her before she could make the attempt.

A desperate wail rose in her throat. Just when disaster seemed certain, a raven swooped over her head. "Nightbird? Rook?" she whispered. "Please. We need help."

The world rippled again and suddenly she and Brendan were in a grass clearing surrounded by trees. Rook crouched beside her, face scrunched in worry. "I saw your feathers. I guessed you would come after Sage and Galin, but why'd you bring *him*?"

"He came with me. I think . . . I think he loves Sage."

Rook's fingers fluttered over Brendan. "Only way to save him for certain is to return him to your realm. I can stabilize him, but there's too much magic in his system. He'll be vulnerable if he remains here."

He whistled a delicate tune and dozens of birds soared through the sky to land near him in a rustling, fluttering cloud. They brought leaves, berries, bits of moss, ragged strips of bark. Rook held out his hands, collecting all the offerings. He crushed them into a rough wad that he tucked under Brendan's tongue.

Within moments Brendan was spluttering and struggling dizzily to his feet. "Gah! Blech." He spat and wiped his mouth. "Why'd you feed me weeds?" His voice was stronger than it had been, though the words were still slurred.

Lark laughed and flung her arms around him in relief. "Those weeds saved your life."

His eyes went wide as saucers and he pointed over Lark's shoulder.

"Oh, that's my friend Rook. Rook, this is Blunder—this is Brendan." The two boys bowed slightly to each other and she swallowed a laugh at their awkward formality.

Rook waved his birds away, but at the motion his sleeve fell back, baring his wrist. Lark spotted a reddened circle of scabs and scars, as though he'd been tangled in thorns. He caught her looking and tugged his sleeve down, eyes darkening.

"Come," he said abruptly. "I need to get you to safety." He strode off, Lark and Brendan scrambling to keep up.

"Where are we going?" Lark asked. "This doesn't seem like the way back to the border." Seeds of doubt took root in her mind and spread like a vine. A tremble ran along her bones as she eyed the vastness of the Fae wilderness they were in, disoriented by the changing illusions of the landscape.

"As you might have noticed, the surroundings of our realm shift like the sea. If you aren't certain where you're going, if you aren't on one of the Twilight Roads, you'll find your destination receding despite all your efforts to reach it. I'm taking a safer detour," Rook said briskly.

Lark glanced back. A wall of rock and dense yew trees blocked the way they'd come. Their only choice was to continue forward, trusting Rook.

Brendan leaned close and murmured in her ear, "How well do you know him? What if he orchestrated all of this?"

"Why would he heal you just to betray us?" Unless . . . maybe he wanted her to use the moonclock for his own agenda? But then why would he have bothered to teach her defensive charms? He'd taken risks to help her, she knew. . . .

"This could be part of some complicated Fae game," Brendan said.

Lark studied Rook as she followed him. It was true that she didn't know nearly enough about the political situation in the Twilight Court, about the details of Rook's motives or his personal life. But she had seen him confront the Briar King's allies when he helped her against the Fae drummers at Mayfair.

No . . . those thorn marks around his wrist proved they were on the same side.

It wasn't fair to doubt a friend . . . even if that friend was Fae, Lark decided.

"I trust him," she told Brendan.

Rook led them through a dense forest, the trees rustling ominously despite the still air. Strange orchids bloomed from forked branches and their perfumes made Lark dizzy.

At one point, they jogged past an oak tree festooned with shimmering scraps of fabric in pink, yellow, pale green, sky blue, and violet. Brendan choked and covered his eyes. Lark understood when she got a closer look and realized she was seeing wings tied in the branches, not ragged silk. They spun slowly, their iridescent membranes casting splashes of rainbow light. At the base of the tree, like a pile of sun-bleached kindling, was a stack of thin, fragile bones.

"Oh no . . . ," Lark whispered, remembering Brendan's story of the Hunt.

"Pixies," Rook said grimly. "One from each clan. A warning to the rest of us not to cross the Briar King, though we tried anyway."

Lark put a hand on Brendan's elbow. "You couldn't have stopped it," she murmured.

He winced and shook his head.

Brendan and Lark stayed close after that, weaving through the trees as quickly as they could. When the trees began to reach for them, twiggy fingers clutching at their faces, Rook warned, "Don't look up!"

Lark squeaked and Brendan grabbed her arm, appearing as shaken as she felt. But they didn't slow and they kept their heads down.

She was starting to get a blister on her foot when Rook finally led them to a small cabin tucked into a clearing.

It huddled like a toadstool beneath the sweeping limbs of massive fir trees and old oaks, with narrow windows like eyes above the faded wooden door. The sod roof was covered in clover and the stone walls were green with moss and climbing ivy. She was delighted to see Nightbird perched on the crooked chimney like a guard.

Rook opened the door, ushering them inside.

"Is this where you live?" Lark asked, gazing around in hungry curiosity as she followed him. Some of the Fae, she knew, lived in tree houses, caves, cottages, huts, or fancy manors, while wildkin lived in whatever natural habitats suited their natures best. She'd never been able to picture Rook's home, though.

Rook glanced over his shoulder, an unreadable expression on his face. "Sometimes."

She scurried after him, staring at a stone hearth with a copper kettle suspended from a hook. A shelf on the wall held a pewter cup and plate, two spoons. A braided rag rug—so prosaic it seemed oddly out of place—covered part of the faded wood-plank floor and a small table and chair were wedged in a corner of the room. A curtain obscured the opposite corner and she guessed that was where he slept.

Rook kicked back the rag rug, revealing a trapdoor set in the floor. He bent to grasp a brass ring and heaved the door open. "Lark, wait down here. I'll take Brendan back and return as quickly as I can."

"Wait! No—where're we goin'? Where's Sage? 'M not leavin' without her!" Brendan cried, but his tongue tripped over the words.

He'd seemed so much better on their walk over here that Lark was now dismayed to see that one of his pupils was dilated and the other constricted to a tiny point of black. Red blotches had bloomed across his skin again and he lurched clumsily as he tried to step away.

He did not look well *at all*.

Rook folded his arms and scowled. "I was able to temporarily counteract the venom from the meadowflits, but Fae magic has compromised your system. You aren't safe here—and neither is Lark, if you're with her. I need to get you to safety so the toxin can wear off, and then Lark and I will rescue Sage."

Brendan's face fell and he swayed to the side, catching

himself on the wall with a thunk of his elbow. "No! I need to—"

He started to slump and Rook caught him. "Afraid not, friend. The longer you stay here, the worse you'll feel. Time to go."

Brendan clawed at Lark's sleeve. "Please!" he cried. And then tears welled in his eyes. "I know you think I'm just a dunderknuckled blunderheaded clunkerfooted—"

Lark grabbed both of his hands. "Brendan Forth, you are a brave and true friend with a kind, loyal heart and a strong spirit. You crossed the border with me even when you had no idea what you were getting into, and I'll never forget it. No one can question your courage. Least of all me. Do you hear me?" She squeezed his fingers.

Then she said, "Just because a tool isn't made for one job doesn't mean it's not necessary for another, right? You're the newest member of the messenger guild, after all. And I need you to deliver a message. Let my parents know where I am—but try not to scare them any worse than they proba- bly already are. Tell them I know what I'm doing."

She didn't . . . but she could make it up as she went along.

He flashed a wobbly smile and tried to nod, but his head rolled and he closed his eyes. Rook swung one of Brendan's arms over his shoulders and said, "Go on down. I'll be back."

"But where are you taking him?"

"I told you. Shortcut."

Lark eyed the darkness below the trapdoor. "Rook, I don't want to—"

"It's the only way to keep you out of sight. Don't you trust me?" But he didn't wait for the answer, nudging her down the stairs.

The door clanged shut.

The moment it closed, the space filled with light as glass globes hanging from the ceiling suddenly glowed amber. Lark let out a relieved breath. At least she wasn't stuck in the dark.

How long did Rook intend to keep her hidden down here?

Cautiously stepping forward, she explored the secret room. It was larger than she'd expected and furnished with a soft armchair, a pile of colorful pillows, a wooden table, and an oil lantern with a box of matches. The walls appeared to be natural stone, but canvas paintings of various birds covered one and a large tapestry depicting a forest full of ravens hung on another.

Lark drifted closer to study the art and discovered a grandfather clock standing in a shadowed corner. It was carved with birds and leaves, the crescent moon and the rising sun. The face was marked with feathers and flowers rather than numbers, but something about the style was oddly familiar. . . .

Peering at it, she found an engraving near the bottom. *For Rodrik, my new brother and the Prince of Birds. With love from Hawsdon Brassman, Harvest King.*

So the Brassman ancestor who'd made the moonclock *was* the Harvest King, as she had guessed. And . . . Lark's pulse leaped like a fractious colt as she put the pieces together. *My new brother.* Rook had said she wasn't the only one worried about a sibling. Could it be possible . . . Was the May Queen one of his sisters? Was this a gift to commemorate a wedding?

If so . . . *Poor Rook.* Poor Rodrik.

Lark chewed her lip, thinking of the thorn scratches she'd seen around his wrist. If he was related to the May Queen and the Harvest King, he might be next in line for the throne. . . . That made him a threat to the usurper. He could be in terrible danger.

The trapdoor rattled and a sliver of daylight illuminated the stairs. Rook's face appeared as the door lifted. "Lark?"

She flew up the steps, nearly knocking him backward. "She was your sister, wasn't she? The May Queen? Why didn't you say so?"

"My tongue was tied, but since I cannot tell a lie and you've already guessed the truth . . ." He sighed and closed the trapdoor. "Yes, she was one of my sisters. Three of us awoke at the same time from the same pool of magic in a willow glen deep in the wilds of the realm."

He rubbed his chin. "I thought I could protect her, but the Duke of Briars killed Hawsdon and demanded that Ariasandra marry him next. She kept refusing, and . . . he lost patience. He took her life and the throne. There was nothing I could do."

"I am so sorry, Rook. Or should I say . . . Rodrik?"

He rocked his weight from one foot to the other and drummed a hand on his thigh, flashing her a crooked smile. "Once I came to know you, Lark Mairen, I would have been happy to trust you with my true name. But honestly, I like Rook better."

She grinned back at him, until concern tugged the smile from her lips. "So . . . why did the Briar King spare *your* life? Aren't you a rival for the throne?" She hadn't intended the questions to sound so suspicious, but she *was* curious. She needed to understand the situation in the Twilight Court better if she was going to confront the king.

He clawed his hands through his hair, standing the tousled curls on end. "Let's just say he doesn't know me well enough if he trusts the terms of a deal forced in haste." A glint in his eye told Lark what he meant.

"Ahhh . . . he thinks you're cooperating, but you're playing your own game."

Rook smoothed the rug over the trapdoor again. "Galin hides down there sometimes," he said.

"What?" she asked, distracted by the sudden shift. "You've actually been with Galin and never said a word? But—" Her head was still spinning. "Where is he now? Take me to him!"

"I wish I could, but I haven't seen him since the May Queen's death."

Lark rubbed her eyes. "You said Galin was friends with one of your sisters. So . . . the golden-haired Fae I saw with him . . . she's related to the queen too?"

How tightly was Galin tangled with the Twilight Court?

He nodded. "You can save us all with the moonclock, but I have to bring you to the castle. Remember what I've taught you—the false king will test you, but time is on your side. Are you willing to face the challenge?"

"Would I be standing here if I wasn't prepared to do whatever it takes to get Sage and Galin back? But I don't know how to *use* the moonclock. I found the keyhole and managed to wind it, but I don't understand what happened. I . . . felt *something*, but nothing changed." She took it from her pocket and held it out. "Show me what to do!"

He clenched his fists. "I can't. But have faith in yourself—you've already proven your skill, strength, and cleverness. You are bound to the moonclock; you're the only one who can use it. When the time comes, you will know."

She frowned and tucked the moonclock away. What if she *didn't* know? "But why does the Briar King want it?"

"He needs the time. That's all I can say for now. Now let's go clear some weeds from the castle. Don't forget your pack."

At the door he hesitated. "Listen, Lark . . . I'm sorry you got stuck in the middle of all this. But you aren't alone. Remember that."

He stepped out and indicated a smooth dirt road

unwinding through an arch of blooming hawthorn trees she was certain hadn't been there before. "You have to hold my hand to travel a Twilight Road. Don't let go."

Lark clasped his fingers and they stepped onto the path. She wasn't sure what she'd expected, but when nothing unusual happened her shoulders relaxed. Then they took another step and everything changed. The road . . . wrinkled . . . and the land around them blurred. Another step and dizziness sloshed in her head.

"Hang on. Just a couple more steps and we'll be there."

No wonder *watch the road* meant be careful.

She closed her eyes and tried not to throw up as the world lurched again.

TWENTY-SIX

The Briar King's Bargain

"WE'RE HERE. YOU can open your eyes." Rook chuckled quietly.

Lark grimaced and dropped his hand. Her legs shook and for a heartbeat she was afraid to move in case she collapsed. That had been the strangest journey she'd ever taken—and the swiftest.

She tried to steady herself with a deep breath, but she was overwhelmed by the sight of a massive castle constructed of living trees, reaching high above her in a tangle of sweeping branches and stretching limbs. Curtains of ivy hung like banners over stone arches set between tree trunks near the entrance.

"Stay strong," he whispered, escorting her across a wide courtyard covered in moss and clover, toward a pair of tall silver gates depicting the seal of the Twilight Court—the May Queen's nested egg, rose, and star on one side with the Harvest King's feather, acorn, and flame on the other.

Someone had taken a hammer to the embossed silver and left the images heavily dented and scarred.

Lark squinted at the gleaming gates. Deep grooves in the flagstone terrace offered evidence that they had stood here for a long, long time, but there was no tarnished patina of age.

Rook spoke a word and flashed a quick gesture with the fingers of his left hand, and the massive gates swung open with a ponderous groan.

Thornguards stood sentinel on the other side, sharp pikes leveled at Lark. Rook waved them off, ushering her through.

Lark swallowed fear as sharp as broken glass when the gates clanged shut behind her, trapping her in a granite cloister amid a tangle of thorns and brambles. Rook held up a hand and the thorns retreated with a rustle of scrapes and creaks, leaving a clearer view of the castle ahead.

The castle appeared to have grown out of the very trees of the forest. Tall trunks formed pillars and columns while densely woven branches created walls and turrets, arches and balconies. Moss and leaves and tightly furled fern fronds filled the gaps like mortar between stones.

"Come," Rook said, and she stumbled after him. Her stomach twisted like a snake in a rotten log, but she was determined to find Sage and Galin.

The two Thornguards beside the palace doors smirked at Lark when they stepped aside so she could enter. Her footsteps echoed as she marched after Rook, down a stone corridor and into a vaulted hall where two thrones stood on a dais at the far end.

To Lark's horror they were not empty.

The one on the left was wrought of ever-blooming white and pink roses twined with ivy and lilacs, eggs and feathers decorating the base. The May Queen sat upon it, still and lifeless. Her lovely features were frozen in a grimace of pain or fear. The hem and sleeves of her shimmering blush-colored gown were torn and ragged.

The throne on the right was formed of oak and maple branches covered in brilliantly colored fall foliage, woven with grape vines and cornstalks. Pumpkins and apples secured the base. Here the Harvest King sat propped, unmoving. A streak of blood marred his chestnut beard and another darkened his pale golden robes.

The light shifted and Lark saw glints of silver at the May Queen's throat and hands. There were similar flashes across the Harvest King's body and she realized spelled silver darts must be holding the Fae monarchs in place on their thrones like grisly trophies of war or a hunt.

In front of them lounged the Briar King on a throne of blackthorn briars, one booted foot propped on the gnarled armrest. A crown of wild roses was tangled in his dark pine-green hair, the blooms so red they looked like clotted blood.

Thornguards in dark leather flanked him, holding blackwood lances with sharp obsidian tips. Hoods obscured their faces, but the hands clutching their weapons did not look human at all. Too many finger joints, with nails as long as talons.

Lark forced herself to step forward.

The king straightened, his black velvet robes shifting to reveal slashes of crimson silk and a hem of gilded brambles. "So, Lark Mairen," he said, in a voice like the last gasp of a nightmare. "I have something you want, and you have something I want. Shall we trade?"

Beside her Lark felt Rook tense. He caught her eye, something dark and fierce in his gaze.

In the back of her mind this had always been her plan if she couldn't work the moonclock—she would gladly hand it over in exchange for Sage and Galin. After all, if Rook was right and it was bound to her, then the Briar King wouldn't be able to do anything with it either. What harm could it do in his possession? And hopefully by the time he discovered it was nothing more than a remarkable curiosity, she and her siblings would already be home.

But an uncomfortable realization had given her second thoughts. Without the moonclock, Rook had said the Fae realm would run out of time. If Lark gave it to the Briar King, rendering it useless, Rook and his sister and all the Fae who might oppose the new king would be hurt—frozen in a changeless eternity.

Lark couldn't buy her siblings' freedom at the expense of so many others.

And even if she *could*, what would stop the Briar King from crossing the broken border and exacting revenge?

She had to *think*. . . .

If only I knew how to make it work! she lamented.

"Well, Lark Mairen? What do you say?" the Briar King rasped.

"Shouldn't I fetch a cage for our birds?" a voice growled from the shadows behind the throne. A slender figure glided forward, wearing a pelt of silver and sable fur.

The Fae's pointed ears swiveled toward Rook, tufted tips quivering as his staring eyes burned gold. He snarled, lips peeling back from teeth like daggers.

The Briar King held up a languid hand. "No, Reynaud Stoneheart. Not yet. After all, the Prince of Birds did bring us the little Mairen meadowlark, didn't he? Perhaps he has earned our gratitude and his freedom. Let's see what bargain she's willing to strike first, eh?"

He surged to his feet, his two Thornguards lowering their lances menacingly at Rook's chest. "But you should have brought *me* the pieces of the moonclock. I could have chosen someone to fix it without all this fuss and bother. If you betray me again, I will let my Thornguards prick you until your blood runs like wine, and then I'll feed you to Stoneheart and his pack of wolf wildkin. Understand?"

A muscle twitched in Rook's jaw but he balanced insolently on one foot and smiled slowly. "Understood."

Folding his arms, the king jerked his chin at the Thorn-guards and they withdrew their lances. The furred Fae called Stoneheart licked his lips and moved closer. "So," the Briar King said. "I have your sister, and you have my clock."

"You also have my brother," she said.

"It was not by *my* hand that Galin ended up in the Fae realm." His black brows folded lower over his eyes. "But if you hand over the moonclock, I'll do my best to return him to you."

Lark slipped her hand in her pocket. It would be so easy to believe him, to do as he asked and be done with all of this. All she wanted was to go home with her sister and brother, for life to go back to the way it had been.

But that wasn't possible. Too much had changed. *She* had changed.

There was too much at stake. And she knew too much now.

This so-called Briar King had stolen the throne with murder and mayhem. His reign threatened the balance between the realms and risked the stability of the Twilight Court itself.

She didn't trust him in the slightest.

She had to stop him. Only, how could she defeat a Fae king?

Rook shifted uneasily and the king flung out a hand, casting a thorny vine around Rook's wrists and neck.

"Well?" the king demanded. "Give me your answer or I'll send my thorns down his throat."

"I'm willing to negotiate," Lark said, thoughts spinning desperately.

"Ahhhhh." The Briar King smiled, but it wasn't a kind or happy expression. "What do you propose?"

"I—" Her tongue stuck to the roof of her mouth. All she had to bargain with was the moonclock, and yet she couldn't let him have it. Could she trick him? Her throat was so dry it felt like she'd swallowed sand. "What use is Sage to you?" she asked, buying time.

He laughed and it sounded like thorns scraping glass. "Other than as bait to bring you and my moonclock here? Or as leverage to guarantee your brother's good behavior? Well, I suppose she can care for my shadowbreds. They seem to be ailing."

"What's wrong with them?"

The Thornguards beside the king shifted their weight, stark gazes locking on her. "If I knew, I wouldn't need her help, now, would I?" the king said. "Stop delaying. Do you agree to trade the moonclock for your sister, or do I let my Thornguards take it by force?"

Lark clenched her fists. "If they come near me I'll smash it to bits!" How could she get Sage, Galin, and the moonclock out of the Briar King's clutches? *Think of a trick . . .*

She glanced at Rook and his lips quirked, one brow raising in a curve.

A daring idea occurred to her. The Fae loved games. . . .

"Your Majesty . . . why don't we play for Sage?"

"Well now." The Briar King sat back down on his throne, crossing his arms. "Your sister as the prize, eh? But I've already said I'm willing to trade her." He raised a hand to his chin, tapping with a finger that seemed to have a dark thorn for a nail. "The problem, little meadowlark, is that I have everything to lose and nothing to gain by such a wager. I *already* possess Sage. If I win, I only keep what is already mine. There's no inducement to play unless you put up the moonclock, and as I said, I've already offered the exchange."

Lark pretended to be deep in thought before she said, "If I win, my sister and I are free to go, along with Galin." She tipped her chin toward Rook. "And you release him. He is not responsible for my actions. But if I lose . . . I will stay as your prize. After all, I'm the one who fixed the moon-clock. It won't work without me."

"Lies!" the one called Reynaud Stoneheart howled. "The mortal lies!"

"She speaks truth," Rook said. The look he sent Lark was worried, but she *had* to tell the king; otherwise there would have been nothing to stop him from killing her and stealing it.

She knew playing games with the Fae was dangerous, but this was the only way she could see a chance.

A fleeting expression of frustration darkened the king's gaze—there and gone so fast she wouldn't have seen it if she hadn't been watching his face so closely. "I do not know where your brother is. I cannot answer for him. But if you find him, you may take him with you and Sage," he conceded. "And I agree to release the May Queen's brother. *If* you win."

Lark bowed her head. "And if *you* win, I am yours to command, along with the moonclock."

He studied her, drumming his thorn-tipped nails against the arms of his throne. After a moment, he nodded. "Then let's play."

Now she had to trust luck and skill. . . . "What shall we play? Cards? Dice? Ball?" She was good at games of strategy and quick on her feet, and after her lessons with Rook she knew that the Fae were easily distracted and often impatient. She could use that to her advantage.

"No . . . I have something far better in mind." A sharp-edged smile crawled across his face.

Dread slithered down the back of her neck. "And what game is that?"

"Oh, you'll like it!" He leaned forward, his red eyes shining like embers. "The rules are simple. I'll hide your sister in plain view. If you find her, you win."

Lark tried to read his intentions in that sinister face. Where was the lie? The trick concealed in his words?

"And what is the game board?"

He swept his arm out. "My castle grounds."

Lark glanced around. The castle itself was sprawling,

and she couldn't guess how far the property spread. She shook her head. "Too big. One room."

"Too boring. Let's say . . . my garden maze. You can see it for yourself, just out there." He pointed out a tall, arched window and Lark saw a hedge labyrinth crowning a low hill. It didn't look too large or too complex, so she said, "Agreed."

"Excellent! Then we shall play."

"Wait . . . that's all there is to it?"

"That's all."

"Do you swear?" Lark sifted through his words, seeking a trap or a loophole. It seemed too straightforward. . . . What was she missing?

"By the light of morning, the stars of night, and all the skies between, I do so swear. Now are you ready to play, or do you forfeit?"

Lark hesitated. She couldn't escape the feeling that she was overlooking a critical detail. She thought back to the things she'd learned of the Fae. . . .

Oh yes: Never take the rules for granted. Always ask or you'll end up playing a game you don't expect.

"What are the rules?" she asked, and Rook let out a breath of relief behind her.

"I told you. Find your sister and you win."

"I want *all* the rules."

The Briar King scowled and Lark suddenly saw the trap she'd almost fallen into. *Find your sister* didn't specify how many times her sister could be hidden or how many tries

Lark had before she lost the game.

She raised her chin and stared at him resolutely.

The Thornguards grumbled and Stoneheart edged closer, but after a moment the king chuckled. "You're a clever meadowlark, aren't you? Very well, then. How about this? I will hide your sister in five disguises. You win if you find her each time."

"You will hide her once, and I get three guesses."

Stoneheart growled but the king held up a fist and stopped him. "A smart bird with a sharp peck, eh? Three times. One guess each time. And you leave your pack behind."

Lark chewed her lip, glancing at Rook. If she left her pack, she'd be completely vulnerable.

"Three times, three guesses. And my pack stays with me."

"Three times. Three guesses. And you may take three items from your pack, or I refuse to play."

His voice was quiet but there was a knife's edge beneath the words, telling her these were the best terms she would get.

"Fine. Three times. Three guesses. Three items from my pack," she repeated. But she wasn't done pressing. "And everything I'm carrying in my pockets."

"Pockets? What do you have in your pockets?"

Reynaud Stoneheart smirked. "Mortals carry bread

crumbs and salt, dried herbs, and feathers for protection against us. The little bird wants her dusty superstitions."

The king roared with laughter. "Bread crumbs and bitter herbs, eh? Done." He leaned forward. "I'll even give you a clue: Once by land, once by air, and once by water is where you'll find the Horsemaven's daughter. She'll take her form when you give her name, and back you'll go to where I sought her."

Lark repeated his words in her mind and tossed a sideways glance at Rook. He met her stare and blinked once, slowly, as if in agreement. "Let's play," she said.

"Excellent!" The Briar King clapped his hands and a surge of prickling magic swept the throne room, blowing Lark's hair away from her face and making her shiver. "And so the game begins!"

Lark crouched with her back to him, rummaging through her pack. What would be most useful in this game? After a moment's thought, she chose her length of red string, her tool pouch, and a small knife. She belted the tool pouch around her waist and slipped the knife and string into one of her pockets, and with a last look at Rook, still bound by thorns, she straightened.

The Thornguards pointed their lances toward a door beneath a shadowed arch in one wall of the throne room and Reynaud Stoneheart cried, "Good luck, poor little meadowlark! You'll need it."

Stoneheart's howling laughter rang in her ears, as the king's thorns tightened around Rook and his panicked breathing chased her out.

Lark couldn't lose. Everyone she loved was counting on her.

But maybe she had an advantage. The king didn't know she carried the moonclock—he must have thought it was still in her pack. He also didn't know how much Rook had taught her.

Squaring her shoulders and lifting her chin, she ran out the door, her hand in her pocket, clasping the moonclock tight.

TWENTY-SEVEN

Wishes and Fish

LARK STAGGERED OUT of the castle tree trunks onto a wide, sweeping veranda of glittering white stone.

Blinking in the sunshine, she surveyed clover meadows spilling down a series of curving terraces. A hedge of hawthorns, holly, and rowan trees lined a twisting path that disappeared for a stretch before climbing a hill to the maze where Sage would be hidden in disguise.

"Land, air, or water," Lark repeated nervously. But at least she knew Sage was in the labyrinth. How hard could it be to find her?

She stepped off the terrace to follow the path, pressing a hand to her throat in anticipation of the road wrinkling and folding the way it had when Rook brought her to the castle. Luckily, it stayed firm, and after the first few cautious steps she began to hurry.

She couldn't ignore the thought that time didn't flow

here the way it did back home. What if she found Sage only to discover that fifty years had passed in the mortal world? And then there was Galin. . . . Where had he gone? Would he agree to return home with her?

One thing at a time.

She scurried ahead, urgency making her clumsy and careless so that when the path veered suddenly past a small stone well she stumbled into it, kicking a pebble against the base with a hollow clunk as she braced herself on the cracked, mossy rim. The basin was no larger than a horse's bucket and a thatched roof perched above it, with tiny silver bells that chimed faintly.

Oh no. A wishing well.

All the stories said wishing wells were dangerous. If you dropped a wish in, it might come true—or it might crawl out to haunt you.

Something deep inside knocked back.

Lark tried to lurch away, but it was already too late to run. Long gnarled fingers grasped the rim. She glimpsed a pointed nose and sharp chin, and then the creature hefted herself from the depths to stare at Lark with milky eyes.

She had dark, lank hair like waterweeds and pale skin the mottled color of a frog's belly. Her mouth was wide and too full of blocky teeth, and she sniffed the air like an animal scenting prey. Then she laughed—a wet, sloppy sound.

"Your wishes taste delicious," she sang in a surprisingly lovely voice. "If you want to walk away, tell me what you're going to pay."

A wishler.

Lark raised her hands and licked lips as dry as dust. "I'm sorry. I didn't mean to disturb your rest. I'll just be on my way."

The wishler shrieked. "Since you knocked upon my well, a wish you must prepare to tell. But nothing of worth is ever free, so pay the price or stay bound to me." She grinned hungrily.

The wishler's thick yellowed teeth made Lark shudder. "I didn't knock on the well. Or not on purpose, anyway. I accidentally tripped into it and—"

"A wish you owe before you go!" the wishler screeched. She heaved herself farther out of the well, dripping water and muck.

"I . . . I . . ." Lark *wanted* to make a wish, but she'd heard too many stories of wishes going wrong. Thinking fast, she took three glass marbles from her pocket and held them so they caught the light. One clear as ice, one translucent green, and one shimmering blue. "How about a payment in return for the trouble I've already caused?" she offered.

The wishler slapped the rim of the well, splashing murky water over the side as she considered. After a moment she nodded and held out her hand, greedily flapping her fingers.

Lark tossed her the three marbles and hastily stepped back—just in case.

The wishler splashed back into the well and Lark raced away, heart still thumping. She'd very nearly failed before the game even began!

After ducking under a tree branch and jumping over a patch of irises encroaching on the path, she spotted a stone arch leading into the hedge labyrinth ahead. She eyed the dense shrubs with trepidation. What might be hiding inside?

She took a deep breath. If Sage could race the Gauntlet and ride the Wild Hunt despite being afraid, Lark could do this. She plunged into the labyrinth.

Green shadows swallowed her, wrapping her in the scent of earth and sap and stone. Shoulders tense as she hurried forward, she scanned the swaying hedges for a glimpse of anything peeking out at her, waiting for a trap or a trick.

But it was just a labyrinth. Just a garden maze.

She extended her right arm to skim the leaves of the hedge with her fingertips. She'd wandered a labyrinth once before, with Sage and Galin years ago on a visit to Millplace. "The best way to navigate a maze is to follow the same wall, no matter how many times it turns. Eventually it will lead us back out," Galin had promised.

Squaring her shoulders, Lark forced herself to stride forward, one hand brushing the hedge. She twisted through the labyrinth, twice passing dead ends.

She started to sweat and her tunic stuck to her back. The blister on her foot began to burn and her tongue felt sticky and dry with thirst. Her stomach grumbled. When was the last time she'd eaten? She realized dismally she had no way to tell how long she'd been in the Fae realm. Or how long she'd been in this *maze*.

She forced her attention back to the task at hand. Where could Sage be? *Once by land, once by air, and once by water is where you'll find the Horsemaven's daughter.*

A tiny flicker of light ahead caught her attention, like a pink firefly. Drawn by curiosity, Lark sped up. Another sudden flash of light, this one lilac-colored, snagged her gaze.

And then a swarm of sparks surrounded her. Blinking blue, gold, green . . . they clung to her legs, stuck to her shoulders, climbed in her hair. Cold, dark, wispy things with glowing eyes . . .

Lark remembered the bloodmoths and the meadowflits and started to panic, but her thoughts scattered and she couldn't hold them. She swiped a hand before her face and found the clambering lights distracting. Where was she? What was she doing?

She spun in a circle and a weight in her pocket bumped her leg.

Bemused, she stuck her hand in . . . and felt the moon-clock. The cool heft of the silver pocket watch cleared her mind and she realized what was happening.

Muddlewisps. A whole hive, scrambling her thoughts and plucking her motivation. Grabbing a handful of salt and sage from her other pocket, she cast it in a circle around her and clapped her hands three times.

The swarm of muddlewisps flickered away, leaving her scratched and shaken. She'd taken her hand off the hedge wall and stepped away, and now she frantically hurried back to it. Hopefully she hadn't gotten too disoriented. . . .

How much time had she lost?

Lark hurried on, doubts dogging her heels, until she rounded a bend to discover a clearing with a huge hourglass in the center.

She lurched to a stop, staring at the massive object. It shimmered in the sunlight, made of some glass with a pearl sheen. Instead of holding sand, it was filled with shining water that poured into the bottom globe and then spilled out into a wide fountain pool. Over a dozen large golden fish swam in the water.

"Once by land, once by air, and once by water is where you'll find the Horsemaven's daughter," she repeated to herself. Could Sage be one of these fish?

She circled the hourglass, bending down to peer into the pool. She only had three guesses. . . .

Lark put her hands on her hips. She knew her sister better than anyone, didn't she? Surely she could recognize her even in another shape.

But she couldn't get a good look. The fish darted quicksilver fast, flicking their tails, and the water distorted their images if she wasn't staring straight down at them.

She knelt, forcing herself not to panic. Taking slow, deep breaths she tried to empty her mind and just observe.

The longer she watched, the more convinced she grew that Sage was in this pool. It was a feeling deep in her bones, the bond between sisters.

Lark dipped a finger into the water, her touch sending ripples spreading. The fish scattered and then swam back to her. She leaned forward, studying them. She just needed to name the right one.

But how would she know which was Sage? They all just looked like . . . *fish*.

Fins, tails, scales, gaping mouths, blinking eyes . . .

Wait. That gold-and-white speckled one . . . there, under its tail. One scale a different color than the others, making a mark like a little hoofprint.

Sage had a birthmark shaped like a tiny hoofprint under her arm. She and Lark laughed about it, because what sort of coincidence had given the Horsemaven's daughter a hoofprint on her skin?

"That one!" Lark cried. She fixed her gaze on that speckled fish with the mismarked scale and said, with all the conviction in her heart, "You are Sage!"

The water in the hourglass fountain turned to froth and foam, and when it cleared Sage stood there, dripping wet in a gold-and-white gown of sequined scales.

Lark flung herself at her sister, clinging to Sage's cold body. "Are you hurt? What happened? Can we—"

But before Sage could do more than smile and kiss Lark's cheek she was surrounded by a swirl of smoke and thorns. Lark stumbled backward as her sister vanished.

"Rust and iron!" she cursed. "Couldn't he have given us a minute to talk?"

Still, at least Lark had found her. Now she just had to do it twice more.

And then the hedge started to bulge and twist, choking off the maze corridor she'd just walked through as it shaped another.

The labyrinth changed around her.

TWENTY-EIGHT

Three Guesses

LARK RAN AS the maze folded, hedges crashing together like green gates. Brambles and thistles burst from the labyrinth in clouds of thorns and shredded leaves.

Her breath whistled in her chest and her lungs burned as she sprinted through rapidly narrowing corridors, dashing around reaching branches and clutching twigs. She lost all sense of direction and it took her several minutes to realize that the maze wasn't simply changing—it appeared to be *expanding* as well.

She found herself splashing through a creek and scrambling up a hill, racing between boulders and massive oak trees that hadn't been part of the original labyrinth. She wanted to wail that the game was forfeit, that the Briar King had cheated, but she wiped a trickle of sweat from her upper lip and swallowed the words. If she complained, he might do something even worse.

Besides, it was her fault. She knew the Fae were tricky—she should have made him promise not to change the playing board. She hadn't been careful enough with the terms of their game.

Pausing beneath a tree, she leaned against the rough bark to catch her breath. Ferns brushed her ankles and wild roses filled the air with a sweet scent. She shaded her eyes with her hand, squinting as she surveyed the landscape. A cliff rose to the north, pocked by caves and marked by steps leading to a grassy meadow plateau at the top.

Wait. What did she know about the Fae? Without time, they couldn't create or change, build or grow.

They were masters of magic illusion, not makers of substance.

When Lark looked beyond the surface appearance of the landscape in front of her, she could still see traces of the labyrinth. The trees lined up almost too precisely, and to the west, a row of hawthorns bent sharply as though marking a turn in the maze.

The Briar King hadn't altered the maze; he'd simply made it harder for her to navigate.

Worry about finding Sage first, and then worry about finding your way out, she told herself.

Sage would be disguised as something from the air or land now. This was the perfect spot for deer, rabbits, badgers, foxes, squirrels, raccoons. . . .

Just then a raven croaked overhead. He landed on a

nearby branch and shuffled back and forth to get her attention. "Nightbird?" she whispered.

He cawed and launched into the air, soaring to an outcrop midway up the cliff. Hundreds of white birds nested on rocky ledges and swallows darted over a trickling stream. Wrens sang their warbling song, redwing blackbirds perched on hedgeroses, and ring-necked doves crooned from the trees. Woodpeckers knocked for bugs and meadowlarks flashed through the grass.

Was Nightbird giving her a clue? Was Sage hidden as a creature of air? Lark's heart rose—and then plummeted. There were just *so many* birds. . . . How could she find her sister among all of them?

She chewed her thumbnail, watching a red cardinal streak through a copse of low cedars clustered near the shadow of the cliff. Then, drifting in a circle, she spotted a bright-bellied meadowlark perched on a rock nearby. The Fae loved to play with words, and since the Briar King had already teased her about her name being Lark . . . how far would he carry the jest?

There were four or five meadowlarks within sight. If a fish with a different-colored scale could remind her of a hoofprint birthmark, would one of these birds also have a marked feather?

Taking a seat on a sun-warmed, mossy boulder and leaning back on her elbows, Lark observed all the birds in view. They spun and circled around her, a few landing in the grass nearby to peck at worms and bugs.

But she paid closest attention to the meadowlarks. She squinted at them, looking for marks on their feathers without any luck.

One of the meadowlarks drifted closer, landing in a clump of hyacinths. It cocked its head to the side, staring at Lark with a bright eye.

Could this be Sage?

Lark held her breath, afraid of startling the bird. She studied the meadowlark's coloring: gray and brown with black speckles and white splotches, a golden belly. . . . Was that black smudge a hoofprint?

The bird ruffled its feathers and spread its wings. Lark tried to get a closer look but the meadowlark flicked its tail and prepared to fly away.

"Wait!" Lark said, leaning forward. She didn't want to miss her chance. . . .

"You are Sage!" she called, trying to convince herself.

The meadowlark gave a sad little warble and flew away. A chime shivered in the air as though a distant bell had rung.

Lark had guessed wrong.

She blinked away the burn of tears and swallowed the sour sting of disappointment. Two guesses left . . . and how many dozens of birds?

Suddenly, a bald-headed eagle dove from the cliff to snatch a snake. Its massive wings beat the air as it rose, clutching the wriggling black rope in sharp talons.

Once by air, the Briar King had said.

Maybe finding Sage the first time had been too simple. The Briar King had obviously decided to make the second challenge more difficult. . . . What if he'd hidden her sister as close to the sky as possible?

Wiping clammy hands on her hips, Lark stood and walked to the base of the cliff.

She'd been foolish to assume the birds would come to her. Maybe she needed to go to them.

She took a deep breath and began to climb up the series of stone ledges to the plateau at the top.

The sun beat upon her shoulders as if it was high noon, though it hadn't moved the entire time she'd been searching for Sage. Flies buzzed around her ears and birds swooped from the cliff, but Lark had to fight vertigo. She could only stare one step ahead; otherwise dizziness threatened to topple her.

One step, then the next.

Lark climbed until her mouth was dry as paper dust, until her calves ached and the blister on her toe hummed with raw pain. She climbed until her vision blurred when she accidentally peered over the edge.

After she finally reached the meadow at the top of the bluff, she had to sit and let her galloping pulse slow to a steady rhythm.

A red-tailed hawk soared past her, riding thermal

currents beside the edge of the cliff, wings spread like sails.

Lark still wasn't close enough to see the details of its feathers. Desperate, she cupped her hands around her mouth and cried, "Sage? Sage! Show me where you are! Sage, I'm here for you!"

A single blue heron skimmed past, legs tucked under its belly and neck folded back. Lark couldn't see individual feathers, but herons were her sister's favorite birds.

Surely the timing of this heron's appearance couldn't be coincidence.

"You are Sage!" she called, hope thumping in her heart.

But the heron ignored her, continuing its flight as that chime sounded once more.

Lark had guessed wrong again.

She collapsed, hiding her face in her hands. Two wrong guesses . . . What if she couldn't find her sister? What if they were *both* trapped here?

What would that do to her parents?

What would it mean for the Borderlands, for Rook, if the Briar King forced her to use the moonclock? What could it do?

She had wagered too much.

A soft chirp raised her eyes and she wiped away her tears. A plump robin with dark feathers and a cheery red breast cocked her head and chirped again.

The robin was standing in a clump of pale green, fuzzy

leaves with a pleasant spicy scent.

A clump of *wild sage*.

Lark was afraid to hope. She'd already been wrong twice and couldn't afford another mistake.

But the robin hopped closer, tipped her head, ruffled her wings, and chirped once more.

Lark couldn't see any marks on her feathers that might resemble Sage's hoofprint, but perhaps the Briar King had been more careful with her disguise.

The robin fluttered and preened, bobbing her head and flicking her tail. Then she opened her beak and sang the two-note whistle the Mairens used with the shadowbreds.

Joy burst in Lark's belly like laughter and she pointed at the bird. "You *are* Sage!" she said, utterly certain.

A swirl of feathers and red sparks surrounded the robin, spinning faster and faster until everything went still and Sage stood there, clothed in a soft wool gown with red insets. Lark leaped toward her, flinging her arms around her sister in another hug. "Keep being brave. Don't let him trick you—stay in the labyrinth. He must not win!" Sage whispered in her ear.

Dark storm clouds surged across the sky as fast as thought, whipping across the meadow and blowing dirt and leaves in Lark's face. She clutched her sister, but she was flung backward and Sage disappeared.

Lark folded her arms across her chest, clutching her

elbows. One more disguise, and then she and Sage were done.

"Nightbird, can you help me?" she whispered.

The raven flew into view, but before he could reach her, a wildkin hawk the size of a small horse dove at Nightbird, screaming a battle cry until the raven retreated, flapping out of sight.

Lark was left alone.

— TWENTY-NINE —

Red String and Rabbit Holes

LARK SPUN IN a slow circle. *I can do this. I just need to think my way through. . . .*

Sage had told her to stay in the labyrinth. Did that mean the king would call the game forfeit if she accidentally wandered outside the confines of the playing board? Though she could see the suggestion of the maze in the shifted landscape, she certainly couldn't trust her ability to continue navigating it.

Then Lark remembered her hagstone. She took it from her pocket and held it to her eye. Peering through the hole in the middle of the stone would strip away illusions, though she'd never faced anything of this scale before. She blinked and . . . yes!

Almost as if she were peeking behind a curtain, she could see the structure of the labyrinth hidden underneath the image of the forest and cliff. Keeping the hagstone pressed to her eye and extending an arm to brush the edges of the maze, she carefully made her way through the puzzle. It was disorienting and made her head ache, but she steadily worked her way forward.

To one eye, it seemed as though she slipped between a couple of elms and into a copse of aspen trees. Through the hagstone, however, it appeared she was still walking down a white gravel path between tall, neatly trimmed hedges with glossy green leaves.

Now all she had to do was find her sister once more and get them both out of the maze.

A small hare bounded over a crimson toadstool and paused to study her, its whiskered nose quivering nervously. Could it be Sage?

The hare stretched itself taller, long ears swiveling backward and forward.

The flicker of hope was quickly extinguished as Lark examined the hare more closely. Her hagstone might not be powerful enough to peel away a particularly strong disguise, but her own intuition told her this creature couldn't be her sister. There was something too . . . deliberate and watchful about it. Dread prickled Lark's arms and teased the hair at the back of her neck. Was this a wildkin?

She patted her pockets. Besides the moonciock in one, she still had string and marbles, bread crumbs and salt and herbs in the other. And dried cherries . . . Would that appease a wildkin hare?

Moving slowly, cautiously, she withdrew a handful of

dried fruit. "I might have something for you," she murmured. "Do you like cherries?"

The hare blinked, a sly gleam in its eyes.

Definitely wildkin, Lark thought with an inner sigh. But the hare hadn't done anything threatening—yet, at least—so maybe she could buy a little goodwill and luck with a tasty treat.

The hare's nose twitched and it hopped closer.

"Here you are, then." Lark tossed a handful of the dried fruit toward the hare, just as she had when she and Brendan passed the bog-sprite sentinel on their way across the border.

The hare pounced on the cherries, nibbling them with evident delight. Tension flowed from Lark's shoulders and she adjusted her cloak, raising her hagstone to her eye again.

Before she could take another step the hare sat up and grinned at her, teeth stained red with cherries. It thumped the ground three times with a long back foot—and the earth heaved.

A hole suddenly opened beneath Lark's feet, dirt and pebbles and dried pine needles crumbling beneath her. She stumbled, swayed, pinwheeled her arms—and fell.

The hagstone bounced from her hand as she tumbled into the sinkhole, scraping her elbow on a rock. "Rust and ruin!" she cried. The hare peered at her, flashed a gleeful grin, licked its teeth, and hopped away.

Dirt filled the hole, and the harder she struggled to kick

her feet and climb out, the more firmly the ground held her. It was as if the earth had simply swallowed her.

A heavy feeling grew in her belly until it crouched like a fat and ugly toad. It wasn't menacing enough to be called *despair* just yet, but it was certainly stronger than *discouragement*.

"You're not playing fair!" she yelled.

A wind whipped through the fallen leaves and pine needles, sending them skirling around her. At the edge of hearing a voice whispered, *"A raven helped you and a hare helped me. Fair is fair."*

"Aggh!" she shouted, slamming her hand on a mossy patch of ground.

A faint echo of laughter followed the wind through the tree branches, tossing leaves and twigs at her.

Lark closed her eyes and took a deep breath. *Frustration only means you aren't seeing the situation from the right angle,* Ma liked to say. *Change your perspective, and you change your options.*

So. What were her options?

She could wait until moonrise and then see what the moonclock was capable of. It was obviously an object of great magic somehow connected to time and seasons and elements, but how would that help her in this situation? How would that help her win Sage and Galin and free Rook?

And the problem with waiting for moonrise was that in the Fae realm, without a consistent flow of time, it was impossible to predict when that might occur. Meanwhile, how much time would pass in the Borderlands? Had the moon back home already risen? Was this all part of the Briar King's plot—to hold her here until there was nothing left for her in the mortal realm? What good would it do to win her siblings' freedom if a century had passed back home?

She needed to move *now*.

Lark braced her elbows on the ground. Since kicking her feet was impossible, she tried to pull herself out of the hole with her arms. Grunting with effort, she strained to lift herself, hoping she could gain enough traction to free her legs.

But the ground held her fast, and panic broke in a cold sweat across her forehead.

When you can't rely on strength alone, you must be smart, Ma always said.

So . . . Lark needed to be smart about this. Maybe she could dig just enough dirt away from the edge of the hole to give her legs a little space. . . .

She scrabbled around the rim of the hole, looking for loose dirt she could start scraping. But the ground was hard as clay brick, and when she clawed her nails in, brambles burst out to scratch bloody trails down the back of her hands.

Hopelessness sank poisonous fangs in her mind, but she couldn't give up. Sage needed her. Galin and Rook needed her. Her parents were waiting.

But she wasn't strong enough or smart enough to get herself out of this situation. She didn't know a charm for this.

Although . . . Rook had taught her that her will was the most important element. Maybe . . . maybe she didn't need a charm. Maybe she had the power to break free on her own, if she wanted to badly enough.

And oh, did she want to.

She closed her eyes and thought about soft, loose, crumbling dirt. Garden soil that sifted through her fingers with the warmth of spring sunshine. Sand and scree at the edge of the Snakesong River and the way it felt between her toes. She focused so hard her jaw hurt and something popped in her ear.

Soft, loose, crumbling dirt.

Soft. Loose. Crumbling.

Soft. Crumbling.

Something gave way around her feet, shifted and released. She flexed her toes, rolled her ankles.

For a moment the ground fought back, squeezing around her knees until she started to fear she'd never free herself. But she didn't stop—she *couldn't* give up now. She kept imagining the dirt loosening and falling away, and with a sudden sigh the earth around her let go and she scrambled out of the hole.

Panting, she lay on the ground until her ears stopped ringing and the dizziness in her head subsided.

She'd done it. She broke a Fae enchantment all by herself, simply by believing she could.

But she couldn't rest. She still had to find her sister. She still had to find her way through the maze.

Taking a deep breath, she patted the pocket holding the moonclock, thankful she hadn't lost it in the fall, and climbed to her feet. The air shimmered and spun, and she realized with a frosted thrill that *she could see the maze*. She didn't need the hagstone or a charm at all.

She marched down the corridor of the labyrinth wearing a fierce grin, ignoring the forest and focusing instead on the green hedges she saw behind the ripples of the Briar King's constructed images.

I'm coming for you, Sage, she thought.

But after walking and walking and walking, Lark's confidence began to erode, leaving behind a widening hollow of dread and desperation.

Was she simply wandering in circles?

She was using every trick of navigation she could think of, but under the shifting Fae illusion, everything looked the same. And she still hadn't seen any sign of Sage.

Perhaps she had been overconfident, thinking she could win a wager with the Briar King. Maybe she had let her unexpected success with Rook's small charms cloud her judgment.

Had she made the worst mistake of her life?

The air suddenly carried a deliciously enticing smell—something sweet and rich with the allure of endless summer. . . . Lark breathed in, mouth watering as she recognized the scents of bright citrus and ripe fruit.

She turned a corner and discovered a tidy orchard bowing over the maze path, every limb hanging low with fruit just within her reach. Golden-green apples with a pink blush, promising the crisp bite of ambition; dusky plums with indigo skin that smelled of dreams; rosy peaches as sweet as a sister's smile; oranges bursting with the tart-sugar temptation of sunshine and lazy sighs. Red cherries, yellow pears, even pawpaws and persimmons. Blueberries and blackberries.

Lark's stomach growled. She was hungry—ravenously hungry at this point.

The fruit gleamed like jewels, impossibly bright and perfect. As she walked beneath the apple trees, she idly raised a hand, simply wanting to know if the fruit was real or an illusion, some mirage conjured by her appetite or meant to tease her hollow belly.

An apple fell into her palm as if waiting for her.

Lark stared at it, her tongue tingling with the desire for a taste. The sweet fragrance blurred her thoughts. But at the back of her mind a warning buzzed—a vague caution she couldn't quite remember. Something about getting stung when picking fruit? Or watching for worms?

She bounced the apple in her palm and took a step. An orange fell in her other hand, followed by a plum and a peach. She gathered them in a fold of her tunic, and then she noticed a thicket of wild strawberries. Trailing grape vines climbed up a wooden trellis nearby.

Hunger gnawed her belly and she eyed a patch of grassy shade. She could sit and enjoy her snack, take a rest and . . .

Again that vague warning prickled her mind, an itchy discomfort she couldn't seem to shake.

Lark looked at the orchard, at the perfect trees with their perfect leaves and perfect fruit. Was there room in her pockets to hold more? She brushed the moonclock with one hand and it was like a splash of startling cold clarity.

Wait . . . these fruits wouldn't all ripen at the same time. Of course, conditions in the Fae realm were different than in the mortal world, so the laws of nature could be bent, but . . .

The whisper of unease she'd tried to ignore grew to a sudden roar and Lark remembered another rule: *Never eat Fae fruit.*

With a cry of disgust, she flung her collection of fruit away and wiped her hands on her clothes. The ripe fruit hit the ground and burst, rotting before her eyes. Fuzzy mold coated the once-gleaming skin of the apple and crawled over the orange peel, pitted the pear, and collapsed the plum. The flesh burst in clouds of tiny flies and maggots wriggled out. She pressed her hands to her belly and bent over, retching.

What would have happened to her if she'd eaten a bite? Nothing good, that was certain. The stories said Fae fruit could wipe away memory, tangle the senses, and trap mortals forever.

Lark wiped her mouth on the back of her wrist, glad her mind had cleared in time.

An ominous rustle swept the surrounding trees, leaves fluttering as twitching branches reached toward her. The blackberry thicket stirred, thorny berry brambles slithering across the ground.

She swallowed a curse, realizing it must have been a deliberate trap set by the Briar King.

She fled, still choking on the horror of what she'd almost eaten.

Lark continued to run until a stitch pinched her side and her breath rasped like dry tinder in her chest, until her muscles burned and dizzy sparks flickered at the edges of her vision. She slowed to a walk, and then the hedge she'd followed as a guide turned in a tight circle and she found herself nearly enclosed in a green cage.

By the time she pushed her way out, the maze had changed again. Now she stood on a stone terrace surrounded by low rosebushes and creeping ivy. It didn't appear to be an illusion . . . just a part of the labyrinth she hadn't expected.

She paused and considered where to go next. Where

should she look for her sister? Sage would be a creature of land this time. . . .

Something rattled the leaves of a small aspen grove nearby. A twig cracked beneath a light step, and a cluster of witch hazel trembled with the passing of something swift and quiet.

Sage?

Lark stepped toward the sound, then hesitated. This might be another trap. She needed to be cautious. . . .

Thinking quickly, she took a bit of red string from her pocket and tied it to the closest rose branch to mark her spot. Then she hurried to the next fork in the maze, marking a twig of low-growing laurel when she turned toward the aspen grove.

Now she would at least be able to find her way back here.

The aspen grove seemed to be a dead end in the labyrinth, but she had to investigate. Walking softly, she entered the graceful copse of trees and listened for any sound.

There! Another quiet footstep. A blur of motion, a bright eye . . .

A beautiful young buck stepped from between the pale, slender trunks. He was a warm, russet brown fading to golden cream around his muzzle and under his chin. Dark chestnut shaded his shoulders and legs, the tips of his pricked ears. His antlers spread wide, though he wasn't as large as the White Stag had been.

Still, he was proud and magnificent.

He caught her gaze with his large, limpid eyes and blinked long lashes. Lark didn't sense any of the malicious magic of the wildkin, but he didn't feel like Sage either. And yet, the Briar King's disguises had gotten increasingly more convincing, so . . .

"Are you Sage?" Lark whispered.

A silvery chime sounded and the stag startled, leaping away until he vanished in the shadows between the trees.

Lark hung her head. One guess wasted.

Dejected, she turned away—and then she heard the haunting moan of a creature in distress.

Another trick of the Briar King?

The sound grew louder, punctuated by a heavy thrashing and then a wail that raised goose bumps on her arms.

She knew it could be a trap, but how could she ignore any creature's suffering?

Lark tied another red string with fumbling fingers and raced in the direction the young stag had gone. She didn't have to run far—just a few paces into the woods she lurched to a stop at the sight of him.

The stag was caught in a net of cobwebs, kicking his legs and tossing his antlers in a futile effort to free himself. But the more he struggled, the worse the net tightened around him.

"Ohhhh no . . ." Lark breathed, stepping close enough to see the white rim of fear around his eyes, the red flare of his nostrils. His chest heaved as he fought the thin cords of the net, and tiny lines of red streaked his coat where they cut his skin.

He opened his mouth and groaned.

"Easy now . . . easy. Lie still and I'll see what I can do," Lark murmured. She knelt on the ground just out of reach of his thrashing hooves. Maybe she could cut him loose with her pocketknife. "Easy now. Easy," she crooned, digging through her pockets until she found it.

The knife was small but sharp and she didn't want to risk hurting him worse. Showing him the blade she said, "I think I can cut the net, but you must lie still or I might accidentally nick you too. Do you understand? I'm trying to help."

He heaved a sigh and blinked his warm brown eyes twice. His legs stilled.

Lark carefully scooted closer and grabbed one end of the net. It stung her fingers, but she ignored the prick of pain and tried to sever the closest strand of the net.

The knife blade wouldn't go through.

"Rust and ruin!" she cursed. The net appeared as flimsy as spidersilk, but it was stronger than she would have guessed.

The stag moaned softly and she hastened to soothe him. "Easy, friend. I'll figure something out."

If the net couldn't be cut, then she needed to find where it was anchored so she could somehow lift it off the stag. Scrabbling through the ferns and fallen leaves on the ground, Lark felt the cool slick of metal. Yanking the leaves away, she discovered a copper stake driven through the ground to secure a loop of the silver net.

She tugged and pulled and strained and stretched and tugged some more until the copper stake lifted clear of the ground and she could loosen the loop of the net. The stag gave a soft huff of hope and flicked his ears. "Patience, friend. Stay still. . . ."

She wrestled the silver spiderweb net away from his legs and off his back, and then untangled his antlers. His sleek coat was soft and warm beneath her hands, but she was afraid to pause and marvel at his beauty. She had to hurry.

Finally getting his front legs free, she took a deep breath and heaved the net off his body. "This . . . should . . . do . . . it!" She gasped, stumbling under the surprising weight of the thing.

The stag clambered to his feet, gave himself a fierce shake from his tail to the tips of his antlers, and then lowered his head to regard her with his fathomless eyes.

Lark smiled. "Go on, then," she told him. "But watch your way this time! And . . . if you know where my sister and brother are, send them my direction?"

He snorted, tossed his head, and bounded away.

Lark watched him go for a moment before turning her attention to her hands. Her palms were red and blistered from where she'd gripped the strange net but she'd left her salve back in her pack. She blew on them and then decided the best she could do was just to ignore the pain and resume her search for Sage.

Tired but relieved she'd at least managed to help the stag, she trudged back the way she'd come, searching for the red string she'd used to mark her path. There, off to her left—a flutter of red. She picked up her pace, aiming for the next red string. Another, to her left.

Wait. That was odd . . . she must have lost her sense of direction when she entered the aspen grove, because she could have sworn the laurel bush would have been closer and to her right. But that's precisely why she'd tied the string in the first place, wasn't it? She knew a labyrinth could be disorienting, especially one wrapped in illusions and Fae enchantments.

Quickening her pace, she walked toward the red string— and froze. It wasn't dangling from a laurel branch as it should have been. No . . . it was clinging to a blackberry bush.

Lark had not tied this.

A prickle of foreboding itched between her shoulder blades as she turned her head. There was another string twisted in the crook of a hawthorn tree. Another dangling from a bird nest. And one caught in the limbs of a spruce.

She took a step to her right and looked around. Red string hung from every tree and every shrub for as far as she could see, fluttering in the suddenly still air like cruel taunts.

THIRTY

Finding Summer

LARK TRIED CLOSING her eyes, counting to three, and opening them again, desperately hoping the red strings were simply another illusion. But no matter how many times she blinked or how hard she wished, they remained.

The Briar King must have used the stag as bait in another trap, and she'd fallen for it.

No . . . that didn't seem entirely correct. The trap had been set for the stag and she'd just stumbled along in time to save him, but her impulse had given the Briar King and his allies a chance to further confuse her.

She'd been outplayed, and now she was hopelessly lost.

"Sage? Where are you? If you can hear me, I need you to give me a sign!" she called, voice cracking.

Wind laughed in her ear and she shivered. She only had two guesses left.

This is just another problem that needs fixing. I can think my way through. She shaded her eyes with one hand and studied the landscape.

"You'll have to forge a new path. What matters is finding Sage," she told herself resolutely.

She chose a direction, mostly at random, and reached to pull the closest red string off the branch. If she couldn't follow a trail marked by knots of string, she'd follow one indicated by their absence. And if she ended up at a dead end in the maze, she'd simply return to the strings and try again. Blazing a trail in reverse.

However, when she grabbed the string, her fingers only closed on colored smoke. In a single blink, every bit of string vanished as quickly as they had appeared.

Caught by surprise, Lark lost her balance and pricked her hand on the branch. A drop of blood oozed from the scratch. "Oh, salt and stars!" she cursed, shaking it off.

A twig cracked behind her and she turned to see the stag regarding her with his gentle eyes. "Greetings again, friend," she said.

He turned his head and tipped his antlers, as though encouraging her to follow. When she'd asked him to send her sister or brother her way, she hadn't really expected him to listen or understand. But now . . . was it possible he knew where they were? Could he lead her to them?

Or was this another trap? A distraction?

When he took a steady step down a low, boulder-clotted

rise she decided to follow. He glanced back at her, flicked his ears, and bowed his stately head in approval.

They walked for some time, Lark thinking about her brother's easy laugh, the way he ruffled her hair and raced her around the house. His habit of spitting apple seeds into the backyard and the tiny tree that had sprouted by chance the year Lark turned five. The way he sang in the rain and whistled when he worked.

She thought about Sage, her sister's sunny smile and dauntless courage. Her fearless riding, and the secrets she whispered to Lark late at night under the quilt. Her love of flowers and fireflies, summer stars and glittering winter frost.

Sudden thunder rumbled in the distance, though the sky was still clear. Lark slowed her pace, afraid she might tumble into another trap. The stag paused and lifted his head, but he didn't seem frightened.

The wild scent of deep magic and roses filled her nose and she suddenly recognized the rhythm of that thunder: hoofbeats. Dozens and dozens of them.

A moment later a herd of black horses poured over a hill in the distance. "Shadowbreds!" Lark murmured, but they weren't *all* shadowbreds. Some of the horses galloping with the herd were purely Fae—starshadow horses, creatures of mist and midnight, starlight and shadow, smoke and wishes. They tossed their heads and flagged their streaming tails, racing with their supposedly tame half-kin.

In a tide of gleaming, shifting darkness, the horses swirled into a valley and vanished.

The stag sighed and continued on, more swiftly now. Lark trailed after him, clambering over boulders and climbing up a cliff of loose scree. Her feet slipped on the pebbles as he bounded ahead, and she worried that he was leading her out of the labyrinth. He moved with such urgent purpose, though, that she felt compelled to follow until they reached a grassy bluff crowned by a ring of stones and a massive, moss-draped oak tree.

The stag tipped his antlers toward the tree, indicating a monstrous knot of briars beneath its branches. "I don't understand," Lark murmured. "Why did you bring me here?"

He snorted softly and leaped over a low hedge, quickly bounding out of sight.

Lark eyed the briars and a terrible sense of betrayal shook her to her bones. Had the stag simply drawn her out of the labyrinth and led her into another one of the Briar King's tricks?

But a soft voice called, "Who's there? Please—don't go!"

Lark froze, shock dropping her mouth open for a second until she clicked her teeth closed. There was a *Fae* caught in those briars and thorns, a slender hand straining to reach through the vines and a face peering through the sharp-edged leaves.

For several long, breathless moments they regarded each

other warily. The Fae's skin was the golden color of summer sunlight, with pale green freckles sprinkled across her nose like the first leaves of spring. Her eyes were a darker green with a cat's narrow pupils. Honey-colored curls tumbled down her back and she wore a diaphanous gown of flame red and orange.

Lark thought she was lovely—and terrifying. There was an aura of restrained power—and temper—about her.

Why had the stag led Lark here? Did this Fae know where she could find Sage and Galin?

Wait . . . there *was* something familiar about her. Could this be the golden Fae Lark had first seen riding beside Galin? Maybe she *did* know where Lark's siblings were. . . .

Just as Lark was about to ask who she was—why the Briar King had caged her in these brambles—the Fae let out a delighted laugh. The smile that blossomed across her face warmed her eyes.

"You must be the one called Lark!" she said in a musical voice. "You look just like your brother!"

Lark's questions took to wing like startled birds. "So you do know Galin!" she blurted. "I recognized you—you're the golden Fae who rode beside him in the Harvest Hunt!"

The Fae laughed again. "Yes. I'm Iselda Summerwind, and I am most pleased to meet you, Lark Mairen."

Lark blinked. Iselda had offered her full, true name. Why would she do that? Was there an implied obligation here?

Before she could respond, the briars shifted and creaked,

one of the thorns scratching Iselda's wrist. She hissed and withdrew, cradling her hand. "I'm sorry. I would step closer, but I cannot."

Lark shifted her gaze from the Fae to the cage woven of briars. "How were you trapped? What happened?"

Iselda sighed and paced a small circle within the thorny branches. "I wasn't as clever as I thought," she confessed sadly. "You see, I intended to deal with the false king before the Wild Hunt, hoping I might be able to restore some balance. However, I underestimated how far his thorns had spread and a wildkin spy revealed my plans. I was ambushed by the king and his allies."

"What happened to Galin?" Lark drifted around the thorns, looking for an opening. Maybe if she helped this Fae escape from her cage, Iselda would help her free Sage and Galin in return.

Besides, Lark couldn't walk away from someone who needed assistance, and it seemed as if the stag had led her here for a reason.

"Your brother is very brave. He helped protect the Harvest King as long as he could to the best of his abilities, and then he tried to defend the May Queen. But he's just a mortal, and when it became clear that he could not stand against the thorns, I convinced him to go into hiding. He and my brother have been mustering support from the shadows, gathering allies. . . ."

"But they left you here?"

"My cage is charmed against them. They couldn't do anything," she said sadly.

Lark tapped a leaf with a cautious finger, leaping backward as though it might strike like a viper or sting like a wasp, but nothing happened. The brambles didn't seem to react to her. She just had to figure out how to break the tangle open. . . . "I still don't understand why—"

"Why the usurper didn't just kill me? Well, I'm the May Queen's sister. The false king thinks he can force a marriage, now that he has started to realize he can't hold the Twilight Court alone. This cage is my punishment for defying him, marriage the price of my release."

"I thought you couldn't speak ill of your own kind," Lark said, kicking a root to see how sturdy the vines were, how firm they stood.

A flash of emerald anger blazed in the Fae's eyes. "We can't lie either, and his crimes against me and my family are too terrible."

Lark studied the briar cage, tugging a small branch to see how it was woven. "If you're the May Queen's sister, then . . . you're *Rook*'s sister! I mean, Rodrik's."

"Rook? That's a perfect name for him. And yes. Where is he? I saw his raven, but I have not seen my brother in a little while."

"He's in the castle."

Iselda's eyes grew sad and troubled. "I knew the false king would do anything for the illusion of a prince's support.

There are some in the Court eager for the novelty of a rebellion, thrilled by the chaos of a usurper king, and delighted by any chance to exercise their malice, but there are plenty of old families who are only pretending to recognize his rule. I suppose he thinks to use my brother to secure their allegiance. And mine," she added sadly.

Lark frowned. She doubted Rook would let himself be used as a tool for the Briar King's wicked reign. "But why is *my* brother involved?"

A glow seemed to light Iselda from within. "He knows that I am the rightful queen of the Twilight Court now that my sister is gone. He understands that the Briar Thief must be uprooted before he brings ruin to both of our realms. And he knows I—" She pursed her lips, the glow in her cheeks turning rose pink.

Iselda's expression reminded Lark of Sage in her silly Brendan moments and an uneasy suspicion slithered through her mind.

But the Fae had turned serious, pacing a tight circle in her cage of thorns. "No matter how much support we manage to rally, though, we are doomed to fail without the moon-clock." A shining tear slipped down her cheek and splashed on the ground. Where it fell, a bright golden buttercup bloomed. "The usurper captured dozens of thralls during the Wild Hunt, but the realm is so far out of balance that there isn't enough mortal energy to preserve the illusion of time. We will lose our ability to change, to experience new

413

things. We might as well be statues. Stones."

Lark paused her study of the cage. "What does the moonclock actually do?"

"Hawsdon Brassman—you would know him as the Harvest King—made the moonclock to manage the flow of time and maintain a balance here. He bound his mortal blood—the power of time and change—to the elemental powers of the seasons and the tides of the moon, linking them to the magic of the Fae realm. The moonclock created seasons in a realm that had none, time in a place outside it. He preserved the balance here . . . but as he became more like us, the moonclock's effects began to fade. And while the Court weakened, it became vulnerable to weeds and thorns."

She kicked the hem of her skirt. "My sister was the rain, the spring. I am supposed to be the flame of summer."

"And the cloud? Is that Rook, for air?"

"No . . . that represented Hawsdon himself. The Harvest King, the once mortal consort of the May Queen."

"What about the snowflake?"

"Wait . . . have you *seen* the moonclock? How is that possible?" Iselda's eyes went wide, her lips parted in shock.

"Yes, I've seen it. I'm the one who fixed it. I found the key and wound it up. Only . . . I don't know how to *use* it. Rook never explained anything."

"Ahhhh," Iselda breathed. "He was bound by a bargain with the Briar Thief and had to swear he'd hold the secret in order to save his life, but Rodrik told me he had a plan. I just never thought . . ." She clapped her hands. "Oh, well done, Lark! Brilliant. Now if you can just get me out of here we'll go find your brother. With the moonclock, together we can set things right."

The thorns quivered, leaves rustling. "Hurry!" Iselda hissed. "When the usurper realizes what you're doing, we'll both be in terrible danger."

Lark reached for a branch, wondering if she could tear it away, but before she grasped it a thorn pierced her skin. "Oh, salt and stars. That hurts!"

Maybe one of Rook's charms would work. . . . Lark took another bit of red string from her pocket and wove it around her fingers in the pattern Rook had taught her. It had seemed like a silly game at the time, but now she realized what a gift it had been. Twisting her hands, she shifted the loops of string and chanted, "Caught and bound, by string surround until the cage comes unwound. Caught and bound, by string surround until the cage comes unwound. Caught and bound—" On the third repetition, she flicked her fingers and the weave came loose. "The power of three shall set you free."

The instant the string slipped off her hands, the thorn cage trembled and creaked, peeling open so Iselda could leap out.

"Excellent. You are as brave and brilliant as your brother said. Come with me—hurry now!"

Lark ran after her, protesting, "But I can't leave the labyrinth! I have to find Sage or else I'll lose the wager and be forced to use the moonclock for the Briar King!"

"You've already left the labyrinth. Besides, he'll never let you win."

Already left the labyrinth! Lark's stomach plunged. How could she save her sister now? "But Sage—"

A raven's cry tore through the air. Nightbird circled toward them, fanning his tail feathers and banking his wings. When he landed, he croaked and ruffled his feathers, in obvious distress.

"What is it, Nightbird? What's wrong? Is Rook all right?" Lark cried, already weighted by a sense of defeat.

Nightbird clicked his beak and shuffled back and forth, toes scratching the ground and wings lifted. "What are you trying to say? I don't understand. . . ." Iselda said.

But Lark noticed that he was gripping something in one of his feet. "Nightbird, what have you found?" she asked, holding out her hand.

He grumbled low in his throat and flew to her, dropping a rolled bit of paper into her palm before flying to a nearby tree branch to watch her reaction.

Lark held the slip of paper up, peering at it in perplexity. It was covered in tiny, precise handwriting she didn't recognize. "What is this?" she asked, and then she realized it must be a message. From Brendan?

She read:

> Lark, not that you need any additional pressure, but I thought you should be aware that the Elders have agreed to allow an expeditionary force armed with salt and iron to invade the Other Side if you do not return by moonrise. They have thrown caution to the sea. Talk of war has drowned out my urging for caution and patience. You must hurry. Luck of the winds, my friend. Signed, BlunderKnuckles.

Nightbird jabbed his beak toward the briars and crawked, but it took Lark a moment to shake off her stunned dismay. An expeditionary force? *War?*

Also, Brendan knew the nickname she had given him, and the guilt felt like stinging nettles of shame in her heart. It had slipped out when she believed the meadowflits had stolen his senses, but she hadn't realized he'd heard.

"Nightbird, is there still time to fix things?"

He flew to her shoulder and spread his wings as though prepared to see what she would do next.

Iselda crossed her arms, hugging herself. Her face had gone pale, her golden shimmer all but disappearing. "Salt and iron? If they separate our realms it will mean disaster for all of us!"

417

Nightbird clicked his beak and shifted his balance.

Lark answered grimly, "I freed you from your cage. Now you need to help me get my sister and brother home before it's too late."

Their whole world faced destruction.

Was she strong enough to save it?

Iselda trembled. "I had no idea things had gone so far," she whispered. "When I heard the White Stag had been shot, and the wildkin let loose, I thought that was as bad as it could get. But now . . ." She covered her face with her hands. "The Briar Thief has no idea what he has unleashed. All he cared about was seizing the throne. He didn't understand the responsibility, the burden of protecting an entire realm and all its people. . . ."

Lark was only half listening, staring at the bit of paper. Surely her parents wouldn't let the Elders start a war? But with all their children on the wrong side of the border, how far would they be willing to go?

"Everything is unraveling," Iselda moaned. Tears like molten gold shimmered on her cheeks. "I do not know if there is still a chance of saving things. It may be too late, even with the moonclock. But we still have to try."

"Then I need your help," Lark said.

"Iselda!" a voice called. Footsteps padded across the grass. And then, "Lark, is that you, little bird?"

A voice she hadn't heard for six moonturns.

— THIRTY-ONE —

A New Game

"GALIN!" LARK CRIED as he drew near, but her brother only had eyes for Iselda.

Lark recognized his expression. She'd seen her parents look at each other the same way. Galin was in love with Iselda.

He ran to embrace the lovely Fae—a Fae who should be queen!—and buried his face in her hair. Iselda clung to his neck as he wrapped her in his arms. "You're free," he murmured. "I've been so worried. . . ."

Lark turned away, trying to ignore a prickle of bitterness, but after a long stretch of silence she said, "Pleasure to see you again too, Galin. Oh, don't worry about the *six moonturns* you've been gone without any word. We didn't mind a bit. And now, if you'll both excuse me, I'll just go and find Sage now."

"Rust it all, Lark, I *am* glad to see you!" He laughed, grabbing her in an enthusiastic hug and sweeping her feet from the ground as he squeezed her ribs. "But I can't believe you're here. You are so clever and courageous. How did you find Summer?"

The Fae rested her hand on Lark's arm, interrupting. "Oh, Galin, we're practically family. I already gave her my true name."

He grinned. "Well, little bird, I have to say thank you from the bottom of my heart for opening Iselda's cage. How did you manage it? Her brother and I were foiled in every attempt."

"With a charm," Lark said. "Listen, you owe me explanations." *And an apology.* "But Sage is missing and the Borderlands are on the brink of war and I made a bargain with the Briar King that I really, *really* need to win so . . . uh . . . I think we've got some serious issues to deal with. Any ideas?"

Galin and Iselda exchanged a look. "Yes, but first . . ." Iselda paused and said, "Wait here one moment. . . . I'll scout ahead. Maybe I can lay a false trail for the Thornguards and buy us a bit more time before the Briar Thief comes after us. We might have a chance after all." Between one blink and the next, she'd become a shifting ribbon of light that darted through the trees and shimmered away like an errant sunbeam.

"What happened to you after the Hunt, Galin? Why didn't you come home?" Lark asked.

In some ways her brother looked just as she remembered:

same mussy dark curls, same freckles dusting his nose. Same friendly brown eyes, though a crease of worry folded his brow.

But a leather vest with copper studs and a cream shirt embroidered in gold had replaced the simple tunic he used to wear, and underneath the fine green cloak slung over his shoulders she spotted a bow and quiver of arrows.

"I didn't plan to leave you all with no warning, I swear. I just wanted to prove that I could keep up with the Wild Hunt. I mean, Iselda was a princess and—" He shrugged, his face ruddy with embarrassment.

"See, the thing is . . . I love Iselda, Lark. I have since the day I met her, and I wanted to spend more time with her. She talked her brother into tearing secret rifts in the border with his ravens so she could sneak across and see me every few nights, but the risks she took made me feel guilty. I thought the Hunt would be an adventure, a chance to show I could be worthy of her. . . .

"Then the Harvest King was attacked and she didn't know who to trust or how many in the Twilight Court were involved, so . . . I agreed to help him back to the castle. I intended to return. But the Duke of Briars was determined. Someone poisoned the king's favorite wine with hemlock and I couldn't leave Iselda and the May Queen surrounded by secret enemies."

He scratched his chin. "I planned to come home with the Mayfair Hunt, at least to visit and tell you all where I was and what I was doing. But—as you've discovered—the thorn revolt was hard to root out. Tendrils snaked through every level of the Court. The queen lost her staunchest allies to strange accidents. Assassins crept through the castle, left venomous snakes in her basket of scarves, waited in dark corners with spelled silver. They threatened Iselda too and tried to force her brother into an oath of loyalty. Luckily, as I'm sure you know by now, he's too clever for that."

Lark just listened, scratching the ground with the toe of her boot. She understood why Galin had stayed—he'd always been fiercely loyal—but she and Sage had also faced danger. Didn't he understand that his family had needed him too?

"I *tried* to get home to talk to you. I asked Rodrik and his ravens to tear an opening in the border for me as they had for Iselda, but the wildkin were causing trouble and everything was so unstable . . . I was afraid to think about what might happen in the Court while I was gone, afraid I wouldn't be able to get back, afraid of losing time."

Frowning, he rubbed the back of his neck and said, "Believe me, it was terrible to feel torn between two worlds. But I knew that if the Duke of Briars took control of the Twilight Court, it would spell disaster for our realm too. I had to help stop him. And I knew Iselda's brother was keeping an eye on you, so I hoped that someday I'd have the chance to see you all again, to introduce you to Iselda and explain everything. I never meant to cause pain."

"You left us for *six moonturns*. Sage thought it was her fault you went missing. That's why she's stuck here now. She wanted to save you."

"I know. I'm sorry. I'm going to help you get her out, I promise."

"All because you fell in love with a Fae. Which, by the way, is against the rules." Lark tried to keep the anger and accusation from her voice because he was alive, after all, and that was a joy. And she liked Iselda too, but . . . still.

He scrubbed his hands over his face. "As far as the rules . . . well, we both know I'm not the only one who's broken them, eh? Besides, no one has the right to tell you who to love."

Something he'd said struck her. He'd said he would help get Sage out . . . but he hadn't said anything about returning with them. "Wait," Lark said. "Are you . . . are you planning to *stay* here?"

"Iselda needs me. You'll understand shortly."

"How do you know she hasn't enchanted you? What if she's just using you? Look, we got her out of the cage and she disappeared!" Furious, frustrated tears blurred Lark's vision and she brushed them away impatiently.

"Lark, sweet little bird, you don't really believe that. Iselda and Rodrik are *good*. If the Twilight Court falls to a king that lets chaos run free, what do you think happens to the Borderlands? They're trying to save all of us and I can help . . . if I stay."

"How do you know you love her enough to give up everything? How can you be sure she loves *you* enough to deserve the sacrifice?" *How can you love her more than the family you've known all your life?* "How did you even meet?"

"She came to Da's shop during Mayfair one year and returned at Harvest. And then she snuck across the border whenever she could." He grinned at his own memories. "But, Lark, I don't want you to think for a moment that I love her more than you. We'll find a way to visit often." He reached out to grab Lark's hand. "We can change things, make them better. Please, try to understand."

Lark thought about Brendan entering the Fae realm with her to save Sage and thought maybe she already did.

A flash of light burst nearby and Lark flinched, assuming it was the Briar King arriving to punish her for destroying the cage he'd wrought. Instead, Iselda's form coalesced before them.

"I set traps of my own for any Thornguards in pursuit and sent messages to our supporters, telling them the time for planning and preparing has passed—we must seize the moment and reclaim the Court before we miss our last chance." Then she called, "Nightbird!" and the raven soared down to her. "I need you to summon the aid of the birds and the pixies. We have to distract the Briar Thief until moonrise, if we can. Hurry!"

The raven took to wing with a fierce cry, but Lark chewed her lip. She'd spent *hours* searching for Sage, yet the sun didn't appear to have shifted at all. "If there's no time here," she said slowly, "how can you be certain the moon will rise? How long will we have to wait?"

Iselda shrugged with forced nonchalance, but Lark knew the Fae couldn't lie and after a heartbeat she admitted, "I don't know, Lark. I *can't* be certain. But it's our only hope. We just have to trust that the moon will take her turn in the sky, and then . . ."

"Then what? I still don't know how to use the moon-clock!"

"You know more than you think you do. When the time comes, you'll see."

Lark grumbled, "You sound like Rook. I hope you're both right. But it won't matter if I can't find Sage in her third disguise."

"Tell me exactly what you wagered with the king," Galin said.

So Lark described the bargain she'd made with the Briar King and how she'd already found Sage twice. "I only have to find her once more and she'll be free of him, but I've already wasted one guess and Iselda said I'm not even *in* the labyrinth anymore," she finished sadly. Although the stag *had* led her to her brother, in a way, so at least she hadn't entirely failed. . . .

He ran a thumb over his chin and said, "You'll never win. The king won't let you. All we can do now is change the game. It's time to play by *our* rules."

Iselda nodded. "I'm afraid the only way to get Sage away from the Briar Thief is to defeat him—once and for all."

"But how?" Lark cried.

A rush of wings filled the air, and the sky suddenly darkened in a storm of birds. Ravens, crows, hawks, kestrels, eagles, vultures—even pigeons and cloudswifts, starlings and magpies. They swirled through the air like flickering schools of fish, darting one way and then another.

Among the flocks of birds, Lark caught glittering flashes of rainbow-colored pixie wings. All the clans must have converged to seek vengeance for the brutal murders of their kin.

"That's our sign. Come on—grab my hands and don't let go. We'll take a Twilight Road," Iselda said.

Lark suppressed a groan. She hadn't entirely recovered from her first trip on a Road and wasn't keen on repeating it. "Why don't you go ahead and I'll keep searching for Sage," she suggested.

"Lark, you have to trust us. Things have been set in motion—" Galin started to say, but a burst of thistles shoved through the ground near them.

"Hurry!" Iselda urged.

In a panic, Lark grabbed one of her hands as Galin held the other. They plunged onto a dirt path as briars choked the hill behind them. Iselda took one step and Lark closed her eyes, letting herself be dragged along a shifting, twisting ribbon of Road.

When Iselda finally stopped, Lark sucked in several

deep, shuddering breaths before opening her eyes.

They faced an arched wooden gate in a low stone wall covered with ivy and sweet honeysuckle. Iselda opened it and ushered them through, leading them inside a garden full of wildflowers and sprawling bushes.

"Our reinforcements have arrived," Iselda said with satisfaction as the first wave of birds spilled from the clouds in a ragged rush of wings, filling the branches of the castle trees with a furious cacophony as they landed.

Lark tipped her chin up, watching the birds congregate on the spreading limbs until the trees seemed covered in more feathers than leaves. Then, with wild cries, dense flocks dove at the heads of patrolling Thornguards marching along an ivy-draped timber rampart just visible from one side of the garden. Somewhere out of sight more shouts and curses rose in response to the shrieks and cries of additional birds.

"The Thornguards won't stay distracted long," Iselda warned, hurrying to the end of the enclosed garden. Lark and Galin followed her beneath a sun-dappled arbor holding grape vines.

She stopped at a narrow door carved with eggs and birds, roses and feathers, leaves and honeybees. "My sister's secret entrance," she explained, tapping on the carvings in a complicated pattern. It swung open and they stepped into an airy, graceful corridor lined with floral mosaics.

They ran down the hall, around a corner, past double

doors carved with the May Queen's symbols, and then to a door with a rising sun carved over the lintel. Iselda laid her hand flat on the polished wood and it creaked open, releasing a glitter of dust and the scent of sun-warmed hay.

Iselda murmured, "Feels like an age since I've last been here, in my rooms. Ariasandra wouldn't let me stay when she realized how dangerous the Briar Thief was becoming. Elementals like us are rare, you see, and she said the realm would have need of me if . . ." Her voice broke and she covered her face.

Galin kissed her forehead, but a dark thought pricked Lark. "Is the Briar King an elemental too? Is that why he can send briars and brambles through the earth?"

Iselda shook her head. "He's stealing power from the wildkin, the last magic from my sister's and her consort's thrones, the realm itself. He's nothing but a wicked, cowardly thief. It's time for him to face my wrath!" She marched to a cabinet against one wall and opened a small copper chest. A golden diadem shaped like a sunburst rested within on a faded cushion of red velvet.

"This helps focus my power," she explained at Lark's questioning look.

A sudden fear struck Lark. "If we defeat the Briar King, will Sage's disguise fall away or will she be trapped forever in whatever form conceals her now?"

"All the illusions he has wrought will crumble, Lark. Do not worry. Your sister will gain her freedom the moment I claim his life," Iselda promised.

"But how will we find her? I left the labyrinth! What if he's hidden her halfway across the Fae realm, or . . ."

Iselda clasped Lark's hand. "If he dishonored your wager by cheating, we will still find her. My brother will send all his birds across the realm until she is located. But I do not think it will be necessary. I doubt she's far. . . . The Briar Thief likes to keep his prizes close."

Only slightly reassured, Lark finally nodded.

Iselda adjusted the diadem across her forehead and Lark felt a warm glow spread around the Fae, like the heat of a candle flame when it first sparked to life or the glow of an ember when she blew on it.

"Let's do this," Galin said, nocking an arrow to his bow.

Moving swiftly and silently through the empty halls, they reached the throne room and huddled near the doors. It appeared empty of Thornguards, but Lark didn't trust the dense shadows in the corners.

Iselda breathed, "Luck of the winds to us," and darted toward her sister's throne.

Three Thornguards stepped from a dark alcove and leveled spears of black hawthorn at her, but she raised her hand. Light filled her palm, sparkling like a sunbeam on clear water, flaming pale gold and white as her sunburst diadem brightened. One of the guards hesitated, only to be pushed forward with a growl from the others.

Iselda grabbed his spear, sending flames racing along its

length. He screamed and dropped it, but embers had already ignited the sleeve of his coat and scorched his fingers.

With a howl that reverberated through the room, he ran out, clutching his burned hand to his chest and ignoring the orders the other two Thornguards barked after him.

Galin drew his bow and aimed at the Thornguard closest to Iselda. "Halt!" he cried. "Or you'll regret it!"

Both Thornguards lunged at Iselda at the same moment. Galin dropped one with a spelled-silver arrow and Iselda cut the other down with a blazing beam of light.

"Quickly!" she gasped. "Help me release them!"

Together Galin and Iselda gently loosened the silver stakes holding Ariasandra, the May Queen, to her throne.

Lark's knees trembled but she forced herself to approach the Harvest King's throne. She'd never been this close to Fae royalty before and seeing him like this—lifeless, drained of power, a feeble husk of the regal, ruddy presence he'd been—frightened her. She clenched her teeth and freed him from the Briar King's bindings.

He slumped in his throne and Lark stumbled backward, closing her eyes. "I'm so sorry," she murmured, heart twisting.

A hand touched her elbow and she spun around, eyes flying open. But it was Galin, wrapping her in a hug. Iselda stood beside them, tears in her eyes. "Farewell, sister," she said quietly. "Farewell, brother. May the peace of the deep woods, still waters, and ancient stones be yours. May the light of the sun, the silence of the moon, and the memory of the stars welcome your spirits into the great unknown."

A wind rose, sudden and startling, to swirl through the throne room. It gusted around the rafters and skirled across the floor, scattering leaves and petals from the thrones. Sparks of light glittered in the air, growing brighter and brighter until Lark had to squint.

With a flash and a rumble, the May Queen and the Harvest King, along with their thrones, collapsed into piles of silk and satin, dust, dried leaves, fragile petals, rotten fruit, and brittle twigs—and then were blown away.

There was a grinding screech and a howl at the edge of hearing, then the Briar King's throne crashed as a ripple of sparkling magic—scented with pine, clover, roses, and raspberries—swept the chamber and dissipated like the memory of mist.

"Thieving snake! He was trying to use them to anchor his stolen power," Iselda snarled, lip curling, before a rumbling quake shook the floor and knocked splinters of wood from the rafters.

At first Lark thought it was the Briar King and his Thornguards marching in to punish them for what they'd just done, but as she listened more closely she recognized hoofbeats. Soon she heard horses whinnying and squealing, and she let out a shocked laugh as she realized that the shadowbreds she'd seen in the labyrinth had made their way into the palace.

The thunder drummed louder and louder until the first shadowbreds burst into the throne room, manes and tails streaming like smoke and eyes gleaming silver-bright with magic. The Fae starshadow horses joined them, surging through the space with wild, reckless energy.

One of the mares was obviously their leader. She rounded up the stragglers, nipping and nagging them until they raced in the direction she chose. She drove them around the walls of the throne room, their hooves barely skimming the floor.

Something about the mare's movements, the flick of her ears or the look on her face, caught Lark's attention. She couldn't have said what it was, exactly, because the herd of black horses looked like a flood of ink and darkness and it was all but impossible to distinguish individual horses in the rush.

But that mare . . . determination and fury burned in her eyes. Her willpower was fuel for the entire herd. When the Fae horses turned to smoke and started to drift, she bared her teeth and pinned her ears and they solidified beside her, anchored by nothing stronger than the force of this mare's focus.

Lark knew someone like that too.

Just as Lark opened her mouth to cry her sister's name, the Briar King lurched in. His fine clothes were rumpled and torn, his cloak a tattered mess. His crown hung askew

from one ear and dirt smudged his face. One of the shadowbred mares kicked at him, only missing his head because
he ducked.

Livid, he stormed toward his ruined throne and pointed
a shaking hand at Iselda. "The Twilight Court does not
belong to you!"

"Of course not. It *belongs* to no one. But it *is* mine to
lead. To guard and guide, just as it was my sister's and her
consort's until you killed them." The shadowbreds seemed
to agree, coming to stand behind her in a protective curl.

The Briar King whistled and two companies of Thornguards marched in, ranging down the length of the throne
room in a menacing wall of spikes and spears and thorn
branches. One of them dragged Rook by the collar of his
tunic.

The shadowbreds tossed their heads and pawed the
ground, nostrils flaring.

The Briar King spotted Lark and growled, "Oh, it's my
little bird, somehow escaped from the labyrinth. Never
mind. Come. You lost our wager and now you and that
moonclock belong to me."

The shadowbred mare who had led the others squealed
and bared her teeth. Lark cried, "Our game is not yet ended."
She pointed to the mare and said, "You are Sage!"

The mare shook her body like a dog shaking off droplets
of water. Glittering black smoke swirled around her—and

when it faded Sage stood there, dressed in a simple black gown. She flung her arms around Lark, laughing through her tears.

The Briar King roared and both companies of his Thornguards leveled their silver-tipped spears. "A sister found . . . and a brother lost. Bring the Prince of Birds to me!"

The Thornguard holding Rook dragged him before the king and Lark yelled, "No! You agreed to release him!"

"But I never specified *when*, did I?"

"You're a liar and a cheater!" Lark shouted.

Iselda cupped her hand and her palm filled with a glowing ball of golden light. "Let him go!" she ordered. "Or burn with all the heat of my fury!"

A raven screamed and seconds later a storm of birds filled the throne room. Nightbird flew to Rook, pecking and tearing at the Thornguard holding him. Eagles and hawks streaked through the doorway and windows, shrieking at the Thornguards. More ravens and crows followed, along with starlings and jays, swans and geese and swifts. Pixies viciously swarmed the Thornguards, their peaceful natures transformed by the grief of the false king's betrayal.

The shadowbreds kicked and lunged, reared and raced like a cyclone of smoke and shadow barely contained in the castle walls.

Rook wrenched himself free and ran to join Lark and her sister, long scratches from the thorns oozing silver trickles of his Fae blood. "Take them to the Hall of Clocks!" Iselda shouted to him.

"Go on now. We'll deal with this," Galin called, raising his bow again.

"No!" Sage cried. "I can help. The starshadow horses and shadowbreds listen to me. See?" She gave a piercing whistle and the panicked horses turned to look at her. With another whistle and a series of gestures, she directed them to isolate a group of Thornguards. Plunging and striking, snapping their teeth, the horses backed the Thornguards into a corner. Two mares kept them pinned in place while the rest of the horses worked to cut off another group of the Briar King's soldiers.

"Come on! You're needed in the Hall!" Rook shouted to Lark, grabbing her elbow and pulling her away. He tugged her behind a curtain and they raced down a small corridor.

THIRTY-TWO

The Hall of Clocks

ROOK LED LARK down dark, twisting corridors and through dim chambers woven from tree roots and twiggy limbs. They ran past halls of mirrors and fountains of music, around stairs that climbed the air with no support, and under vaulted ceilings made of butterflies. They ducked behind a waterfall of colored light and raced over a bridge of woven spidersilk.

Lark's heart thrummed in her chest, and her ears rang with the distant sounds of battle. Outside the windows, the Briar King's wicked allies had arrived. Lark saw pixies fighting wildkin while sprites tried to distract rocktrolls and goblins. Magic currents ebbed and flowed through the entire castle and she hated to think about the danger her brother and sister faced.

"Nearly there!" Rook said.

Finally, when Lark's breath burned in the back of her throat and her stomach cramped with fatigue, they skidded to a stop in front of a massive grandfather clock carved from different woods. Instead of numbers the face showed flowers and fruits, trees and wild shrubs. The case was embellished with dozens of animals: rabbits and field mice, foxes and wrens, horses and wolves and small cats with whiskered faces.

Rook darted forward and pressed the carving of a small owl perched in a tree. The entire case swung open and Lark breathed, "It's a door!"

"Of course it is. How else would you get into the Hall of Clocks?" He beckoned her inside.

Lark tiptoed through, gasping as she emerged in a huge room that was indeed filled with clocks. She saw cuckoo clocks with live birds on tiny perches, grandfather clocks carved like forest glades or castle turrets or thatched cottages. There were clocks with glass faces and symbols she'd never seen before, clocks with dozens of numbers or none at all. Sundials and water clocks and even the old candle clocks her grandmother used to speak about stood on tables along one wall while cases contained pocket watches and bell clocks.

But the chamber was completely silent—no ticking, no chiming, no marking time. None of the clocks were moving.

"This is madness," she muttered.

In the center of the room stood a massive hourglass, a larger version of the one in the labyrinth. It was filled with translucent, glittering sand. . . . Only, instead of spilling downward, the sparkling sand rose from the bottom of the glass and swirled into the top, where it seemed to vanish.

Around the strange hourglass stood a linked circle of mortals bound in thick branches and thorny vines. "Thralls, captured during the disastrous Mayfair Hunt and now held in service to the Briar King," Rook told her. Their faces were frozen in expressions of fear or pain or dread, eyes blank and glazed. Glossy leaves tangled their hair; roots knotted around their legs. Silver collars enclosed their necks.

Sick horror drained Lark's courage.

"He's consuming their mortality through the lifeglass to fuel his power," Rook explained grimly. "Without the moonclock, he needs them to create the illusion of time. But it can't last—they will die, or freeze in stasis."

"How do we free them?" Lark demanded in a shaky voice. If she could cut their connection to the hourglass— or lifeglass, as Rook called it—she could save their lives *and* further weaken the Briar King.

Before he could answer, a scream echoed from elsewhere in the castle and Nightbird flew in to perch on Rook's shoulder. His feathers were ruffled and a thorn had pierced one foot. He croaked in Rook's ear, flapping his wings in distress.

"Oh, stars and sorrows. All right, you stay here and help." To Lark he said, "Iselda's in trouble. I'll be back as soon as I can. See what you can do for them."

As Rook dashed out of sight, Nightbird fluttered to

Lark. He cocked his head as if asking a question, but he couldn't rest his weight on the injured foot.

"What are we going to do with you, bird?" Lark asked with a fond smile. "Give me your foot." She held out her hand until the raven hopped closer and awkwardly lifted his leg. She could tell he had tried pecking the wicked thorn out of the skin, but it was in a tricky spot between his toes and must hurt like fury.

"I'll try to be gentle," she promised, "but I'm in a hurry." Pinching the thorn between her fingernails, she gave a sharp tug and yanked it out.

Nightbird squawked and tried to pull away, but blood welled out of the puncture and she held on to him, keeping pressure on the wound with one hand until the bleeding stopped and she could let him go.

With a relieved croak, Nightbird hopped a few times and then gave himself a quick preen.

Lark turned back to the lifeglass. "Let's see what we can do for all these people. . . ."

The only weapons she had were her small silver knife and a pocketful of charms. Desperate to free them as quickly as possible, she stabbed her knife into the closest thorny vine. The instant the blade touched the vine, a shriek at the edge of hearing shook the entire hall. The lifeglass trembled, the glittering sand within spiraling in a sudden whirl. Every thrall's mouth opened in a silent scream as the briars imprisoning them thrashed and writhed.

"Sorry!" she cried. Clearly that wasn't going to work. The magic holding them was too closely tied to everything else, too interconnected. If she used the knife to destroy the briars restraining the thralls, she might end up injuring the people.

Lark sifted through the salt and herbs in her pockets, wondering what she could do. What charm could she try? When she cast a sprinkle of salt and vervain at the thicket of thorns to see what would happen, however, another tremor shook the vines and they tightened around the thralls.

Anything she did to damage the briars would hurt the thralls too.

Maybe she just needed to loosen them. . . . Remembering the charm that had released Iselda, Lark pulled out a bit of red string and wove it around her fingers, twisting the loops as Rook had showed her. "Caught and bound, by string surround until the cage comes unwound. Caught and bound . . ."

But the briars only swelled and grew, leaves rustling ominously as the thorns drew fresh beads of blood from the mortal thralls.

Despair gnawed away at her determination. Why wasn't anything working?

Think, Lark, she told herself. *It's not a cage. . . . It's some kind of binding, linking their life forces to the glass and draining away their mortality. So how do I break that connection? How can I interrupt it?*

As she examined the lifeglass, a flicker of motion near the wall caught her attention. She lost her breath when she realized she was seeing spiders—*hundreds of wildkin spiders*—creeping through the hall. Wolf spiders, jumping spiders, weaving spiders, widow spiders, venomous spiders— too many spiders.

Lark's teeth chattered and she scrambled backward. They were *so fast*.

Nightbird shrieked and a furious cloud of birds swooped into the hall. They fell on the host of spiders, pecking and tearing, snapping and smashing.

Some of the birds clawed at the tangle of thorns holding the thralls, but the briars slashed back, tearing feathers and fragile skin as the mortals caught in the midst screamed silently.

Identify the problem and fix it.

While the birds kept the spiders back, Lark kicked the glass to see what would happen. As she'd guessed, it was too strong to crack. And she couldn't tear the briars away. . . .

She needed to understand how it worked.

The lifeglass sat on a silver plinth, and if she looked past the glass and glitter, the magic and thorns, she discovered that it was connected to a series of rotating gears set within the floor. Each of the thralls, though they appeared to be standing motionless, was actually balanced upon a small platform above similar gears. These cogged wheels drew the glittering life-sand into the translucent globes as they turned.

If she ignored the magic, it was just another clockwork mechanism—and Lark had spent countless hours learning all about clockwork mechanisms at Elder Brassman's shop.

She yanked off her tool pouch and found her favorite small screwdriver. Working as quickly as possible, she knelt on the floor and began attacking the gears. She unscrewed small silver bolts, loosened pins, jammed cogs.

The sand swirling in the lifeglass slowed, then stilled, settling in the bottom. A low groan filled the Hall of Clocks and a rumble vibrated under Lark's feet.

Gritting her teeth, she pried a gear loose and the screech of metal grinding metal made her ears buzz. The lifeglass suddenly tilted, wobbled, and collapsed with a terrible clatter as the plinth it had stood on fell. When it hit the floor, the glass cracked and sparkling sand spun through the air.

Color and consciousness returned to the thralls as they inhaled the glittering life energy, but they were still tangled in tightening ropes of briars and brambles.

"What do you think you're doing?" the Briar King suddenly roared, storming into the Hall of Clocks with a host of Thornguards behind him. He held a shining sword of black obsidian and his thorn-tipped spear, which he swept in a menacing arc to clear the space before him as he led the charge toward the circle of thralls.

Iselda and Galin chased after him—her hands radiating golden light, his bow nocked with one last arrow—but the king's fury had given him fresh speed and strength.

The Briar King faced Lark with an ugly sneer. "All of this is your fault, you know," he said, the words hitting her like sharp stones. "If you'd just left the moonclock alone, your family would have lived in peace. But no . . . you had to meddle in things that were none of your concern, and you've made a mess of everything."

Lark flinched.

Rook ran into the hall, joined by Sage and a shadow-bred. They lurched to a halt as they saw the Briar King advancing, pointing his spear at Lark. "And *then*, after taking what was never yours, you refused to give it up. You hid it and conspired against me, and now look." He swept the spear around the room and Lark winced at the number of wounded.

"This is *your* fault. You bound the moonclock to your blood. You are responsible for all this conflict—but you can stop it too," he said.

Rook opened his mouth to protest but a Thornguard lunged, pressing his spear against Rook's throat. Night-bird and his feathered army swooped and dove, harrying the guard, but the king laughed with a sound like chewing gravel.

"The Prince of Birds has shown his true colors, eh? I knew you'd never join my Court. You have brave friends, but they can't save you now." He took a slender flute—was it carved of bone?—and played an eerie, wailing melody.

The hair on the back of Lark's neck rose and her body

quivered. "You're supposed to release him!" she cried again. "You *promised*!"

Rook closed his eyes as though in resignation, and that frightened her more than anything else. "Go, Nightbird," she heard him say. "Take the flocks with you. *Please*."

Nightbird screeched, but a second later a chill gusted through the hall and a creature of cloud and frost flew in.

A stormdrake. Lark had heard stories of such creatures but had never in her wildest dreams expected to see one. They usually lived in the deeplands of the Fae realm, hidden in mountain nests.

This one wore a finely woven silver collar, fury blazing in her white eyes. Her wings were thin and pale as mist, her long, sinuous body like a curl of blue smoke.

She opened her mouth and screamed a fog at Rook, encasing him in frost.

"No!" Lark shouted, but Rook was still as ice.

The stormdrake spun through the hall, her wings lashing wind and freezing pellets of hail at everyone below as she chased Nightbird and his followers out.

"A king can be merciful and forgiving," the Briar King continued, "but he must be practical and strong for the good of his people. So here's where we stand. If you agree to use the moonclock as I direct, I will recognize you as a trusted member of my Court. You will be granted all the privileges of a royal adviser, given quarters here in the castle. And your family will remain safe."

He stalked around Rook's frozen body in a slow, menacing circle. "If, however, you persist in your stubbornness, your loved ones will pay the price."

"But I won your game! I found Sage. You agreed that I could take her and Galin home with me!" Lark cried. "That you would let Rook—Roderick—go!"

He shook his head. "No, silly bird. You identified Sage Mairen here in the castle, not in the maze. You broke the rules and so I've decided our little wager is forfeit."

"No! You can't do that!"

"No? I *can't* do that? *I* can't do that? I AM THE BRIAR KING," he roared.

Lark thrust a hand in her pocket. Her only hope was a charm that might—

An invisible force wrapped around her arms and squeezed so hard she thought her bones might crack. She glanced down in shock as another tightened around her legs, and a third filled her mouth like a gag so she couldn't speak.

Her gaze flew to the king, who smirked at her. "You thought you were so clever, fixing the moonclock, eh? But who do you think helped you?"

A Fae glided from behind him—the same Fae who had sold Lark the case for three hairs. She smiled and held up a glass jar.

Lark was perplexed. She'd felt the Fae trying to peek through her eyes already—three times, once for each hair. What did she have in the jar?

Something fluttered behind the glass. Something small, red, and black. Lark squinted, and then sudden dreadful understanding swept chills across her skin.

Oh no. A bloodmoth. Not just any bloodmoth either—the one that had taken her blood months ago.

"Now, let me say this again in case your pitiful mortal mind is still confused. You can help me willingly and I will let your loved ones go, or I can kill everyone you care for and force you to use the moonclock. Either way, you *will* use the moonclock. All we need is mortal blood."

The Fae shook the jar and the bloodmoth inside beat its wings.

Lark's thoughts scattered like startled rabbits. What choice did she have? She hated the idea of helping the Briar King after all the horrible things he'd done, but Rook had said that without the moonclock the Fae realm would slide into timeless stasis and all the Fae would suffer.

If helping him meant saving her sister and brother and giving the other Fae a chance, Lark had to agree to remain in the Court.

Her heart ached.

She glanced at Galin, surrounded by Thornguards, and Rook standing frozen and helpless. At Sage with briars around her wrists.

Lark raised her chin to nod agreement, but Sage tilted her head toward the window. *Keep him talking*, she mouthed.

Puzzled, Lark flicked a glance at the window. The sky was filled with a peach-colored glow, rapidly cooling to plum purple. Was the moon about to rise? Had their luck just changed, or had releasing the spirits of the May Queen and Harvest King and destroying the lifeglass set things in motion?

The Briar King changed his tone, lowering his spear slightly. "You are just a frightened child who stumbled into something far bigger and more significant than you could ever suppose. And I am a great king. Join me and you will see." He held out his hand, twisting his face into a smile he probably thought was kind and benevolent, though it came out like a leer.

Lark glanced around the Hall of Clocks again. Half of the clocks lay broken, gears and springs and pendulum weights scattered among the fallen forms of Fae Thornguards and mortal thralls still caught in briars. Smears of mingled silver and crimson blood stained the floor, and her stomach twisted.

She hadn't saved anyone or fixed anything.

If she hadn't been tied motionless by some charm, Lark would have collapsed beneath the weight of despair.

Movement behind Rook caught her eye and she realized Iselda was creeping closer, her warm sunlight glow thawing the stormdrake's ice as the shadows grew longer and sharper.

Dusk definitely approached.

"The moonclock is far too much responsibility for a

mortal child," the Briar King said. "Too much weight to carry. But with my guidance—"

Lark stopped listening. Her spinning thoughts clicked into place. *Time is what the immortal lacks.* The inscription and everything she'd learned about the moonclock, one tiny piece at a time, made sense. She'd known for a while that it didn't *measure* time and had suspected that instead it somehow *made* time, though she hadn't been certain how.

Now she knew what she had missed. One simple detail she'd forgotten. . . .

The moonclock had a two-part winding system.

She wanted to laugh in triumph. She held the power of *time* in her palm. Right now the king had more to fear from her than she had of him.

And thanks to her lessons with Rook, she knew she had a will strong enough to break the charm that bound her.

The Briar King demanded, "What is your answer? Will you join me as a trusted subject or as a prisoner?"

Across the hall Rook met her eyes and nodded encouragement.

Iselda had freed him, and now the rest was up to Lark.

Remember your will.

She clenched her jaw. Ignoring everything else around her, she focused all of her intention on freeing herself. *Unseen bind must now unwind. Unseen bind must now unwind. Unseen bind must now unwind.* . . . She imagined

448

the invisible knot-charm coming loose, her body liberated, freedom restored.

Nothing happened.

"You have tried my patience long enough, foolish girl," the Briar King growled.

Lark tried again, throwing every ounce of determination she could into her effort. *By my blood and bone, my breath and hair, the bonds I feel weigh less than air.*

And suddenly she felt them fall away as the sun slipped from the sky like butter melting. One last shaft of dying sunlight struck the hall before it faded.

The king's voice sharpened, every word like another thorn. "You are out of time, Lark Mairen. My wildkin are strongest in the dark, and if you do not make your choice they will tear your brother and sister apart. And then they'll—"

"You are the one running out of time," Lark said. "And since I'm the only one who can give it back to you, I think you'd better reconsider your offer."

"What?"

The Fae beside him held up the bloodmoth jar, shook her fist, and scowled as if to remind Lark what they had taken.

"Oh, sure. I see you have a few drops of my blood. But that moth can't wind the moonclock. Can't set it. Can't carry it. Smashing its wings won't do anything but make a mess and waste a sad little life."

She put her hand in her pocket and withdrew the moon-clock, holding it up so they could see. "The Twilight Court needs to share our time as much as we need to share your magic. And I'm the only one who can make that happen."

Shifting, muttering suspicion mixed with awe rippled around the hall, but several Thornguards lowered their weapons. One with owl eyes and feathered wings faced Iselda. "Summer sister," he growled, "tell us true."

Iselda's sunburst diadem gleamed in the darkening hall. "The moonclock holds the power of time, yes. And Lark Mairen is its true and rightful Keeper, as our Harvest King was before this usurper caused the accident that broke the clock. As he was before he was killed."

The Briar King snorted. "Of course she is . . . *now*. But that doesn't mean another can't hold the clock. Guards, kill the child and—"

Iselda laughed. "Oh yes. Another Keeper can claim the moonclock—but only if they construct it themselves, oil it with their own blood and the sweat of their labor. And by the time you find another capable of that—another willing to do that—this Court and all of us in it will be frozen in stasis. Immortal, unchanging, and . . . alive but lifeless."

Rumbles of discontent grew stronger, but a voice growled, "We managed just fine in the time before, when Hawsdon Brassman was still a mortal clockmaker and we ruled our-selves. We can do so again, without the moonclock."

Iselda snorted and waved a hand in disdain. "I remember the time before. You captured mortal thralls, forced to rely on their flickering life force to feed your cravings for changing time. You stole children and thought their energy could fuel this realm. But you see how well that works, can't you? And the mortals have salt and iron—already they are prepared to storm the Oak Gate and rip our worlds apart. We need the moonclock, and Lark is the only one who can use it."

The Briar King's expression shifted as he tried another approach. He stepped closer to Lark again. "Perhaps being in my realm has given you a taste for more than your simple home and endless days of mucking stalls for your mother, eh? I'll give you a manor by the sea, a herd of your own shadowbreds, jewelry and candies and . . . and . . . anything your heart desires!"

Outside the castle, dusk fell.

Lark smiled through her fear. "My heart desires peace between your realm and mine. My heart desires happiness and health for all those I love. My heart desires freedom for everyone. Safety. Security. Trust. Honor and respect and compassion. Can you give me those?"

The Briar King slammed the butt of his spear against the floor and roared, "I am finished with patience! You have rejected my generosity and now your chance to bargain is gone."

"So is yours," Iselda said, and she raised a glowing hand. A host of sprites, pixies, and other Fae rushed into the hall, pressing the Thornguards back.

"You stole a throne you had no right to take. You are a murderer and a thief. As sister of the May Queen and rightful heir to the Twilight Court, I declare you outcast and exiled," she called in a ringing voice.

"I AM KING." Before anyone could react, the Briar King lunged for Lark's brother, wrapping his arms around Galin's neck. Between one breath and the next, brambles twisted through Galin's skin, erupted from his muscles, oozed blood as they tore through his mouth and nose.

"*Nooooooo!*" Lark and Sage screamed, echoed by Iselda's own wail.

Galin coughed, choked, and collapsed in a tangle of thorns and sharp-edged leaves.

Iselda flung herself at the Briar King, enveloped in a blaze of light. Her hands were like torches, her breath as hot as summer wind. She touched his robe and it burst into flame. His hair scorched; his clothes singed black.

He tried to fight her with his thorns and briars, but the heat of her fury and sorrow was too great.

With a gasp and a burst of blackened vines, the Briar King died.

Lark and Sage clung to each other, sobbing. Iselda's scream still reverberated through the Hall of Clocks. The thorns binding the thralls shriveled and fell in clouds of dust.

The fallen king's guards turned on Iselda but lost their

courage when confronted by her blazing wrath.

"We waited too long!" Sage wailed. "We should have attacked him before he—" She broke down, tears streaming.

Lark couldn't seem to stop shaking. She'd only just found her brother again, and now he was dead. What could she tell their parents?

And how could she live with the knowledge that all of this was her fault?

Rook appeared beside her, Nightbird croaking sadly. "Lark!" He gave her shoulders a gentle shake. "The moon-clock."

She blinked at him in a daze. His words seemed muffled, as though her head were full of cotton and nothing could penetrate her overwhelming grief and regret.

Rook grabbed her by the hand and tugged her to the window. The moon, still nearly full, was rapidly rising. "Quickly!"

Dazed and brokenhearted, Lark listlessly took out the silver key. She held the moonclock up, shifting it until a slanted moonbeam struck the surface of the clock's case. She turned it until the secret keyhole appeared, and then carefully fitted the key into the slot.

She had already turned the key as far as it would go, but she'd forgotten the winding knob on the top of the case. Now she twisted it gently, feeling it vibrate beneath her fingertips.

The entire world seemed to lurch sideways for a second.

Lark's stomach swooped and plunged as though she'd dived off a cliff into cold water and lost her breath. The moonlight dimmed and flickered, dimmed and flickered—spinning faster and faster.

"Keep winding!"

She gave the knob another turn.

The clocks still hanging on the walls shook and rattled into sudden synchrony, the rhythm of their workings like a quiet heartbeat in the room.

She turned the knob again and the stormdrake soared through the hall, her silver collar clattering to the ground.

Lark turned the knob once more and felt a click. The moonclock was completely wound.

But what good had it done? Galin was still dead. People were still hurt. Skirmishes and arguments outside the Hall of Clocks still filled the castle with clangor and conflict. She gave the moonclock a gentle shake—it had been a shattered collection of tarnished parts not that long ago, so perhaps expecting it to flick into action immediately was unfair—but the hands remained fixed and frozen.

As quickly as it had come, night poured from the sky and morning sun took its place. A warm breeze smelling of sweet grass hay, flowers, honey, and ripe peaches swept through the hall and berry bushes burst from the corners. The drone of summer bees hummed behind the sudden ticking of the clocks as the chaos briefly dwindled.

"Our Summer Queen!" a Fae called, bursting into the hall with Lady Mist. "I'm sorry," the emissary cried. "We couldn't get here sooner—he had us locked in a prison of mistletoe and thorn. Oh, Lark Mairen! You have the moonclock! Brave girl."

But Lark didn't feel brave at all. She felt broken.

Her brother was never coming home again.

She sank to her knees and buried her face in her hands, letting the moonclock tumble to the floor.

Iselda flashed beside her, crouching down to peer into her face. "Lark, sister of my heart, calm yourself. You hold the moonclock, my dear. *You hold our time in the palm of your hand.*"

Lark didn't understand. She didn't *want* to understand. She wanted to go home with her brother and her sister and pretend that none of this had happened.

"Lark. Trust me." Rook rubbed a circle on her back and handed her the moonclock again.

She let him put it in her palm, but she made no move to do anything with it.

"You wound the moonclock, but you haven't set it yet. You can undo what time has wrought," Rook said in her ear.

And suddenly a dazzling possibility bloomed in her mind. Was he right? Could that be true?

Lark raised the moonclock to her eyes and studied the symbols again. She considered the wheels and the winding knob. "But what if I go too far or the wrong way or—"

"It was bound to your blood. It will answer to you," he promised.

Holding her breath and praying for luck, she adjusted the hands on the face of the watch. Just a bit—nudging one, tapping the other. She moved the set wheel, turned the winding knob, calibrated . . .

The Twilight Court was built on balance, wasn't it? She thought about Iselda's summer sun, about the May Queen and her mortal consort . . . about the snowflake and her brother.

Galin and Iselda. Winter and Summer.

The realm needed him.

The world spun. Colors blurred, sounds melted together. . . .

She didn't want to reverse the Briar King's defeat, but maybe if she just sped up a few seconds here and there she could move her brother just out of his reach. . . .

She tapped one of the hands on the moonclock again, a sliver of adjustment, setting it square on the snowflake symbol. And then she closed the case.

A chime sounded and the air turned to ice and wind, mist and sun all at the same time. Lark closed her eyes and when she opened them a moment later her brother stood whole and healthy beside Iselda—whose glowing hand was still raised, her final declaration ringing in the air. The Briar King was just about to—

"Galin!" Lark screamed. "One chance!" She hoped he remembered. *Don't waste the moment.*

A flash of understanding lit her brother's eyes. He nocked an arrow and Iselda touched the shaft, igniting a ribbon of flame.

In one smooth motion, faster than thought, Galin drew and released his bow and the Briar King was suddenly falling, an arrow in his chest and tendrils of smoke curling from his robes. Before their eyes, he turned to briars and brambles, trying to rise even as smoldering embers burned through the vines and bracken holding his spirit together.

And then, in a flicker of sunlight and fire, he was gone.

"I am Iselda, sister of Ariasandra, Summer Queen of the Twilight Court!" Iselda cried, her diadem blazing like the setting sun above her brow. "I will restore balance to our realm, peace between—"

She was interrupted by a stirring near the door. Two shadowbred mares raced in, followed by a giant stag. His coat was a rich, warm brown that lightened to cream at his nose and throat, his crown of antlers forked like tree branches.

Soft murmurs dwindled to silence as he continued to approach, until he stopped before Lark and lowered his head. Lark recognized him. Driven by impulse, she reached out a hand and touched his shoulder. "You did lead me to my sister and brother, didn't you?"

White spilled from her fingers and she pulled her hand

away with a stifled cry. *Oh no.* She'd left a perfect white handprint on his coat. "Did I hurt you?" she moaned.

The white spread, seeping through his coat in a rush. "The Guardian of the Forest," someone whispered. "Lord of the Wildkin."

"The White Stag!" another Fae cried, the words repeated in an awed echo through the hall.

The stag, now a gleaming snow-white, nudged Lark with his nose and then majestically bowed his head to the Summer Queen before calmly leaving the hall.

An owl-eyed Fae looked at Lark in surprise. "You have found us another Guardian," he said. "The White Stag is back."

She blushed and shrugged. "I found him caught in a net, so I turned him loose. That's all."

Iselda beamed. "A new Keeper of the moonclock and her Guardian, Lord of the Wildkin, to repair the border and balance time. This is an auspicious moment for the Twilight Court. But I have some announcements. First, Lady Mist, my dear friend, I must tell you that you are no longer the Fae emissary. Instead, you shall be my personal adviser and trusted counselor. Your time with the mortals will help me guide our lands into a closer friendship, governed not by rules but by understanding and mutual cooperation."

Lady Mist curtsied and hurried to her side. "As you wish, Your Majesty."

She continued, "Lark Mairen, I appoint *you* our new emissary. You have demonstrated an ability to fix not just clocks but the bonds of friendship and community as well, and with your help I hope to build strong connections with our mortal neighbors."

Lady Mist smiled warmly at Lark. "We shall have many conversations, young Lark," she said. "And you may call me Nieve Mistsong."

Lark bowed her head at the gift of Lady Mist's true name, but her mind was reeling. Emissary! *Her?*

But the Summer Queen wasn't finished. "And I hereby officially declare Galin Mairen Threadneedle my consort, and your Winter King, if he agrees."

Galin laughed and swung her into the air. "Yes, of course, my queen. Sky of my heart. Breath of my life." Cheers and laughter filled the hall as goodwill replaced the menace that had lurked earlier.

"We will hold a coronation in due time, but first we must clean this mess and return these mortals to their own land. And then we have work to do. It's time we revised the Accords."

THIRTY-THREE

The Next Moonturns

LARK ADMIRED THE play of moonlight across the silver case of her moonclock for a moment before turning the key and giving the winding knob a few twists. She set the fragile hands of the clock pointing to the dragonfly moon and the summer sun, and smiled when a stardancer sprite waved to her from the honeysuckle vines climbing the garden gate.

Light spilled from the windows of her family's home in golden pools across the yard and music swirled through the air. Galin and Iselda were visiting to plan their joint wedding and coronation ceremony.

So much had changed in just a few short weeks. Lark was getting better at understanding the moonclock, though she had a feeling it would take more practice to master all of its mysteries. But Elder Brassman was helping her—he had been astonished to discover that his ancestor had been the Harvest King and that the moonclock was, in fact, real.

With Lark's help, he and his son Simon had thrown

themselves into new designs melding mortal mechanics with Fae magic. Their first project was a special clock mounted on the Oak Gate. Instead of marking time, Lark had suggested a design to stabilize timeslip between the realms so that the Gate could be left open permanently, allowing Fae and mortal visitors to travel back and forth whenever they wished.

As part of her diplomatic duties, she had proposed new guidelines for these visitors, and both Fae and mortals were eagerly taking advantage of the opportunities. Megrim Inkler, the head librarian, had become fascinated by the Fae's general aversion to writing and the prohibitions surrounding their sacred First Words. He had offered to listen to their stories and transcribe them on paper so that they could be shared more widely. His scrawling, untidy penmanship amused the Fae as much as the stories.

Already, trade and friendships flourished.

The White Stag patrolled the border in case wildkin slipped through the Gate, but the malice and mischief of bored Fae had mostly been replaced by creativity and ingenuity fueled by the moonclock's production of time and by their welcome access to the mortal realm.

Rook and Lark remained friends, of course, but he'd been busy too. He sent his birds winging throughout the Borderlands and the Other Side, making sure everyone knew that new rules—based on respect and appreciation rather than fear and mistrust—were being introduced.

She missed him and Nightbird.

As Lark now tucked the moonclock inside the special pocket Da had sewn in her clothes to hold it safely, the front door creaked open and she heard her sister's soft giggle.

Lark grinned, knowing Brendan would be right behind her. Sure enough, he whispered, "Quiet or someone will hear!"

"Don't worry! Someone will hold her tongue!" Lark responded in her loudest, most obnoxious whisper.

Sage and Brendan stepped off the porch and flashed guilty grins when they saw her. "We just didn't want to distract from Galin and Iselda's wedding," Sage said, "so we need you to promise to keep our secret."

"I promise. Erm . . . what secret?"

Sage held up her hand, and on her third finger—beside the copper ring she wore for tradition's sake now—was a thin gold love-band. "Brendan asked me to be his bride as soon as we're old enough to wed, and I said yes!"

"Oh, I am so happy for both of you!" Lark said, and she truly meant it.

She hugged them and laughed when Brendan whispered in her ear, "I guess your sister decided she likes Blunderknuckles, eh?"

"Brendan, believe me. You are still one of the bravest boys I've ever met, and I'm so glad I'll get to call you brother. Just . . . stay away from bees and wildflower meadows, hm?"

Then she laughed. "And I was actually hoping you'd come out here. I have a gift for you. Come to the barn."

"What are you talking about?"

Sage grabbed his arm and smiled. "Just follow us."

Inside, Lark lit a couple of lanterns and led him to Journey's stall. She rubbed the mare's nose and then stepped back. "Brendan, I'd like to introduce you to your new horse. Her name is Journey. She loves rose petals, hates flies, and likes to dunk her hay in her water bucket."

"But, Lark . . . ," he breathed.

"I already talked it over with Ma and she agreed you deserve a shadowbred, and Journey deserves a braver rider than I could ever be. Besides, you're a messenger! She'll help you make the fastest deliveries in all the Borderlands. Consider her an engagement present."

Brendan flung his arms around her and squeezed. "Thank you, little sister."

Lark left them in the barn and returned to the house. She found Galin sitting in the backyard, staring up at the stars. She plunked herself down beside him and said, "I've been thinking about your motto and I've decided you're wrong."

"Oh? And how's that?"

"Well, it's not about one chance and only one chance, right? Sometimes we have to keep trying."

"But that's the whole point! Do you know who first said

'one chance' to me? It was Da, when I'd started helping at Threadneedle's. I was so afraid of making a mistake, so afraid of doing something wrong, that I could hardly do anything at all. And one morning, as I was standing at the table staring at a piece of brocade so beautiful I was scared to cut it, he told me that it was only one chance—and that there would be others. He said that if I made a mistake we could either fix it or fashion a new garment out of the same fabric and try again."

He brushed a firefly off her sleeve and chuckled. "Sometimes our best successes are made from the failures that came before. You know those divided riding skirts Ma loves to wear in the winter?"

Lark nodded. "Yes?"

"They were supposed to be a Solstice gown, but I misread the measurements and cut in the wrong place. I was devastated . . . until I realized the fabric was in Ma's favorite seafoam green. Serendipity, eh?"

"All this time I thought you meant we only had one chance and shouldn't hesitate in case we missed it."

"No, little sister. I meant that there's no need to hesitate because you'll get another. Failure is simply a step on the path to triumph. We just have to try." He rose and reached a hand down to pull her to her feet. "Care for a cup of cocoa with me?"

"Galin, it's the middle of summer!"

"What difference does that make?"

She laughed. "All right, then, I would. And Galin?"

"Hm?"

"You're going to be the perfect Winter King."

Iselda and Galin had planned their wedding and coronation ceremony for the Summer Solstice, the longest day of the mortal year.

The town green was crowded with both Fae and mortal friends when Lark arrived. Huge arches of flowers—poppies and sunflowers, red roses and tiger lilies, all woven through honeysuckle vines and ivy—were spaced along a path leading from the Oak Gate to the pavilion at the far edge of the square, creating a tunnel of sweetly scented blooms.

The pavilion was curtained in drifts of white, black, and pale blue cloth and festooned with evergreen boughs tied in silver and black ribbons.

Galin waited within.

Lark spotted Sage and Brendan beside the Gate and hurried toward them. "When will you make your own announcement?" she asked. Sage glanced at the love-band on her finger and blushed.

"Soon," Brendan said.

Before Lark could respond a bugle called a fanfare and the Gate opened. Rook and Lady Mist rode out first, followed by an entourage of pixies and other Fae who had been instrumental in brokering the new peace between the mortal and Fae realms. Musicians and dancers followed, and

465

then came Iselda, the Summer Queen.

Da had made her a gown of golden satin that slowly darkened to a deep crimson. An emerald-green silk sash fluttered around her waist and green leaves swirled along the neckline.

She glided forward, trailing a train of laceflowers and rose petals. Sparkling light swirled around her. When she reached the pavilion, Ma and Da gave her warm hugs before bowing and stepping aside.

The Elders of Tradewind Junction then came forward and ceremoniously pulled back the drapes surrounding the pavilion to reveal Galin in robes of pale blue and white satin with black velvet trim. Silver embroidery—stars and snowflakes—traced his hem and collar, and pine-green ribbon accented the tunic and pants he wore beneath.

The Elders recited the words of an old oath-chant. Lark was too far to hear it clearly, but she knew it was a binding of love to mark the marriage of her brother to Iselda.

Galin and Iselda exchanged rings—he gave her a silver one, she gave him a golden one to symbolize the balance of summer and winter—and then she presented him with a silver crown wrought in the shape of snowflakes and pine cones.

Lark had discovered a trick with the moonclock and now she gave the winding knob a little twist as she set one of the hands to the snowflake symbol. The instant she did, feather-soft white flakes danced from a clear summer sky to drift around her brother.

Galin beamed at her, dusted with glittering snow flurries that quickly melted in the sun.

"Behold the Winter King!" someone called.

Fae voices sang a lilting, magical song and when Iselda placed the crown upon his head they gave a cry of joy.

There was a sudden stirring at the edge of the crowd and Lark was afraid that someone—a rebellious Fae, perhaps, or a jealous mortal—might be causing trouble. But then the White Stag emerged from the Gate, roses and summer ivy twined around his neck and antlers.

"The White Stag blesses this union!" the luckwitch cried, and cheers resounded through the square.

While the crowd dispersed—some to dance, others to feast—Rook darted up to Lark, holding something covered in a wicker frame draped in canvas. "I have a gift for you, Emissary Lark."

"A gift?"

"Yes. For your service to my sister—both my sisters." He yanked away the wicker frame and canvas cover to reveal a small meadowlark with bright eyes. "She's yours, so you can send messages or scout the woods or whatever you need to do. She's faster than feathers and can reach me any time. She'll find me or Nightbird wherever we are."

The meadowlark trilled a little song and bobbed her

head, and Lark's heart soared. She laughed in delight. "She's lovely!"

"She'll come to you whenever you whistle. Like this." He pursed his lips and blew a clear, three-note signal. The meadowlark ruffled her feathers and clicked her beak. "Now you try."

Lark gave the whistle on her first attempt and the meadowlark launched into the air, soaring in a sweeping circle before flashing through the pine trees at the far side of the town square. Was she flying away?

Then, with a trill, the meadowlark streaked through the trees and dove straight for Lark's arm. Rook snapped a leather cuff around her wrist a moment before the meadowlark landed. "She's not very big, but she's enthusiastic. This will protect you from scratches," he said.

"Oh, brilliant!" Lark breathed.

"She'll stay within hearing distance unless you send her away, and if you need her to fly farther than you can whistle, you can use this." He held out a tiny silver whistle on a long chain.

"Marvelous!" Lark bent her head and let him drape the chain around her neck. Then she raised her arm and the meadowlark flew off, quickly joined by a shining black raven.

"Rook . . . thank you."

"You should never thank a Fae or you'll end up owing them a favor!"

"I know. And still. *Thank you.*"

His cheeks flushed and he rubbed a hand across the back of his neck. "Well. Um. I . . . I mean, it's no big deal. Do you have time for a game?"

"I always have time." She grinned.

Rook laughed and together they dashed off, following their birds.

Acknowledgments

I should have known that a book about tricky, troublesome Fae would also prove tricky and troublesome to write. But every time I wandered off the path I was fortunate to have talented guidance and friendly support helping me find the way again. There is powerful magic in being part of a creative team and participating in a writing community, and I am inexpressibly grateful to everyone who has cheered me on and made this book possible. I owe so many people thanks it would be impossible to list them all, but I especially would have been lost without:

Sarah Landis, my brilliant agent, who patiently answers my long, rambling emails and frantic questions with kindness, practicality, and encouragement no matter how many ideas I try to juggle at once—thank you for everything!

Alice Jerman, my incredible editor, who first gave me space and support to find the shape of this story and then offered keenly insightful comments to clarify and polish it—I would still be caught in the brambles if you hadn't helped me find the way through. You are an absolute joy to work with and I'm so grateful for your patience and hard work!

Clare Vaughn, talented assistant editor, whose cheerful comments and pointed questions helped me see things hidden in the shadows—Lark's relationships owe a lot of their strength to you and I so appreciate your careful, thoughtful reading and enthusiastic support. It was a delight to work with you!

Christina Kraus, artist, and Jessie Gang, cover designer, who have wrapped my story in an absolutely stunning piece of art—thank you from the bottom of my heart for giving this book such beauty to wear!

Jon Howard, production editor, and Stephanie Evans, copy editor, who helped a messy manuscript become a real book and saved me from embarrassing myself. I appreciate your sharp eyes and patient formatting! And Rosanne Lauer, whose proofreading polished these pages. Thank you for your attention.

Everyone at HarperCollins Children's Books who have been involved in publishing, producing, or promoting this book—thanks for letting me do this again!

Kelly Jones and Edith Hope Bishop, who always offer exactly the sort of encouragement or comfort I need no matter how many thorns I find myself tangled in. Your brilliance and creativity are matched only by your compassion and kindness, and I am so grateful to call you friends.

Marin Younker, who keeps me on target with daily accountability texts and friendly cheerleading. Thanks for the horse conversations!

All of #TeamLandis, but especially Meredith Tate for coffee and long conversations about the twists and turns of publishing. It's not an easy path but having friends to walk it with makes all the difference. Thank you!

All the bookstores who took a chance on a debut author and supported my first book, but especially Main Street Books in St. Charles, Missouri; Edmonds Bookshop in Edmonds, Washington; Books of Wonder in New York City, New York; and Water Street Bookstore in Exeter, New Hampshire. Thank you for helping readers find their next new adventures, and for supporting authors so we can continue sharing stories.

All the writers, librarians, teachers, bloggers, parents, and readers who have supported me and cheered me on—I couldn't do this without you, and I am so grateful for your enthusiasm and encouragement. From the bottom of my heart, thank you.

Abby and the staff at CMB—thank you, as always, for your friendship, support, sympathy, celebrations, and conversations. You take care of me as well as you do my horses, and I am forever grateful.

My parents and siblings, who believe in me without question and cheer me on no matter what I decide to attempt next. Love you all!

My mother-in-law, whose outspoken support of my first book is probably responsible for as many sales as any official bookseller or store employee—thanks for enthusiastically spreading the word!

Taryn, who gave me Sage's name and talked me out of countless panic attacks before I saw the shape of this story through the weeds and thorns, and Alec, whose cheerful encouragement was often a light in the dark. I love you both more than words can express and I'm so proud of you. I wish you luck as you walk your own paths and discover your own adventures.

Andy, who—after more than half my life—remains my best friend and true love. You have sheltered me through storms of sorrow, supported my impossible dreams, and celebrated unexpected successes with me. Every day is an adventure with you and every season brings new stories. Want to go on a road trip?